WATER RITES

Janet Carroll

Pen Press Publishers Ltd

© Janet Carroll 2007

All rights reserved

No part of this publication may be reproduced,
stored in a retrieval system, or transmitted
in any form or by any means, without
the prior permission in writing of the publisher,
nor be otherwise circulated in any form of binding or cover
other than that in which it is published and without a similar
condition including this condition being imposed on the
subsequent purchaser.

First published in Great Britain by
Pen Press Publishers Ltd
25 Eastern Place
Brighton
BN2 1GJ

ISBN13: 978-1-905621-87-3

Printed and bound in the UK

A catalogue record of this book is available from
the British Library

Cover design by Jacqueline Abromeit

*Down she came and found a boat
Beneath a willow left afloat,
And round about the prow she wrote
'The Lady of Shalott'.*

Alfred, Lord Tennyson

CHAPTER ONE

The recipe to forget had been a simple one for Lily. For fifteen years she had immersed herself in the banality of earth and toil. She had surrounded herself with the smell of soil, muck and grass. Her chores were a balm to old wounds. She slept without dreams.

But the past was about to tap her on the shoulder. It has a will of its own. And it never forgets. It had been waiting – or sleeping perhaps.

Later, it struck her as an odd day for a slumbering demon to wake.

The day was cold, white and hard. A day that bore grudges. Footsteps crunched, breath froze, but to Lily it was just another day of labour like all others.

She hooked out a crescent of clay from the horse's hoof and then leaned against the rough stone of the byre while the animal shifted its weight, his shoe scraping at the cobbles underneath. Lily pushed wild strands of russet hair from her face with the back of her hand. Grit scratched at her skin and her cheek glowed with the insult.

She worked at the horse's coat and talked quietly of nothing noteworthy. To the animal this was important. This nothing reassured him that today would be the same as yesterday and all the days before that he could remember. And Lily took comfort too – for just the same reason. Praises and chidings were muttered in the same tone: 'good boy'; 'you mucky old bugger'; and she slapped his rump with the same ambiguity.

As she stepped into the swallowing fog her eyes sought the invisible window on the gable end of the farmhouse.

Dominic was home from his first term at university. He would brighten up the lifeless house for a couple of weeks. Lily pondered on the reason for this. He was after all quiet enough with that calm, unhurried voice of his. A boy with a stillness within him. One that had never banged a door shut. In fact, she had never known him close one. It was because he had no need to block out anything; no need to hide.

She stopped herself thinking. It could lead anywhere – usually a place she had no wish to visit.

She had an easy gait: long strides for a small framed woman. But this day she trod awkwardly over the unyielding ridges of frozen mud. She pulled her hands from her pockets, the better to balance herself. The day was soundless as if nature had forgotten to wake up or just decided not to bother. Life held its breath and waited for the thaw.

The pond took up half an acre of Lack Farm. It was still and white. Less threatening that way, Lily thought. Locked away beneath the ice crust, its malice was trapped. Not that the farm pond was particularly sinister. It was just the way she viewed water in general. She squinted at the fog. The duck house on its tiny island was shrouded like a mocking replica of a distant building. That one was moated not by a blanket of still water but by an unpredictable river. It lay in mist in Lily's mind. She flinched slightly feeling the memory brush the back of her neck. 'This bloody weather's slowed me down. My mind's got far too much time to go wandering.' She kicked at the ice, but her boot scudded unsatisfactorily off the surface.

A chiding cackle erupted from the gloom. Lily hoisted out a branch over the pond and thrashed at the ice until a dark stripe appeared. As if at a signal the ducks launched themselves at the freed water and were on land hoovering up the scraps before she had tugged herself loose from the mud. Lily counted the birds absentmindedly as she did each morning. She counted again.

'We're one missing.' Her breath hung in the air and stung her cheeks. 'Where is she, girls?' Lily waited a moment with her head to one side as if they might answer her. Tales perhaps of a quarrelsome night in the duck house.

She looked back into the fog and called out softly, making a noise with her tongue and the roof of her mouth. Only a moorhen's grating call echoed back. She trudged back to the pond and yanked at a rope. A boat looking like a craft from an adventure playground sat rigidly on the ice. It rocked violently as she stepped inside.

'Don't be daft,' she scolded herself loudly, gripping the sides as the vessel grew accustomed to its guest.

'It's only a pond – two foot deep at most.' Lily peered over the rim. 'I probably couldn't drown if I tried.' She sucked in the last words. They had floated up from a mind that had been tamed to forget.

Battering at the ice, she fetched the oar through the splinters, scuffing at the reeds. Barely a few metres in, she saw it – the pitiful object, encased in rime. Grim faced, she pulled the bird onto her lap and cradled its flopping neck. Her fingers were numb, but she could feel with her palm the velvet plumage. Wasted beauty now. She lifted the lifeless creature to her cheek.

'Water's no sanctuary – it's a treacherous friend,' she whispered, her breath ruffling the feathers. She put a finger to a disobedient eyelid, imagining her father's words, 'Don't waste your tears,' as if the salty water were too precious to fall on this bleak earth.

With dead-cold hands buried deep in her pockets and head pulled down into her shoulders, Lily loped to the farmhouse. There was breakfast to look forward to now.

At the back door she tugged at her boots and hollered out an expectant 'good morning', but the smile tumbled as she padded to the kitchen table. Instead of the debris of toast, she saw a small box, open and revealing its red lining like an angry mouth.

"What are you doing?" Her voice cracked the stillness of the room.

Dominic's head was bent over an object in his hand, but registering the sharp tone he shook the mess of dark hair from his eyes. By the time he had straightened his long limbed body and looked up at his mother she was already studiously washing her hands at the chipped sink. The splashing failed to fill the silence. With the fluttering of panic rising in her chest Lily picked up the kettle and set it down again in the same spot. She opened cupboards and moved mugs around noisily on the battered worktop. And while her hands worked she tried to summon up plausible answers.

The questions would come. She knew her son well enough. He had a healthy curiosity about everything around him. So unlike a Weaver.

"I was just up in the attic, looking for my sleeping bag..." Dominic's voice trailed off and his gaze returned to his palm.

"Looking for your sleeping bag? Oh and of course it's likely to be in something the size of..." Lily swallowed the last words: a jewellery box. It made it sound something precious, something treasured.

"I thought it was some old chess set or something. Something of Granddad's." He turned his attention to his mother, his grey eyes clouded.

"What's up, Mum? Has something happened?"

Lily barely heard him. Her eyes were fixed on the box. She was rigid, spellbound.

"It just looked interesting. I've never noticed it up there before," he explained. "Tell me what this is then." He held out his hand.

Lily wrenched herself back from another world and tried a thin smile, but she felt it fail. Her face, she was sure, was contorted, its muscles seemed to be mismatched. An imperceptible tremor ran from her thumb to her palm, but she took the braid of hair and held it at arm's length, coming face to face with an old enemy.

The plait was cleverly wound into a ring so that no end could be seen. Small enough to fit Lily's finger, it was made up of three miniature tresses: two russet coloured; and one much darker. With the ring in her palm, she let her thumb touch the strands for a moment before putting it back with its partner – almost identical but a little bigger.

She closed the dusty lid and rubbed her hand hard against her thigh. Dominic leaned carelessly against the table, a bare foot perched on the chair in front of him. Lily felt his eyes on her. He was waiting. He had always been a patient child.

"Just old things. Old things from the past. I thought I'd thrown them out years ago," she lied.

She had hoped they would be buried forever in the jumble of old toys and memorabilia, to be found some time in the future when she was long gone.

Dom grinned.

"From your wild youth, I bet. They've got that sixties look about them. It's about time I heard a few tales about the old times."

"No tales to tell. Anyway I was still a schoolkid in the sixties."

"You can't fob me off just like that – I already know a few. Aunt Trin tells a good story after a couple of glasses."

"What story?" Lily regretted the undisguised panic in her voice.

Dominic put a hand to her shoulder. "Nothing awful, Mum," he reassured her. "Just about the two of you in school – something about you bunking off to go to some festival."

No doubt the account would have been colourful, but Lily was unconcerned. It was a story of no importance. "Oh, that," she said simply.

"So whose is the black hair then?" Dominic teased. With both hands he pushed his own back from his eyes and shook it up with strong but slender fingers. He had inherited his mother's undisciplined locks, but not her fiery colouring.

There. The first question had been uttered.

Lily dodged it. She hoped that she seemed preoccupied with her father's appearance beyond the small-paned window. Leaning extravagantly to one side of Dominic she screwed up her eyes and bent her head.

With back stooped, Jack had emerged from the murk as he walked back across the yard. The eldest Weaver of the house had the rolling gait of a farmer, legs bowed and arms lengthened by the years of labour. As he disappeared from view Lily moved quickly. She was used to hiding things. She picked up the box and clutched it close to her waist while her eyes scanned the room – a worktop, bare but for the kettle, teapot and mugs; a scrubbed table; the glowing stove and an old-fashioned radio. But there were no shelves filled with the homely clutter of collected ornaments. There were no souvenirs of happy holidays on the window sill – no place where a small casket might be quickly secreted.

Sensing Dom's scrutiny Lily reached for the table drawer casually. The room was so quiet, her breathing seemed so loud. With a shaky hand she pushed the box amongst the keys, screws and fuses, and shoved the drawer shut giving it an extra nudge with her hip. The table and box scraped at each other as the porch door whined open. Her complexion had returned to normal in the benevolent climate of the kitchen, but now she felt her cheeks colour again as she caught Dom's cocked eyebrow.

"Now then," her father pronounced as he strode into the room. It was said with gravity as though it preceded words of importance, but none came. They never did. He brought the morning post with him and now passed it to Lily, taking her hand in his and depositing the letters there securely as though he feared they might take flight.

"Bills for you to pay, lass," he told her, falling heavily into his captain's chair. The postman had evidently caught Jack at the door, but Lily doubted that he had elicited even a 'morning' from her father. In his seventy years Jack had failed to acquire the normal skills of greeting, having avoided all opportunity to practise.

Lily counted her breaths, trying to slow them down until one escaped her control and she made a small gasping sound. She was glad of Jack's poor hearing for once. With her head bent to the letters, she sneaked a glance at Dominic. He leaned against the table still, a wry smile aimed at Lily. With arms folded he was an amused spectator. Lily relaxed a little. The day had started badly: those eerie memories out on the pond and then the box. But she would bury it again and all would be well.

One envelope in her hand was much larger than the rest. At first Lily thought it was a Christmas card. These were rare arrivals: the Weavers sent none and expected none in return. But some charitable friends and family still kept Lack Farm on their lists.

With his hands above the stove, Jack rasped his palms against each other and glanced up sideways at his daughter. And then turned his head, staring hard at her.

Lily's hand had jerked, her fingers stretched rigid. The French stamp and extravagant handwriting seemed to jump out from the white paper and she almost threw the letters onto the table.

She felt that hand on her shoulder.

Four grey walls, and four grey towers,
Overlook a space of flowers,
And the silent isle embowers,
The lady of Shalott.

                Tennyson

CHAPTER TWO

Standing at her bedroom window with the unopened letter in her hand, Lily scowled. The frost at the pane had thawed, mottling the glass. Lily wiped away at it with her sleeve and wished she could erase Felix's handwriting as easily. For years she had waited with dread to see that elaborate script again, had waited for the morning post. But no news had arrived, no letter begging her to return. And she had forgotten.

The fog had lifted and she could see again the neighbouring farm on the other side of the valley. She could not see the farmhouse: it hid behind a wall of conifers planted against the raw weather. Lily knew it protected a garden of sorts – roses and a mock orange. Here at Lack Farm there were no roses; no flowers at all.

The dry-stone walls snaked down the valley sides to the road at the bottom. If Lily had been standing in the field and turned three hundred and sixty degrees she would have been able to count on both hands all the trees visible. They were misshapen and abused by the wind. The landscape was laid bare.

She gazed at the horizon as though she could see that other place, enclosed and detached from the world where the aspens rustled like rain showers. Lily exhaled a sigh and tore open the envelope.

"Ma chère Lily," the letter began. It had been fifteen years since Lily had used any French, but Felix had made no allowances. The language was as elaborate as the hand. Occasionally she re-read a sentence to be sure that she comprehended its meaning.

"My dear Lily,

This letter will perhaps unnerve you, but that is not my intention after all these years. I write to you now, because it is my duty to do so and because there is so little time. But I have examined my soul, dear one, and in truth, the real motive is selfishness for I plan to please God before the end.

Although we lived as man and wife for five years, you never fully consented to that role."

Lily made a noise somewhere between a grunt and a sigh. Man and wife – is that what you still kid yourself, Felix? Her mouth pulled itself tight in expectant irritation. She lifted the letter again, her fingers twitching against the thick paper.

"But now I am on the threshold of death and I need you to come here. I am writing this not from Chez Reynat, but from the little hospital at La Grande Aubaine where the noble doctors are doing what little they can."

Oh for God's sake, Felix – give me a break. Lily glared out of the window, unseeing.

"I have been diagnosed with liver cancer, Lily.

I have not drunk from the well for two years – that is, since I began to feel the weight of my guilt. Can you imagine? You do not comprehend now Lily, but you will when you come. How could I drink that blessed water with such a sin dwelling in me? But I want to taste it once more before I go and that I cannot do until you absolve me. I must confess to you my sin."

The letter had fallen to Lily's feet. She looked out at the naked fields, but saw instead aspen, a weeping willow, and a towering house with a roof the colour of faded roses.

*

She first saw that place twenty years earlier in the last summer of love and the first of a new decade. She and Trinity had arrived in the late afternoon of a June day. The two seventeen-year-olds had escaped the last few weeks of school and headed to France. They planned to hitchhike as far as Perpignan, but the journey was slow going. Hours were spent sitting on road verges, sometimes in the rain. And they had had their fair share of perverts as Trinity called them. But her friend had a variety of insults to throw at men as they unzipped their flies. Lily's favourite had been, 'Did you grow it yourself?' Most had shrunk back in their seats; some hurled abuse in a French neither girl understood. Always they drove away at speed, leaving Lily and Trinity to catch their breath before the local farm dogs came skidding and yapping towards them.

Felix stopped in his dull blue Renault van and his eyes twinkled like a child that had found two stray kittens. Trinity and Lily rolled their eyes at each other and sighed, already world weary travellers. They had sat with their backs to two oak trees since morning, singing all the Leonard Cohen songs that they knew by heart. When they had finished their lunch of bread and yellow plums Lily sat cross-legged, leaning forward as Trinity tamed the red hair into a heavy plaited rope. The sun disappeared behind the tree canopy and Lily faltered in her singing. Only three cars had passed that day, the drivers not seeming to see two young women in bright embroidered cotton. When mosquitoes danced up from the ditch and teased their bare legs, songs were exchanged for curses and they slapped at the air and shook their long dresses in vain.

They stood beside the old car and eyed each other, weighing Felix's enthusiasm against the possibility of a night with the insects. Trinity made the decision for them both and Lily sat in the back as she always did. She bounced around with a crate of wine and a net bag of provisions – ripe cheeses and cured sausage by the smell of it – and she watched Trinity's head nod and her many-ringed fingers play with the air as she entertained their driver. Lily let herself relax. She loved conversation – she had none at home – but she left the speaking to others.

With his keen eyes fixed to the rear view mirror Felix asked Lily her name, shouting over the rattle of the engine. Lily told him and his hands danced around on the steering wheel.

"In that case, you will stay at my house."

Lily leaned forward. Surely he had used the wrong phrase – although his English was very good. Then he added, "It is fate. Happy fate."

Trinity sat bolt upright and Lily knew the words before they were delivered curtly – 'We'll get out here, thank you.'

"I will cook you an excellent dinner – coq au vin. You know it? Chicken with wine." Felix looked from Trinity at his side to Lily in the mirror and back to Trinity. He blinked and smiled.

"You cook?" Lily leaned further forward. The girls had eaten nothing but bread, cheese, fruit and chocolate for two weeks.

Trinity swivelled in her seat. "Chicken? I haven't had chicken in ages."

At that the conversation stopped. The girls both thought of their stomachs and Felix watched the passing countryside of chestnut coloured cows, oak and corn.

As they bumped over a narrow stone bridge Lily glimpsed the dove coloured house through the trees. It stood on the bank of a wide river.

Felix flung open his door as the car jolted to a halt. Lily thought he looked like a small boy as he loped across the gravel, eager to point to the R carved into the massive lintel above the door. He pronounced proudly, "This stands for Reynat – my family name. This has been known as Chez Reynat for at least four hundred years." He turned back to Lily and she saw some doubt on his face as if he had let his pride get the better of him. "Well, so it is said," he added.

Lily easily believed him. The lettering looked old, medieval even. The builders had chosen an almost white stone for the lintel. She walked up to look more closely. A late June sun caught the granite. The wall glittered.

"So, it's been in your dad's family all that time," Lily said from behind her sunglasses. Trinity had wandered off and she felt obliged to say something. She knew family history was important to rural people. Her own father took every opportunity to recount their own at Lack Farm.

Felix's head bobbed sideways several times while he weighed up the necessity to tell Lily more. His round cheeks flushed and a frown creased his forehead.

"It is my mother's family I talk of," he conceded. "It is my mother's name that I bear. My father is of no importance." His smile returned, an awkward lopsided one. "But that was a long time ago. And those days are gone." He waved his hand aloft as if to blow the past away like an irritating fly.

Lily shrugged – perhaps other families were as odd as her own. She could think of nothing else to say. Instead she breathed in the scented air, gazing around to discover the source. It was a mixture of woodsmoke pouring from the tall chimney and the thick green smell of the river. And perhaps too the lush vegetation, lolling at the riverbank. As she screwed her head round she spotted Trinity. Stooped under a clay roof, her blonde hair fell like a curtain down the circular hole of a wellhead.

"Ah, your friend has found our well – the most important possession of the Reynat family."

With a hand Lily stopped the laugh as it erupted. Above her fingers her eyes giggled at this absurd man. He was a lot older than she and Trinity – older than her brother probably – and he was nothing like the adult men she knew.

Felix's eyes sparkled, willing her to laugh again at him.

"Will you look at the well, Lily?" He emphasised her name, making it sound melodic. So different to the way her father and brother hollered it, the middle vowel dropped as if it were of no importance.

Trinity seemed satisfied with her cursory investigation, because she ambled off with swinging arms towards the river and Lily followed with Felix trotting beside her.

"Now you see why you were meant to come here," Felix called to Lily above the noise of the water. "You see my Île des Lys," he sang out.

"The Island of Lilies," Trinity jumped in, nudging Lily and grinning.

In front of them the indolent river forked around a small island. In the middle sat a building, too small to be a house, but as a child raised on a farm Lily knew that it was an odd place to build a byre or a haystore.

"What is that?" she asked.

The dressed stones framing the door suggested it was too well regarded by its maker to be any sort of outbuilding. And yet the shuttered window was meagre and plain. All around the grass grew long and the path to the door was barely visible. Lily's eyes followed the track down to the platform at the water's edge.

The river moved slowly, creeping westward. To Lily it looked bottomless, but then she saw the causeway. It threaded across the water, stretching from the island to a spot a little downstream from where they stood. Waves lapped gently over the shining stone and then they rushed on, becoming white and high spirited as they met rock and boulder. Swaying with the hypnotic water, Lily unconsciously moved her feet apart to brace herself.

She was cold – cold through to her bones. Her eyes went back to the humble house. Across the river it lay and yet she felt her bare feet flattening the damp grass as she trod up the path. She knew already the weight of the door. It willed her to open it. Her hand curled unconsciously as it measured the round knob.

"What is that place?" She heard the tremor in her voice.

Lily turned to Felix. He had been studying her she realised.

"That is La Maison des Lys. And here we are in the valley of lilies although it is rarely called that anymore. So you see why I was so excited to hear your name."

He almost hopped from one foot to another.

"But what is it? I mean what's it for?" she persevered.

"It is my hermitage."

He had mistaken her look of bewilderment for one of incomprehension. "I am sorry," he said in competent English, "it is a sort of monk's house."

"Oh yes," she nodded, keen to show she understood. "It's the same word in English – hermitage. But what's it doing out there?"

Felix answered with the same word: once delivered in French and then in English, to be sure of her understanding. "Refuge. Refuge."

And Lily knew that she wanted to be there.

"I will show you everything later, but now you must meet the other guests. You are not my only visitors, you see. And now we are a house party."

He laughed and spread his arms magnanimously, puffing out his chest. Lily laughed too – at his halo of golden curls like spun sugar framing his face; the two spots of pink pricking his cheeks; his dungarees, baggy at the knees, looking like a work of modern art with their patchwork of stains.

*

At the misted window Lily blinked away the image of a healthy, happy Felix and bent to pick up his unwanted news. She turned to the dressing table and slipped the letter underneath a frayed mat, smoothing out the linen with both hands. It was hidden now and she would forget it. At least for a while. And then finding it again with her cleaning cloths in hand, she would throw it away.

Her hairbrush was the only other item adorning the rosewood top. Lack Farm had belonged to the Weavers for generations, but there were no photographs in silver frames, no perfume bottles, no candlesticks. When Lily was just six her mother had died and the day after the funeral Jack Weaver had emptied the house of his wife's possessions. Lily liked to think that this was the action of inconsolable grief. But she had no idea. Jack never spoke of his wife.

She attacked her hair, brushing out the tangles with more vim than she would have used with her beloved horses. With her arm swinging relentlessly she heard her father's creaking climb up two flights of stairs and then he appeared at the open door.

"Now then, lass," he announced. Lily knew the rest of the unsaid sentence: 'What does he want after all this time then?'

Jack said as little as possible in life as if there were only a finite number of words in a body like a finite number of heartbeats. He waited patiently, leaning on one ailing hip and then the other.

Continuing her assault, Lily winced, fixing her reflection with a fierce glint.

"He's dying – so he says."

Her father answered with a barely visible half-nod that in another might have been vocalised as 'ah well, that's the way of it'.

"I don't know why he's written. He still feels bad about Dom and me, I suppose. There's no need to. I always told him it wasn't his fault. I left him, not the other way round. We didn't belong there – we never did belong there." As her voice rose the words rushed out more quickly. Lily closed her mouth trapping the rest of the torrent.

She stopped brushing and glanced through the mirror at her father. She had almost said too much. Lies were so difficult to maintain, especially unspoken, unpractised lies.

She has heard a whisper say,
A curse is on her if she stays,

                Tennyson

CHAPTER THREE

A dusting of snow by day and frost at night brought Christmas Eve hard and glittering. For two days Lily had fidgeted with the letter, picking at it like a sore, unwilling to read it and unable to leave it. And for two days she had tried to distract herself, brushing her hair so that this night it shone amber with the fire's reflection as she sat with her father.

They ate a late supper in the dining room and Lily had built up the fire as high as she had dared without losing logs to the hearth. Lack Farm coped without central heating: that is, Jack and his son managed well enough with Lily there to light and keep fires and clean out all the hearths each day. The high ceiling'd room was normally used twice a year: Christmas day and Easter Sunday, but tonight Lily had persuaded Jack to sit in this loveless place with a bowl of lamb stew and a bottle of Burgundy between them. Trinity had given her the wine the previous New Year and this was Lily's first opportunity to open it. In the glow of the flames and candlelight, the shabby wallpaper and the sun-bleached curtains looked more like faded tapestries lining the room. Even the worn and curling rug at the hearth seemed sumptuous to Lily's eyes, which sparkled in gratitude.

The Weavers lived in the kitchen, a large, brightly lit, but grubby room. The men trailed in hay and muck, the collie left brown smears wherever it flopped down. Every day, the rasping and grating of dirt under her shoes offended Lily. She waxed the bumpy tiles weekly just to give the place an odour other than that of manure.

This night she was in a room that smelled of wood-smoke and wine. She breathed it in deeply and let her eyelids drop.

"And what's the meaning of these, then?" Jack enquired gruffly, pointing to the candles on the table.

Lily opened her eyes, but hid her irritation. Jack's cheeks were flushed and he leaned back into the chair curving around his broad back. He had consumed most of the

Burgundy and now sat with a bottle of port cradled in his swollen hand. His eyes shone. He seemed pleased with the break from routine that his daughter had engineered. But he was a man in the habit of complaining: he had perfected it in gestures and grunts. Lily had grown up recognising the signs: the way he moved sullenly from one foot to another; his peevish sighs of discontent; fretting about the newcomers across the field; nagging her about the telephone. 'Answer the bloody thing or we'll have folk at the door.' Lily often wondered how she had been blessed with such an easy going son. The Weaver family enjoyed the struggles of life far too much.

Dominic was not at Lack Farm for Christmas. He would spend it at Lily's cousins' in town. It was a tradition now. It had been her brother's suggestion that first time when she had arrived home with a borrowed suitcase and a small child. 'It's no place for a kiddie here at Christmas.' And Lily had relented. There would be no need for a Christmas tree or any of the other unnecessaries.

A loud long sigh from Jack brought Lily back to the present, but on this night it was a sound of contentment, tinged perhaps with happy memories of a wife and the promises he once had of life ahead.

Lily stared out at the black night through the window, now edged white with snow.

"Let's face it, Dad, tomorrow's nothing special, is it?"

Christmas would pass uneventfully: a morning of milking; lunch at twelve prompt – eaten quickly and in silence; and in between jobs listening to the Queen's speech.

"I know you'd rather be out there than in the kitchen," her father answered her as though accepting in advance an apology. Yes, she usually burnt the turkey. But if she were honest – it hardly mattered to her.

Jack rubbed his chest with his palms and murmured, "No clocks to watch tomorrow though."

Lily had been playing with the glass in front of her, but now stopped and smiled at the quiet man. Jack had officially retired from the farm that Michaelmas, and not a day too soon for his son.

"You're not going to help with the milking tomorrow?"

"No, your brother can manage. He's told me often enough. I can enjoy tonight with no worries about a thick head tomorrow." His eyes glinted mischievously.

Jack poured more port into the Georgian glass he had inherited from his grandmother and used normally only for that rare breed: guests.

Lily had not bothered to invite her brother David to eat with them this evening. At most he would have closed his door sharply in reply. His would be spent, like every other, in the old parlour. It had become a sort of bedsit for him. Lily dared enter each morning to clean and relay the fire, but otherwise the room was off limits to her and her father. The tinny blare of David's television seeped from his room each night. Jack had no television, and no need of one, he said. He counted out the hours of the evening in the kitchen, listening to the BBC. Even when her son was at home, Dominic was rarely in the house: he seemed always to have either a saddle or a guitar in his hands. Horses, music and friends filled his life. Without knowing it, he sang out to the world that he was no Weaver. A bittersweet song for Lily.

Felix's letter with its talk of confessions had unnerved her and that was the reason for the change in routine. Felix needed no absolution, but she would one day. Memories again. She left Jack at the table and restlessly walked to the window, ignoring the cold air blasting in through the thin panes. A milk white moon played hide and seek behind racing clouds.

"Tomorrow might not be much, but Christmas Eve has a bit of magic though, don't you think, Dad?"

Jack's eyes rested on his stubby fingers tapping the table lightly, but his mind wandered elsewhere.

"There is magic, you're right, lass, if you've got the time to see it." He stared into the candlelight.

His fingers stopped. He leaned to one side to look at the grandfather clock in the corner of the room and then pitched forward to squint at it more carefully.

"And we've got just enough time if we're quick," he said in a different tone.

His hand abandoned the glass and slapped the table. Gripping both arms of the chair, he hoisted himself up, pausing halfway and then continuing with a grunt.

"Let's go and toast 'em now. We've got a bit of time afore midnight. Takes me longer now to get out, but we can still do it." He pushed the chair away with his knee. "We'll do what I used to do with my old granddad when I were just a bit of a thing."

Lily stared at her father. Jack kneeled at the old cupboard, bottles clattering and clinking in protest as he carried out his search.

"Toast who?" Lily was pleased to be curious. Relieved to be amused. She had almost forgotten the letter.

He stood up slowly grasping a dusty bottle in one hand while his other comforted a knee.

"We'll toast my girls, of course."

He waved the whisky as though this was explanation enough. His lips moved silently as though practising and then he chanted aloud, "At the stroke of midnight, toast their health, but heed not their speech."

He looked wide-eyed at his daughter.

"Any beast that were there that night. You know, any that witnessed the birth. Don't gawp, lass – like I've gone daft. I'm talking about Bethlehem and the little babe. You toast those beasts that were there, and they in their turn bring good fortune and health to your house and kin." Jack stopped, breathless.

Lily opened her mouth slightly, but then closed it without a question being uttered. Her father's face glowed with an emotion she did not remember seeing before. She had no wish to change it.

"I remember well – seeing the cows kneeling afore my old granddad, but he made us leave as soon as he'd said his piece to them. 'If you're not quick, you can hear them speak,' so he reckoned. Ay, they speak in English just like you and me. But only at the last stroke of midnight. And you don't want to hear them or they'll tell you your own doom."

An unfamiliar look of fear crossed his face. Lily poured some port into her glass and saw her father snatch another look at the clock.

"Dad, I don't know what to say. But David won't be pleased if you go and disturb them in the middle of the night."

She looked away from him quickly and took a gulp of port to rid herself of the taste of betrayal. What did she care about her brother's fussing? "Dad, you know how David thinks everything affects their yield. He gives more thought to those bloody cows than anything else."

Jack dropped back heavily into his chair. Lily joined him and they sat in silence, listening to the clock. Jack pushed away his grandmother's glass.

"Ah well, I'm off," he said and Lily knew he meant upstairs to bed and not out to the sleeping beast. His tongue had retreated again and he shuffled from the room without another word.

She took her own turn to study the clock. Its filigree hands reached to each other as though in prayer, but the usual grinding that preceded the first stroke had not yet begun. She heard the floorboards creak above her head – a slow melancholic sound. In one movement she emptied her glass, pushed back her chair roughly and jumped to her feet.

Lily plucked up the whisky bottle and raced through the house, making for her boots, sentinels at the back door.

The yard was glazed white, but Lily ran across it thoughtlessly. She reached the stone byre with cheeks pink from the wine. The half moon gave enough light to make the doorbolt visible, but the frosted metal was reluctant to shift and she needed both hands. With the bottle held between her knees, she jiggled the catch free.

Lily breathed in the sweet smell of hay and warm bodies and beamed at her own animals, unseen in the darkness. She had left the heat of the house, not to visit her father's beast, but her own creatures that bore witness. For an instant she stood, enjoying the moment.

On the far side Lily sensed but did not see the old horse lift his head from the straw bed and then drop it again heavily, his curiosity appeased. He stretched out a hind leg and snorted.

"Only me, old boy – no need to get up. Anyway it's not you I've come to see."

As her eyes became accustomed to the dark, she focused on the space immediately in front of her and laughed out loud at the spectacle. Two donkeys, inquisitive of their unexpected visitor, were in the process of raising themselves from the straw-covered floor. Having straightened their hind legs first, they now knelt on their forelegs before standing up.

"The old man was right," she sang out jubilantly, clapping one hand against the knuckles of the other as she clutched the bottle. They rose from kneeling in unison and the paler of the two approached Lily, sniffing optimistically at the object in her hand. His lips quivered around her fingers and the glass until he gave up hope of food and instead stood quietly by her side, waiting for whatever the human needed to do at this strange hour.

Lily unscrewed the top and lifted the whisky to her lips.

"Here's to all of you," she started. The custom required particular words probably. Pondering on this, Lily took another swig, but then thinking of the clock's hands she burst out quickly, "And may we all have a good and happy life at Lack Farm." Yes, she was pleased with the hurriedly chosen words. A good and happy life.

The horse uttered a consenting snicker in response. Lily took a last look at the two donkeys. With their heads brought together as though confiding in each other they seemed to weigh up her wish.

A sudden draught bothered the door behind her and as it groaned and banged, Lily heard, "There'll be no happiness here for you, Lily."

She almost dropped the bottle, but tightened her grip quickly. The quiet insistent voice came from the stable. Somewhere in the stable – or was it in her head? The pale donkey passed his trembling mouth again over her hand, but this time Lily pushed away his soft lips and turned round quickly to the swinging door.

Out in the icy air, she secured the latch behind her with cold fingers and she heard again, "No happiness for you Lily."

She knows not what the curse may be,
                              Tennyson

CHAPTER FOUR

Trinity held the letter mid-air and scrutinised it. "What do you want me to say? Felix always loved amateur dramatics – but it's a good last scene, isn't it?" A laugh sparkled in her huge green eyes.

Lily had read it aloud – twice. She had hoped to convey an equal measure of incredulity and indignation, and had paused several times to allow Trinity to pass judgement. Sat on the other side of the oak table with her eyes fixed on the baby at her breast, Trinity had been in her own world of motherly bliss and was not budged easily. But cooing and purring, she had eventually plucked the letter from Lily's outstretched hand.

Now Lily wondered whether she had been listening at all. She had escaped Lack Farm for a few days to celebrate the turn of the year at Trinity's house on the Welsh Marches. It was a custom started when Dominic was not much older than the toddlers playing in the wild garden beyond the kitchen door. This year she came alone – Dominic had outgrown Trinity's parties.

Lily nudged her elbow sideways to avoid the trail of yoghurt sweeping across the table like pink Chinese calligraphy, and let her eyes rest on Trinity's generous breast and the contented infant suckling there. But she could not enjoy the moment. She fidgeted and waited for Trinity's agreement – that it was water under the bridge now, a long time ago, no use in looking back. This was just a portion of the list Lily had recited to herself on the long train journey.

Trinity's house was – in Lily's opinion – perfect in every way. For one thing, it smelled of new wood and beeswax. She had married a furniture maker and his craftsmanship filled the house. But more importantly to Lily, the windows were draught-free; the silent oak floors perfectly sanded and sealed; the walls were as smooth as plate glass.

"Still – I suppose we can allow Felix his melodrama as he's on his deathbed," Trinity remarked at last, continuing from her last thoughts. "Poor soul," she added without conviction.

She pushed her breast back into its proper place and stroked the child's down-covered head. A ribbon of milk dribbled down her emerald coloured cardigan. Trinity put her thumb to her mouth and rubbed at the stain vigorously, scowling at the garment as if it had behaved capriciously.

"I'm not going obviously. I mean, would you?" Lily had another attempt at coaxing an opinion from Trinity. "I'm not obliged to, am I?"

Lily had begun pulling at a coil of hair. She twirled and yanked it, making a bizarre spring on the top of her head. Catching Trinity's lopsided grin, she pulled her arm down and then – to be certain – sat on her hand.

"I can't believe he's done this."

"Done what? Written to his one and only love, you mean."

There was a disparaging tone in Trinity's voice that Lily tried to ignore.

"What was he thinking of?" Somehow Lily felt more vexed now in Trinity's kitchen than she had done on every other reading of the letter. She snatched it from Trinity's hand and put it back in its now shabby envelope.

Trinity arched one eyebrow. "Death probably. Anyway, why are you asking me? You're not going to take a blind bit of notice of what I say. You never have in thirty-two years, not since I showed you how to tie your laces in a double knot."

Lily had met Katrina Bell on their first day at school when they were both five. At the age of seventeen, Katrina rechristened herself Trinity. Proclaiming her new name, Trinity had likened herself to a bell ringing out into the world. 'A bell in every tooth more like it,' Jack had said.

Lily remembered the tussle over her shoes in the playground. Trinity had been a confident child. On all the school photographs she stood proud of the rest of the class, her size and huge grin impossible to ignore.

"You don't have a choice, Liliput. You have to go. It's one of those 'must do' obligations – you know, dental appointments, weddings, deathbeds." Trinity had been speaking with her head bowed to the baby, but now she sneaked an upward glance at Lily. "Funerals," she added.

"Let's be practical – that's what Felix is being, after all. I don't believe all that guff about the water and forgiveness for one minute."

Trinity had once believed though. She had been a witness. Lily studied her friend for any sign of disingenuousness. Perhaps she too had trained herself to forget.

"His mind's going – the drugs probably. Felix is shutting up shop, setting things in order," Trinity added firmly.

Trying to convince yourself, Lily thought. She had expected Trinity to dismiss Felix's words; to read the letter and toss it away. Instead, Trinity was interpreting it for Lily.

Trinity's tone changed – serious for once. "Dom will inherit Chez Reynat. You do know that don't you? In France the children automatically inherit."

With the tiny body attached to her chest, she moved to the window seat as if to distance her baby from Lily's unease. "And there is only Dom, isn't there? I mean there was no one after you?" Unable to keep in mood her eyes narrowed in amusement. "There isn't a Felix junior out there somewhere with the same taste in clothes, is there? God forbid – another Felix roaming the countryside in that little car. Can you imagine it? Sorry am I being insensitive again? I'm just making sure, Liliput. You never tell me anything. How would I know?"

Lily had taken a breath half-way through Trinity's questioning and now realised that she had held it there in a rigid chest. She let the words jump from their cage. "Dom won't want to have anything to do with that place."

The baby stirred, pushing up doll-sized fists. She curled and uncurled her fingers, but already used to clamour in her young life, she settled again.

"Of course he won't want to be stuck with a house in the middle of *la France profonde* at his age," Trinity soothed. She flexed her toes against the wood of the window seat and leaned her head back. "It's not like it was twenty years ago. Half the world seemed to be sticking their thumb out at the side of the D roads of France. We made our own entertainment, didn't we?" Her eyes teased Lily. "Nowadays they're off to educate themselves in other cultures, backpacking around Peru or Nepal. We both know Dom'd be bored witless in Achallat."

It was not boredom that Lily worried about. Dominic was only four when they walked away with a pre-war suitcase borrowed from Felix's neighbour. His memories would be hazy at best. But that curiosity of his would get the better of Lily.

"Go and make peace with Felix – hear what the poor old sod wants to say. Doesn't he deserve it? Liliput, you would've gone once without thinking. It's me that's the callous one, not you."

Lily barely heard Trinity. She was remembering two schoolgirls crossing France at a snail's pace. Curiosity of other cultures had very little to do with their travel. She recollected wet afternoons at Chez Reynat when Trinity had done no more than flop on the sofa and smoke joints with the others. They had said no more than a dozen words to the neighbours; had ventured to the local town only to buy provisions; had had no interest in the nearest city or its sights.

Trinity's feet walked up the wood and she smiled up at her toes. Lily said nothing. This was not just a case of stone and mortar; wood and clay. Chez Reynat was not just any house. A clammy ripple ran down her chest.

"What's the matter? You look like someone just walked over your grave."

'A watery grave,' Lily mumbled and shook her head to dispel the vision. She had wanted Trinity to support her; to tell her that a visit to a dying man was pointless. After all, that was why she had confided in her friend in the first place.

"Liliput, I know I'm venturing into forbidden territory here – but the paperwork's all there, isn't it? I mean Dom being Felix's son. You know what I mean."

Lily knew exactly. Only Trinity could have asked such a question. From that first day at Silsby school when they had clutched each other's hands by first break, Lily had confided in the girl with white blonde hair, standing head and shoulders above her. She was as close as a sister. Lily clenched her jaw and Trinity seemed no longer pleased with her toes.

With unsmiling eyes and a hard edge to her voice, Trinity said, "Are you going to answer me? No, bury your head as you always do. You're an obstinate soul, Lily Weaver, and you won't take telling, but you should have been open about it all from the beginning. If you'd told Dom when he was little, you wouldn't have all this bother now. Life comes back to haunt you." In a quieter voice, she added, "It's too late now, Liliput, I know."

*

As schoolgirls they had stood between the wellhead and the river Vamaleau at Chez Reynat, waiting for life to amuse them. Felix had beckoned both girls into the manor house with outstretched arms, gathering his armful of kittens to show off to his other guests.

"Come, come. Come and meet the others," Felix fussed.

He put a palm to Lily's back and thrust her from the austere hall into a vast room. Lily pressed her back to the door to let Trinity pass – and to take in her surroundings. In the gloom Lily made out carved wood-panelling reaching up past man-height. Massive beams hung overhead – the room was half as tall again as those at Lack Farm. Two sofas huddled together close to the fireplace, and behind them, Lily saw a refectory table stretching out towards the far wall. On one side of the table was a row of three French windows, gaping open to reveal the grassy bank and the river. Three flashes of brilliant water shimmered back at Lily. Opposite the doors sat a wide staircase, and either side of that a wall of books.

The dark room was filled with the scent of wood-smoke and something else that had an herbier aroma. Logs blazed in the fireplace, deep enough to accommodate a small household. In fact, there were benches either side of the recess for their comfort. But instead of a cosy family, Lily saw a figure curled up awkwardly on the hearth.

At first, Lily thought they had interrupted a speech. A booming monologue came from the man squatting on his haunches. It was a voice that was used to an audience – one that wanted to enlighten and entertain at the same time. Hearing the newcomers, he stood slowly like an insect unfurling itself from a cocoon. He was a stringy man, all elbows and knees. A wide toothy grin emerged between moustache and shaggy beard.

Trinity did not wait. She launched herself at the group. "I'm Trinity." She threw her hair behind her shoulders. "A trinity of women in one – I'm mad, bad and heavenly to know."

She delivered this seriously, in her peculiarly throaty voice, but after a second's dramatic pause, her raucous laugh engulfed the room.

It was at this point that Lily read the slogan on the beanpole's canary yellow T-shirt: Jesus, the Water of Life, and she wondered whether this time Trinity's proclamation would fail. But the men reacted as all others had before – not by laughing too, but with a look of focus and concentration.

Trinity had whetted their appetite. Only Felix seemed bemused. Perhaps he had failed to understand the English, Lily thought.

*

Trinity had spread from that nubile girl into a woman with an hourglass figure. With each child she had put on weight, but the fat served to emphasise her curves. She bit her lip now and turned her attention to her infant daughter.

The silence between them was brittle. With nothing to distract her from Trinity's last comments, Lily escaped outside, and instantly regretted not taking her coat. But she shivered rather than return. In the skeletal garden a few early snowdrops peeped through the unkempt grass; pink stars of winter cherry stood out against the anaemic sky.

Lily saw neither blossom. She scolded herself – how childishly she had behaved. She consoled herself – her best friend had no understanding. She congratulated herself – she needed no advice: her own good Yorkshire common sense told her to ignore Felix's emotional pleading.

As a hazy sun slunk back below the horizon, Lily sheepishly crept back into the house and tiptoed past her friend. Like a bitch and her pups, Trinity lay on the sofa with a book in hand and several dozing children gathered around her.

Trinity and Guy threw a party every New Year. And so that evening, Lily helped Guy to hurriedly empty food from supermarket bags onto plates while Trinity picked and nibbled, sucking her fingers and singing snatches of songs. Then Lily placed herself carefully in the sitting room as the guests arrived. With her bare feet under her, she snuggled into the depths of the sofa, content to watch the revelry acted out before her.

"Playing the observer as always," Trinity scolded, jumping up and down on the cushions until she was comfortable. "At least you haven't got your sunglasses to hide behind here. Have you spoken to anyone at all?" She wagged a finger.

Lily grinned. She and Trinity played a game – one as old as their friendship. Trinity knew Lily would not socialise – and it did not matter. Lily did not spend each New Year with Trinity to make new friends. She came to see a happy ending – Trinity's happy ending to the French adventure. Trinity had come back from France even more confident – she had blossomed. She had finished school, gone to university and gained a two-one in English and politics. She had met a reliable, handsome man – and married him.

Trinity's finger jerked closer to Lily's face. "And I know why you didn't marry Felix. You took it all too seriously – that – what should I call it – rite, ceremony, whatever it was. Was he even a real priest or vicar? Those days, eh. Crazy or what? But you're a serious woman, Liliput. You were a serious child – always with a paintbrush or a pencil in your hand. Where on earth did you get that from? I wouldn't have thought it was in the genes. Look at your brother..." She laughed suddenly, tossing the red liquid over the rim of her glass.

"You're drunk, Trin. Forget about Felix tonight." Lily wished she had never brought the letter; wished she had thrown it in the fire as soon as Jack had pushed it into her hand.

Trinity reached to Lily's wayward hair and stroked it back. "He made you happy though – even for a short while – and that's got to count for something."

Lily flinched and Trinity pulled back her hand.

"Felix tried his best. It was unfair on him," Lily said coldly, draining her glass.

"No, I didn't mean..." Trinity started, but then took hold of Lily's hand, its size incongruous with the calluses and texture of sandpaper. "Parties aren't what they were, are they,

Lily? Come and dance with me," Trinity goaded. "I promise not to embarrass you – I won't strip anything off tonight."

The taller woman pulled Lily to her feet and, for an instant, Lily saw a young girl, arms up-stretched with chest bare and hips swaying to the music.

Two days later Lily checked the station clock again, and wished Trinity would leave her to wait alone. With foggy breath, both women hugged their coats to their chests. Lily wore the only decent coat she owned – it was black velvet with a deep hood and a fitted waist. Trinity had passed it on after the birth of baby number two. Its hem had barely grazed Trinity's calves, but on Lily it was almost floor length.

The drone of the approaching train gave relief to both women and they unclasped themselves to clutch each other. Trinity stooped a little and hugged Lily so ferociously that Lily's arms flapped out like chicken wings.

"Give Dom a big fat kiss for me. And stop worrying! Go and see the old bugger – he can only bore you to death."

Lily had already made up her mind, but there was no need to quarrel about it now.

"While you're there, see an estate agent – an *immobilier* or whatever they call themselves. Don't look at me like that. Somebody has to talk sense into you. You could get it all sorted out in one trip. It could all be done and dusted in a few days. Look, I'll dig out the number of the solicitor we used when we bought the cottage in Brittany. Before you know it, you'll be back at the farm – everything back to normal."

Trinity smoothed Lily's hair down and kissed her on the brow. "Put the past behind you once and for all, Liliput – and then forget all about it. Don't let it chain you down. You won't be happy until it's sorted out. I don't suppose Dom'll even need to go over there. Really."

As the train scuttled away from the platform Lily watched Trinity throw her arm in a sweeping arc of a wave.

Something in her expression disquieted Lily and for a moment she heard again that voice in the stable.

CHAPTER FIVE

The headlights flashed twice before Lily recognised the old Land Rover outside the station. Bowing her head, she set her body against the sleet and made for the glare. She slammed the door shut against the weather and saw Jack in the driver's seat. The engine was running, his hands on the steering wheel as if he were only making a pit stop. Without a sound of welcome he kept watch on the wet snow sliding down the windscreen.

"You should've made Dom pick me up," she told him, shuffling her coat straight underneath her. Lily knew that her father hated driving in the dark and she now felt automatically at fault: she had put him out with her gallivanting, as he would call it. And he would make such a fuss if she offered to drive home. She could hear the indignation – "So you don't trust me at the wheel? My old body may be past farming, but I've still got my wits about me." Too tired to listen to the complaints that would come, she tried to stay silent. But guilt made her tongue restless.

"I didn't mean for you to have to come out on a night like this. I expected Dom to pick me up."

The car bucked as it pulled away and Jack waited for the engine to quieten before he spoke.

"Now then, lass. Had a fancy time of it, sitting around with nowt to do, eh?"

Jack was ignorant of Trinity's house and life, and Lily was sure he did not exercise his imagination on the subject. Lily's flighty friend had gone to university and married a public school type – that was all Jack cared to know.

"It was alright," Lily answered, well trained to sounding unenthusiastic. She rarely spoke about Trinity and felt irrationally disloyal to make too much of her visits. It would be as if she were complaining about her own home.

The journey passed without another word, Jack straining to study the road and Lily mesmerised by the squeaking wipers and looming arrows of sleet. As they pulled into the yard, Lily looked up automatically at Dom's bedroom window. It was as black as the night.

"So has he gone off to the pub then?"

Jack had switched off the engine while they were still on the lane, and he coasted the car into its parking spot in the yard. With screwed up eyes he bent forward to pull the keys from the ignition and, like a dog with a rag, he shook them as if freeing them took all his concentration. Lily's hand paused on the door handle. Unusually, Jack was wearing this silence badly – it sat awkwardly on him. He was being evasive, she realised. She shifted her body around to face her father squarely.

"Dad?"

Not even glancing at Lily, Jack opened his door and shivered noisily. "Let's get inside, lass, and put that kettle on," he said over his shoulder.

The telephone was already ringing in the unlit kitchen and Lily lifted the receiver, still examining her father as he switched on the overhead light and then made for the sink.

"Je voudrais parler à Monsieur Dominic Weaver, s'il vous plaît."

The French took Lily by surprise.

"I'm his mother. Who is this?"

"Madame Weaver, I am speaking from the hospital at La Grande Aubaine. I am sad to tell you that Monsieur Felix Reynat has died this evening. It was expected." The voice had softened before it reached the end of the sentence as if its owner were suddenly aware of its message.

Lily was mute. She felt nothing at first – and then guilt at the nothingness. She listened to the emptiness on the line, hoping some other words would be delivered to fill up the void in her head.

"I'm sorry," she muttered. Was it appropriate to offer an apology to Felix's doctor?

And then one thought arrived. She would not after all be forced to make the decision whether to visit him or not. But she was being dishonest – she had already resolved not to go. Lily glanced back at her father. Jack had turned down the flow from the tap so that he could listen more carefully. He stood motionless, the kettle in his hand, his eyes lowered discreetly.

Lily wanted to drop the telephone receiver; to end the contact with Felix, even such third-party contact. Poor Felix, she thought, I'm even escaping you now when you've left this world for good.

As though aware that he had stretched out his time at the sink for long enough, Jack began to busy himself with the business of tea making, but as he moved around the room his head was orientated towards her, her words, and the inaudible words at the other end of the line.

Lily could think of nothing to say. She was light-headed with an intoxicating mixture of relief and shock. "Do you know what the arrangements are for the funeral?" she heard herself ask.

"Madame, surely that is your domain. I have contacted you because your son is named by Monsieur Reynat as his next of kin. It is the family's duty to make such arrangements. I am aware that you are some distance away, but evidently we expect to see you as soon as possible."

Lily realised that Jack was staring at her.

"Are you alright, lass?"

Lily put her hands to her cheeks. She did not hear her father's fretting. He seemed far away in a cavernous kitchen. A wave of remorse surged up from the pit of her stomach as she remembered the pitiful letter. Felix had died after all without tasting his beloved water from the well – the well so precious to all in Achallat, to all of Felix's neighbours. They had a duty now to do one last favour for Felix, the owner after all of Achallat's liquid treasure.

Lily took her hands from her face. She scoured her memory for names. One of the neighbours was a cousin or second cousin – surely she could take charge.

"Bad news, lass? How about a spot of tea?"

Lily offered her father a grim smile. The problem was solvable – she would recall the name or even prod Trinity's memory for it. Her eyes fell on the kettle: the water had boiled; the tea waited in the pot. She remembered the question of Dom's whereabouts. Jack judged the situation well. He lowered himself into his chair in preparation.

"Now don't get yourself all in a lather. I dare say that phone call you just had has some'at to do with it all anyway. The boy went off this morning. We got a call from France – New Year's Eve. I couldn't make head nor tail of what the chap were trying to tell me so I handed it over to Dom – the lad were just about to go out."

Jack shook his head, and his face flushed with embarrassment. "Could hardly make out a word. I said to the boy – your mother goes away for two days a year and this happens," he grumbled.

"Was it Felix?" Lily asked simply. She wanted to hear the full story as quickly as possible. She had no wish to slow her father down.

"The boy was put out when he put the phone down. I suppose it upset him, hearing his Dad in such a bad way. He went straight upstairs to his room – didn't even bother seeing the New Year in. He must have brooded on it all night, because the next morning he were packed and ready for the railway station."

Lily heard a loud humming in her head like a swarm of house-hunting bees.

"He did right, lass."

"You're telling me that Dom has gone to Achallat or wherever Felix is in hospital. Is that what you're saying?"

"Caught the train," Jack affirmed. "How long will it have taken, do you reckon?" Jack had never before been interested in the geographical location of the small hamlet of Achallat where his only daughter and only grandson had spent five years.

Lily was not estimating the duration of the train or ferry journeys, nor the changeover in Paris. She was wondering what a dying man would say to the person who believed himself to be his heir.

CHAPTER SIX

'Fate' as Felix would have said, had brought her to the hospital at La Grande Aubaine. Although not happy fate.

The brightly lit office was bare, leaving Lily very little to occupy her eyes as she sat and waited. The flight to Paris and then Limoges had been followed by a night in an unremembered hotel close to the airport. She barely noticed the train journey that had brought her to the town. The taxi driver had quickly abandoned his attempt at light conversation, but had smiled sympathetically as he dropped Lily at the hospital. He was after all used to the quietness of visitors of the sick.

Lily wriggled under her layers of clothing and tugged at her collar. She pulled at the buttons to free herself of the coat and rolled it neatly, placing it on top of the holdall at her feet. She tried to recall the bag's contents. It had been packed for a New Year break – the clothes were unlikely to be suitable for this visit. She rolled her eyes at the empty room. Well, her coat was black at least – and so was the dress she wore for the party, she remembered. She had indeed packed for a funeral. Perhaps Felix would be content enough with fate this time.

A tall, slender doctor entered and shook hands with Lily. As she strode across to her desk she reminded Lily of an elegant wading bird. Lily formulated her question carefully. She had surprised herself – her understanding of French had not deteriorated during her years of absence, but the words came less easily to the tongue.

"Do I have your son's address here at La Grande Aubaine?" the doctor repeated. With perfectly arched eyebrows she expressed mild surprise at the enquiry, but diplomatically she did not ask how Lily had managed to mislay her son. "Well, perhaps we will find out."

Lily had half hoped to see Dominic sitting in one of the neon orange chairs at the hospital reception, waiting for Lily with a look of expectation as he had done at school – here was his mother to take care of everything. Instead he had acted like a grown up and had dealt with the bureaucracy of death. 'The son of the deceased has already signed all the papers' she had been told.

The doctor swivelled in her chair and flipped some pages. "Certainly he did visit Monsieur Reynat – in fact I remember a nurse telling me so, because Monsieur Reynat had been so contented afterwards. You see, he had been getting more and more agitated."

Lily imagined a serene Felix, unburdened by whatever had tormented him. The doctor's eyes flicked to Lily's hands gripping each other for succour. Lily untangled her fingers and spread them flat.

"Naturally enough he had been waiting," the woman explained. The half-smile bidden on her entrance to the room hovered tentatively. "It must be very distressing for you, Madame, to have failed to get here in time. It happens so often now – with families so far apart. And I know it is one of the things that people find so upsetting."

"Did Felix and my son speak for very long?"

The doctor could not guess the motive for her question, but Lily squirmed at her own words.

"Monsieur Reynat was quite tired by then – and of course the medication takes its toll. I remember he had had a busy day. Another foreign visitor – I mean besides your son – had spent some time that morning with him."

The doctor gazed at Lily and waited for a question. She received none. "Such a shame that you did not arrive in time for Monsieur Reynat. He held on as long as he could – his little bottle of water, waiting on the bedside table. His beloved water!"

The half-smile had widened and was now accompanied by a sparkle in the keen eyes. Lily felt as though she had failed to recognise a joke. The doctor leaned back in her chair, wanting to share it.

"An interesting man, your ex-husband – with an interesting history too. And so proud of it. At least so proud of his mother's history and the house of course. But, from your son's point of view, you should make enquiries about the paternal line. Monsieur Reynat told me that his father was a German soldier, but that he knew no more than that. Is that true?"

"Who knows?" Lily found herself saying. She had been curious at seventeen – curious, but incapable of probing. She had wished then for Trinity's bluntness.

"Perhaps he preferred not to know more. That part of our history is often difficult to uncover, but I must advise you to make the effort. After all your ex-husband's medical history is significant to your son."

"He's not my ex-husband – he wasn't my husband."

Lily's rebellious hands jumped around on her lap. She had no interest in Felix's history: it was of no importance. The doctor cocked her head to one side and regarded Lily with curiosity.

"So, do you think you and your son might live at Achallat? Too early to say, of course – I apologise for the question. It's just that Monsieur Reynat impressed on us all here the age and history of the place and Chez Reynat in particular – and I know the English love historic houses. I have English neighbours myself. You love to buy anything old – barns, farmhouses, stables. Ruins especially, eh?" The doctor's eyes narrowed mischievously at the unseen joke. "I have never been to Achallat – it's very remote and its road leads nowhere else, I believe. Monsieur Reynat made it seem quite magical though."

The woman tapped briefly at her keyboard, her eyes fixed to the monitor. "Yes, we have a telephone number for your son, but it is in England. That must be the one used to contact you, is that so?" She turned the screen so that Lily could see.

"I think I can help you," a voice said from the doorway. From his dress, Lily guessed that the young man was a nurse. "I spoke to your son – he asked me where the youth hostel was." Grinning, the nurse looked over at his colleague and shrugged his shoulders. "This is Aubaine – there are no hostels; we are not on the tourists' itinerary. But I told him that the cheapest place would be the Hotel des Pénitents."

"Is it still in business?" the doctor asked.

The nurse shrugged again.

"I think so – though you wouldn't think so to look at the windows." He looked over at Lily. "But he is a student, I think. He'll have seen worse. It's on the market square – you won't have any trouble finding it. Felix will be pleased you made it. He had visitors, of course – his neighbours mainly. He was an important member of that close-knit little community, I think."

He loped away, half-turning with a wave and Lily rose, her bag skidding along the floor as she pulled at it, eager to be on her way.

The long-limbed doctor blocked her path. "Here, we didn't know what to do with this."

Sheepishly she offered Lily a small glass bottle. Without even looking at it, Lily stuffed it quickly into her coat pocket.

"We could hardly pour it down the sink. I'm not even sure if it's holy water – you know, blessed in some way. I believe Monsieur Reynat half expected to be cured. That one sip would take away the tumours. Or perhaps it was more spiritual. What do you think?"

Lily could not tell the doctor; could not formulate the words. She had spent too many years expunging all memory of Achallat. Instead she shook her head as her hand crept to the cold glass.

Outside the hospital Lily took her bearings. The sky was cloudless, the shadows long under the poplars. Lily hoisted her bag over one shoulder and, as pilgrims had done for centuries, she set off for the church of Sainte Marie des Bains and its sparkling white spire.

Lily found the hotel easily and, as the bells dolefully proclaimed the midday, she swung open the ripple glass door. Standing on the threshold, Lily felt her senses punched. The aroma of French cigarettes and pastis; the brown varnished chairs and tables; the thick lace curtains – all said welcome back.

Dominic was not alone. He sat with a small child who, having leaned across from his own chair, now set both knees on the wobbling table and began to draw a thick purple line down her son's nose. Dominic pulled his features into those of a terrifying monster and the child squealed – probably at the absurdity of seeing such an angelic face transformed. He took up another crayon from the table to add to his creation.

Hearing the door, Dominic looked up and smiled casually at his mother. It was as though they met here every lunchtime, and Lily was content to smile back in the same fashion. She crossed the room and stood over him, putting her hand to his untidy curls.

"Your Granddad's worried sick." She off-loaded her own nauseous anxiety to Jack. "Why did you go off like that without waiting for me?"

Dominic raised one eyebrow carefully. "I don't think catching a train to France is regarded as high risk these days. Papa asked me to come – it was as simple as that."

The toddler, restless at his playmate's inattention, began to climb down from his perch. Dominic aided his descent and put a protective hand over the child's head as he ducked carelessly under the table. He waddled away and a high-pitched female voice greeted the child from the other side of a door.

Lily dropped herself into the vacated chair and studied her son for signs of change, signs of new knowledge, but Dominic looked back with an open smile and a purple nose.

"So you spoke to him?" she plunged in. She had almost said, 'Felix spoke to you?'

"Yeah."

Dominic's smile vanished and she saw in his eyes the image of Felix – yellowing skin and eyes sunken into their sockets.

"He looked awful. And he was as confused as hell."

"What makes you say that?"

A bubble of panic bobbed up in her chest. Swallowing it back, she said, "I'm sure you're right. He must have been very confused – with all the drugs they had to pump into him, I suppose. He must have been in a world of his own."

Her words rattled out quickly and her eyes darted from her son's face to empty space and back again to his intense eyes. He shook his head and Lily did not want to hear any more.

"Here's the odd thing, Mum. When I got there he looked up at me as if he recognised me – stretched out his arms to hug me. But I thought afterwards – he hadn't seen me since I was four – how did he know it was me after all that time. Then he asked me if I'd got his letter. 'What letter, Papa?' I said. In the end he figured out who I was. All the drugs, I suppose."

Like a glimpse of sunshine, Dominic's eyes flashed a smile. "But you know what? He seemed really happy to see me. Said I was my father's son. Funny expression that, isn't it – when you think about it. He kept pulling at my hair and laughing really loud. Weird – this incredible noise coming out of this shrunken frail body."

"But what did he say?" Lily realised she had failed hopelessly to hide her impatience, because Dominic's shoulders jerked back at her words.

"What do you mean?" he teased. "Did he tell me where the treasure was buried?" But seeing her expression, he screwed up his mouth in apology. "He really didn't say much – nothing really. Just kept looking at me and smiling. He didn't seem so pleased that I couldn't speak French – well hardly. After the mix-up about the letter and him mistaking me for someone else I asked him to speak in English – said my French wasn't so hot. He said, 'a boy of Achallat does not speak his own language? Anyway that was when it all got really confusing. I think his English was as rusty as my French."

The bubble of panic in her chest had divided and multiplied into a rising and swelling froth.

"I'm sure you're right." Lily kept her voice level. "His English was never that good," she lied. "What did he say?"

"He grabbed my hand." Dominic fixed bright eyes on his mother. "Held it really tight. What a grip from just skin and bone. He said that I must remember two things: that I must put my faith in someone or something called Oddo; and that I must surrender to the water."

Dominic leaned back and looked at the ceiling. "I've tried to think since what word he must have meant when he said surrender. It doesn't make sense does it?"

Lily was silent. Her eyes were on Dominic, but it was not her son she saw.

"And that was it. He was falling asleep by then."

The froth of panic subsided; the bubbles dispersed. On his deathbed Felix had not felt the need to burden Dominic.

"I don't suppose anything he had to say was important. What matters is that he saw you – that you were there. That was good of you, Dom. It's something you can feel good about."

The church bell thumped out the hour. Lily needed to change the subject – she needed to talk about practicalities.

"You've signed all the papers, so what's next? I'm in the dark – tell me what else there is to do." She stopped herself from saying 'before we can go home'.

Dominic slapped his hands on the table and sent the crayons rolling. "Yep, all sorted. The old boy sorted out the funeral himself, bless him. Down to the last detail. Nothing much to do, but turn up at the church, eh?"

The door from the kitchen creaked open and the owner of the high-pitched voice approached the table. She walked slowly with a pronounced sway to her hips: not the seductive swing of a siren, but the walk of someone used to long hours and heavy duties. Leaning on the table with her fists to relieve herself of her own weight for just a little while, she withdrew one hand to pat Dominic's head.

"Your mother has come, after all. I've made some extra pie, so there's enough for both of you. I'll bring it through now."

"Madame's potato pies are famous," Dominic informed Lily.

When the plates arrived Lily plunged her fork in and nodded at the hotel keeper, who had been waiting with folded arms for the verdict.

"So shall I keep your room for you?" she asked Dominic.

Lily jumped in. "Just for tonight – he's leaving in the morning. But I'd like a room for myself – for a few days at least." She looked at her son. "You don't need to stay. You've got exams next week, remember."

He gave her a look of disbelief, but before he could speak, the hotelier's soprano voice sang out, "I have a nice room in the back, Madame. It was papered in time for Toussaint. Such a lot of people come back to town then to visit the graves of their loved ones." Her face fell suddenly and she put a hand to her mouth. "I hope I haven't upset you saying that. Your son told me why you've come to Aubaine. He tells me you're from Achallat."

"No – we're not. We lived there for a very short time only."

"There's a lot said of the place by some of the old folks, but I can understand why you're not boasting about it." She laughed and walked away, shaking her head.

Dominic gripped the edge of the table with his fingers, his eyes had not wavered from Lily.

"You have got to be joking. I came all this way and I'm staying for Papa's funeral."

"You were here when it mattered." Lily tried to sound sincere – she had wished he had not come at all. "I want you to go home – you can catch a train in the morning. Missing a funeral isn't like missing a party – the host won't be there either. Let's face it, you won't know a soul there, and you won't understand anything of the service anyway."

"I don't need to understand anything. It's the sending off that's important."

"No, what was important was that you saw Felix when he was alive – and that he saw you."

They ate in silence. Lily watched Dominic from under her lashes, wondering whether more persuasion was needed.

Dominic pushed his empty plate away and drummed his fingers for a moment. "Hey, they gave me his stuff – you know – identity card, wallet and things, but..." and he stopped as his hand pursued something behind him.

He dug down into the pocket of the jacket draped carelessly on the back of his chair and pulled out a soft leather wallet. Once opened on the table, it revealed two keys. Both were oversized, but one was much larger than the other and this Dominic took from its holder.

"What do you think? They look like the keys to a castle or a dungeon or something." He grinned and pulled a face not dissimilar to his earlier creation for the toddler.

The key straddled Dominic's youthful palm, its grey metal polished by many hands before him.

"Do you know what they're for, Mum? Do you recognise them?" He thrust out his hand.

Lily's eyes were on the other key still resting on the worn leather. From far off, she heard Dominic repeat the question and she shifted her attention to the key in his hand.

"That is the key to Chez Reynat," she told him. Her dark eyes grew blacker.

"He gave them to me before I left. He was almost asleep, but he had them under his pillow." Dominic frowned slightly. "He put the wallet in my hand and said, 'this is yours now.'"

Lily's finger touched the key and her shoulders dropped. She could no longer sustain the tension. She gave in.

"Yes, I suppose it is."

CHAPTER SEVEN

Despite bowed backs, ailing feet and failing hips, Felix's well-wishers scurried to the safety of the village square, leaving him in his small vault with his mother and forbears. Lily trailed after the mourners and then stopped to watch them pass through the tall iron gates. Behind her, the pallbearers finished their task. So that was an end to it, then. All around fresh flowers decorated the serried tombstones. Lily wondered who would bring blooms for Felix next week, next year.

The squat houses of Saint Bénigne les Fontaines shunned their dreary graveyard. It hid behind high grey walls as if its contents might offend the living. Lily hung back from the sombre-clothed throng, threading its way up the narrow alleyway. She had been ushered down the aisle of the church for the Mass and had sat alone in the front row – she had no wish for more attention. She was, after all, just someone from Felix's past.

She would telephone for a taxi from the small bar – no need to prolong the 'must-do obligation', as Trinity had put it. She had said her farewell to Felix – it was done. Heads turned as they had done in the graveyard, but all eyes avoided her.

A feeble sun struck the thick walls of the church, leaving the rest of the square in cold shadow. The hushed congregation settled itself briefly beside the warm stone and then, as though by some unseen command, it deserted the church. That building had served its purpose, guiding Felix from this world and offering succour to those left behind. The people inched their way towards the bar on the corner of the square, pausing every few steps, looking around and, with a pat on a fellow shoulder, shifting again. It was as though no one wanted to be the first to end the grieving nor to be the first to start the consoling in the 'Bar des Voyageurs'. A disingenuous name Lily thought – she doubted whether many travellers came to Saint Bénigne – until it struck her that Felix was now on a journey of sorts.

Lily's eye was caught by a woman standing back from the throng. This other outsider surveyed the gathering through dark glasses, a silk scarf covering her head in the fashion of a nineteen fifties' starlet. She wore black like everyone else – in her case a badly fitting suit, the buttons straining across her chest, but what made her stand out were the scarlet stiletto heels.

Lily pulled her black velvet coat tight about her and stomped her feet on the uneven cobbles. She wore her flat brown loafers, mud splattered still from the yard at Lack Farm. Mismatched with the coat, but ludicrous with the short black dress she wore underneath. It had been a hasty decision that morning in her hotel room – the strappy black sandals still packed for Trinity's party or the warmer loafers. Now she wished her feet had suffered frostbite.

The arm around her neck took Lily by surprise and she crumpled sideways as the strong hand gripped her shoulder. Lily recognised the owner's face instantly. It had seemed ancient twenty years earlier, but it had not aged any more in that time as though it had been given a second wind. It was a robust face; a ruddy, smooth face in rude health. The nose sprouted short dark hairs, not just from the nostrils, but also from its bulbous claret-coloured tip. Above the slack jaw, a thick protruding lower lip quivered. The double-breasted pinstripe suit seemed as old as its wearer although it was not in the least worn. A layer of pale dust on the shoulders betrayed the suit's history. Underneath, a frayed flannelette shirt and pilled sweater kept the cold away from the old man's chest. Pin-prick eyes fixed Lily firmly.

"*Bonjour*, Baptistin."

Lily writhed free and offered her hand, but the old man pushed it aside, clasping her shoulders and delivering an insistent wet kiss on each cheek. She smelled that day's lunch – garlic and wine – on his breath, but the stronger scent was earthy, as if he had grown out of the deep brown soil in the fields behind them.

"And where is your son?" he demanded, swivelling his head this way and then the other, scanning the now almost empty square. Lily knew that this was a little charade: Baptistin would have seen her sitting alone in the church.

"He couldn't come. He's got exams coming up – he's at university." Lily tore her eyes from Baptistin's gaze and studied her offending shoes instead.

"What are you saying? He's not here? His father's funeral?"

The old man's voice was as vigorous as his body. Lily felt her cheeks flush as the mourners at the bar door turned their heads.

"It was a long time ago, Baptistin. What I mean to say is, we left here a long time ago. And besides Felix and I never kept in touch."

The last few words were delivered with a hint of defiance. It was none of the old man's business, but she felt hampered by politeness and the respect due to his age.

"A long time," he repeated, sounding bewildered. "It doesn't seem so long to me."

Lily squirmed under the scrutiny of his piercing eyes.

"So he's at university? He's grown up then. Big, I suppose. They all are today." Baptistin's eyes softened as he scrutinised Lily. "It doesn't seem that long since you first came here. You would've been about the boy's age."

Lily's hands fluttered nervously at her side. She had no wish to revisit old times. Over Baptistin's shoulder she watched the last of the swarm disappear through the door as bees to a hive entrance.

53

He saw her attention stray. "Come on then – let's get in," he ordered. "A little cognac is necessary on occasions such as these. Let's get out of the cold."

And Lily let herself be led inside. In the narrow space the stools had been pushed aside to give more access to the bar extending the length of the room. Tiny glasses of golden liquid lined the wood counter. With a hand again on Lily's shoulder, Baptistin plucked at one as if it had waited just for him. The barman smiled benignly at all. These were not his regular customers although he recognised some faces from previous funerals – and from a few happier occasions too. He watched the old man throw the drink down his throat. Lily watched too. Baptistin's hand found another glass, his rheumy eyes on Lily, hinting at intrigue known only to him.

He drew his mouth into a crafty smile and moved his hand to cup her flushed cheek in his rough palm. "You're back then."

Lily felt like a captured bird.

Shaking his head, Baptistin brought the glass to his lips. "To Felix – too young" he said, "I've never known one of Achallat die so young. It's unknown," he whispered hoarsely. "Yes, there have been accidents in the past – my uncle burned in his bed and there were drownings, they say. But I think perhaps we're cursed, not blessed as we've always believed." Baptistin jerked his head to one side and dropped his voice further. "Don't let the others hear me say it though. The river doesn't talk the way it used to. And not one of us has children. After all, aren't children supposed to be the greatest blessing."

Suddenly his voice boomed, discretion forgotten. "All childless – except Jopert and his wife, of course. But their daughter went off to Paris to join the sixty-eight protests, and she never came back. Married a Parisian by all accounts. Anyway she's long forgotten now – even by the river." He looked intently at Lily. "But then there was Felix's. Yours and Felix's. And yet you say he's not coming."

Lily caught the sharp ring of anger in his voice and she opened her mouth to say some empty words of sympathy, but he stopped her, his eyes hardened. "The curse of Achallat," he spat out.

This was not the Baptistin that Lily remembered. Not that she had taken much notice of him that first summer. He was just one of the elderly neighbours that gathered each morning and evening at the wellhead.

*

"Don't they have their own water?" Lily had asked Felix one day as she sat on the grass by the well, listening to the villagers' chatter.

Lily guessed that Baptistin had been in his late sixties then, perhaps older, but his face was no more lined now, twenty years later, his hair no thinner.

"Of course they have their own water," Felix had answered. "Achallat is not such a backwater. But they come here for drinking water."

"Theirs isn't fit to drink?"

Felix had smiled patiently as if Lily were a small child, ignorant of very obvious truths.

"Theirs is from the same source, but Chez Reynat's is blessed – I've told you. It was there that the spring appeared – where they laid his body. Oddo's."

That name again, Lily had thought then. Wells, springs – these people take water so seriously. Barely more than a week into her stay at Achallat and she was already tiring of Felix's stories. Trinity had taken to wandering off as soon as that particular light came into his eyes. The other houseguests had obviously had to sit through the tales for weeks before Lily and Trinity arrived, because they seemed not to hear him at all.

Lily had noticed that Baptistin was always the storyteller of the gathering at the well, his trumpeting voice echoing through the small valley. The others listened, sometimes grinning and nodding in anticipation of the ending, sometimes making noises of disapproval – especially the women.

'*Ah non*, Baptistin,' would be the cry, and the men would laugh raucously. When the travelling shops arrived – the boulangerie, the épicerie, the charcuterie – the tales would be all the wilder and the women would march away huffily with their heads in the air and their turned backs as straight as the surrounding poplars.

*

Lily watched Baptistin throw back another cognac.

"Death is not a curse," a low voice said liltingly behind Lily.

She wheeled round to see the priest who had performed Felix's farewell so magisterially. He towered above everyone else. Not that there were many left – most had deserted the bar after their first nip of cognac and made their way to the adjoining room. Lily could just make out through the archway, tables laid with starched white cloths, wine glasses and silver cutlery. Felix would have approved of the attention to detail. The aroma of soup wafted through to the bar and Lily's stomach suddenly complained of its neglect.

Grudgingly, she turned back to her two companions. A smile flickered briefly and awkwardly on the priest's face. Having got the attention of Lily and Baptistin, he now blushed to the tips of his ears.

"You don't need to lecture us of Achallat about the web of life, Father," Baptistin grunted. "It was because of one man's death that we are blessed."

The priest beamed. "And we receive everlasting life from our Lord."

Baptistin shook his head, his loose lips just one beat behind. "That is so, that is so, but I'm talking about the particular blessing of Achallat."

The priest raised a hand to stop him in his tracks. "Of course – the story of the monk. Legend has it that his bones lie in that river there somewhere. Now let's see – that would be the Vamaleau flowing through Achallat. Am I correct?"

Baptistin did not attempt to hide his irritation at the cleric's ignorance. "Not a monk, Father, no. A saint he should have been, but he was a holy man all the same – and still is to us."

Lily found herself entranced by Baptistin. He turned his attention to her.

"But you, Lily, you already know all this. Felix would have educated you in this. You remember?"

Remember? She had spent fifteen years forgetting.

"That was a long time ago, Baptistin." It was an age ago, a different time. She tried to meet his gaze. "Felix told me those stories so long ago. I really can't remember much."

But she did. Here, back in the landscape that she had fled, the memories were floating to the surface like wreckage from the river bottom. Baptistin smiled in recognition and Lily searched for escape – a friendly face amongst the mourners – but she found none. She was a gatecrasher. These people were gathered to share memories of a man that had lived all his life among them. She had no stories to share. None she wanted to share.

"These legends are deeply ingrained, especially in such backwaters, but I see that you are not impressed, Madame." The cleric spoke in a satisfied tone as though he had found a kindred spirit. He licked his meagre lips and waited for agreement.

"Nobody could be unimpressed by Chez Reynat," Lily answered. Even here several kilometres away she felt its walls oppress her. "The stories about Oddo and the water…" Lily tried a shrug. She wanted to be an unbeliever. "Felix

57

saved them for visitors. He liked to entertain," she said haltingly, searching for the correct word in French. She smiled thinly back at the sceptic.

"You left sometime ago, I believe," the priest continued, colouring again as he saw Lily's reaction, and he pulled his shoulders back defensively. "I barely knew Monsieur Reynat. He was not a regular church attender, but we did become acquainted during his final weeks. Felix talked to me." He closed his mouth firmly.

"Here, my girl, drink to your man. It's unbecoming to stand there without a drink in your hand," Baptistin interrupted, thrusting a thick glass in her hand.

Lily welcomed the cognac and gulped it quickly. She reached for a second glass. The priest regarded her intently – perhaps he knew her secrets as well as Felix's. It did not matter – Dominic was back at home.

Baptistin thumped his glass down on the counter and straightened his back. He pulled at his stiff jacket, rearranging his body inside it, and loosened his collar.

"Felix was a thoughtful neighbour. A good neighbour yes, Mon Père Guillaume. Felix may have had his faults, but he stayed true to Achallat. And now you'll have to excuse me, I can smell my lunch." He winked at Lily. "Second lunch."

Lily saw her window of opportunity. She scanned the room for signs of a public telephone, and instead spotted the woman with the red shoes through the open door. She had removed her headscarf to reveal hair stiff and spun into an untidy chignon. Moving from one table to another, she leaned her head in towards the seated diners. Knives were waved in the air in the direction of the bar, heads nodded in the same direction. The enquirer craned her neck and directed her eyes at the bar. Lily glanced behind her – perhaps it was the priest she sought, but like everyone else he had followed his nose in search of a good meal.

Lily was not alone for long.

"I'm so sorry for your loss, sweetie," the stranger cooed to Lily in English, transferring her cigarette to her left hand as she reached out with her right.

Lily was so surprised by the language that her hand had not moved to greet the other. The woman turned her unwanted instrument to good use and stroked Lily's arm as though she were an orphaned puppy.

"You must be devastated. Your husband was so young – by today's standards anyway," she said and swept away the ash from the front of her labouring jacket. "We all hope to live to be a hundred, don't we," she laughed. "It's at a time like this you must miss home – I mean England. Where is your son by the way?"

The question had jumped out so unexpectedly that Lily's head had bobbed backwards. Her lips fumbled with the glass and then she dabbed at the drop of cognac on her chin.

"I'm sorry, but are you a friend of Felix?" Lily felt embarrassed by her ignorance. "I mean, were you a friend of Felix?"

Without food the cognac had had an instant effect and now Lily felt disorientated as if the inside of her head were failing to keep tempo with its exterior.

"I never had the pleasure of knowing your husband…"

A short laugh exploded from Lily's mouth and several heads turned curiously. She shook her head, shocked at her own reaction.

"I'm sorry. It's just the occasion. The funeral, I mean – and I haven't eaten." Lily put the glass on the counter. "It's just that you're the second person today to call him my husband – he wasn't. We were never married."

The woman drew one last time on the disappearing cigarette and dropped it gently to the floor, stubbing it efficiently with a scarlet toe. She flicked at her skirt briefly.

"That's none of my business. Husbands, partners, lovers, – who cares about the name. The fact is you've been left bereaved in about the worst position you could – alone out here. Then there's the paperwork. But I can help with all of that – no problem. Listen, phone me whenever you like. I know it's early days yet, but in my experience people in your situation are keen to get back. It's this sort of thing that makes us homesick. The French dream is wonderful while everything's going well. I've seen your place – just from the bridge. A lovely spot." She stopped and held her head to one side. "By the way – how old is your son?"

"Who on earth are you?" Lily asked and, as she did, she felt a small card pressed into her palm. She flipped it over and read,

Venetia Crow
Waterside Idylls
French Property Specialist

Lily read it several times before she grasped the situation. She looked back at Venetia, too stunned to speak. The estate agent patted Lily's hand.

"As I said, when you're ready, sweetie. I'll leave you now anyway – you're busy with the business of giving your husband a send-off."

The draught from the opened door was too short-lived, and Lily tugged at the scarf at her neck. An hour earlier the conversation had been muted, but now the mourners laughed, raised their voices and howled with delight.

Lily left the bar easily with no one noticing. Venetia was still clipping across the cobbles with stiff steps, coils of hair trailing from their tether.

"You can go and see the house tomorrow if you like," Lily shouted out to the woman's back.

Venetia turned and said nothing for a moment. Then, at Lily's side she found a pen and another card and scribbled something quickly. She looked at Lily with a practised expression that portrayed sympathy and practicality.

"Right, sweetie, give me your number. I can't make it tomorrow, I'm afraid. You should see my diary! But I'll call as soon as I can. Then I'll look the place over and we'll take it from there."

"I don't know the number."

Venetia Crow blinked, but did not remark on this ignorance. "No problem – I'll get it from the phone book." Venetia pushed the card back into her bag.

"Actually, I'm staying in Aubaine – at the Hotel des Pénitents. I want it sold quickly. I'm not bothered about the price, I just want to be rid of the place. You see, I don't belong there."

Venetia patted Lily on the shoulder and glanced her powdered cheek against Lily's. "Of course," she answered as if she understood everything.

Willows whiten, aspen quiver,
Little breezes dusk and shiver
Thro' the wave that runs forever
By the island in the river,

                        Tennyson

CHAPTER EIGHT

Lily turned a circle on the cobbles as Venetia's black car glided away. Her eyes moved from the bar – a beacon in the January afternoon, to the clock tower, to the carved church door, and then to its high arched window. The sun lit up a stained glass figure. Tending the golden corn at his feet, the labourer held his hands up in devotion, but Lily saw it differently. She saw arms thrown up in anger, eyes wide with resentment. She shoved her hands into her pockets and kicked the toe of her shoe at the granite.

Her body was in the habit of occupation – it hungered for physical labour to still the mind. Restless legs took her to the end of the square and down the alleyway until she reached the crossroads.

On the narrow lane that led west, bare trees arched into each other, a cluster of sparrows scuttled around at the base of the wooded tunnel. Lily looked back to the square and then to the tilting signpost beside her. 'Achallat 3 kms', it read. A mere three kilometres, it seemed to say – an afternoon stroll, an escape from Felix's friends. Come on, the black lettering urged, stretch your legs. Her first steps were reticent – two or three. She paused and took a few more. Then with a flick of her hair over her shoulders, she moved briskly, her steps calling out loudly to the graveyard as she passed its walls.

She fell into a comfortable gait – some exercise would do her good, she told herself. Spotting an imposing oak in the distance, she decided to use it as a marker. 'Just to the tree and then I'll turn back and get a taxi to the hotel. With luck they'll be leaving the bar by then.' But she reached the oak and passed it and each turning point along the road was ignored. The overhanging trees were left behind and the land opened up. At a low bridge, she stopped and crouched over its wall to watch the garrulous stream. She had brought Dominic here in the evenings – a device to wear out the toddler before bedtime and an opportunity to escape the resentful eyes of Felix. Dominic had been a child at ease with the world around him and as he grew this seemed to irritate Felix more and more. She had seen Felix glare at the child's black hair; seethe at his steady grey eyes.

The brook gurgled good-naturedly beneath Lily. She sat on the wall, gathering her coat up from under her and placing the folds on her outstretched legs. Ahead, she glimpsed ruddy roofs through the trees and knew these to belong to the two cottages that stood as sentries at the entrance to Achallat.

Time passed. The sun hurried westwards and the sky coloured. And Lily was almost motionless – her hands had occupied themselves while her mind dithered over which way to direct her feet. A flock of doves spun overhead and their whirring brought her out of her reverie. Wings flashed white and turned as one, and then they were gone. Lily looked down to see the key case in her palm. She held it as though weighing it, measuring her choices. Angry with herself, she jumped from her seat and stared over the bridge, the keys clutched in her fist, her arm thrown back. If only it were that easy. Cast them into the stream – let the waters take them back to Chez Reynat.

Instead she let the road take her west. She passed between the two guardians and stopped on Achallat's ancient arched bridge. Below her the birch and aspen were bare and silent, the banks of the river brown with winter's sleep.

Chez Reynat stood resolute.

Leaning out over the stone, Lily could just make out the wellhead between dark branches. The chestnut tree stretched its old arms out to reach both the well and the river as if trying to unite both waters. Under the bridge, the Vamaleau moved lazily and then it broke into agitation just past the house, tumbling past the aspen trees.

Lily hugged her arms to her chest and looked down on the great house. Its walls seemed to spring from the riverbank; its rust roof – angled this way and that – rose through the aspen.

Facing east and the approaching road, Chez Reynat's massive door proclaimed its importance.

A glorious crimson seeped from the western sky. Lily kept her eyes on the house, not daring to let them fall to the other side of the river. There, the building on the island glowed like rose quartz in the sunset. Lily did not look. She pushed herself away from the wall and continued her walk past the square white house on the corner, past Baptistin's little cottage until she came to Felix's home and Dominic's burden.

Chez Reynat loomed above her, lead coloured and cold. Across the Vamaleau, the little blue boat swayed about in water stained red by the setting sun.

Lily climbed the one step of the well. It was here that Oddo was struck down. Or so Felix had told her. Legend did not say who was the assassin or what the motive, but Oddo not only forgave his assailants, but blessed them with a spring where his blood fell on the ground. His body was due to be taken to the nearby monastery for burial and no doubt the harvesting of his bones for relics, but the residents of Achallat were loathe to part with their holy man and so they laid him in the river at moonlight. And so Oddo had rested for over thirteen hundred years, keeping Achallat safe. Felix always told the tale as though it were a bedtime story, a comfort to small children, Lily remembered. It was because of Oddo that Chez Reynat's well belonged to all in Achallat, he recited.

A damp chill rose from the river and Lily pulled the hood of her coat up over her head. Here Lily had learned about life and almost discovered death. It seemed to her as though a cold hand reached out from the water, sneaking under her clothes and gripping her bones. She turned her back on the Vamaleau, turned her back to unseen eyes. With the key in the lock, Lily put one hesitant hand to the knob and another to one of the wide oak planks – and pushed open the ancient door.

*And up and down the people go,
Gazing where the lilies blow
Round an island there below,
The island of Shalott.*

                    Tennyson

CHAPTER NINE

Lily heaved the door shut and it whined its way to the frame. She felt as though she were buried with Felix in his vault. It had always seemed more like a church than a hallway, the stone basin its baptismal font. She braced herself for the next door.

Even after Lily had opened the shutters of the French windows, the vast room was still dark. On the long table a posy of forget-me-nots, dried the summer before, welcomed her. *'Ne m'oubliez pas'* Felix still reminded her. 'I have forgotten, Felix,' she whispered to the silence. She strode back to the hallway, the keys still in her hand.

But then Lily realised that the house was not without noise. An oscillating sound, light and erratic, came from one of the upstairs' rooms. Her eyes to the high beams, Lily crept to the foot of the staircase and then, with a smile of recognition, she ran up two steps at a time.

On the bare wood floor a dove surrendered to defeat and lay with its wings outstretched, its beak open. Lily snatched up a blanket and flung out her arms, tossing it like a fishing net over the wretched bird. With the bundle under her arm, she wrestled with the window latch and pushed open the shutter. In a moment the palpitating body was free and it swooped across the water. Lily watched the dove dip and rise until it disappeared past the high meadow on the other side of the river.

She turned round to face Felix's room.

His carved bed stood against the opposite wall. Lily imagined Felix, propped against his hard pillow, looking out at the square framed sky. Beside the bed was a marble topped table, top heavy with a pile of books. Lily picked up the first – *Les Essais* by Michel de Montaigne. Inside, Lily found an inscription, 'Émeline Reynat 1938'. Felix had taken to reading his mother's books in his last days at Chez Reynat.

The script was childlike, written before a soldier had befriended and made love to a young country girl.

The room was simple – austere even, Lily thought now, but it was unchanged since she had last seen it. An armoire stood against one wall and a small fireplace against another. The only furnishings were a hard bolster, the blanket, and a plain cotton bedspread.

"You were always so tidy, Felix." It was a trait that irked her, but that was just an excuse, she knew. Any habit of Felix's would have annoyed her. In the end it was even the movement of a hand that could fill her with contempt. She opened the wardrobe and, finding it empty, a wave of anger and pity pulled at her face.

"Always thinking of others, Felix. Always being so bloody good. You're not supposed to sort out everything yourself – not when you're dying. Didn't you think anybody would do it for you?"

She imagined his last days at his beloved home as he must have filled boxes with his folded clothes and polished shoes. Lily pushed the hair back from her face and rubbed at her brow with the palm of her hand as if to wipe away the pictures in her mind. She hurried out and closed the door behind her.

She did no more than glance in the other rooms from the corridor – all were neat, but smelling stale and unused. Outside the final room at the south-east corner of the house, Lily stopped and leaned against the bumpy plaster wall of the corridor. With her fingertips, she pushed open the door and waited to recognise her room.

It was as she had left it – she could see that even before she opened the shutters. With the daylight blinking in through the window, her eyes fell on the two small beds, both curtained against the chill of the winter. These had been hers and Dominic's. The heavy mirror above the chest of drawers looked too imposing for such a modest room. The threadbare floral rug at the foot of the larger bed was more in keeping.

On the chest was just one object – a ring with tiny rubies studded around it. It had been placed carefully – in the centre of the polished top, the red stones sparkling out to face the room. Lily opened up the top drawer and swept the band into it with the edge of her hand.

"This doesn't belong in here, Felix – it never did. You should've packed it up with the rest of your things."

The bitterness on her tongue shocked her and she avoided her own eyes in the mirror – she had only just left his wake. Dropping into the armchair, Lily turned to face the outside world and the treetops of Achallat. She watched the pink sky grow grey and closed her eyes.

It seemed she heard the laughter downstairs of the Americans that had strayed here twenty years earlier. Set out to explore Europe they had discovered that their real goal was to escape. And then they found Achallat. Or perhaps Achallat had found them, Lily mused dozily.

In darkness Lily woke confused and cold to the bone. She tried to rise from the chair, but her legs were like dead tree limbs, and she wobbled sideways, bruising her ribs on the heavy wood arm. A sliver of light from a crescent moon crawled into the room and Lily groaned, recognising at last her surroundings. As an owl hooted wearily, Lily limped to the nearest bed and crept under the covers. She ignored the rough ticking of the mattress and pillow and curled herself up into a ball like a dormouse disturbed from hibernation. She slept again.

Hunger woke her before the sun rose and, wrapped in a heavy blanket over her coat, she descended the stairs in search of food.

The main room occupied almost all of the ground floor, with the hall at one and the narrow kitchen at the other. The French windows opened to the south and the Reynat's library lined the north wall.

Lily's stomach cried for attention. A thought flicked through her mind that Felix may have been as ruthless in the kitchen as he was in his bedroom and cleared out the cupboards there too. Opening one empty cupboard after another, Lily began to lose hope, but then she discovered a canister of coffee beans, an unopened packet of toasted bread, and a whole shelf of homemade jams. Bouncing on the soles of her feet to keep warm, Lily swivelled the jars to read the labels, but then, defeated by Felix's unintelligible decorative handwriting, she picked one at random.

As she crunched through dry toast and fig jam, she finished her inspection of the other cupboards, all bare but for one filled with wine bottles laid on their side. Felix had cleared the house of his own inconvenient belongings, but had thought of the comfort of whoever came to stay – and he had expected it to be Lily. She hurried past the thought.

Grinding the beans, Lily ate at the counter and waited impatiently for the water to filter through the ground coffee. Felix's kitchen still smelled of garlic, of herbs and cooking, but the damp green scent of the river soaked through the three-foot thick stone walls and hung in the air. She lit the four gas hobs and held her hands out over the steady blue flames.

*

She had stood in the same spot before, hovering beside Felix as he had chopped vegetables and stirred the contents of saucepans. As he cooked he told her his tales and flapped his hands at her.

"No, no, no. I have no need of help. *Tout va bien, je t'assure,*" he had sung out, glancing at her sideways with shining eyes. He wanted no aid, but he was pleased with her company. She was glad to escape the relaxed party atmosphere of the living room. An upbringing on Lack Farm had not equipped her with the skills to talk casually of serious things. Discussions had been confined to the classroom and conducted by the teacher. Her father and brother never spoke of anything that did not take place within ten miles of the farm. Livestock prices, the weather, the suspected folly of the new veterinarian – these were appropriate subjects if you felt the need to talk. But better by far, was to remain silent – especially at the table.

In the summer of nineteen-seventy at Chez Reynat the gangly American orchestrated discussion. Lily had been intimidated by him from the start.

She and Trinity had entered the house as newcomers to a party already started. Trinity had introduced herself and taken the attention of all – this was just as Lily liked and expected things to be. The guest with the spindle legs and large teeth then did the same. He pushed his long yellow hair behind his ears and grinned, smoothing down a luxuriant beard.

"Bienvenues," he said with a voice that was accustomed to an audience. "I'm the Reverend Mason A Black. You can call me Rev – crazy Rev."

A laugh came from the sofa next to the window. Lily had not noticed anyone except the tall figure at the fireplace when she had first entered the house. In the gloom she saw an oriental looking man cradling an acoustic guitar. He was perhaps a little younger than the preacher.

"Call him crazy Rev if you want, but he's Mason to everyone. He's nuts – but that's another story," the seated figure said. He rubbed at his eyes as if Lily and Trinity's arrival had woken him from slumber.

"Are you a real reverend?" Trinity asked. She sounded bewildered, undecided whether this was a matter of humour or not. The only clergyman Lily and she knew was the vicar of Saint Cuthbert's. Lily watched Trinity pull her arms in tightly around her breasts, ready to deny them. She obviously regretted now her flamboyant performance of a moment ago.

"As real as any other," Mason replied. "A theology degree and ordination got me out of the draft. You could say I'm a travelling pastor at the moment. We have a cool little service here down by the river on Sundays. And I do marriages if either of you young women ever feel the need."

"The need of marriage?" Trinity scoffed. She unknotted her arms.

"You never know," he answered, regarding Trinity intensely. "Free love's just great, ain't it, but weddings can be cool too. I did one in some woods last fall. The river'd make a fine spot."

Trinity threw her head to the side and smiled. "Yeah, far out – I can dig that, Rev."

Lily blushed a deep vermilion for her friend, whose accent had flitted and skipped in just one sentence from Yorkshire to somewhere on the other side of the Atlantic. It had travelled badly. Mason's eyes strayed from Trinity towards Lily and hers in turn moved to the corners of the room. She studied the architectural detail – at least, she hoped that was the effect.

On the other sofa another guest studied a record sleeve, his booted feet on a tapestry cushion. Lily noticed that he looked up periodically as if to keep up to date with the social gathering and whenever he did look up, his eyes fell on Trinity.

In the days that followed, Mason refused to allow Lily to stay in the shadows of the room, literally or figuratively. She would have been happy as an observer, but Mason had other ideas.

"And what do you think, Lily of the Valley?" he would ask her as she sat in the darkest corner. "Come on, our ungilded Lily, give us your views." And Lily would stumble, not because she had no opinion of the war, or civil rights, or Jimi Hendrix, but because she had never practised speaking them aloud. And then a mischievous glint would surface in Mason's eye.

"Lily, why don't you sing us a song? I heard you this morning down on the riverbank – our very own songbird. Or, how about a picture? Ken, hey over there, Ken. Are you with us, man? Would you like your portrait painted?"

The reticent American would put down his record sleeve for a moment and nod. "Sure thing."

"Now, Lily, don't go all shy on us. You're always carrying your little sketchbook around so we know you have a talent for the thing. We all have talents, isn't that right, Trinity?"

Trinity, eyes sparkling, would pull at Lily's hand and bring her tumbling onto the sofa, kissing her friend's cheek in reassurance. Ken and Oki would smile good-naturedly as though they forgave her lack of social ease. The moment would be forgotten until Mason became bored of the others and let his eyes wander to Lily again.

This scenario had become a habit in little more than a week and so she increasingly sought refuge in Felix's kitchen.

One hot still evening, Felix set his cook's knife on the chopping board and, wiping his hands on his apron said, "Lily, I want to show you your island."

Since her arrival, Felix had teased Lily about the Île des Lys, but she had only looked at it from the water's edge. Felix would not let anyone across – 'it is not for parties,' he would say.

"Come, the cassoulet will be fine for a while. Now is a good time to take you to the hermitage."

Untying the apron, he reached for an ancient looking key hooked above the low door and beckoned Lily. He ducked through the weeping willow that grazed the house wall and spread to the water's edge, and Lily trailed after him towards the rowing boat. Before he reached the vessel Felix stopped and took a step down into the river. Instead of submerging, his feet rested on the surface of the water.

"What are you doing? We can't walk across," Lily spluttered.

Felix stood square on the causeway, his hands to his hips.

"Calm yourself," he soothed. "We can walk Oddo's way, I assure you. The water will never be above the ankle."

Lily shook her head, her eyes fixed on Felix's feet. The clear water splashed gently over his toes. She shook her head again and took a step back. "I don't know, Felix. I'm not that keen on water – I don't swim that well. It looks slippery."

She peered down, holding her hair from her eyes.

"Slippery?" Felix repeated the word as if it were unknown to him. "Yes, I understand. No, not at all." He moved a foot back and forth along the stone. "Look. Don't worry, the Vamaleau will look after you. Believe me, if you have faith in the river, you will be safe." His eyes had not left her and now he held out his hand and waited.

"Faith in the river?" Lily looked at the dark water and back at Felix again. "Are you talking about your monk again?"

He shrugged his shoulders. "Faith should not be discussed too much – it is not something for analysis. It is. And he was not a monk. This I have told you."

He took another step further out and motioned to Lily with his out-held hand. Lily suppressed a nervous laugh. The weir just downstream of the house roared a challenge to her, but here the water was quiet and lapped placidly around Felix's ankles. With an intake of breath, Lily extended a shaky hand and stepped down onto the cold walkway. She slid her foot tentatively over the smooth stone, testing its safety.

"Ça va?" Felix asked and Lily nodded. She kept close to her companion, clutching his hand, grasping his arm, seeing only her feet and the black stone. Felix stopped halfway and Lily bumped into his back, so concentrated had she been on her steps. His shirt smelled of starch and lavender, mixed with the odour of an afternoon's body heat.

"He lies here," Felix whispered and Lily followed his eyes into the deep green. She had no need to ask over whose grave they solemnly stood. She tried to make out the river floor as if she would glimpse Oddo's white bones, but saw only surface ripples and darkness below. Felix's expression suggested that he saw more than Lily.

"Why here?" she asked.

Felix nodded back towards the riverbank and the hamlet.

"Oddo had baptised them here in the Vamaleau. They had been blessed and renewed by the water." His shoulders rose as if he had said enough in explanation.

When at last they arrived at the island, Lily trod the soft turf with relief. She bent to examine tiny flowers of white and blue pinpricking the grass path.

"They look a bit like forget-me-nots," Lily said, plucking a trailing stalk and handing it to Felix.

"Aimez-moi," he answered and took the sprig. He noticed Lily's blush and seemed pleased. "That is the old name. *Ne m'oubliez pas,"* he articulated carefully and handed the tiny blossom back. "Now, come and see the hermitage." He pushed the key in the door as he spoke.

"How old did you say this place was?"

It seemed to her that it could have been a hundred years old or a thousand. With walls built of massive boulders, it stood squat and square with a steeply pitched roof and a doorway barely taller than Lily. She wondered that the minuscule window let in any light.

"Probably not that old. We call it the hermitage, but it was not Oddo's. He died hundreds of years ago and this building is not that ancient. But Oddo was not the only person to live on the island at Achallat. The river has chosen others, and one of those built this place of stone." Felix's fingers stroked the lintel above the doorframe. "Probably twelfth century," he added in an offhand manner. He swung the door open. "Come inside now. I will show you the beautiful interior. Like many people its real beauty is inside." His face flushed, and he pushed his hands through his fine hair self-consciously. Lily was unsure whether he alluded to himself or her.

While Felix fussed with the window shutter, Lily gazed around at a plain room, rough plastered up to shoulder height, and above that, the rubble and boulder walls reached up beyond the rafters to the clay tiles of the roof. An iron bed took up most of one wall; a fireplace occupied another. Lily was perplexed. She had expected gloom, but the room was bathed in an amber light.

"Look at the window," Felix said with delight.

Lily followed the direction of his pointing hand to the top of the gable wall opposite the bed and saw the trefoil leaded window. A beam of orange blazed diagonally across the room, illuminating the blank wall above the bed with a fiery picture in the shape of a Fleur-de-Lys.

Felix perched on the edge of the bed, the palms of his hands brought together as if he were about to clap.

"I have decided, Lily. This room needs a mural. It's beautiful, but it needs art and you can give it."

He looked at his hands on his lap and waited.

Lily tore her eyes from the picture painted by the setting sun and raised her eyebrows pointedly. "Art? Felix, I'm not an artist. I draw – just sketches, that's all. I wouldn't know where to start." She frowned, suddenly aware of her own smallness. In little more than a year she would be an art student and perhaps then she would feel more capable.

Felix rose from the bed and stood beside her. "It needs a painting and the person who does it is important. These things aren't decided by technical achievement. I could go to La Grande Aubaine or even Limoges and find someone. Chez Reynat decides. Achallat decides on these things." He put out his hand to stroke her hair and then stopped himself. "I have great faith in you. You must tell a story with pictures. A story of this time and place, these people. It will be your task. Have you not noticed that everyone is allocated an occupation in the household of Chez Reynat?"

Lily gave a look of submission and hoped that her excitement was not too obvious.

"No, I hadn't. What job does Oki have?"

"He is the musician. He is our troubadour although his voice is not audible at times."

"Okay, what about Ken?"

"You must know, for sure. Ken drives to the town for our provisions."

Yes, she knew that Ken had been given the keys to the Renault and was sent every morning to fetch groceries. Since Trinity had volunteered herself as his assistant, the car returned back late in the afternoon, Trinity smugly radiant and Ken always silent.

"Why did you take so long?" Felix had asked the first time.

"Sorry, did we go AWOL?" Trinity had answered, grinning at the beams overhead. She had spent the rest of the afternoon sat close to Oki, her thigh pressed hard against his while letting her eyes rest on Ken, who took up his usual position next to the burning logs. A fire glowed every day at Chez Reynat whatever the weather. 'The fire keeps away the damp,' Felix had said. Ken had unfashionably cropped hair and equally unfashionable muscled arms. A tattoo decorated his right arm, but Lily did not have the temerity to study it. Trinity told her that he had only just returned from a tour in Vietnam when he packed and left his home in Washington State to see Europe. How much of the continent he had explored before arriving at Achallat Lily did not know, but he spent his days at Chez Reynat watching the flames. Trinity gazed at him and Mason studied them all. Perhaps he really does regard himself as some sort of parish priest, Lily had pondered – and we are his flock.

"And what about our man of the cloth?" Lily asked Felix. He looked perplexed. "What about Mason – has he got a chore to do? Or is it just to see to our spiritual well-being?"

Lily coloured at the sarcastic tone in her voice, but Felix ignored her comment. She had noticed he seemed wary of

Mason, usually retreating to the kitchen when the preacher cast about for participants in his performance.

Felix had tired of talking of his other guests. His hand hovered again, this time at her cheek. Lily stepped back and put her heel in the ash filled hearth.

"So, Lily, we will buy your paints and brushes tomorrow."

"But I've got my bag of stuff with me in the house." She shuffled sideways and found space.

He laughed. "Your little satchel? Enough for small pictures, sketches. Here you will paint a mural. It will be like the Bayeux Tapestry." He drew an arc with his outstretched arm to convey the panorama he expected of her.

Lily dropped onto the bed and her feet dangled above the floor. "Don't be so daft. The Bayeux Tapestry is just what it says – a tapestry. I know because Trin and I went to see it on our way here." She swung her legs and gazed at her canvas. She was light-headed.

Felix tapped a wall with the back of his hand. "This will tell a story in just the same way. You will be our storyteller. No wools or threads, Lily. You will not weave a tapestry, but paint. Your painting will illuminate – it will please Oddo."

He trotted to the open door and stood on the threshold. "Come here and see."

Lily stretched out on the bed and let her eyes rest on the blackened beams above. She felt euphoric as though her heart was as big as the room, as though it enveloped the tiny building in its expansiveness.

"Come, Lily," Felix cajoled and she joined him at the opening with a wide smile. "You see. You can watch us all at Chez Reynat and tell the story."

Into the grey dusk, an amber light seeped from the row of French windows of Chez Reynat. She could just hear a guitar – it was Oki's, coming in fitful bursts. And in the interludes a sonorous voice floated across the river – Mason's. It was a duet of sorts. Down from the well a village dog barked – just once, his ears pricked in the direction of the open window. Was it the guitar or Mason's words that he found troubling? His owner called with a word and a slap of the thigh and the two disappeared, leaving the well chain to rattle in the still evening.

Lily let out a deep breath. It was relief, she realised. She would be an observer without fear of Mason's shadow. With the key in his hand Felix stooped to the barely visible keyhole.

"Life is good, Lily Weaver, and God is good. But now it's time for the cassoulet to come from the oven. We must make haste now."

"We're not going to walk through the water again, are we?"

He gave her a quick smile over his shoulder as he scurried down the path ahead. "Do not worry. Was it not easy to come here? Why should it be different on the return journey? I will hold your hand again and between us the Vamaleau and I will look after you. You have my word and Oddo's. And tomorrow you will come back and begin the story."

The next morning in the darkness of the shuttered bedroom, Lily packed her belongings into her rucksack, tiptoeing back and forth across the floorboards and inching open the heavy drawers. From Trinity's bed, movement and moaning suggested that Lily had not been quiet enough. A ruffle of blonde hair poked above the quilt and a slender arm flopped out to hang in the air above the wooden floor.

"What are you up to, Liliput?" a languid voice inquired.

"Sorry, Trin. I didn't mean to wake you. It's early yet – go back to sleep."

Trinity's full head emerged and she pulled herself up, leaning on an elbow. The crumpled sheets fell back to reveal a mop of spiky black hair.

"Where do you think you're off to?" Trinity's voice was indignant as her eyes spied the rucksack.

"Only across to the hermitage," Lily whispered. "I told you about it last night, if you remember. There's a bed over there. It'll be better all round. You know – easier," she said awkwardly, looking at the top of Oki's head.

"What do you mean? We're okay as we are, aren't we?" Trinity sat up, her arms folded across her bare chest. "I'll miss you if you're all the way over there. It won't be the same. We're supposed to be on holiday together, aren't we?" A hand surfaced from below the covers and fondled Trinity's tanned right breast. "Not now, Oki," she complained, her mouth pulled into a sullen pout.

Lily heaved the rucksack over one shoulder. "We'll still be together, Trin – I'll have to come back every day to eat." A flutter of panic rustled in her stomach as she thought of crossing the river every day. Waking before light, she had already resolved to take food with her to the hermitage so that she could restrict her journeys to one a day – for dinner. She blew Trinity a kiss and mouthed, "See you later."

"You guys, listen up – we have our very own hermit," Mason announced that morning over a late breakfast. "We'll have a celebration in your honour. The feast day of Lily of Achallat – I like the sound of it. And if anything should happen to you, well then, we'll make relics of your bones and treasure them. Or then again, we could sell them to the highest bidder. Isn't that what they did, Felix? Hawk old bones around Europe?"

Felix either did not hear or ignored the question. He and Lily had returned from an early expedition to La Grande Aubaine with cans of paint and an assortment of decorators' brushes. Lily sat herself on the end of the long table and helped herself to the last of the bread. While Oki ate, the heel of his hand rubbing at his eyes, Trinity laughed heartily at Mason's humour. She swayed back and forth, sweeping away crumbs as they fell down her chest. Catching sight of Lily's pink face, Trinity stopped suddenly and concentrated on her plate.

Lily turned her attention to Ken who was enjoying Felix's cooking – a meal of fried eggs and leftover vegetables. He shovelled at the food lustily with his fork.

"So how long is this trip around Europe going to take?" Lily asked him.

She was less timid with Ken than the others – he was unlikely to fire a question back at her. Ken looked into the middle distance. Lily noticed that he never made eye contact – except perhaps with Trinity.

"Don't know. Haven't done much so far. But that's cool. This is time out." He waved his hand and fork towards the door and his eyes followed. "Still waiting for Gabe anyway."

Lily turned her head round as if she half expected another guest to walk in that moment. But she knew that they had been waiting for their companion, Gabriel, for weeks. She and Trinity had grown used to the refrain, "when Gabe comes" from all three Americans, but no one had asked about the whereabouts of the elusive friend. Felix seemed incurious and Trinity was only interested in the flesh and blood to hand.

"So where is he, your friend? What's he doing?" Lily asked Ken.

Mason leaned forward towards Trinity, his eyes straying from her hair to her tanned shoulders, but he listened to the other conversation at the far end of the table. He bent his head fractionally in Lily's direction. With his eyes still on the blonde girl across the table, Mason answered for Ken.

"Our friend Gabriel is a restless kind of guy. He gets bored sitting around staring at blazing logs like some of us are apt to do. So he took off for a while. He's the kind that needs a little adventure in his life."

At this last remark, a ripple of laughter ran down the table. "If he hadn't had so much adventure he wouldn't have had to run away to Europe," Oki piped up, looking more awake than Lily had ever seen him.

"Is he on the run from the police or something?" Lily almost whispered to Ken, trying to evade Mason's ears. She was uncomfortable with loud hailer conversations down the length of the table.

"Nothing like that – just a woman."

Oki shouted down the table, "Got too close to somebody else's wife. Trouble was, the somebody was his best friend. So he skipped town – decided discretion was the better part of valour. That's the phrase, right?"

"Quit it, Oki," Ken said. He almost looked at Lily. "Life can get kinda messy. I know one thing for sure, he felt like a shit about the whole thing. Anyways it's mostly talk. Some guys have got nothing better to do than talk."

Ken gave his food the attention he thought it deserved, hunching over the plate and cradling his fork.

Whether or not the others had heard Ken's words, the topic was not quite finished.

"He'll be back when he's got bored with pretending to be some olde world knight or whatever he's into," Oki announced.

Trinity raised her eyebrows melodramatically and, with mock bewilderment, said, "Explain please to us ordinary mortals, who haven't the faintest idea what you're talking about."

Lily knew Trinity was making an attempt to rise out of her ignorance. She hated to feel at a disadvantage, and possibly foolish. Oki shook his head wearily and put down the chunk of bread. He looked bored with the conversation.

"Gabe took off on some old farmer's horse – that's all. Packed up some camping gear and a map and took off. A horse trek, I guess you'd call it."

Felix reappeared from the kitchen with a fresh pot of coffee, but nobody had noticed his absence. He said over the heads of his guests, "He has borrowed Claude Jopert's horse.

Claude's wife is a distant cousin of mine and so Claude was happy to let the American have the horse for a short while. But I doubt he thought that it would be such a lengthy loan."

"I don't suppose he's too troubled," Mason muttered. He sounded irritated with Felix, but he barely raised his head to speak. Then looking down the table at his friends, he added, "Gabe and that old guy got on pretty famously, didn't they? Did any of you guys hear them talk together? Gabe's French must be a whole lot better than I thought."

"It's the horse thing," Oki said, his mouth full. "You get two people together and if they have a common love they speak the same language. Know what I mean?"

Felix refilled Lily's empty cup. "Drink up. I will put your supplies in the boat while you finish your breakfast. I will wait for you there. Do not be long."

Lily caught Trinity's smirk and frowned back: Felix's fussy attention embarrassed her. "He thinks he's helping, but he's a pain, honestly," she mumbled and then immediately felt guilty.

*

The coffee machine's gurgling ended and the sudden silence in Felix's kitchen brought Lily out of her reverie. Her hands were pink with the heat from the gas flames and the air wavered in front of her. She turned off the hob.

Disorientated for a moment, she shook herself as if to throw off the memories and then went to the telephone sitting on a rickety table underneath the staircase. In its shallow drawer, her hand scrabbled about until she found a card advertising a local taxi company. With the receiver in her hand she began to punch out the numbers. She stopped halfway through.

She had intended to go straight back to La Grande Aubaine, to the hotel room with the newly papered walls. She could perhaps get away with never returning to Chez Reynat.

Venetia Crow was surely used to seeing herself around properties.

Lily put down the receiver, took a few steps and flopped onto a stair tread. With her hands on her knees she let her eyes survey the room, quickly at first and then she scrutinised more carefully. She knew nothing of selling houses, but she knew how to clean; how to touch up paint; how to mend creaking floorboards. She was almost expert at repairing cracked plaster and fixing rattling window panes. The kitchen tap dripped; the front door dragged at the stone floor. These things she had noticed without wanting to.

The fire needed lighting first – then she would attend to Chez Reynat's minor ailments. She would rid herself and Dominic of the past. Lily replaced the card and pulled out a box of matches.

As she pushed the drawer shut the telephone rang. Lily listened to the rings, counting them, unwilling to convey the news of Felix's death. Backing away, she imagined the caller to be an acquaintance, perhaps hoping to arrange a visit that afternoon. Then she remembered Venetia Crow. She lunged forward and plucked up the telephone, eager to reach it before the estate agent hung up.

"Hello. Halo."

Lily waited. There was no answering voice, but she listened to the long silence at the other end before the dialling tone murmured in her ear.

CHAPTER TEN

Scowling up at the unseen beams, Lily tried in the blackness to estimate the time. Her nose and cheeks seemed less cold than on that first morning at least – four days of a blazing fire had warmed the old house. Lily slipped a hand between the bed curtains and her fingers fumbled on the rug until they found her socks. Then she dared throw back the covers. She descended the stairs in her velvet coat. Already each small act felt like a habit: first the coffee machine to see to; then the fire to light; and finally something to eat. But this morning she took some satisfaction in breaking her new habit. She delved into her handbag and found the business card given to her the day of the funeral. The telephone had rung each day, but it had not been Venetia Crow. Not that Lily knew who the silent caller was – she almost imagined it to be Felix, too sullen to speak, still brooding on her flight.

Venetia's answer machine was switched on. The honeyed voice announced that she was presently at a property exhibition in Birmingham. Lily started to speak after the beep, but changed her mind and dropped the receiver with her mouth screwed to one side. There was nothing to be said; nothing to do but wait.

For four days Lily had chivvied the old house. She washed and waxed; sanded bumps and patched up holes. Hinges were oiled; screws tightened. She freshened up the bed linen despite the weather. The laundry hung forlornly in the barn, drying too slowly for Lily. She pestered the sheets, turning them this way and that, scraping the barn doors open as far as they would go. In her head Lily itemised the chores that would fill her few days at Chez Reynat. It was a satisfyingly long list.

She was polishing the huge timber mantelpiece when a trumpeting motor horn broke the quiet of the house. The repetitive blast grew louder and louder until it seemed its owner would thunder through the walls. Recognising the sound, Lily jumped down from the chair and lurched to the table and her bag. She shuffled across the floor, kicking her legs sideways and cursing under her breath. Extravagantly flared jeans flapped around beneath her feet, folding themselves under the soles of her shoes, polishing the floor again for her. On the first day she had used Felix's Renault to fetch her belongings from the hotel and to buy some basic foodstuffs. The same little car that had first picked her up hitchhiking, she realised with astonishment when she found it in the barn.

With only the clothes from her New Year break she had been forced to dig into the chest of drawers in her bedroom. Her bedroom. It had become her room again, much more easily than Lily wanted to admit to herself. Having dismissed the cheesecloth smocks and long cotton dresses, she pulled out a few checked flannel shirts, some T-shirts – more tightly fitting than she would have liked, and the problematic jeans.

Lily threw open the door and hopped down the steps, hoisting the jeans up at the knees. The epicier's blue and white van had parked up a short distance from the wellhead on the other side of the gate pillars. This open space was known as the couderc: a common piece of land that all the residents of the hamlet used.

Lily stumbled to the pillars in her eagerness. She was reluctant to travel again in the ancient car. Its engine had started easily enough, but the drive was noisy – almost everything that should have been fixed in place rattled, keen to loosen itself, and the petrol fumes had compelled her to gasp for air through the open window on a blustery January day. She need not have worried that the grocer's visit would be a brief one for a queue had formed along the length of the vehicle and it would probably be some time before they were all served. Oddly, the line of customers did not face the glass display with its bounty of cheeses, hams, sausages and pâtés, but all stood facing Chez Reynat. Like hushed theatre-goers, they had been waiting for Lily's appearance.

A watery sun had risen as far as it would that day. Ochre leaves gathered in a sodden mass around the doorstep and Lily kicked them away as she shambled to the back of the queue. A cold easterly blew up the lane towards the house, but the grocer had parked his van in consideration of his patrons' well-being. While the other customers stood in the lee of the wind, Lily at the end of the queue felt its full thrust. Her neighbours eyed her with wonder. Lily pulled up the collar of her shirt and turned her back to the wind.

Taking up the prime position in the queue was a frail looking woman perched on a mobility scooter. When Lily heard the shrill voice hailed at the van, she bent forward and turned her head to get a better view. At the same instant, the others – who up to this point had been mesmerised by the newcomer – suddenly swivelled their faces towards the food on display. But the grocer's eyes stayed on Lily even as he listened to his customer's requests.

A haughty voice interrupted the order. "For goodness sake, Séverine, why the delay? You get the same thing every time, so stop pretending the decision is difficult."

Standing erect with her disciplined hair pulled back into a chignon, the owner of the voice looked to the shopkeeper for sympathy, but already the seated woman was driving her little machine towards Lily, sending the ragtag troupe of hens on the couderc into a noisy panic. She glared at Lily.

"I don't remember you," she squawked.

Despite her physical frailty, her eyes flashed with vim. Wild white hair shot out from her tiny head and heavy walking boots thrust out from her spindly legs. She reminded Lily of an old peg doll.

Extending her hand, Lily began to introduce herself, but the woman flapped her own in irritation at Lily.

"I know who you are, but I don't remember your face. You don't look at all familiar. You must have changed a lot – time isn't kind to everyone. Felix told us to expect you – and your son." She looked back at the house.

Baptistin stepped forward, but not before putting his basket on the ground as if to reserve his position. "You remember nothing, Séverine. The boy's not here. I told you, remember. He's at school and that's everything these days. More important than family. In our day burying your own father would have come first."

Lily winced. She had never thought of Dom and Felix as members of the same family.

"And you will be here while he's at school in England?" Séverine asked with disbelief.

Lily's mouth opened and closed several times. She had not rehearsed an explanation of her decision regarding Chez Reynat. Practice was needed before she felt able to relay the information diplomatically.

"He's not a child anymore. Dom's at university, not school," she dissembled.

A heavily set man glowered from beneath his wide brimmed hat, a feather quivering in its band. Perhaps he guessed the truth. Lily recognised Claude Jopert – a farmer with a deep love for his horses and a talent with the accordion. Stretched over a heavy sweater, his braces tugged at sturdy trousers. Lily turned to Baptistin and her eyes searched for the kindness she had found in the past. But she saw only wiliness in his steady gaze.

"Felix expected you to come. He needed to talk to you before he died, but you stayed away," Séverine accused. She clutched her basket on her lap with bony hands, the knuckles white and swollen.

"I'm sorry I didn't get here in time." Lily flushed from the shame of the falsehood.

"It's too late to go over all of that now," Baptistin interrupted. "Felix lies in Saint Bénigne with his mother and grandmother. He won't be talking to any of us again – at least not until we join him. Whatever he would have said will have to wait."

"But what about the tea dance?" Séverine stabbed her scooter forward towards Lily.

"Tea dance?" Lily's eyes shot from one to the other. Had she misunderstood or missed a vital part of the conversation? Although she had barely spoken to anyone since her arrival, she found that her grasp of the language had returned mysteriously on its own as if her mind, recognising the surroundings, recalled five years of speaking only French.

Hearing the refined woman with the chignon begin to recite her order, Baptistin wheeled round. "No, no, no. It's my turn, Honorine – I got here first. Even Jopert's cows know their place in the line. You think you can lord it over all of us still after all these years. It was your father who was a teacher not you – acting as if you're *d'en haut*. You're just one of us, no different."

"As usual you're being ridiculous, Baptistin. Why do you always bring my father into everything," Honorine almost whistled through her teeth.

"I may live in a smaller house than you, and I didn't go off to work in Paris, but I was in front of you in the queue. It's my turn."

Baptistin marched back to his place beside the glass counter and shuffled himself backwards so that Honorine was forced to step back too. Patting at the scarf at her neck, she smiled disdainfully.

Lily relaxed her own tense smile, grateful for the reprieve until she looked back to Séverine. The woman had not moved her scooter, but continued to study her new neighbour. Baptistin and Honorine made their purchases and joined Séverine in a loose huddle. Even the hens re-congregated at their feet as if eager to be in the know. And Lily kept her eyes to the goods on display. Jopert and the grocer settled into a lengthy discussion about the unusually wet season. Not cold enough, Jopert said in a doom laden tone. No, the grocer agreed, it would bring consequences in the spring. They continued to confer on their observations of the weather and its effects on Jopert's beast, and Lily relaxed more, feeling at home, as though she listened to her father.

"Welcome to Achallat." The grocer turned his attention to Lily. "I'm not a resident, but I'm very glad to have a new customer."

"You don't have a new customer," Baptistin hollered from the huddle. "She's just replacing Felix Reynat. You haven't got any more than you had a few weeks ago before he went off to hospital."

The polite smile vanished from the shopkeeper. "I didn't say an extra customer, you old fool, just a new one. I wish I could replace a few more sometimes. The young lady and I haven't met before so she's new. And no one here has the manners to make the proper introductions. You're all so wrapped up in yourselves here. There's more to life than Achallat, you know."

Like an upbraided child, Jopert turned to Lily sheepishly and offered his hand. "*Bonjour*, Madame Reynat, I'm Claude Jopert."

"I remember. But my name is Weaver not Reynat."

"For goodness sake, Jopert, I meant introduce her to me."

The shaking of hands and exchanging of names over, Lily rattled off a list of items she wanted. She had studied the display for long enough: she wanted to make her purchases and retreat.

"So will you live here permanently?" the grocer asked. "All the year round? There are some that are like swifts – they come for the summer only. It makes things hard for us travelling shops. What are we to do in the winter?" He waited.

Feeling her chest tighten, Lily composed her face. "Everything's been so unexpected – I mean Felix's death was such a shock. And everything's so complicated. Life's so complicated, isn't it, these days? I have a son at university in England." She was nervous and her tongue worked hard to hide it. "And then there's my father – he's getting older." Who isn't, for goodness sake, she scolded herself and reddened. "And I have to help on the farm too – there's a lot of work." She turned to Jopert as if he would understand. "I know it would be so much better if Achallat could have a permanent family – you know, children. It's what these places need, isn't it? To keep them alive."

All now studied her more intently. Where was this rambling speech going, she could see them wondering.

"And I know Felix would have wanted Chez Reynat to be lived in properly – to be a real home." Lily gulped. "Dom was so young when he left Achallat and, of course, it's Dom who's inherited the place, not me. So," she said, pushing out her chin and mustering some courage, "it's completely his decision, of course. But young people have so much they want to do. It's not like in our day when we just settled down and that was that." She cursed her own lameness: she could hardly believe she had used that phrase 'in our day' – she sounded like her father.

Lily swallowed again. "If Dominic chooses not to keep Chez Reynat then I'll have to go along with that."

With some of her provisions under both arms and her fingers strangled by flimsy plastic bags, Lily retreated gauchely, saying quickly, "We might sell."

*"The curse is come upon me," cried
The Lady of Shallot.*

                        Tennyson

CHAPTER ELEVEN

Lily pressed her face to the pane of the French window. A chalk blue sky blanketed a still landscape – even the river seemed placid. She had looked to the glass as a bird began its wary song, hesitant, doubtful of its timing. January – the quietest month – was silent in Achallat. Lily wished for the rowdy winds that buffeted Lack Farm. She searched, not to identify the singer, but to see what had caught her eye – a movement, not the quick fluttering of wings on a willow branch, but something farther off – across the Vamaleau.

Below the hermitage, the little boat tipped about in the slow water. It had been there when she first walked over Achallat's bridge, Lily recalled. She rubbed at her brow trying to find a memory of the days since. She had seen it by the chestnut tree, she was sure. Inspecting the squat building and the little garden that surrounded it, Lily saw only a shuttered window and stark fruit trees.

She turned back to the room, and her book on the sofa. The blazing fire, the sunlight brightening the rug coaxed her back. Alone, Lily had done what came naturally to her: she had cleaned; she had scrubbed away at life as she had taught herself to do. As a child she had dared not rebel – the bucket and brush were hers by right. It was a matter of pride to Jack that she should follow in her mother's footsteps. 'As good as your mother could do,' he would say, patting her head, and praising her in the same fashion as he did with his sheepdog.

Waxing Chez Reynat's banister and polishing its floorboards, Lily felt Felix rebuking her. And she found herself making excuses to him. "I don't belong here, Felix – we have to sell,' she apologised. She saw his reproachful expression and felt the weight of it in her chest.

Lily hoped for a call from the estate agent and waited with dread for a visit from Baptistin. She received neither. The matter of the tea dance had bothered her – Séverine's caustic tone implied that it was not an invitation that Lily had received. Well, if it was, they would no doubt change their minds, she was sure.

Her days were measured with chores. She had scrubbed out cupboards; had taken every book from Felix's copious library, dusting each jacket; had polished the floors until they gleamed with a soft lustre. She had shivered and gone without a fire for a day while she repainted the stove with black enamel. In the barn she searched Felix's shelves for inspiration – some tool that would suggest another chore – but she found herself at a loss. The house was cleansed and purified and she was still restless.

Bookshelves lined the entire northern wall either side of the staircase. She had scanned the books and ran a finger along the spines, eventually pulling out a small blue book. She read the title, *Le Cid* by Corneille, and then replaced it. She took down books by Maupassant, Souvestre and Balzac, but had settled for a study of local history.

Lily returned to the sofa and Felix's book and stopped herself from looking back to the window. "This place is full of ghosts, Felix. Have you joined Oddo in the hermitage – or at the bottom of the Vamaleau?"

With her legs drawn up beside her, Lily flicked through the pages, pausing at grainy black and white photographs, studying the lopsided cottages with smoking chimneys and women in preposterous looking bonnets. She looked up at the threesome staring down at her from above the fireplace – a man in a dark suit and wide brimmed hat not dissimilar to Jopert's, and a woman in a sombre bonnet tied under her chin. A child in a plaid dress and laced boots – Felix's mother – gazed at the camera with a look of sullen bewilderment.

The telephone rang – it was the voice she hoped to hear.

"I hope you didn't think I'd forgotten you, sweetie. What a week I've had! Anyway do you still want me to come out? Haven't had second thoughts, have you?"

"Yes – I mean no. I haven't changed my mind. When can you make it?"

"Don't worry. We'll get everything sorted out in a jiffy," Venetia crooned. She seemed to sense Lily's desperation – her tone was relaxed: no need to woo or court her client anymore. "I may be able to fit you in tomorrow, probably a.m., but I can't promise."

Lily heard a fluttering of paper down the line.

"Sometime tomorrow probably. Can't be sure. You didn't have any plans to do anything, did you?"

"No," Lily replied lamely, looking around at her ordered surroundings.

"Good. We can discuss the legal situation then."

When the bell rang Lily almost ignored it. She had forgotten the soft ringing of the brass bell at the entrance, so long had it been since she had been a resident of Chez Reynat.

Venetia Crow strode past Lily. The estate agent's eyes flicked quickly around the cold hall and continued their scan in the main room. She spoke enthusiastically of the house's best features and remained mute on its weaknesses. She loved the oak floor.

"I think it's chestnut," Lily suggested.

Venetia peered more closely and then gave a quick shrug of the eyebrows. She adored the stone fireplace, so typical of the region she said, but ignored the blistering scaly white patch creeping up the east wall. She enthused about the stone sink in the kitchen and drew a blind eye to the mismatched cupboards and miserly daylight. Upstairs, it was more of the same.

"What a delightful room and a perfect view," she gushed, stooping to look out of the square window. Straightening up, she averted her eyes from the large crack that ran from the ceiling to lintel like a river seeking lower ground.

"Such lovely country furniture. Will it go with the house?" Venetia stroked the washstand with one lingering finger.

Lily nodded.

"Been in your husband's family a long time, I suppose. Or did you buy it together?"

Lily looked at the washstand, the high bed, the armoire. "All of it was here when I came. I've always assumed it's old family stuff. Felix was very proud of his family – he wouldn't have parted with any of it." The last words came out dryly like thorns on her tongue.

Venetia drew herself up and smoothed down her skirt. "I've enough experience in this business to know guilt is not helpful or practical. This place was special to him. Whether it is to you or not is none of my business, but you're the one left making the decisions and he's somewhere else – having better things to think about, eh, let's hope."

Venetia caressed the washstand again and let her eyes rest on the carved headboard. A cherub smiled back at her.

Lily had squirmed inwardly at every reference to Felix as her husband, but she had kept her silence on the subject. Not because of any embarrassment but because of guilt. Standing in Felix's bedroom, by his bed, the guilt overwhelmed her. He had entreated her often enough.

*

"There is no obstacle, Lily," he had said in his oddly formal English. "Lily, will you be my wife? I do not see that you are anyone else's wife." And she had glared at him, forbidding him to continue.

"Lily, marry me. Only marriage in church – in the eyes of God – counts. There aren't even any legal papers. It's absurd – the whole thing is absurd."

"So God only has eyes in church. What? He's blind everywhere else or he doesn't venture outside the building? He can't see us here on your bed, Felix?"

Felix had risen from the bed and left the room and Lily was left with the hollow victory of sarcasm.

*

Venetia Crow brought Lily back to the present with a rumbling sigh of contentment. "We'll have no problem," she muttered almost to herself and marched from the room and down the stairs, clomping heavily on each tread.

Lily made coffee and they sat at the table, not quite opposite each other. Instead Lily sat diagonally across from the buxom woman in her silk blouse and pearls. They spoke at a courteous distance – at first of the weather and then Venetia leaned forward, her hand smothering the tiny espresso cup.

"It's a rural idyll – a lost England."

"What do you mean?"

"England as it was fifty years ago – England as it should be. I mean, our countryside's gone hasn't it? Ruined."

"Are you from the country – back home in England, I mean?"

Venetia picked up the cup and then put it back again. "Not exactly. But I used to be able to see fields from our house in Cheshire – there's an industrial estate there now. See what I mean?" She rolled her eyes and took a sip with pursed lips. "Sweetie, this coffee's a bit strong for me. You don't have any instant, do you?"

Disappointed with Lily's negative gesture, Venetia lifted her eyebrows, blinked and pulled the corners of her mouth upwards as though forcing herself into a more positive attitude.

"So tell me, what are the neighbours like here? You can be honest with me. They're not going to be a nuisance, are they? That's the one drawback of this house – our property searchers are usually looking for privacy. They don't want a lot of nosy parkers hanging around."

An image of the huddle of neighbours, gossiping at the wellhead appeared in Lily's mind and she beamed back at Venetia too enthusiastically. The agent pushed the saucer away and folded plump arms on the table.

"Things probably weren't very different when you first came here. Not like the rest of the world – this part hasn't changed in years." She simpered at Lily with her head tilted to one side.

Lily thought for a while. "Things were a lot different to the way they are now – I mean back in 1970."

"1970? Gosh, you must have been a young slip of a thing. Must have been a bit staid for a young girl in those days, surely?" Venetia looked Lily up and down as if trying to ascertain her age.

"Staid?" Lily laughed and remembered the first days for a seventeen-year-old from a Yorkshire farm. "I met people from the other side of the world – or almost anyway. And they'd just come back from killing some other people on the other side of the world again. No, it wasn't staid. I discovered life, sex, love and drugs." There was a hint of nostalgia in Lily's voice that surprised her.

Venetia pulled her arms back from the table and tucked her chin in close to her bosom. Her eyes were suddenly more interested in the garden through the window. Lily saw her mistake. She looked afresh at the other woman with her grey suit and her high collared blouse. The chasm between them brought them both into a catatonic state. At last Venetia moved.

"Time's getting on and I must be moving. I know we haven't sorted out the legal side, but there's plenty of time." And she rose awkwardly from the bench, catching the heel of her shoe as she tried to extricate herself.

Outside, like a flag announcing her presence, Venetia's BMW had drawn the attention of Achallat's residents. Honorine and Baptistin stood together on the step of the wellhead, patiently facing the house. They were a mini-delegation, Lily realised.

The sun that had bathed the hamlet in brightness if not warmth the previous day, had yet to appear. A low mist hid everything but the nearest trees standing like black silhouettes against the grey. Honorine stood poised with the collar of her wool coat turned up against the damp, a scarf just under her chin. Baptistin, round-shouldered, had apparently been summoned quickly – he wore only a thin blouson jacket, half unzipped, revealing a cotton vest.

Venetia turned her back to them and faced her client. Her warmth had returned. "It's quite enchanting out here too. What is that?" She pointed to the climbing shrub arching around the entrance.

Its stems, as thick as saplings, twined around each other before its branches spread exuberantly in all directions, dipping here and there in front of the doorway so that Lily and Venetia were forced to stoop to avoid its leaves.

"I think it has white flowers in the spring," Lily replied, not very helpfully. She tried to remember what Felix called it – it seemed important suddenly as if by forgetting she had allowed something else to die with him.

"It looks like it's almost in flower now. Aren't they buds there?"

Venetia crouched to inspect the plant, but kept at a wary distance from the wet foliage. "That'll go down well with viewers. Everyone loves blossom round the door – very romantic," she sang and nodded with approval.

Lily's eyebrows shot up with alarm. "It won't be in flower for weeks yet. It's not going to take that long, is it?"

Baptistin and Honorine conferred, smiling with knowing eyes, pleased that perhaps things were not going smoothly.

As Venetia began to march towards her car, Lily called out to her back. "Don't you want to look around outside. There's the garden and the barn. There's a potager round the other side and…" She stopped herself before she gave the full inventory – she could not bring herself to mention the hermitage.

The agent half turned and looked down at her polished shoes. She picked up one foot, studied the heel and made her decision. "It all looks quite lovely – I can see that much from here. Not a lot of land, but charming." She waved a hand in no particular direction. "But a little tidy up wouldn't go amiss. How about a couple of pots – something either side of the door there?" As she scraped a shoe across the ground to rid herself of the coagulated leaves, she muttered, "It's not the best time of year for viewing anyway. The property season doesn't really get started until spring." Seeing Lily's expression, she added, "But I have a very good list of people on my books already so there's no need to look so glum.

"And what's over there?" Venetia squinted at the river, a hand to her eyes as if it aided her sight through the mist.

"That's just a building that goes with the property. An outbuilding of sorts."

Lily had not looked, but she knew where Venetia's eyes were directed. "It's locked and I don't know where the keys are."

Venetia studied Lily for a moment, but said nothing.

"It's just a wine store really. Do you need to see it? I'm not sure where Felix kept the key."

Lily glanced at the two bystanders. They studied the English pair intently, but their expressions suggested that they had not followed the conversation well.

"An odd place to keep wine," Venetia laughed. "But then this is Achallat and you do hear stories. How romantic – as long as you're not too thirsty. And you have to get to it by boat, I suppose?"

Lily's eyes were still on Honorine and Baptistin.

"Yes, but I'm not sure what state the boat is in. It's probably not safe. I don't suppose Felix used it much lately and you have to maintain these things. He wouldn't have been able to do that much while…" Lily's waffling dried up as she thought of Felix, frail like a matchstick, trying to cope with living. Honorine's eyes narrowed as though she read Lily's mind.

"It looks pretty watertight to me," Venetia replied.

Lily saw a wry smile on Venetia's face, her eyes still in the direction of the river and the Île des Lys. Lily followed the gaze and stepped back instantly, tripping on the doorstep. Her fists had been clenched, tense with the pretence of indifference to the hermitage, but now they fluttered around like moths disturbed by daylight.

The little vessel glided towards them, its prow bobbing rhythmically. A dark figure rowed effortlessly, his back to the shore. Lily's breath had stopped, but she gasped now, and the sound made Venetia turn for a second from the approaching boat. It escaped the hovering mist and floated into the just emerging sunlight. Lily could see that it was not Felix come to scold her for her long absence. She smiled at her foolishness. There were no golden curls, reflected in the sun. It was not Felix rowing vigorously and busily.

The figure stood before he reached the riverbank and turned to face Chez Reynat. Lily saw the man and her face fell. The prow bumped the landing platform and he stepped lightly onto the planking.

Venetia's eyes turned from the visitor to Lily and then back again, but this time more intently as though she saw something in Lily's expression that intrigued her. But Lily was frozen, her face and body motionless. Her hands had halted their frenetic activity and rested now mid-air.

Loose-limbed, he walked up the grassy bank with a long casual stride, his dark hair damp around his face.

"Hello, Lily," he said grimly as he came to a stop.

Lily was incapable of moving her tongue or her jaw. She felt she had become a pillar of salt and any movement would cause her to crumble to the ground in a heap. Somehow her mind still worked. Gabriel had hardly changed. This was less because time had been kind to him in the intervening years, more that experience had been cruel before. His hair was streaked with grey and now stopped short of his collar. The stern face was lined around the eyes and brow, but the rangy figure was the same. The scar that ran from mouth to cheek was no longer white and fresh, but the grey eyes were still steady and keen. These features were ingrained in her buried memory and now they stood before her, refusing to be suppressed.

He leaned against the stonework of the wellhead, his thumbs in the pockets of his jeans, his boot brought up against the short wall behind him. Honorine and Baptistin moved slightly towards him and suddenly Lily saw them as a threesome. He had not magically arrived through the mist, an apparition from the past. And Lily found that she had not disintegrated into a corrosive pile to be kicked and blown about.

She turned away from the intruder and attempted to pay attention to Venetia Crow, whose hand was waiting in farewell. Lily pushed up her own mechanically to meet it. This took all her concentration so that she was unable to hear the words mouthed by the other woman, but she kept her eyes steady and she hoped that her expression was appropriate.

"As I said, sweetie, we have to be patient. You've got to remember our viewers will be coming from Britain, but that'll give you all the time you need to do all the finishing touches." Venetia waited for the usual farewell words of no importance. But none came.

"Okay, sweetie? I'll give you twenty-four hours' notice at least so there'll be no need for last minute running around with the duster and polish. And don't take offence – I say this to everyone, it's not you – but if you could make yourself scarce on the day, that can only help. Our buyers need to see this as a little bit of unspoilt France – their little bit of a French dream. They like to think they've stumbled across heaven. No need to remind them you found it first."

Venetia gave a short practised laugh, but she saw that Lily had not reacted to this last remark as sellers always did, with some umbrage.

"I'd take myself off for a spot of shopping if I were you. You could probably do with a break from all of this." Venetia glanced at the bystanders at the well.

Lily heard little: the odd word about dreams and shopping penetrated the salt filled brain, but she nodded and kept her eyes fixed on Venetia. She needed to escape.

As Venetia heaved herself into her car Baptistin spoke out with a brittle voice. "So you've not changed your mind. I thought that perhaps it was just the grief speaking – the other day at the grocer's van. How do you know what you want? How do you know what your son wants? You've only just buried Felix."

Lily looked away from the glassy eyes, filled with disappointment or perhaps resignation, and ran to the door, slamming it behind her.

She strode to the French windows and then to the fireplace. Her eyes searched wildly for a salve to her panic. One emotion surged above all the others churning her stomach.

"Hello, Lily," she repeated, imitating his slow speech. She wanted to slap the words as they left her own lips.

Bowed over, concave, she pressed down on her wild hair with flat palms as though she could crush the charge of anger. She felt it like a bolt of lightning, shooting from her head. Storming up the stairs to her bedroom, she closed the door – and then slammed it when it refused her. It had never shut properly and would not obey now even when violence was shown it. Aimlessly, her eyes roamed the room and then went to the window and the view of the hermitage. Now the mysterious movements of the boat came to mind.

The thought of him loitering outside, chatting to the neighbours infuriated her. None of the bedrooms looked onto the wellhead and she needed to locate him. She remembered the attic room – little Dom's playroom.

She scrambled up the primitive staircase – not much more than a ladder – and knelt on the floor by the small window. The walls of Chez Reynat were so thick that she was forced to pull most of her body onto the windowsill in order to look down to the ground outside, but she still failed to see him – the top-floor window was too high and the wellhead too near the house. She screwed round awkwardly and slouched to the floor, blinking at wet lashes.

The room stretched the length of the building. It was here that Dominic raced his tricycle boisterously over the floorboards and made all the exuberant, uninhibited noises of toddler delight with his garish toys. Here, Felix was free of the sight of the child's dark curls and easy grin.

Lily picked herself up and descended the house. She took a breath as she opened the door and saw the company of three still not yet disbanded. Baptistin stopped talking as he heard the door open and they all turned to face Lily, without surprise, as though they fully expected her return – in fact they had waited for her.

"You should have been here to hear what Felix had to say on his deathbed," Baptistin shouted to her although she stood only a few feet away at the door. He was a man that had churned over his displeasure and now thrust it out at his first opportunity. "If you'd been here, been with Felix at the end, you would not be selling Chez Reynat." The old man said the last words with difficulty as though they disgusted him.

Lily's face was pinched. "He has no right to be here." She looked fixedly at Honorine and Baptistin. She imagined herself a horse, blinkered to avoid being spooked.

"Who?" Baptistin asked, looking confused. He looked at his companion. "You mean Gabriel? You know what right he has. Perhaps not legally, but in the sight of God?"

Gabriel put a hand up to interrupt. "I'm sorry if my being here is…" He hesitated while he searched for the word, "offensive to you, Lily."

Lily saw his eyes clouded and unsure, but his voice was confident.

"I got a letter – a puzzling letter. You could say it made me curious." He gave a brief smile. "It'd been some time since I'd given a thought to Felix. I'd about forgotten the guy – and then this letter came straight out of the blue. I didn't think I'd get the chance to revisit Achallat."

A forlorn feeling soaked through Lily's insides as she heard the word. Forgotten. It was a cruel word to use – you forget keys, perhaps even birthdays. Her eyes escaped to the space behind Gabriel, to the trunk of the birch tree and its bark, curled and stained like old paper.

"He told me he was dying and would I come out here – he had things he needed to say. I figured if it was that important after all this time, I was obliged to come." Gabriel gave up his leaning position at the well and moved closer to Lily. "I'm sorry it didn't work out for you guys." The words were of condolence, but Lily heard sharp rock in the tone.

She shook her head as though a wasp bothered her. "This is all wrong!" she shouted, but it started somewhere deep inside and emerged hoarse and breathy. She shot an angry look at Baptistin.

"This is Dom's house," she told him, speaking deliberately in French. "It was Felix's and now it's my son's. It has nothing to do with this man." Lily's eyes were fixed on her neighbour, but she felt Gabriel flinch.

Baptistin scratched his nose with an arthritic hand and raised an eyebrow. "God recognises marriage as for ever. You and Felix never married. For those of us who have always lived in Achallat, life is simple. More simple than for

105

some of you, it seems. My parents met, married, and had me – simple. They died and I inherited my fine little house and the field with seven oak trees – simple."

Honorine took in a noisy breath. "Baptistin, this isn't about you. For goodness sake, just shut up for once." She put her hand to her throat as if to stop the irritation bubbling up. "And what about the well?" she asked Lily.

"You and Baptistin both have wells of your own. Baptistin's is in front of his house and yours is in your garden. You use it, Madame, to water your vegetables. And probably everyone else in Achallat has their own. What's so special about this one? You're all obsessed with it."

Honorine and Baptistin glanced at each other.

"And the Île des Lys and the hermitage?" the elderly woman persisted.

"You know it belongs to Chez Reynat, Madame."

"The well and the hermitage belong to Achallat, Lily. You know this."

Lily understood that they were discussing a different type of ownership: not legal; something not of paper, pen and ink. She felt a moment of shame. Felix had talked endlessly of his precious Chez Reynat. Its documents were so precious to him that he kept them under lock and key in a little cupboard in the chimneybreast. There too, he treasured the documents written by his predecessors. He had shown them to her with pride, but also love. He would never have imagined that anyone would argue about the ownership of his heritage. That these things were his, was evident. That they belonged to Achallat, was beyond any doubt.

"I'm sorry. I'm sorry Felix died. I'm sorry this has happened. I don't know what else to say." Lily felt drained and inadequate. Her determination to ignore Gabriel was failing; his presence sucked at her.

"You can say what's right," Baptistin suggested.

The shy sun had warmed Lily's face and its rays seemed out of place in such a frosty meeting.

"I'm sorry," she repeated, and put her hand out behind her to reach for the doorknob.

"And the tea dance?" Baptistin said quickly, seeing her intent. "We'll be having it as usual at the end of next week – in honour of Felix this time. It'll be the first since he died although he couldn't make the last one either."

Lily was puzzled. Was this an invitation after all the acrimony? Honorine saw the expression and nudged her companion.

"She doesn't know, Baptistin." And then to Lily, she explained, "The tea dance is held at Chez Reynat every month – without fail. They are Felix's tea dances."

"Oh," was all Lily could manage. And then she added, "Of course, that's fine. While it hasn't been sold, you can have your tea dances. Felix would want that." And finally she closed the door behind her.

*There she weaves by night and day
A magic web with colours gay.*

                          Tennyson

CHAPTER TWELVE

Lily bounced the pruning saw on the grass in front of her – it made a satisfyingly distracting thrum as it hit the turf. But not distracting enough. She closed her eyes against the afternoon sun and a negative image of the hermitage flashed against her eyelids. It was the last thing she looked at when she shuttered up the house after dusk and the first thing she inspected in the grey dawn.

Her fingers drummed on the tool's handle. She felt jangled up inside as if she had drunk too much coffee: her feet twitched; her hands twittered.

"Where are you?" she yelled and, unnerved by her own voice, she jumped back, splaying out her legs and putting her hands out to the stone step.

The day had been spent pruning shrubs as best she could. With no garden at Lack Farm her scanty knowledge came from five years of watching Felix tend his plants. She regretted remembering so little. Taking note of Venetia's advice, Lily had tackled the climber arching around the oak door, tying in its wayward stems and clipping those that refused to obey. As she snipped and pestered the shrub, she imagined house buyers sighing with pleasure seeing the results of her handiwork.

On her cold seat the pacifying work was forgotten. She walked to the river. Pacing up and down, she tapped the saw against her thigh like an irked cat twitching its tail. Gabriel's materialisation out of the mist had been eight days earlier, but he had vanished again. For a week she had waited for his reappearance – those days were too much of a reminder of a longer vigil twenty years before.

She gave the saw a final slap against her leg and marched to the house. With the iron key clutched in her fist, she returned and almost ran to the water's edge. She did not want her nerve to fail her. Awakening gnats rose in the sun above the river, but Lily rubbed the goosebumps on her arms, so close to the Vamaleau.

"One hundred paces across Oddo tells us in his journal," Felix had said, and then laughed as he added, "but our beloved Oddo must have been a very short man – I make it eighty at most."

Lily ignored the causeway and walked upstream to the boat still bearing her name. The faded gilt lettering was only legible to those already acquainted with it. Beyond the three arched bridge the shallow water was noisy, frothing at pebbles; downstream past the willow it eddied, sucked downwards and spewed back in angry swirls. But at Lily's feet it was still like a sheet of green glass.

The air was calm and the sky bright. She stepped into the boat, holding out her arms to steady herself, the pruning saw still in her hand. Out of kilter with the boat's rhythm, she dropped herself clumsily and lost the saw to the river. It caught for a moment on the shining causeway and then tumbled over it, jigging through the foam until it disappeared, swallowed up in white water. As her arms worked the oars, Lily searched for it in vain.

Chez Reynat receded. Through the slapping of wood against water Lily heard Felix reassure her and she replied out loud, "I know, Felix. Oddo will protect me, so you say," and she squinted down at his burial place as she rowed over it. Felix had told her that Oddo could bless, but the river could curse. The holy man had saved her that day – so Felix insisted, but she banished the memory and sung to herself as she pulled at the oars.

It had been twenty years since she last stepped foot on the island. She had left it in despair, abandoning everything and Felix had never asked her to return there. After the incident with the boat, he had been careful to keep her on Chez Reynat's bank. In those five years they never spoke again of the Île des Lys.

Lily thrust the key in the lock and took a breath. Her hand dithered at the knob. She half wanted it to be different; half wished that Felix had whitewashed the walls, thrown out the bed. She half hoped to find cases of wine, baskets of stored fruit. She threw open the door and stood back. It was unchanged.

The room still smelled of ancient wood-smoke and a scent that reminded Lily of hay – flowers and grasses baked in the sun. Other than the bed in the middle of the room, the only other piece of furniture was a stubby three-legged stool. There was no sign of an unwelcome guest. She should have felt relief, she knew. Gabriel was as elusive as ever.

She leaned against the open door and remembered.

*

Her painting had consumed her. Waking each day as the cockerel crowed, eager for dawn, she had worked with her brushes, crouching on the stool in the crumpled T-shirt and briefs that she wore to bed. Oddo's room – that was how she thought of it – was even-tempered, like the man himself, if Felix's accounts were true. It took no notice of the heat of summer and shrugged off the cold dampness of the river. Even the flag-stoned floor had been kind to her bare feet.

The very first brushstroke was placed on the wall opposite the trefoil window. Excited and anxious at the same time, Lily wanted to see her work lit up by the afternoon sun, and so she dragged the metal bed into the middle of the room. It was not a hindrance to her – she had few belongings. She kept a collection of candles, some stuck in wine bottles, some in thick jars, and these she lined up on the blackened mantelpiece. The hook at the back of the door took care of her clothes, and regularly she would return from Chez Reynat to find these exchanged for a neat pile of clean laundry on the bed. Felix mothered her – a girl unused to the attentions of a mother.

At the clattering of shutters opening across the river, Lily would leave her brushes, pull on a dress and make for Chez Reynat. It was Felix who banged wood against stone and let in the light. First to rise in the house, he would fret if she delayed. Once he crossed the causeway on foot to fetch her, scolding her with bright eyes and a near smile. The boat had become her property: Felix happily walked across the river, treading lightly and quickly on the submerged path; the others were too absorbed in their own activities at Chez Reynat to be bothered by the humble dwelling on the island.

Lily crossed for breakfast and again in the evening for dinner. Trinity went through the motions each day of sulkily trying to coax Lily to stay at the house, and Lily obstinately refused with a screwed up smile. She was happy at a distance. From the Île des Lys she could listen to the chatter and laughter, the music and uproar. She began to find it difficult to focus at the close range of the dinner table.

"Stop watching the world and join in," Trinity chided her one night as Lily set off home again, swinging her candle lanterns in each hand. Felix had set them in glass jars for her and attached string handles.

"But I'm happy, Trin," she almost sang in reply.

Claude Jopert, harvesting late into the night, saw the candlelit boat and knew its occupant to be the wide-eyed elfin girl, rowing to her cell. Lily saw the headlights of the tractor as it worked the field and knew it to be the farmer with the feathered black hat.

From her doorstep she observed the world of Achallat, studying everyone and giving them life again on her painted wall. She watched by day and by night. In the dark it was not only Jopert out of doors in the hamlet. To the sound of the crickets, Trinity led Ken away from the lamp-lit house and guided him under the canopy of the willow, its weeping branches embracing their secret.

By day, Lily observed the Renault rattle across the stone bridge on its way to Saint Bénigne or Aubaine. In the morning, she spotted the farmer's wife arriving at the great door, one shoulder pulled to the weight of the milk churn she bore. In the evening, she witnessed the small gathering of neighbours at the Reynat well or heard them beyond the gate pillars on the couderc. There stood the round farmer with his plumed hat; the lopsided one called Baptistin slapping his leg with joy as he retold an old story; the grey haired ladies knitting as they stood and conferring with heads pulled together. Sometimes a row would break out and, like a flock of starlings, they all cried out and hopped on the spot, arms waving. Sometimes they sat quietly on the wall of the wellhead shaded by the far reaching limbs of the chestnut tree, the farmer swishing a stalk of grass or chewing it.

Lily saw Felix at the windows of the grey house, shaking blankets and eiderdowns. She watched his progress as he moved from room to room, and she recorded it in simple strokes of the brush. She viewed Trinity and Oki, prostrate and passive, worshipping the sun, or so entwined that it would have been impossible to slip a sheet of paper between them. Mason with his yellow hair and pale skin avoided the sun, but sometimes Lily saw him leaning against the jamb of the French window. Not so often, Trinity and Oki led Ken in a game, playing noisily like children, chasing each other with water bombs, Trinity poking out her tongue and squealing. Always the game ended in a tangle of legs and arms in the long grass. Lily's favourite view was of Trinity dancing on her own on the grassy slope, her face hidden by the swishing mantle of sun-bleached hair. Trinity had forsaken clothes after the first week at Chez Reynat and for the rest of the time wore only a minuscule pair of shorts. Her skin had toasted to an even nut brown, and as she swayed to the music, Lily imagined her a Celtic queen with her attending consorts.

All these scenes she laid down in bold colour in a two foot panel running along the walls of the square room. And she was happy.

When the sun sank Lily would sit on the still warm flagstone and wash out her brushes. Without running water at the hermitage she was obliged to fetch two buckets of water from the river. She washed the brushes first in one bucket and rinsed them in the second before pouring the strange coloured liquid into the brambles behind the hermitage.

Lily and her small island were intimate now. She tried not to think that this blissful life was finite. In a few weeks she would return to Lack Farm and finish her schooling. Like someone on the verge of waking, she tried to etch the details of this dream to memory. She knew each fault in the timber of her small boat; her hands knew the smoothness of the oar handles. She was familiar with every flagstone in her cell and avoided the chips and dents that might graze her foot. And as she painted she became acquainted with the bumps and lines in the plaster.

With her legs splayed either side of the bucket, Lily sat to her cleaning ritual and rested her back against the rosy stone. It was a July evening and the sun lit up the northern wall, bathing Lily in golden light.

Chez Reynat sat in shadow, smoke ribboning from its chimney, but two miniatures of it shone out from Lily's mirrored-lens glasses. Swallows darted low over the green water and chattered in their mysterious language. Achallat's residents had taken their last draught from the well and had retreated to prepare their *souper*. All was quiet.

With her hands still playing at the bristles, Lily closed her eyes and, leaning her head against the pink granite, she breathed in the scent of seasoned pear logs drifting across from the great house. The Vamaleau murmured quietly and the aspen whispered back to the sleepy river. As if enthralled, the birds hushed their singing and Lily listened to her own breathing.

She was unsure what made her bring her head up and look across to the house – perhaps it was a noise or a vibration from the ground. As she opened her eyes she saw across the river, a bay horse and its rider.

The heavy-hoofed horse trotted confidently, making straight for the water's edge. They stopped, the rider loosened the reins to let it drink and he sat back as it sated its thirst. Lily put a wet hand to her brow and watched closely as they kept close to the river, passing under the willow and making their way to the bridge. When she saw them turn back, Lily wondered whether the rider searched for something in the grass, but then he pulled the horse to a halt at the causeway. The animal put a sturdy foot out into the inky water and, having felt solid ground with the first hoof, took a few steps onto the invisible path.

Lily held her breath as if this might help her see through the sun's dazzle as she struggled to read the minuscule movements between rider and mount. The figure stooped to stroke his horse's neck and in response the animal lifted its head and whinnied. They crept out into the Vamaleau, the rider stooped forward, a hand held under the mane. Lily held her breath again, straining to catch the words that a rider would use to charm an animal onto Oddo's path. Perhaps Oddo could hear them as they reached his resting place, but Lily only heard the docile river. They left Oddo and moved from Achallat's shadow into the red glow of the sun. The horse's coat shone, its mane glistened, and Lily saw now that the man rode without a saddle. She had no thought to paint this scene. She had no thought at all – she was awestruck.

At last, the horse stepped up onto the island and, above the whisper of the river, Lily heard clearly – the rider had enchanted his horse with a slow deep song. The animal shook its head of some imaginary water and the rider gave up his serenade.

In one supple leap, he dismounted and climbed the bank, ignoring the baked clay path – his frayed jeans and muddy boots cutting through the high grass and wayward flowers. Lily had been watching his approach with fascination – her hands holding the brushes mid-air, but, at the dull thud of his feet touching earth, her shyness brought her back to her senses. With equal nimbleness, Lily jumped from her seat on the flagstone and, wheeling about, she searched for a plausible retreat from the imminent meeting. In her panic, Lily forgot the half washed brush still in her hand; she forgot the bucket between her knees. Helplessly, she looked down as it clattered over and watched the iridescent water tumble, spilling over her bare feet, and washing down the stone step. She kept her eyes to the mess at her feet, but she saw his legs approach anyway, the rein in hand, his horse following meekly.

With her cheeks hot, her hands and feet damp, Lily kneeled to remedy the situation, but her dress now slapped around in the kaleidoscopic water, soaking it up like a mop. Breathily, she plucked at the hem and wrung it. The liquid escaped, slopping onto the path, but the colour only rose further up the cloth. As they always did in a crisis, Lily's hands reached for her hair. A finger caught the arm of her glasses and she watched them fall and break on the flagstone, splintered mirrors flashing up from the polychrome water.

The horse, so steadfast on the Vamaleau, reared at this shattering sound and it dug its hind hooves into the soft turf. It pulled back from the rein, its ears back, the whites of its eyes flashing, but the man at its side put a hand to its muzzle and spoke softly, pressing his mouth close to the creature's face. Its nostrils still flaring, it stilled itself, but looked askance at Lily, prepared for more surprises from the unpredictable human.

He seemed not to notice the upturned bucket – or the broken sunglasses. Hardly taking in the flustered drama, he dropped the reins and, ducking his head, he walked uninvited into Lily's hermitage. At the threshold, he surveyed her unfinished story, his eyes pausing at each scene – but he passed no comment. A smile flickered across his face as his eyes moved along the panel. There was Mason at the door, keeping watch on his flock; there were the two secretive lovers disappearing behind the curtain of willow leaves; there were three dancers, legs and arms extended to the sun. When his eyes reached the half-painted sketch above the stool he turned back to Lily. Her dress clung to her calves; her toes blushed a lurid purple. She hid one foot and then the other behind the stained hem and wished for the safety of her sunglasses.

"You must be Lily," he said.

Lily's eyes went straight to his mouth, arrested by the timbre and the quietness in the tone. Her father and brother were quiet too – especially with strangers, but theirs was an awkward self-conscious quietness born of shyness. This man seemed comfortable with himself and the world.

"Felix says dinner's about ready. I guess he likes everyone round the table together."

Lily listened to each syllable.

"Mason sent me to fetch you," he explained as he rubbed the horse's shoulder with the back of his hand.

The animal had followed him to the doorway and hung its head inside as if it too were interested in Lily's artwork. It snickered, perhaps enticed by the scent of Oddo's herbs.

Without waiting for a reply, Mason's messenger picked up the hanging reins and turned back to the river. Man and animal waited for Lily, the horse's mouth inching along at the lush grass. With luminous eyes, Lily watched him for a moment and then she took the key that hung by a thin cord at her neck and locked the small door, tugging the handle with the weight of her body. The lock refused the key at first, and then she felt the satisfying click. She turned and saw his amused expression.

"I know I don't need to lock the place up." Her eyes pointed out their surroundings to him. "I mean – out here in the middle of nowhere. But I think of everybody that shut this door before – all through the ages. Perhaps they had manuscripts to keep safe." Her eyebrows shot up – her words had surprised her and she gave him a grin. "And it's a beautiful thing too – too beautiful not to use," Lily explained. She cradled the key between her palm and thumb before returning the warm metal to her neck. At the platform Lily knelt down at the rope securing the boat and began to unfasten it.

"You can ride with me – Bayardo won't mind."

He mounted and reached down a hand. From the ground Lily looked up into the horse's eye and saw a knowingness that all was well, that nothing untoward could happen with this man on his back. His hand waited outstretched, his eyes unsmiling.

She hitched up her wet dress and climbed up, squeezing herself between the withers and the rider. He adjusted himself into the horse's back and pulled her towards him.

"Let's make life easy for my friend," he said to the nape of her neck.

He pushed her hair to one side to see more easily and she felt his breath at the tip of her ear. They crossed in silence. Lily listened to the splishing of hooves kicking water and the rumbling weir downstream. Her hands held the black mane, but her eyes saw a strong hand, thumb over leather, fingers clasped.

At the other side, she slipped down onto the cool grass and he jumped down beside her. And she found herself looking him in the eye without her usual discomfort. Lily thought that some would find his face intimidating with such angular features, but she saw a vulnerability in the jaw line that softened it – his mouth seemed to say sorry. A thread of pink ran from the corner of his mouth to just below the prominent cheekbone. She took her eyes away and coloured.

Lily wondered often in the days and weeks that followed as she studied each inch of his face what had drawn her to him. She came to the conclusion that it had happened minutes before any feature had come into view. It occurred as the horse stepped into the river, the figure swaying slightly with the rhythm of the gait when man and creature seemed as one.

As they stood in the shadow of Chez Reynat, each silent, Mason walked towards them, bent arms swinging awkwardly, legs bowed. His freckled face wore its habitual grin.

"I see our Water Lily has received a visitation from the angel Gabriel."

Lily looked up at the rider, wanting to say his name aloud, but whispering it to herself instead as she would do all that night as she lay in her bed at the hermitage. Gabriel's face was transformed by a smile directed at the pastor – far from daunting, he now had a look of playfulness as if he waited for the start of Mason's game. Lily watched his hand stroke the horse's glossy shoulder as he grinned at Mason and she felt a dart of jealousy aimed at the animal.

An hour earlier Lily had known contentment and now she knew love.

At dinner she watched everyone else's eyes as they gazed on Gabriel – she had lost her nerve to look at him directly. Suddenly it was important whether he looked back – or not. She took courage once and from underneath her lashes she glimpsed his eyes on her. She put down her fork. Her insides panicked so much she put a hand to her waist.

"Come on, Gabe, old friend, tell us all about your equine adventures," Mason declared in his patriarchal fashion.

Gabriel rested his hands on the edge of the table. "I see you've got yourselves company since I left."

Lily ventured a glance, but his eyes were not on her and suddenly she felt a lead weight plummet. But his eyes were not on Trinity either and Lily took in a little breath of comfort. With her head resting in her hand, Trinity looked dreamily at the newcomer while Oki absent-mindedly stroked the white-blonde hair.

Gabriel looked up from his cleaned plate with a minute smile creasing his eyes. "Mason I swear you're paler now than when we left Oregon in spring," he said, dryly. "You should get out more – farther than the doorpost."

"I can see more clearly standing in the shade than in the harsh glare of the sun, my old buddy."

"And what do you see?" Gabriel asked, beginning a game played by old friends.

"Tonight is not the night for revelations – however revealing they might be," Mason answered, letting his eyes scan round the table.

"Enlightenment tomorrow – celebration tonight. Our adventurer has returned – let's break out the weed and get stoned. I know guys, supplies are getting low. No offence, Felix, but this sleepy little hamlet of yours has its inconveniences."

Ken dutifully climbed the stairs and returned shortly with a small cloth bag. The joint was made lovingly and silently by Ken, who had propped himself against the wall of the chimneypiece. He was a man who was comfortable when his hands were occupied. Lily had watched him whittling at sticks on the riverbank or skimming stones across the Vamaleau. With his eyes to a task, his features relaxed, the permanent crease on his brow softened.

Lily hesitated. She normally said her goodbyes as soon as dinner was over and now she felt Felix's knowing eyes search her face. She looked everywhere but back at him and joined Trinity and Oki on one of the sofas, allowing Trinity to rest her brown feet on her lap. The two lovers snuggled their heads to each other, Trinity's hand to Oki's cheek, his to her waist. Mason stood by the fireplace, his arm raised to the mantelpiece, his ice blue eyes surveying his congregation.

Lily was relieved to notice that Felix had withdrawn from the room – and then she felt a surge of guilt. She picked up one of Trinity's feet and stroked the painted toes to calm herself. She did not look, but knew that Gabriel, ignoring the free sofa, had joined Ken on the floor.

As the joint was passed around, the lively conversation became less spirited. Trinity's eyes had been sparkling with the anticipation of her first cannabis experience, but were now lazily focused on Ken across the room. Oki played with the rings on Trinity's fingers.

Lily had been less enthusiastic. She remembered her disgust with the only cigarette she had tried, but she drew tentatively on the reefer and managed to suppress the immediate cough. At each turn she found she could inhale a little more easily and she settled into the sofa, pulling her legs up beside her to scuffle with Trinity's.

She was no longer a detached observer, but a silent member of a group, bonded by unspoken thoughts. Her eyes were drawn repeatedly to Gabriel, but as his met hers, she turned away quickly, convinced that her mind was unconcealed, to be read like a children's book, her thoughts in large, bold print. Lily saw the embarrassing letters and squeezed the painted toes, making Trinity squeak. She searched for safety, but found Mason grinning at her. Am I that foolish, she asked herself. But she glanced back at Gabriel and his eyes were solemn.

As the next joint was lit, Lily quietly pushed Trinity aside and sidled out of the room. She need not have been so surreptitious – no one seemed to notice. But as she ambled dozily down the pathway to the riverbank Felix appeared out of the darkness. Lily almost lost her balance.

"Where did you come from?" Her voice was harsh, she realised too late.

"Are you alright, Lily?"

"Of course I am. I'm fine. It was only some dope," she answered in a casual tone and tried to walk more briskly, keen to be away from him.

When they reached the water they both looked at the empty mooring – Felix blankly and Lily in dismay.

"How can it be – the boat has gone," Felix said with disbelief in his voice.

"It's not gone – it's still on the other side." She tried to sound nonchalant and then stood limply, listening to the water still busying itself, even in the night. She had no idea what to do and yet she felt no urgency to think of a solution.

"I don't think I can get Bayardo to go back in the dark."

Lily recognised the voice in the blackness behind them and whirled round. But it was a slow pirouette she performed and Gabriel was beside her by the time her eyes focused.

"But if you want to go back tonight – if you've a need to, I'll walk you across."

Felix stepped towards Lily with a little hop, turning his back to the other man at the same time. "No, no," he stuttered. "I will take you, Lily. I know this river. I have walked the causeway since I was a small child. It is not safe for people who do not know it in the same way. And you trust me, Lily, don't you?" He looked at her expectantly.

"But you said it was safe for anyone who had faith," Lily answered. His boastfulness irritated her – his presence irritated her.

She felt as though she could float across, hovering above while her toes skimmed the cool water. Felix was already on the causeway with his hand outstretched towards her. She looked back – Gabriel had taken a step back and now took another.

"Come, come," Felix urged.

She did not float. The river was icy – it gripped her ankles, or perhaps Oddo did with his bony hands. Felix stepped quickly and lightly and Lily stumbled to keep up. When they reached the other side her feet were numb.

"Thank you, Lily" he said.

"What?" she asked, confused.

"For trusting in me," he replied, his emphasis on the last word. Me and no other.

She stood and watched him retreat and then saw Gabriel still at the river's edge and, even at one hundred of Oddo's paces, she felt him read her thoughts.

Halfway across Felix shouted back to her, "Go to bed now." Although turned away from her, he knew she had not moved.

*

Lily heard more shouting and realised it was not Felix. He was dead and lying next to his mother in Saint Bénigne. Standing on the hermitage doorstep, she turned her head to the melancholic sound. The hollering came from beyond Chez Reynat – it was Claude Jopert, calling home his cows.

The sun had dropped while she had wasted time, punishing herself with memories that should have been left to wither. Like weeds their roots clung to life. She locked the door behind her and walked back to the boat. The sky turned from copper to puce as she rowed over Oddo's grave. "Where are you hiding?" she asked. The river whispered back to her as the hermitage was lost to twilight.

CHAPTER THIRTEEN

It was already February. Lily had tamed every bare twig and stem; had climbed to the last but one rung of the ladder and painted every shutter and window that she could reach. And so she turned her attention to the contents of the barn.

She cleaned and oiled all the tools arranged neatly above Felix's work bench, swept clean the shallow shelves and threw out anything she failed to identify. This labour she managed to draw out to two days.

The barn stood on the north side of the house. It was a cavernous space whose tapering ladders stretched up heavenward to the rafters. On the top floor Felix kept old woodworm speckled furniture that he, no doubt, intended one day to repair. Lily scaled one of the ladders and, in half light, made out beds, armoires, a pile of rush-seated chairs. On the platform she scrutinised each piece, but then clambered back down onto the dusty floor.

The lawnmower caught her eye and, when it failed to start on the first attempt, Lily smiled triumphantly. She had only a rudimentary knowledge of petrol engines, but had watched her father and brother often enough to feel confident that a repair was not beyond her skill. Well into the morning, the machine was still in pieces and she had no idea how to put it together again. But she knew from long practice that manual activity kept the mind from straying and in recent days hers had wandered too far, too often. Memories itched, waiting to be scratched.

With a collection of parts laid out in front of her, Lily pulled herself up from the barn floor and rubbed oily hands on her lower back. "Okay I give in, Felix. I've buggered the thing for good by the look of it. At least the grass won't be growing for a while – and I won't be needing it by the time it does." She stared down at the miscellany for a moment and then turned her back to it.

At the kitchen sink she scrubbed at her hands, but the oil refused to budge – the second failure of that day. She ate her lunch of bread and cheese with blue-black fingers, gazing out at the rain that had been falling since dawn. Before she had finished eating, Baptistin arrived, thumping at the door to attract her attention.

"There's a bell," Lily said to his shoulder as he barged past her.

"I thought I'd bring these over while it wasn't bucketing down," he shouted. Water trailed down his face, dripping from his nose and chin. He carried two plastic kegs of red wine in one hand and two light wooden chairs, back to back, in the other. Lily watched his wet trek across the floor. The wine he set on the table. As he placed the chairs against the bookshelves, he caught her expression.

"You know we'll be moving furniture around, don't you?"

Lily's mind suddenly focused as she remembered the *danse du thé*, and she gestured understanding. He scrutinised her with an odd expression, his eyes on her hair and face at first, and then her hands.

"I thought it was a tea dance," Lily said, frowning deliberately at the kegs and the puddles on her waxed table.

"It was Honorine who decided to call it that and Felix liked the idea. You know what she's like – no, perhaps you don't. Anyway, she likes to go and buy the stuff from one of those new shops in Aubaine. Brings back all sorts – oddest names, some of them. What's that one now...?" His hand gave up the scratch on the top of his head. "I never drink it myself, but we get more women than men – and they seem to like the stuff."

"So did Felix," she countered.

"Yes, well, he had his bourgeois notions from his mother – we'll forgive him for those. He was never one for wine anyway – preferred his water. The wine's for the rest of us."

Baptistin slapped his chest. He and Lily stood facing each other in the middle of the room – for more than a moment. He waited. And then Lily's hands jumped to attention.

"Oh, I'm being rude – can I get you a coffee or something?" she asked.

Before she had finished the sentence, Baptistin reached the table. "Coffee? At this time of day?" He glanced down at an imaginary watch. "I can manage a little glass, thank you," he said and pulled out a chair.

Lily went to the kitchen and returned with a bottle of Felix's Medoc, a corkscrew, and two small tumblers.

"Ah no, ah no, ah no," Baptistin protested, each syllable uttered more loudly than the previous. He waved his hand vigorously. "You don't have to go and open a new bottle for me. After all, we're old friends, you and me. Whatever you just had at lunch will be good." And then his eyes took in the tea plate, breadcrumbs, and the bottle of water. He brought his thick eyebrows together and pushed out a lip.

With pink cheeks Lily opened the bottle and poured out two glasses. They sat opposite each other, Baptistin leaning forward, his elbows in the middle of the table.

"I thought women liked to look after themselves these days," he remarked, nodding at Lily's hands.

She forced a smile and hid the black nails and stained fingers under the table. "And what do you know about women these days, Baptistin?" she asked, pretending to be amused.

"You think I'm a hermit – like old Oddo? I have a woman friend, you know. I don't see her very often, it's true, but we've known each other a long time now. She lives in an apartment over in Aubaine."

He sipped at his wine and looked at Lily over the glass. "Good stuff," Baptistin nodded appreciatively. "She comes over now and then. Oh, I know what she's after – they all like to tell me, but I already know. She's after my inheritance – the house, my field, the twelve oak trees. I'm not an old fool. I told Jopert, 'I'm not weak in the head yet, *mon frère.*' But she brings me a cooked chicken and washes the bed sheets for me while she's here." He winked at Lily mischievously and then played with the glass, swivelling it round on the polished wood.

"I know she likes to spend money on face creams, perfumes, clothes. Money, that's what she's after." He gulped his wine and, as though wanting to steer the conversation elsewhere, he leaned back in his chair and turned his attention to the female before him.

"But look at you. You should look after yourself more. It wouldn't do you any harm to spend some money on yourself. Is that what selling Chez Reynat is all about? You need the money?"

Lily shook her head. "No, Baptistin – I don't need the money. I like the way I am," she said hoarsely, smarting at his remarks, and then irritated that she had acknowledged them.

"I know Felix left a little savings too. He told me. Well, you'll sort all of that out with the solicitor, no doubt. Get it spent on some clothes for yourself – some creams and stuff." He surveyed her. "You're still a pretty woman, you know, underneath."

His frankness stung her and she blinked at watery eyes. Draining his glass, the old man stood, pushing the chair noisily away from himself.

"I'll bring the rest of the things over later," he grunted as he shuffled to the door. "You haven't thrown out the glasses or plates, have you?"

"What? Of course not."

"Just asking. I've noticed you're such a busy person about the place. So keen to get everything shipshape." With his fist at the doorknob, he half turned. "By the way, what are you going to do this afternoon?"

Lily looked blankly at him for a moment. So there was no invitation, after all.

"Oh, I need to get a few things in town." She dug her hands in her pockets and looked out at the rain. "What time does it start?"

He pushed his wet hair from his brow. "This time of year we have it early – about three."

He waved behind him as he trotted down the muddy lane.

At two o'clock Lily went to the bedroom to change and by half past she had not chosen anything to wear. Every piece of clothing was strewn on the bed. It looked a sorry collection – lots of frayed jeans, washed out woollens, and shapeless shirts. She chose the neatest sweater she could find and the trousers she had travelled in from England. She brushed her hair and swept it back into a knot, studying herself in the old mirror, peering closely at her features, and then standing back, pushing herself against the bed. A small woman with wide anxious eyes and hair that tried to break free blinked back at her. She pulled out the tortoiseshell clasp and brushed her hair again, this time leaving it fall loosely around her shoulders. Her work had made it as glossy as conkers.

"Bloody cheek," she cursed, still bruised by Baptistin's comments.

She slipped on her coat – Trinity's cast-off with the capacious hood. This one item of clothing pleased her. After all, she might have brought her only other coat – a grubby waxed jacket that – at best – smelled of damp animal. Lily forced a thin smile to her reflection.

"Never mind tea dances, girl – you look like you're off to a party yourself."

The worn-out Renault took her to Saint Bénigne. "Me and you have something in common," she said, patting the steering wheel before she got out. "At least according to Baptistin."

At the church square she pulled up outside the Bar des Voyageurs. Even from outside she could see that she was about to be its only customer. The barkeeper put down his damp cloth and greeted her warmly.

"*Bonjour*, Madame. Not the weather for visiting loved ones." He nodded at the steamy window.

"No, I suppose not," Lily answered vaguely, and then remembered the graveyard down the alleyway. He gave a sympathetic nod. She brushed at the raindrops on her precious coat and felt a fraud. With the order of hot chocolate made she sat at the window and stared through the condensation at the empty square. Rain dribbled down the pane. Lily sipped at the drink slowly, lingering over it, glancing up now and then at the clock behind the bar. Eventually the cup was drained and she ordered a second, but this time she asked for a cognac in it. The barman brought it to her table and stood over her, smiling.

"You don't remember me, I think."

She looked up at him with fresh eyes. He wore a black shiny waistcoat and a bowtie as though he was unaware of his rural surroundings.

"The other day – the funeral?" Lily was unsure of what he meant.

"You used to come here every market day. You sat outside in all weathers – with the pushchair."

Lily tried to smile politely, but failed and turned her gaze back to the window. They were not happy days, but he was not to know.

"When you never came again I guessed that you'd moved away. Or someone told me, perhaps. How is your son? It was a boy, wasn't it?" he persisted with the conversation. He spoke in staccato, each word bruising as it entered the dark room.

"He's fine, thanks. He's nineteen now. He's at university," Lily told him, not hiding the pride in her voice.

"Not had a chance to do anything with his life yet. The world's his oyster. As long as he doesn't get stuck in a place like this."

Lily's eyebrow lifted at the bitter tone.

"Oh, I love it here," he reassured her. "But a nineteen-year-old should see a bit of the world, don't you think? How about you? You were just a girl then. Did you do much travelling after you left here?"

"No."

The man seemed not to notice Lily's scornful tone. She had his attention, and he waited for a fuller explanation.

"I haven't been anywhere," she said flatly.

"That's two of us then," the barman laughed. He leaned against the bar behind him. "It can be a burden being a son. When your parents die, that is," he explained. "Look at me – my father died and left me this place."

Lily looked around the room and the neat glass shelves full of bottles. "It's a good bar."

"I've made something of it now – not much choice. Too late to get out once Papa died. There were expectations of me. Left it too late to do anything else."

Trying to be discreet, Lily glanced up again at the clock.

"You've got to be somewhere?"

The barman seemed not to notice Lily's sardonic smile.

"Quite the opposite. But I'll make a move all the same."

She could sit in the barn, she thought for a foolish moment. No, she would walk into her own house – at least her son's.

Lily turned off the engine outside the barn and heard the music before she had stepped out of the car. As she reached the great door she recognised it as one of those old big band tunes.

Like an intruder she turned the knob quietly. In the hallway she picked her way through a row of boots and half-opened umbrellas, and pulled off her hood at the sitting room door.

The room that had seemed neat just hours earlier, glowed. She was stunned. The partygoers had lit all of Felix's odd assortment of table lamps and the fire gave out a ferocious light. It seemed a wonderful indulgence to someone who was used to her father complaining if she switched on a lamp before dusk, no matter what the time of year or weather. She saw Chez Reynat as a beacon of welcome in the rain-sodden landscape. The house had probably always been the hub of the hamlet, its dour walls needing the warmth of people as much as the heat of the fire.

There were more than she expected – at least twenty, she guessed. Several couples danced: some in formal ballroom poses with ramrod straight backs; others wrapped around each other in a friendly bear hug. The table had been moved to the back wall, its white cloth barely visible between platters of food. A few men hovered over the dishes, napkins in hand. Others were seated around the room, tapping their feet as they watched the swirling couples. One woman caught Lily's attention – it was Séverine, the scooter rider. Wearing thick woollen socks and the sturdy boots that seemed to act as weights to her feet, she energetically clapped along to the music, yelling encouragement to the dancers.

Lily was entranced. For an insane moment she saw herself, arm in arm with Felix, playing the part of hostess. She shook herself – it would not have been like that. There would have been no happy endings here with Felix.

With small clipped steps, Honorine approached Lily.

"Does she do much walking? She uses one of those mobility things, doesn't she?" Lily nodded at the enthusiastic member of the club.

"Séverine can barely walk a few steps, but her cousin bought the walking boots for her, thinking they would help.

She's ga-ga – the cousin that is. Séverine wears them to please her."

Lily spotted Baptistin's friend standing by the staircase. With a florid face, he waved his feathered hat about as he talked animatedly to someone seated on the stairs. Scarlet braces over a starched white shirt pulled his trousers to his chest.

The music came to a halt, but only briefly, as a bare-boned man with snow white hair stooped over the old fashioned record player and carefully lowered another vinyl disc onto it.

"Who are all these people?" Lily asked Honorine.

"Surely you can remember some of us. We were your neighbours after all – and we haven't changed that much, have we? I remember you well enough – you're not very different. Perhaps wearier, yes."

"I remember my neighbours okay. But who are all the other people here. Achallat is a tiny hamlet and there are... Well, the room's full, isn't it?" Lily looked around her.

"Let's see. That's Claude's wife at the table with the teapot. I'll understand if you don't remember her, because she's always been a bit of a recluse. She brings – I mean brought Felix his milk in the morning, but she never comes to the couderc or the well." Honorine stopped for a moment and she flashed an anxious look at Lily as if suddenly aware that she had strayed onto a contentious subject. She sipped her tea quickly. "It was Felix that got Marie to come to our little dance after a lot of coaxing. And it's done her the world of good. Probably the happiest she's ever been since her daughter ran off. Now, who else? Well, dancing together are the twins – Florence and Florette – from over the bridge – but you must remember them." And sitting by the window are Jopert's cousins with Séverine's sister Honorine put a genteel finger to her lip as she thought, and then waved an arm expansively as if bored by the task. "Everyone's related to somebody or another."

Lily had an image of Felix, with eyes twinkling, welcoming one and all to his ancient home and, for a moment, she thought she heard the floorboards creak above her, the host about to descend and greet her, forgiving her for her abrupt departure.

As if she heard Lily's thoughts, Honorine said, "We owe it all to Felix. He was a generous man. Too generous, sometimes – easily taken in. He would share his last loaf with anyone. Look at the people he had here all those years ago." She pursed her lips as if the memory were a sour taste, but she savoured it again and looked Lily up and down.

"He should have married. If only he'd made an effort – there were plenty of opportunities. He would have had a respectable wife and children. And all this wouldn't have happened." She let Lily see the anger in her eyes.

"You're right." Lily's cheeks flushed and she turned her head, first to the door behind her, and then to the staircase.

"There are obligations in life, young woman. Not legal ones perhaps."

The music and the dancing stopped and Honorine looked down at the empty cup in her hand and shifted restlessly in the sudden quiet. Lily fidgeted too – she had not been offered a drink and stood at the threshold of the room, an uninvited guest. At the fireplace, Jopert's cousin, on his knees, closed the stove door and moved the empty log basket to the back of the hearth. He lifted his eyes to the small woman standing in her damp coat.

"I hope it's alright. I went to the barn," he explained with a sheepish expression. "Normally Felix would see to the fire."

"Don't worry," Lily reassured him. "There are enough logs in that barn for a lifetime of fires."

Honorine had slipped away and Lily saw her erect figure heading for the table and the teapot. Left alone, neither host nor guest, Lily made the decision to escape and took a few steps across the empty floor.

Baptistin bellowed across the room. "*Mon frère*, enough tales told over there. Come on." Claude Jopert turned his head to his old friend and Baptistin pointed to an accordion propped on a chair near the fireplace. Jopert nodded in agreement. Lily quickened her step – it would be impossible to leave while Jopert was performing – after all, he was the official musician of Achallat as his father and grandfather had been before him. A Jopert had played at all the important occasions of the hamlet, be it baptism, wedding, or funeral. On the other hand, her departure was probably expected – and wanted – by most of the guests.

Heads turned as she moved self-consciously towards the staircase and she offered a dutiful smile and a muttered greeting to those who made eye contact. Concentrating on her escape route, Lily reached the middle of the room and then she saw a pair of boots on the lower steps. She stopped mid-stride. There was no mistaking the legs casually outstretched at the bottom of the staircase. She heard her own heavy breathing like a cornered beast. Claude Jopert was still waving his hat like a flag, reluctant to return to his instrument. Lily looked beyond the farmer talking excitedly – Gabriel's face was partially hidden by the newels. He leaned back, one elbow on the tread behind him, focused on Jopert's tale telling, comprehension ebbing and flowing across his features. Catching some movement, his eyes flicked sideways and as they found Lily, he frowned. It was a look of pain tightening his jaw.

The accordion player swivelled round to discover the source of the distraction, but Lily had already retreated. She retraced her footsteps quickly, not stopping when she reached the door. The rain fell still. Under the dripping branches of the chestnut, Lily's eyes rested on the circles playing on the river's surface.

CHAPTER FOURTEEN

With her fork hovering at her lips, Lily shifted her chair for a better view – a better view of the night beyond the glass. Her eyes searched for a flicker of candlelight across the river, but there was none.

Clutching a bottle of wine and a glass awkwardly in one hand, Lily abandoned her surveillance and went to the pile of old records. She flicked through record after record and eventually chose Leonard Cohen. The quiet night demanded something sombre.

There had been no sign of Gabriel since the dance, but she imagined him lurking around every corner. Just thinking of his boots on the staircase made her head ache.

With her second bottle of wine since she had arrived at Achallat, Lily stretched out beside the fire. She had opened the first bottle to please Baptistin and avoid the humiliation of seeming bereft of the small delights that her French neighbour took for granted. This one she had uncorked to distract herself – she was an expert on avoidance. Her toes curled and uncurled as she finished her third – or was it her fourth – glass.

Lily held the telephone receiver to her ear, waiting for a pause in Trinity's comical story so that she could pour out her own – she needed Trinity's blithe reassurances. She swirled the ruby liquid around in the glass and heard her father's admonishments. "Drinking on your own, lass? Back to foreign ways already." This time she did not shy from the disapproval, but raised her glass to him. She sighed as she waited for her turn to speak.

"So you're getting some R and R at least over there, then," Trinity said, as if aware of Lily's posture on the sofa.

Lily sighed again, but this was not one of impatience. She had a knee-jerk reaction of guilt to the comment. The Weavers did not do R and R – they kept themselves occupied. 'Life is an uphill struggle, lass,' her father assured her often. Lily shifted on the sofa, its deep cushions suddenly uncomfortable.

"There's not much I can do anymore. I'm stuck here – waiting," she said lamely. She bit her lip. "But Trin," she began again.

"You could get out and about. Do something interesting."

Lily was at a loss for words. She had no idea what something interesting might be.

"So is it all the same – the house, the place?"

Lily recognised the excitement so easily aroused in her spirited friend.

"Exactly the same. Same neighbours, same furniture, same river." As an afterthought, she said, "Felix is gone." But it was not quite true – Lily still saw him. That morning he had been standing in the inglenook fireplace. Lily had turned away, unable to look at the anguish in his face. She fretted that he had not pleased his maker after all.

"Poor old Felix." The voice at the end of the line failed in its attempt to sound sympathetic.

Lily tried to get the words out, 'He's here, Trin,' but, before she could, Trinity's voice sparkled. "I thought I was in Paradise – our very own Garden of Eden. You don't know when you're seventeen that it won't always be like that. I thought that was the way it was going to be in the grown-up world."

Trinity let a brief silence fall and now Lily felt unable to fill it.

"And we had those boys all to ourselves for the whole of the summer. We didn't think of them as boys then – they seemed ancient compared to us, but they must have been all of twenty-four. But then, we were still in school and they'd already been to war – except the crazy reverend, of course. I thought they knew everything there was to know about the world – and then some. We hung on their every word. We were awestruck, weren't we? Oh, to be seventeen again."

Lily could not muster up any noises of agreement. She had needed to tell someone about Gabriel's' appearance. There was no one else she could tell.

"You're awfully quiet, Liliput. Are you alright over there on your own. If it weren't for the kids I'd come over – you know that. Look, are you sure you should be selling the place so soon? More to the point, are you sure Dom wants to sell? You haven't given yourself enough time."

Lily pulled at the telephone cord. Time? She had wandered from window to window for days, weeks.

"Why don't you sit back and take stock…" Trinity continued.

Lily jumped in before Trinity could finish. "That's why I rang you," she lied. "I got a call from the agent this afternoon. She's bringing some people out – she thinks Chez Reynat will be perfect for them."

"So what do the neighbours think of it all?"

"It doesn't matter what they think," Lily answered bluntly.

But she had summoned up the courage to tell Baptistin that afternoon. He had rubbed his unshaven chin for a while and, looking at her from the corner of his eye, said, "I can show them around if you like. They can have someone who knows what he's talking about to show them the old place – just like Felix would have done. I know Chez Reynat inside out. And I can tell them all about the history of Achallat, and the water, and…"

Lily had shaken her head quickly to dissuade the old man. "You know estate agents – they have their own way of doing things. This woman doesn't even want me around, let alone anyone else." Lily rolled her eyes, hoping for sympathy from Baptistin. "You know what these people are like."

"No, I don't know. I've never met an estate agent. We've never had one in Achallat before."

Lily had left him at his door, but when she turned at the gate pillars, she saw him trotting up the lane towards Honorine's house.

Trinity's response to the news was not as enthusiastic as Lily expected. "Well Liliput, if you're sure, I suppose." She sounded as if she only half listened anyway. "Not getting nostalgic playing those old records of ours, are you?"

"They weren't ours."

"I know, not literally. But it felt like everything belonged to all of us, didn't it? There was something magical about the place that made you never want to leave."

A distant whine down the other end of the line grew progressively louder like an approaching siren.

"Actually, it isn't the same at all," Lily almost shouted. She wanted to swipe at Trinity's nostalgia. "Chez Reynat has become a dance hall."

The siren grew into a wail and then a piercing scream.

"Got to go, Liliput – the kids have started a riot and Guy's trying to get the baby to sleep. Speak soon."

Lily lost the battle for Trinity's attention and the news remained untold.

The insistent ringing eventually punctured Lily's fretful dreams and she hobbled to the window with one hand to her head. She knew she had overslept – daylight crept in through the cracks of the shutter. Lily stared at the clock in disbelief. Scrubbing at her eyes, she turned on the spot, for a moment unsure of the whereabouts of the telephone.

"They're eager to get started so we'll probably be there before lunch," Venetia uttered in a rush down the telephone.

Usually she basked under the hot spray, letting it heat her body through, but now she galloped out of the steamy bathroom and dressed quickly, hopping down the stairs as she pulled on her socks. She ate her breakfast of bread and jam at the kitchen sink – much easier to clean up.

Lily lit the fire, swept the hearth, plumped up cushions. She picked up a breadcrumb from the rug and surveyed the scene with satisfaction. Skewed squares of sunlight lit up the floor and, at the window, Lily recognised one of those mid-February days that promise spring. 'Ah, but there'll be a blackthorn winter next week,' her father would have told her with the satisfaction of a pessimist. The air was still. She pressed her face to the glass and saw a few white anemones in flower under the chestnut tree.

Crouched in the hallway with a dustpan and brush, Lily pulled herself up and put an ear to the door. A noise that she could almost identify came from the other side. It was a soft, snuffling sound. She threw the cleaning tools into the corner behind Felix's gaunt houseplant and stroked down her hair, ready to greet Venetia and the potential new owners of Chez Reynat.

The muzzle of a bay horse met Lily at the open door, a leafy stem slowly disappearing past its whiskery lips. It turned its head to one side so that it could direct one eye on her and, finding her unremarkable, it returned to its browsing beside the doorway. In shock, Lily jumped back into the hallway and then craned her neck to peer round at the object of its attention. The wall, which had been clothed in glossy green leaves and promising flower buds, now had its stonework bare to the sun. Lily stared at the denuded clematis stems twining round each other.

"What the hell…" she began, spluttering curses and glaring at the animal, but she stopped, her breath held at the top of her chest.

Her eyes followed the line of the tether from the horse's head collar to its origin. It ended in a strong knot around the wellhead's roof support. As it attempted to reach the leaves above its head, the horse strained the thick rope, taking a few steps backwards and then forward again, sure of its strength to either break the rope or the timber strut.

Lily threw out a gasp. And then sucked in air again, holding it in disbelief. Her eyes must be lying, she decided. When she saw the tent she could not register it. It was a mistake – or a joke. The grey, stained canvas, sagging along its ridge, was pitched on the south side of the well. It looked like something from a previous century – something from a sepia print. Lily's hand sprang to her mouth and nose as its rancid odour reached her. Shaking her head as if denial would help, her eyes took in the tripod at the entrance to the tent. On the apex of the metal structure hung a chain and, on the end of that, a small black cauldron spat its contents above a smouldering wood fire.

The telephone brought her back to her senses. "Don't you eat one more leaf," she wailed at the horse, pushing her hair from her face and running back to the sitting room.

"You're still in? Get your hat and coat on – I've had to do some juggling. We'll be there in ten minutes," Venetia sang, and put down the receiver.

Lily pressed the palms of her hands to her skull and stared back through to the hall and the contented animal. It had pushed open the door and puckered its mouth over the brass tap at the stone basin. Lily was shell-shocked. She pulled herself enough together to shove at the horse's muzzle, grunting at it as she pushed it from the doorstep.

"Domage, uh?"

Baptistin stood by the gate pillars, sighing noisily and dramatically raising his arms up in harmony with the sound from his pursed lips. "It's that time of year. There's nothing to be done."

"What time of year? What are you talking about?"

"It's the Romany. He comes to Achallat every year at this time." Baptistin ambled forward, his arms folded in front of him. As though it were too heavy for him, he cupped his chin in one hand.

"A gypsy? I don't remember any travellers coming here. I'm sure of it – there were never any while I was here. Felix never mentioned any either."

"He didn't? I'm surprised. They've been coming for centuries. Achallat is a traditional stopping place for them. Yes, I do remember now, there was a short time when they stopped coming for some reason. That would have been in the early seventies. Yes, that must have been when you were here. A coincidence." He looked at the tent and then sideways at Lily.

She took in the scene again, still disbelieving. "Where's the cart or caravan or whatever they live in?"

"Oh, he's a simpler type of traveller."

The horse nuzzled at Lily, pushing her hair aside, as if it might be home to an interesting shrub. It snorted derisively as she shoved its head away with both hands. A pungent aroma rose from the ground and Lily groaned at the steaming pile deposited at her feet.

"It's just nature." Baptistin shrugged his shoulders and turned to walk away.

"Hang on a minute."

He swivelled awkwardly on one foot to hear her. Lily pulled herself together and, leaving the stench at her feet, she jogged up to the old man.

"You must know him quite well after all these years, then. If he's been coming as long as you say. Can't you ask him to move a bit – not very far. Just across the lane to Jopert's field would be fine. I'll help him move if he wants." She looked back at the festering canvas and swallowed.

Baptistin put a hand on each hip and shook his head mournfully. "You don't understand the Romany mentality. This place is sacred to him. You should remember – the spot where Oddo fell? Jopert's field wouldn't do at all. And then there's the water... but then you never did understand the water. I saw that bottled stuff on the table. Felix'd turn in his grave if he knew."

Lily squirmed slightly under his hard glare.

"Bottled is safer and, besides, I prefer it," she answered defensively. "Look, Baptistin, it's a bit hard for me to believe that this gypsy just turns up here today of all days."

"What? You think I conjured him out of thin air? You have a high opinion of me if you think I can rustle up Romanies overnight."

"You might have put him up to it. He might have been pitched up somewhere down the road. How do I know one of you didn't just come across him on your way to Aubaine and bribe him to come here." She blushed from her neck to the tops of her cheeks at the absurdity of her words.

Baptistin seemed not to be too bothered by her remarks. His eyes drifted past the grimy tent and to the chestnut tree and the river beneath it.

"Listen, Lily. There's a natural course of events in the world. You listen and watch for the flow of life. It flows one way only. You're trying to go against that flow and it will defeat you. Felix had a wish and you have decided to deny him. Stop and listen to the current. You should be keeping Chez Reynat in the family – you know it in your heart." He seemed about to say more but stopped.

How could she tell him that there was no Reynat family anymore? The line was already dead – the last of it lying in a fresh plot in Saint Bénigne. But her attention was caught by the cauldron. Its liquid had begun to spit and hiss – the meal needed attention by the look of it. With her weight on one leg and her arms folded, Lily waited for the owner to appear from his shabby home. Baptistin's eyes followed hers.

"They're secretive people."

The distant hum of a car engine became louder and Lily saw the black car coast over the bridge. She did a sort of pirouette as she looked first to the horse, then to the tent, and then to Baptistin.

"Do something," she urged the old man.

Baptistin put his hands in his pockets and gazed up at the sky as if admiring the spring-like day. The horse ceased its carefree browsing and turned its right ear back as the car entered the lane. By the time the BMW stopped just inside the gate pillars, Lily had untied the tether and was now tugging at the head collar.

"Hi, there," she shouted out manically to Venetia, clambering out of the driver's seat. Two passengers stepped out warily and eyed Lily and the horse.

"Sorry about this, Venetia," she whispered, waving vaguely behind her. "I decided to air an old tent I found in the attic – bit damp. I meant to take it down before you got here, but you took me by surprise with that call. I hope it's not too much of a nuisance."

Venetia Crow looked from Lily to Baptistin, but said nothing as her eyes rested on the bubbling pot.

"Anyway, we'll leave you to it," Lily said, beaming at the chary couple and leading away the horse as she tugged at Baptistin's sleeve.

"You can't steal a man's horse," Baptistin chastised her as they crossed the couderc.

"Don't be ridiculous. I'm not stealing it – I'm giving it some exercise."

"You don't think it's had enough exercise getting here."

"It can't have come very far – it looks fat to me." She looked back at its ample rump swaying easily.

They halted outside Baptistin's cottage and Lily hitched the rope to the gatepost. They looked at each other for a moment.

"You'll have a drink then," Baptistin eventually said.

Relieved at the request, Lily made herself comfortable on the wooden bench – she had no wish to wander the lane alone with the gypsy's horse. She listened to her neighbour moving around his kitchen – the window was open as always. On the stove, a pot of soup simmered, but Baptistin ignored it, knowing it would be ready in time for his lunch. As his parents and grandparents did before him, he took lunch at eleven thirty – and it always started with soup.

He returned to the tiny garden with a bottle of pastis, a heavy looking pitcher and two tumblers. Baptistin handed Lily a glass and poured out a thin layer of the golden liquid, but as he was about to pour the water, Lily gave him a vigorous shake of the head. He took back the glass, seeming displeased with the small quantity of liquid now there, and poured in a more generous amount of pastis. They sat together, looking out towards the river. Little of it was visible. Glints of sunlight sparked off the Vamaleau through the silver tree trunks.

Lily had sat on the same bench twenty years earlier. Then she had been distraught and feeling sick. She had walked from Saint Bénigne les Fontaines and found Chez Reynat empty and locked. Baptistin had sat with her then too, waiting for Felix's return from a rare trip to Limoges.

Her mind had strayed to that memory and she suddenly said, "I'm not a girl anymore."

"I know you're not. You're a woman and you should know better. What have you been doing all this time?"

Lily looked away from him and turned her gaze to the half-hidden water. "I should have gone to university."

Baptistin's shoulders barely twitched and he raised his glass to his mouth. "Should have, would have – what does all that mean? You should have finished the painting."

"Tell me about the people who drowned."

Baptistin gave her a look of bafflement.

"The day of the funeral – you said there had been drownings in Achallat. Felix never mentioned any."

The old man swirled his pastis. "Well he wouldn't. For one thing they were before his time. His aunt – no great aunt that would have been – got swept away."

"It must have been high then." Lily waited for a confirmation and got none. "Was the Vamaleau high? Had there been a storm?" There was urgency in her voice. Her mind had been rubbing away for weeks at Baptistin's almost throwaway news. "So, was she on the causeway or in a boat? Baptistin?"

Perhaps Baptistin had not heard Lily. Perhaps he was lost in memory. "Célestine – that was her name. She hated the river, hated Achallat. All she could think about was getting away from the place. It was as though she never belonged here – that's what they said, anyway. I don't remember anything really – I was too young. But you pick up snippets of grown-up conversation when you're a child.

"And the others who drowned. You said there were drownings."

"Let's not spoil a good drink, Lily." His eyes rested on his glass.

They sat without talking and Lily hugged her drink between her knees, listening to the murmur of the river.

A sudden slam of a door and a stifled scream ripped into the silence.

"What was that?" Lily asked, but this time the shrug of Baptistin's crooked shoulders was an exaggerated gesture accompanied by a rock of his head.

The scream was followed by shouting, but Lily could not make out any words. And then more bangs – this time of car doors. The BMW pulled up beside them and Venetia got out alone. The habitual smile was missing.

"I suggest you sort yourself out if you're serious about selling. You've wasted my time and my clients' time this morning."

"What do you mean? Of course, I'm serious. What's happened?" Lily peered past Venetia to the couple in the back of the car. Clasping hands, they leaned towards each other.

"Look, put your hippy past aside and get rid of that dubious friend of yours."

Lily looked across at Baptistin. Was Venetia so xenophobic that she objected to the neighbours sitting in their own garden?

"And I thought you seemed a sensible enough young woman when I met you."

"Sorry, Venetia, you've lost me. What friend am I supposed to get rid of exactly?" In her dull head, clarity sparked for a second. "The traveller! Of course, the traveller. I'm really sorry – he arrived out of the blue. Look, I promise I'll get rid of him today. It won't be a problem. Can't you explain to your clients…"

"A traveller is he? A traveller in the garden is one thing. That'll make it pretty impossible to sell a property. But a naked, wild man wandering around through the house? He looked at home enough to me – in your husband's bedroom. Babbling about goodness knows what. What language is it? If you ask me, the man is completely deranged."

Venetia opened her door and, with one hand, dismissed Lily and her traveller. Desperate to right the situation, Lily jumped up from the bench. Skittle-like, she swayed for a second before her legs moved, and then her foot caught on Baptistin's extended leg. Pitching forward, she threw out a hand to catch anything secure and found Venetia's chest. Lily realised that in her other hand, she still clutched the glass – its contents had been ejected. Venetia looked down at the aniseed scented liquid soaking into her jacket and then back to Lily. No word was uttered by either woman, and Baptistin too seemed satisfied that nothing needed to be said. He put one arm around Lily's shoulder and a hand at her elbow as though she needed support.

Lily watched the estate agent retreat into her car and drive away.

CHAPTER FIFTEEN

"Some water will calm you – you shouldn't have taken the pastis neat." Baptistin lowered Lily to the bench, but she sprang up again and was on the lane before her neighbour could put down the glass.

"Don't you worry yourself about our visitor," he hollered after her, trotting with his hands stretched out in front of him as if he meant to catch her.

Lily had been striding, her arms swinging, but she stopped at the gate pillars. "Is he likely to do anything violent, Baptistin?"

Breathless, he reached her. "Violent? No, no, no. You're not going to do anything rash though, are you? Look, he'll be moving on soon – I know these things. He's travelling north like a migrant bird, like a swallow. When he's rested and sated he'll fly on. Achallat is just a staging post for him. When the weather warms up he'll be on his way." Baptistin's words struggled between the gasps for breath.

"You mean I have to wait till spring?" Lily's eyes wandered wildly as if she searched for the season.

"It'll be spring soon enough. It's best not to aggravate the situation. Just think – if you offend him he might be difficult to move – might dig his heels in."

"And what about roaming the house? Venetia thought he was deranged. He sounds dangerous to me. Don't you think we should get in touch with the police?"

Baptistin shook his head so violently that the veins on his nose protruded like puce coloured rivers on a map. "No, no, no. Why would you call the police? He's harmless – just a travelling man living his own little private life. I'll talk to him. He won't be a problem to you, I promise."

"He's already a problem. He was wandering around the house naked!"

Baptistin had recovered from the chase down the lane. He rocked his head from side to side as he weighed up the validity of Lily's argument. "Now, there's an explanation for that if you think about it. For one thing, he probably doesn't know Felix has passed on – after all, who could have told him? And you remember how easy going Felix was with his guests? He probably just wanted to use the bathroom – I imagine that would be a real luxury to a man in his situation. And the lack of clothes? Well, when you live a solitary life, you forget about polite behaviour. I know what I'm talking about. Me, myself, at home, I sometimes forget to dress in the morning. Often have breakfast naked as the day I was born."

He left his head bowed to one side, waiting for a positive response from Lily. She blinked to rid herself of the image of her neighbour at his table.

"I promise you – no more uninvited guests." Baptistin smiled with determination and, relenting a little, Lily returned the gesture.

Nevertheless she returned to Chez Reynat and locked the great oak door behind her. She bolted the French windows and the kitchen door.

In the days that followed, Lily saw no sign of the encamped trespasser. Occasionally, she stopped outside the tent, trying to sense his presence, straining to hear any sound, see any movement through the canvas. The campfire burned and a pot simmered, but there was no other sign of life. The horse was not returned to its tethering post. Lily had inspected the wellhead's timber post for signs of damage, but saw none. She discovered the animal's whereabouts when she heard the familiar sound of grazing as it worked the generous pasture of Jopert's field.

On the first day of March, Lily roamed the house restlessly, eager for the grocery van's arrival and the small talk with its owner – it would dispel the memory of the conversation she had just had with her father.

"You're still out there?" He had said it at least three times, failing to understand how this could be. He had never become accustomed to speaking on the telephone – it was as if being out of his sight made his daughter a stranger.

Lily enjoyed the aimless conversation with the grocer about his mother's health – which could have been better, but spring was on its way after all; about the Mardi Gras carnival in Aubaine; and the weather – it was far too good and would surely mean a terrible March. With elbows on the counter, the grocer leaned out of the window, his eyes returning again and again to the tent. He rolled his eyes and shrugged, but neither made a comment. Lily tried to pretend that her uninvited guest did not exist.

She turned for home with her purchase of a piece of *fromage de brebis* from the Pyrenees, some wild boar pâté, and half a dozen eggs. Before she had taken more than a few steps, Séverine brought her scooter to a halt in front of Lily.

"So, you think you'll sell?"

"My son's made up his mind." 'Do we have to go through this again,' Lily wanted to add, but she pressed her lips shut and sidestepped the scooter.

In a flash Séverine reversed and blocked Lily's path. "I'm sure you've both made up your minds to sell – but that's not what I'm asking you. You don't understand, do you? Do you think that any one of us is master of events? Do you think you could alter the course of the Vamaleau just because you'd made up your mind to?"

Lily was baffled and her forced smile dissolved. The older woman did not wait for an answer – she spoke again with a fierce voice.

"Our lives are as the water, our wishes but a breath of wind.

Flustered, Lily struggled to keep hold of the collection of paper bags bundled under her arms. She managed to manoeuvre herself around the machine and heard the bewildering proclamations repeated as she closed the door behind her.

As she dropped her shopping on the table, Lily repeated Séverine's chant and then at the bookshelf her hand wavered along one row until it found the book it was seeking.

The Guiding Waters – The Life of Oddo of Achallat. The letters, picked out in gilt, had faded badly, but Lily would have recognised the green book without its title. Wedging herself into the corner of the sofa, she placed the heavy book on the seat cushion beside her and turned the pages slowly, searching the handwritten text. It took a while for her eyes to become accustomed to the scrolled script weaving across the page, but eventually her finger stopped at one line halfway down.

She read out the sentence slowly. "My life is as the water and my desires but a breath of wind." She glanced through the French window towards the hermitage. "Well, Oddo, you're still being quoted in Achallat, even though your most devoted fan's no longer here. But perhaps he's still singing these words somewhere."

Lily knew each page. Her fingers had followed these words before, her hand had held the paper firm when the breeze blew up teasingly. She had read the words aloud, not to Felix, who had the words imprinted on his heart, but to Gabriel.

*

Felix had guided her back across the Vamaleau and Gabriel had watched them both from Chez Reynat's riverbank. She had woken before dawn and, for the first time, she did not pick up her paintbrushes. The silver light filtered through the little window, but Lily did not look at her tools, did not glance at the painted panel. Instead, she went to the doorstep and, resting on her haunches, she waited. With her eyes on the grey house, she did not move until Felix's shutters opened.

She found Felix alone as usual, at the table with the first pot of coffee of the day.

"What is the matter, Lily? You do not look well."

"Don't I?" She put her palms to her cheeks as though ashamed. Lifting her leg over the bench, she sat beside her host, sharing the strawberry jam, butter, and the previous day's bread. A plate and large breakfast cup were waiting for her.

"Why don't you leave the painting today, Lily? Stay here at Chez Reynat. Perhaps you have become too engrossed in your work. A day of relaxation would be good for you."

Felix had allotted a task to each of his guests, but his own task, Lily realised, was to watch others enjoy themselves.

"Why are they here, Felix? I mean the Americans."

"Because I met them in town one day – in La Grande Aubaine. They were sitting at that little café by the train station, and I think it was Mason who called out something to me. And then I invited them to my home. Just as I met you and Trinity – and brought you here."

"I understand that – but why did you invite them?"

Felix put down his bread, and the coffee that had soaked through it now dripped onto the table. Golden curls flopped around his high brow as he shook his head.

"Achallat was not always like it is now. Look at us – Baptistin is unmarried and probably past the age to bother. Jopert – the farmer across the lane – do you know who I mean? He farms most of the land in Achallat. Yes? The Joperts' only daughter went off to Paris two years ago, and she hasn't written or got in touch since. Went to protest, she said, about the government. Jopert is convinced they'll never see her again. His wife has turned away from the world – she hides herself away as if she's to blame. Jopert says always they should have had a son. They prayed for one at the well, but Oddo has other plans, for sure. Jopert prays for a son and perhaps Oddo will give him one yet, somehow. Honorine and her husband were not inclined to have a family. She has a good job in Paris, you know, at one of the couturier houses. And it's the same with the others. We have forgotten something in Achallat. I don't know why it's like this, Lily. There used to be many people here. All the houses upriver were once all occupied by busy little families. Now they're almost all empty or used as storehouses."

Felix pushed his coffee bowl away with an elbow and cupped a cheek in his hand. "Then there was the big farmhouse near Jopert's – it burnt down when I was a small boy. The family moved to Saint Bénigne – they said they would come back – rebuild the place – but no, they did not. All these people took the noise of life with them – took the sound of Achallat with them. And we stopped making any of our own. It's good to hear voices; it's good to hear people in Achallat. Life is good, Lily."

He said the last words with emphasis as if he suspected that she was ignorant of the fact. Lily dipped the last of her bread into her cup and popped it into her mouth.

"I know what you mean, Felix. At home there was only my brother and me when we were children."

"You're still a child," Felix said, laughing.

"No, I'm not. Do I look like a child? Do I act like a child?"

"No, but you are still young. That is what I meant."

Lily pulled out a strand of red hair that had strayed into her coffee. "At home we were the only young people for miles around. Or at least, that's how it felt. I played on my own. My brother only ever wanted to help Dad on the farm so I got used to just being on my own."

"It is why you are like you are, Lily. Do you not know this?"

A stair creaked and Lily turned to see Gabriel sauntering down, his body loose and relaxed, but his eyes dark with concentration. Passing behind her, he disappeared into the kitchen and reappeared with a coffee bowl. He pulled his long legs over the bench and seated himself opposite them.

"You speak good French," he told her.

"It's talking to Felix – I get lots of practice." She flushed.

The common language in the house that summer had been English, but Lily spoke French to Felix when they were alone at breakfast. Trinity spoke the language with more flamboyance but less accuracy, and the Americans went no further than simple phrases and Mason's own hybrid of Anglo-French.

"How's yours?" Lily asked Gabriel as he poured himself coffee, and then finished the pot by emptying it into the other two cups.

"My Spanish is better. I've had some fun trying to communicate with Felix's neighbour, Claude. I'm not sure how well we understand each other, but we seem to be better acquainted so I guess it's worked. Anyways, it's good to listen – and if I get lost I'll let you know." He had a thoughtful voice as though he measured each word before speaking.

Felix made a spluttering noise as he took the cup from his mouth. With puckered lips he took his bowl and the drained coffee pot to the kitchen.

Lily and Gabriel said little to each other. They sat in silence, sometimes with their eyes on their coffee, sometimes on each other. Lily felt as though they were in their own bubble of quietness. She let her lids fall to enjoy the moment, and then, opening them, saw that Gabriel had left the table.

He wandered over to the bookshelves and pulled down a map. Already he was planning another adventure, Lily thought with dismay. But he replaced it and stood with his thumbs in his jeans' pockets. His hand grasped a heavy green book and he took it across the room to the French windows, reading its faded title in the better light. He turned to her before going out onto the grass. "Why don't you join me?"

Lily screwed up her eyes against the sun and saw him sitting cross-legged near the chestnut tree with the book between his knees. With closed eyes he waited for her. Lily found herself beside him, knees drawn up, watching his stillness. His smile appeared before his eyes opened and he handed her the book, leaning back on one elbow.

"Would you read some?"

She recognised Oddo's journal – or at least that was Felix's name for the weighty volume.

"It's Felix's favourite book."

"I guessed as much. He keeps quoting from it, so I thought I'd take a look. My French isn't so good – I need a translator."

"I'll do my best. It's lucky it's not Oddo's original journal – that was written in Latin apparently. And my Latin's pretty hopeless. And then it was translated into Old French. Felix keeps that copy locked away in his little hideaway in the fireplace – I don't think anyone's going to steal it. But you're doubly lucky, because my Old French is worse than my Latin."

A giggle escaped, but she caught it quickly. She fixed her eyes on the book, but when she darted a glance at him, she was relieved to see that he had not noticed, or had not minded. She straightened her face and hauled out a serious expression.

"How old are you, Lily?"

He was lying on the grass so near to her. She wanted to tell him she was nineteen – twenty would be pushing it.

"Does it matter?"

He shook his head and smiled back at her. "Still at high school though, I guess."

"I'm going to university next year," she said, too defiantly. "Don't know what to do yet, though. I want to do medieval history and art, but Dad's going to have a fit when I tell him. He'd be happy enough me going to agricultural college – that's where my brother went. But university?" Lily shook her head and looked skywards. "Now, if I wanted to be a vet, okay."

"Do your own thing," Gabriel said and turned to look at the river. "Or as my friend Claude might say, plough your own furrow. But as I don't know the French for plough or furrow, I can't be sure. Whatever you do, make the most of it – and do some work. I flunked my exams and I ended up in deeper trouble than just being out of a job."

"What do you mean?"

"I got drafted. Uncle Sam sends his failures to fight his war for him. Perhaps it's supposed to be poetic justice. Some world, eh?"

He took his time to study the girl with the book on her lap and then said, "Read me some."

"I can translate Felix's favourite bits. Or at least the bits he's read most to me." She turned the pages slowly, stopped, and smoothed down the paper with a palm. Through lowered lids she saw that he waited for her to start.

"On my journey in that part of France, I came to a quiet place by a wide river," she began. She surprised herself – her voice sounded confident, the words rolling out effortlessly. *"There are shady oaks and aspen, growing by the waterside, like Paradise above the Flood. Here I built a path to cross the river and a small house, no grander than the peasants' honest dwellings, and no less humble than the beasts' byres. By my endeavours may I row to Heaven, by my path let others find new life in the water. It is here, by this river, that I will end my earthly journey."*

Lily looked up from the writings of Oddo and saw that the man beside her had stretched himself out on the grass. Through shuttered lids he seemed to see Oddo's boat rocking beneath the aspen. She put the book to one side and rolled over onto her elbows. Scrutinising his face, she resisted the temptation to touch it, instead following each line, rise, and hollow with her eyes. Even relaxed it held on to its troubles. Eyes shut, he smiled as though aware of the examination.

A few metres away the river whispered. Lily could feel its murmuring inside her head, flowing through her body. She felt each blade of grass, each stalk of clover between her toes. Her skin differentiated between daisy and sorrel, between leaf and stem; her hand, resting on the green between them, sensed the soil beneath it and knew the earthworms moved, shifting the earth itself, churning rocks and stones to the surface. And the river spoke and the aspen rustled. Lily leaned forward and found his mouth with hers.

With his shoulder against the window frame, Mason squinted against the sun, his expression inscrutable. He put a hand up to shield his uncertain eyes.

At the wellhead, Felix put the heavy container down on the wall. Straightening himself, he turned round towards the riverbank as if a noise had caught his attention. The morning was silent but for the Vamaleau. Felix saw two people lying in the cool grass, but it was not Trinity and Oki. Shadows of leaves danced across Felix's fallen face; he mouthed something, but no one heard. His hand suddenly jutted out sideways as if he were about to gesture to someone or call out. It thumped against the bucket, spilling the water over the granite floor, but Felix did not hear it, or feel the wet soaking into his shoes. He saw the girl stand and lead the man down to the river. They stepped on to the causeway, one after another, and walked out to the island.

Mason uttered a short sharp sound and slapped a palm against the timber. "Oh Lord, do you see that?" he shouted out, turning for just a second into the room, not wanting to miss the sight. There was no one to share his wonder. He watched the couple walk across a dry stone path whose pink stone shone out in the sunlight for the first time in living memory.

Lily took the key from around her neck and opened the door to her refuge. The river had guided her across its clear waters, and perhaps it guided her still – she had no experience of taking a man to her bed. But the aloneness that

Felix had recognised that morning at breakfast was no longer. For the first time since she had left her mother's womb she was connected to another human being. He was inside her, his tongue was in her mouth, and she felt his cells flow with hers. It seemed to her that their molecules mingled, just like the water molecules of the Vamaleau. And at some point it was no longer physical. She floated above him in a dark, wondrous place. She was formless, stretching across a black universe, a part of all creation. The sound she uttered was not the moan of a young woman, but the sigh of life.

*

Lily woke herself from her memory with numb legs knitted underneath the heavy book. The wood stove was grey but for a faint glow at one side – she might save the fire yet.

The sound of Baptistin and Honorine arguing at the well sent the past scuttling away. She pulled up the book cover and closed Oddo's journal. Was it true? Had it been she who had kissed him? Had she led him across to the island? It had been the first time that she had allowed the memory to surface and she shook her head, denying it. She flipped the book over and read the last page.

"And on the first night of August the clouds scattered and the holy soul sailed to its author. The uncorrupted body is left for those who loved him to keep and cherish. And it is to the water he loved that we have entrusted it. And Achallat will remember its guardian each year, as he remembers us. And the first of August will in Achallat be Oddo's Feast Day."

*

Lily could not recollect how much time had passed between that first day with Gabriel and Oddo's feast day. She knew that she had painted no more of her story. Her brushes remained on the doorstep of the hermitage; the three-legged stool squatted next to the last scene – Felix at a high window of Chez Reynat, his hands held out as though waving.

Every moment in time existed only in relation to Gabriel. She measured her days by him. From the moment before he woke, feeling the dizzy anticipation of seeing him smile at her as he stretched out on her bed, to the day's end, his sleeping body at her back. He was her timepiece. She soaked up his presence – watching him wash, splashing the water from the bucket vigorously over his face, watching him swim and dive into the brown water. She watched him take shad from the Vamaleau and cook it over a makeshift campfire on the bank of the Île des Lys. She watched him breathe.

"I think you've cast a spell on our Gabe," Mason said one day as she sat with Gabriel by the reeds in the calm inlet of the river. She tightened her lips, awaiting mocking words from their bowlegged pastor. He stood above the two of them, casting them in shade as though he were one of the spindly trees. Lily concentrated on the string of daisies in her hand as she split a stem with her thumbnail and threaded the other flower stalk through. One chain already hung around Gabriel's neck. He sat bare-chested and barefoot and watched her with a look of mild amusement.

"Let's call it an enchantment," Mason continued. Lily looked up sideways, relieved at the softer tone in his voice. He had ventured further from the house than normal and she saw that his gaze was drawn to the sparkling Vamaleau.

"The place is enchanted – look at it," he whispered.

Gabriel skimmed a stone across the still water. The three of them watched it skip and spin.

"So what have I said to put a spell on you?" she asked, disbelieving that she may have any power over him.

Gabriel put a finger to her lips. "Hell seemed a lot closer before than it does now."

"You're not going to hell – you're a good person. Why do you say that?" Lily's voice caught.

"We don't have to die to find hell, Lily. I've learned that much. There are hells here on earth of our own making and I know two of them. I've come back from one. I didn't think I'd get away. But I haven't dreamt about it since I saw you sitting in the sun with your bucket and brushes." He pushed his hand through her hair and pulled out one of the daisies there.

Behind them Mason fidgeted on the spot, his elbows pumping.

"Hey man, don't frighten the girl with all of that."

Lily put her hand to Gabriel's face and traced her finger along the pink scar. He took her hand in his and kissed the fingers. "It's okay, Mason. I'm not going to make you uncomfortable."

"And what about the other hell? You said you knew two." Lily waited for his reply.

Gabriel looked up at Mason and then down at the grass at his feet.

"The other one doesn't matter here," Mason jumped in, looking hard at his friend. "We're in Oddo's enchanted land now – we've crossed the Styx." Mason turned from the couple and shouted out to their host, "Hey Felix!"

Ducking under the weeping willow with one hand shielding his stooped head, Felix looked up.

"Hey there, Felix," Mason called out again.

Felix stopped and waited, but came no closer.

"Isn't it Oddo's day about now? You said something about it a few weeks ago. When is it?"

Felix walked reluctantly towards the trio, but his eyes were fixed elsewhere. He stopped near enough to speak without raising his voice, but distant enough so that Lily could not read his face.

"The feast of Oddo is the first day of August – the day after tomorrow."

"And what happens at that feast, man?"

"We celebrate. All of Achallat – and more – celebrates life. We eat, we sing, we dance – here at Chez Reynat. There will be many who come – it is a long tradition. There will be music and food and wine." Felix's face lit up as if Oddo himself had wafted away his previous mood.

Mason rubbed his beard with the back of his hand, his elbow out at right angles. Putting an arm around Felix's shoulders, he guided the smaller man into the house.

"Felix, *mon ami*. We're talking about a celebration of God-given life itself here, if I'm getting the picture right. That means more than just music and dancing. We need a ceremony to honour life."

It was that time of year when the birdsong had almost ceased and the hamlet of Achallat seemed to have stopped breathing. But Oki and Trinity erupted from the house, tumbling down the bank and falling into the river. Trinity squealed, rising and falling in the broken water like a bronze fish. Lily put down her flowers and watched them dive under the froth.

"Ken hasn't been rescued though, has he," she said suddenly. "He was out there with you – and he's still in his hell."

"Maybe."

Lily wondered whether Trinity still led Ken in the dead of night to the weeping willow. She was even unsure if they went to town together in the Renault – she had stopped being a spectator of others. But sitting on the floor of the sitting room, listening to Oki play a wistful tune, Lily saw Trinity's eyes on Ken and knew that she still took him by the hand while Oki slept. The company forsook the weed that night. Mason said he was saving it for the big party.

Under a fat yolk-yellow moon Lily and Gabriel walked to the riverbank. He pulled her round in a dance, humming softly to the music drifting out from the house.

"Would you marry me?" Lily asked.

*

Lily thumped the book shut.

"No," she breathed, glaring at the stove. Its logs jostled with each other, spitting and hissing with complaint. She ran out, stumbling over the threshold at the French window, sliding down the dew heavy grass.

In the sun the river flashed silver at her. Heavy and metallic looking, it seemed to be in no hurry. It showed her the causeway.

Hatred engulfed Lily. She remembered Célestine – she had hated the river too. Lily looked down at her feet, toes curled over the grassy rim, inches above the languid water. As she jumped back, it whispered to her. It would claim her yet.

CHAPTER SIXTEEN

"Would you marry me?"

The words had tumbled carefree. She had been dreaming of a world in which she and Gabriel were married – a world that did not entail finishing her education or even going home to Lack Farm. It was just a daydream, but now the question had taken form. It could not be unspoken. What she had meant was, 'is it possible that someone like you would ever be married to me?' Lily held her breath.

Gabriel's eyes darkened, but his mouth opened to a child's smile and he laughed out loudly, picking her up in one movement. He turned towards Chez Reynat with his bundle in his arms and they both saw Mason – or rather they knew the dark figure to be his silhouette, standing with the light of the room behind him.

"How about it, Mason? Will you marry us?" Gabriel shouted up to the door.

Lily could not see Mason's face, but he answered with no tone of surprise in his hardly raised voice. "It's what I've been waiting for, Gabe. We'll do it the day after tomorrow – it'll be a toast to life."

Felix spent the next day in the kitchen, preparing food for the party – his house guests had to content themselves with cheese and cold meat for supper. On the morning of Oddo's Feast Day the women of the hamlet brought trays of food: hams; pies of potatoes, garlic and herbs; quiches; *tartes aux fruits*; and flans. Baptistin brought a keg of home-made pear cider and Felix fetched wine from the outhouse. Pushing everyone out of the kitchen, Trinity closed the door and emerged later with a tray of small cakes.

"What kind are they?" Felix asked, taking one and nibbling at the edge.

"Special ones," Trinity said, winking at the others. "In fact, they're wedding cakes. No matter what, there are traditions to uphold. There should be a veil, confetti, terribly boring speeches and much drunkenness." Trinity had been hovering over the table as she recited her list, undecided where to deposit her baking. Wide-eyed she shoved the tray at Oki. "And rings! Has anyone thought about the rings?"

Felix pushed past Oki, sending the cakes into a little dance on the wood surface. They all watched his back as he strode from the room. Lily pressed her face to Gabriel's chest and heard only his heart beat.

"What are you up to now?" Lily asked, seeing Trinity approach with scissors in her hands. Trinity had found Lily and Gabriel under the chestnut. She snipped a tress of hair from both heads and marched back up the bank to sit with her back to the house wall. Lily turned to see Trinity unusually still, her head bent to her fingers moving deftly on her knees.

The visitors started to arrive before noon. Claude Jopert came early, playing his Hohner accordion as he processed down the lane towards Chez Reynat, a straggle of followers moving self-consciously to the music. Behind the musician, two children held hands and giggled as their father half danced, kicking his heels together and shouting out to anyone who would listen. Towards one side of the little parade, the curé marched in a more dignified manner. His expression suggested that he had better things to do, but he was willing to appease the country ways of his congregation.

They gathered around the curé at the wellhead and sang a cheerful song.

"À la belle fontaine
m'en allait promener,
J'ai trouvé l'eau si belle
Que je m'y suis baigné."

Even the smallest child seemed to know the refrain,

"Hands on water still the river,
Hands on water, praise our giver,
Bless our well and give a son,
Bless our lives till life is done."

Lily watched them sing the next verse with earnest faces, knitted brows.

"What's it about?" Mason asked her.

"About finding Oddo's well – and bathing in the river – about being blessed by Oddo and praying for a male child. Weird."

Lily looked up at Mason, expecting another question, but the American had forgotten his curiosity. He gazed solemnly at the singers.

Gabriel leaned against the chestnut tree, Lily leaned on him, and as one they watched the festivities. Oddo's followers sat in groups – the first to arrive, at the tables set up near the river, the rest on the grass. Trinity and Oki had taken a child in each hand to dance around the well and they led their chain of young revellers to skip and weave through the picnickers.

There was no sign of Ken – Lily's eyes searched for him. Then she saw a figure sitting on the first stone of the causeway – he faced out towards the river, his back to the party. She watched his arm swing back and forth as his small missiles scudded and bounced on the water.

When there were only crumbs left on the table and dregs in the glasses, the feast day celebrants made their way home. The accordion player ambled up the lane. Achallat's residents and visitors chose not to swing their hips or kick their heels – they had danced enough under the beams and under the chestnut tree. They strolled back – arm in arm, or carrying worn-out children.

Trinity brought out her cakes – saved for the real party, as she had put it. Felix stood at the edge of the group. He had spent the day with his fellow believers, attending to their needs – Lily had caught glimpses of him with trays of glasses or uncorking wine. But he was not in a festive mood. Holding the cakes out, Trinity pinched off lumps and was feeding them to Oki when Felix beckoned Lily into the house.

"I have something for you." He held a wooden chest in his arms. "Open it and see."

Lily took out a long veil. It was very simple with just a little embroidery traced around the top and bottom. It had been stored in tissue paper in a velvet lined box – it was cherished. Cherished by the Reynats.

Seeing Felix's smile harden she spoke quickly. "Felix, you can't give me this. It's lovely, but it's not right. Whose is it anyway?"

"It was my grandmother's. I want you to wear it today on your wedding day. My grandmother always wanted to see my mother in it. She grieved about that, but it was not to be."

Lily took in a breath. She held the delicate fabric in both hands – it felt like a heavy burden.

"This belongs in your family. You'll use it yourself one day – or rather your bride will."

Felix put the chest down. The house was so quiet that Lily could hear his fingers rustle the tablecloth.

"It is meant for you, Lily. I know this."

"Great – that's another thing to tick off the list," Trinity called out from the doorway, and before Lily could say anything Trinity had plucked the veil from her hands.

She wore it with her favourite dress – long and white with scarlet birds and flowers decorating the hem and wide sleeves. Trinity had teased flowers through the veil and into her russet hair. Under the chestnut canopy Mason told Gabriel and Lily to love and cherish each other. He spoke in an almost tender voice so that, for the first time, Lily believed him to be qualified for such a sacred act. They exchanged their vows and then the plaited rings that Trinity had woven that morning.

Trinity and Oki threw the white petals they had collected from the rose growing up the west wall. It was in its second flush of summer. There were no speeches – boring or eloquent. The small wedding party was silent. Lily felt as though she were part of a living tableau. Her eyes moved from one participant to another. Mason silent, with folded arms to a job well done. Trinity beamed – her green eyes were just slits as the vast smile took up the whole of her face. Oki rested his guitar against his legs. He had played 'Greensleeves' as Lily came to her groom, and now he waited to begin his next piece. Ken nodded at Gabriel with a shadow of a smile and then returned with wet shorts to his seat on the causeway. Pale faced, Felix stood apart as if he were undecided whether to witness the event. He looked limp as if the long hot summer had wilted him. From the wellhead, the old neighbour called Baptistin looked on at the strange end to Oddo's feast day.

Lily's eyes went back to Gabriel. He was unsmiling. It was the face she had first seen when he stepped inside her hermitage and read her painted panel. Behind his head, Lily saw the last rays catch the hermit's wall. The sun was setting – this day had been a little shorter than the one before. A yellow leaf, a premature sign of autumn, spiralled down and she brushed it from Gabriel's hair. Before she had pulled her hand away a thought crept into her head. Summer will end.

CHAPTER SEVENTEEN

Lily had woken to remembrance, the path from dream unbroken. The wedding played out to her as she lay in the shuttered room, the scenes vivid like photographs that had been hidden away. She let the tap run and held the tumbler under the water, gushing bad-temperedly, spitting up at her and spilling over the edge of the glass. The last of the Evian had been emptied the previous morning and she had drunk wine and coffee for the rest of the day. Now, she put her fitful night's sleep down to dehydration.

She gulped at the water – the water she had stubbornly refused to drink. At least it's not straight from the well – who knows what lives down there, she complained to herself. With the icy liquid flowing over her hand, she stared at her fingernails. They were uneven and mis-shaped, but they were long. There were white talons where there should have been brown stubs. She could not remember the last time she had cut her nails – work had always done the task for her. With kitchen scissors pulled from a drawer, she began paring away the nail.

A loud rap at the other end of the house vibrated through the house and a familiar voice bellowed out.

"Anyone there? Are you in?"

She found Baptistin on the doorstep. He had his back to her and, at the sound of her footsteps in the stony hallway, he spun round to her, still chuckling at something known only to himself.

"I brought you these." He handed her a small bread basket filled with speckled eggs. His expression changed quickly to one of apology. "I saw you buying some from Dufraud's van. I didn't think before – Felix wasn't keen on eggs so I didn't give him many – just now and again when he made mayonnaise or baked those little cakes of his."

Smiling, Lily took the offering, but then her eye caught the sagging grey tent and she felt her face harden. "He's not gone."

"Spring is a little slow this year – it hasn't warmed up yet. What's the poor man to do? We're into March now – he'll be gone soon enough."

Lily made a noise through a tightened mouth. "Most people wait for the swallows to come. In Achallat you wait for travellers to go."

"Always in such a hurry, girl. Would you hurry the Vamaleau on its way to the sea. Don't answer – knowing you, you would. Things have a natural course of events."

"So everyone in Achallat keeps telling me." With her arms folded, Lily began to turn back to the house, but then she stopped, her eyes to the ground. She needed to know. "And what about him? Is he still around or has he wandered off?" She placed emphasis on the last two words, but the meaning was lost on her neighbour.

"Who are we talking about?" Baptistin opened his glassy eyes wide to show his ignorance, but she could clearly see the gleam of humour in them.

With ill temper, Lily pulled at her hair and glared at him, tired of the charade before it had begun. "You know who I mean – that American. I haven't seen him since your dance. You must have invited him to it – he wouldn't have just turned up." She heard the hurt in her voice. He had been welcome, not her. "And anyway, what's he still doing here? One of you lot must have him ferreted away somewhere?"

"That American? That American? You have a way with words, Lily! Is that what you call your husband?" Baptistin cackled, his cheeks pink with pleasure. "He is still your spouse, you know – after all there was no divorce."

"I would have divorced if I'd needed to. It wasn't legal – there were no papers. I don't suppose he was a real pastor even. The whole thing was just a pantomime." The words came breathily. She felt winded and she put a hand to her chest to comfort it.

Baptistin's shoulders did their habitual rise and fall and his arms rose in support. "You were married by a man of the cloth in sight of God."

"It wasn't in Church. How do you know it was in the sight of God?"

"Do you think He confines himself to damp buildings with dry rot and leaking roofs. He exists here among us, among our little drudgeries. Your marriage was witnessed by Oddo himself on the very day we honour him." Baptistin sounded wounded. "We are blessed here in Achallat. You deny Oddo; you deny the river. I know nothing, but you were married to one man and then chose another – and you couldn't even keep to him. Is there another one over there in England?"

"You're right you know nothing. It was a stupid day and a summer of fools," she hissed at the old man as she charged off, not back into the house, but past the pillars and down the lane. She marched over the bridge, but at the twins' cottages the anger began to ebb and she came to a halt.

Flora, standing by her green gate, turned at the hurried sound of Lily's approaching feet. An anxious expression broke out on her face and she hurried down the flower-edged path to put some distance between herself and the Englishwoman. Florette, across the narrowing road, put down her hoe and attempted a smile. They greeted Lily quietly and in unison.

She could think of nothing pleasant to say. Looking up, she thought she should mention the weather, but her chest still ached with bitter words. The sky was ash grey, unmoving and refusing to break one way or the other. The twins exchanged glances and looked heavenwards too, but kept their thoughts to themselves. Lily returned to the bridge and stared blankly at naked trees and stone, sombre in the dull light. She felt hemmed in, unable to breathe.

Footsteps echoed on the quiet road – a light but adamant tread. Honorine wore a cream raincoat, neatly belted, and an emerald scarf at her throat. Her lips were pink, her cheeks powdered, and her hair just arranged. When she stopped, Lily realised that her destination was not a neighbour's house or town, but the bridge itself and, in particular, the spot where Lily stood.

Lily's hands pulled at her unbrushed hair as with shame she registered the muddied hem of her jeans, the frayed espadrilles. Self-consciously, she turned towards the river.

"It looks so insignificant from here, doesn't it?" Lily's head nodded in the direction of the hermitage.

"Insignificant? Do you measure the importance of something by its size?" Honorine's tone was cool, but when Lily looked back at her eyes she did not see hostility. She remembered Honorine as the part-time resident, who worked in Paris and only came back to her family home for the month of August. Lily had once been invited to the white painted house when Dominic was barely walking. In the kitchen the two women had watched the toddler crawl around, trying and failing to reach gleaming copper pans hung at the fireplace. He had abandoned the quest and had sat still, mesmerised by the soft striking of the inlaid longcase clock. Honorine had served tea in Limoges porcelain cups with langue de chat biscuits. Lily had wished that the older woman would befriend her, but she shut up the house and returned to her job in Paris.

"Perhaps Achallat doesn't look at its best now," Honorine said. "She is an old woman sleeping, her beauty apparently perished, but it's dawn and she is about to wake. Look, the birch is hung with catkins and the aspen is in budburst. Everything is about to happen. Do you feel it?"

Lily did not know why, but the tone of anticipation in Honorine's voice made her fearful. "No," she said simply.

"Then perhaps you are sleeping too." The lines on Honorine's face deepened as she gave a just perceptible smile. "By the way, the *danse du thé* is tomorrow."

"I remembered," Lily lied. "Actually, I have to go into town anyway so it works out fine. Shall I leave the key with you or Baptistin?"

"There's no need to remove yourself. You should remember Felix's way – open house. Everyone is welcome. Why don't you stay? You may even enjoy it."

The following afternoon Lily found herself sitting between the Joperts. With hands clutched, the reclusive wife fixed a stubborn gaze on the feet of the dancers while her husband tapped a foot to the music.

Baptistin trotted past, the heels of his shoes barely touching the floor. Carrying a plate of food in one hand and a jug and glass in the other, he acknowledged Lily with a nod of the head as he hurried to the door.

"For the *pauper*," he explained without stopping.

"It really is open house," Lily said to Honorine standing above her. "I mean showing hospitality to the traveller..." She stopped when she saw Honorine's blank expression.

"You look very nice anyway," Honorine said back. Lily pulled a face – she was ashamed to be reminded that she had taken so much care to dress. The morning had fled as she tried on possible outfits. She had emptied the drawers again, but somehow the cheesecloth tops and woollen sweaters were exactly the same as they had been the last time she looked. 'I should shop,' she told herself. 'But I'll be back home soon enough so it's not worth it,' she reasoned. In the end, she chose the black dress she wore to Felix's funeral – and Trinity's party. She felt like someone else, and her hands fidgeted with the hem. Worse, sitting beside nervous Marie, Lily felt as though she were waiting for an interview.

Her hair had at least behaved. She had brushed it into submission, but strands still wafted skyward and, in the heat of the busy room, the flattened waves began to bounce back with new vigour. She had applied mascara and vaselined her lips, and hoped she looked more like a guest at a party than a job candidate. Quietening her fretful hands, Lily scanned the room again and again.

Seeing Séverine arrive, walking stiffly between two sticks, Claude Jopert put his plate on the chair beside him and jumped up, wiping his hands on the back of his trousers. "Here, sit here, my old love. It's time I got back to my accordion anyway before Baptistin tells me off for taking too long over my food."

Jopert rolled across the room. In one movement he slung the instrument over a shoulder and sat on the edge of his chair, the accordion resting on one leg, while the other stretched out before him, the toes pointing to heaven.

Séverine freed herself from her rucksack and, settling down, she rummaged inside it to bring out needles and an unfinished garment. Lily watched as she knitted with brightly coloured wools, the balls skidding across the floor as she changed yarn. Lily at first stooped to bring them into line, but then used her foot to flick them back to Séverine.

"Who is it for?" Lily asked about what seemed to be a scarf. The white-haired woman looked bewildered. To Lily, the multi-coloured work looked like something Trinity might wear.

"It isn't for anybody."

"For yourself then?"

Séverine anxiously pulled the knitting away from Lily as though she feared theft of her handiwork. She studiously turned away and peered at a couple, spinning giddily at the edge of the room.

"It doesn't have to be for anybody, young woman. It's the knitting that gives pleasure," she said over her shoulder. And then, forgetting the dancers, she flattened the scarf on her knee to admire her own artistry. "It's too flamboyant for me. I'm more of a practical type, you know, I like to wear sensible things. But it lifts my heart to look at such pretty colours and if I find someone that wants it, so much the better."

Lily fingered the wool with her red, rough hands.

"You don't paint anymore then," Séverine said flatly, tapping Lily's hand with a needle. "Not the hands of a painter."

Lily began to say something, but the old woman waved the needle, sword like, almost striking Lily's chin.

"Don't tell me – you don't have the time. Life's too full. Too busy, leading a purposeful life." She spoke the words with disdain. "Magic only comes when there's emptiness. Stillness. Purposelessness. I thought you would understand." Failing to get a response, she nodded in the direction of the French windows on the other side of the room. "Your painting in the hermitage – it has no purpose. It just is."

Lily shifted uncomfortably on her seat. She tugged at the dress drifting up her thighs, surprised to see her legs.

"It's still there," the woman continued. "But, of course, you know. You've been over. But just the once, eh? Back and fore, back and fore, you used to be."

It was not only ghosts that watched her then.

Séverine recognised the look of astonishment. "What? You think we've all fallen off the tree, don't you? Just old withered leaves, ready to be blown away to dust."

Lily's mouth opened uselessly. The telephone saved her. At the first ring Jopert's fingers stopped and all faces turned to the present resident of Chez Reynat.

Venetia's voice was cool as if she expected to be disappointed. "What I need to know is, have we resolved our little problem?" She wasted no time tiptoeing into the conversation.

Lily turned her back to the room and, hunched over the receiver, whispered into the telephone. "I'm sorting it out, I promise you." She dared not mention that the weather was against them; that their traveller was as free as a migratory bird. "Are you calling about a viewing? Is someone interested?"

"Now, sweetie, be honest with me. Never mind saying you're sorting it out. Is he gone or not – our colourful gitane?"

"My neighbour tells me he's leaving very soon. Apparently he has some sort of schedule he keeps to."

"Not good enough, I'm afraid. There's a couple I would have brought out tomorrow, but – no matter – I've got a few other places for them to see."

"Tomorrow?"

Baptistin had arrived at Lily's side and, as he put a paternal arm to her shoulder, he murmured in her ear. "*Demain*? Did I understand right? She wants to bring someone tomorrow? No problem, no problem, tell her. We'll put everything right." His stiff fingers squeezed the top of her arm. "Tell her to come – bring the people."

Lily hesitated and yet Baptistin beamed at her, nodding encouragingly. She repeated to Venetia, "No problem – we'll have it sorted out." Then in a more confident tone, she added, "Bring them tomorrow. They'll be impressed. Some of the shrubs are in flower and the place is really beginning to look lovely."

Baptistin tapped his foot and beat his hands against his side. "Come and have a dance with an old man, now that we've got that cleared up. Tomorrow you can get out of the way and go shopping. It's been a worry for you, all of this. I can deal with the difficulties."

Jopert pulled up on the couderc at twenty past eight and left the engine running. They had arranged to pick up Lily at eight thirty. Baptistin had insisted that Lily be chauffeured to the market at La Petite Aubaine and she was glad not to have to drive Felix's clattering car.

"You won't remember the way to La Petite Aubaine," Baptistin had said on her doorstep. "The route's very complicated – and there are no road signs to speak of. Better to go with Claude and Marie."

Lily took the front seat when she saw Marie in the back and swivelled round to comment on the wonderful day. But there was no reply. The driver occupied his seat as though it were his throne, fat hands draped across the steering wheel, legs gaping at the knees.

"Don't worry about my wife," Jopert told Lily, his eyes fixed on the windscreen, "she's a nervous passenger – prefers to sit in the back where she can't see the road."

They passed a vista of rolling hills, grazing cattle and wooded valleys during the half hour journey to La Petite Aubaine, but kept silent. Lily dared not think that the day might go well, that the business of offloading her burden might begin. But she was to lose her gypsy and that was a good start. They arrived in town sooner than Lily expected – modern houses, naked without the adornment of greenery or age, ribboned the road and a boxy supermarket flanked a new roundabout. Jopert pulled into its deserted car park, muttering that it would be busy in town, and anyway it was only a short walk to the square. Lily followed the couple who set out as though on an arduous trek, heads down and wordless with an empty basket each.

At the bustling square, Jopert said something incomprehensible to his wife and strode off towards an already busy bar on the corner. Lily watched Marie Jopert's plum coloured hat disappear into the crowd.

Lily remembered the market. She had pushed the infant Dominic up and down the rows, glad of the noise and banter around her. 'Not yet, Felix,' she would beg when he arrived to take her back to the quiet of Chez Reynat. Not until the last vendor had packed up his empty crates would she agree to leave the cobbled square, strewn with fallen flowers, squashed fruit, lost feathers.

This time she ambled haphazardly from one stall to another, buying mussels, asparagus, fresh greens – there was so much. The smells and sounds lifted her spirit. She bought bunches of purple and white tulips and, weighed down with bags, she scanned the perimeter of the square for somewhere to sit. Seeing Claude Jopert playing a game of cards with several other men, Lily decided to avoid embarrassment and she trundled on towards the church, finding a smaller café with just one outside table.

Lily stretched her legs under the metal table and looked at her beer, a glass of sparkling liquid and creamy froth. She might have been on holiday, she thought, smiling through closed eyes to the benign spring sun. With her head against the wall and an empty mind, she listened to the disorderly chorus of hollering stallholders and gossiping shoppers.

The scraping of a chair leg on the paving interrupted her pleasure. Lily pulled up her head and squinted. She had expected to see the waiter or perhaps another fatigued shopper, but it was neither. Gabriel put a beer down next to hers and made himself comfortable in the other chair.

Her first thought – after the shock of seeing him – was that he seemed so at ease – an onlooker might think that they did this often, that it was just a regular date. Then she noticed how he shuffled around as if he could not quite get comfortable. His brow was furrowed and he held his jaw stiffly, not quite in line. At least, he had said nothing this time. There was no casual 'Hello, Lily.' She turned her head and concentrated on two young women who had stopped to chat, kissing each other as a reflex action. Her task proved impossible. She felt his gaze, felt the edge of his shoe against hers. Surrendering, Lily allowed her eyes to return to the man at her table. She looked at the most beautiful face she had known. He wore a T-shirt and a sheepskin jacket. Lily was still surprised that he seemed so unchanged.

"What do you do?" she asked bluntly.

He smiled sheepishly and picked up his beer. An odd first question, she realised, but she could not imagine what sort of life he had made for himself. She had never – except in rare moments of weakness – tried to picture him in a different world. Seeing him now, she half suspected he was still wandering across Europe, borrowing horses, and searching for adventure.

"I've got a kite shop – back in Oregon, on the coast." He smiled almost shyly.

His low voice had a strange effect on Lily – but it always had. Somehow the exact pitch reverberated somewhere between her chest and diaphragm like an old song picked out on a guitar.

"So that's what you do? Sell kites? Fly kites?" Incredulity flew from her voice.

"Pretty much. Some snowboarding, surfing." He stopped and looked into the distance as though he could smell the sea, or perhaps feel the snow. He seemed to reflect on each word and phrase. Mason had said that 'Gabriel lives in a different time to the rest of us – perhaps a theoretical physicist could explain it.' It had the effect of slowing down the other person in the conversation. Lily remembered that her breathing always seemed slower when she was with him.

"That's it?" she scoffed, refusing to be affected.

"Not what you expected?" He looked apologetic. "And how about you?"

Her life was not so impressive, either. But then she blamed him. It was the first time Lily had articulated the thought.

"And the others?" she asked.

Gabriel took a moment to catch up with the leapfrogging of his question. "Mason's still a pastor. He's a family man now, got a great wife. She keeps him in tow." A smile came and went as if, for a brief moment only, he thought to share the joke.

"And the other two – Ken and Oki?" She had no curiosity, but the questions and answers kept her emotions at bay. Lily saw her fingertips white against the beer glass.

"Oki went back to college – works for a law firm in southern California." Gabriel shoved his hands in his pockets. "Ken's doing okay." He nodded at the ground as if assuring himself of this truth.

"So what are you doing here?" Lily snapped at him.

"Felix asked me to come."

"But the funeral's over. He's dead – gone. Why are you still hanging around?"

"I was with Felix before he died. You have to respect a man's dying wishes, Lily."

She studied his eyes, but failed to read them.

"So what did he tell you? What did he say?"

Gabriel's eyes wandered to the bar window behind her and then returned. "Felix was a man with a lot on his mind. He wanted to leave with all the boxes checked – you know – get everything off his chest?" He tipped his head to one side. "He didn't make a whole lot of sense. Just said the same thing over and over – 'Life is good'."

"What else?" Lily jabbed the words at him, dismissing what he had already told her.

Gabriel winced at the urgency in her voice.

"He said something about me thinking I'd lost something, but he'd stolen it. I don't know – he spoke some French, some English – and my French is pretty lousy these days. It's been a while since I spoke any."

"You'd lost something? At Chez Reynat? You didn't leave anything. You remembered to take everything with you." She hurled the words and waited for them to strike.

"It wasn't a great way to go," he answered. He had heard the unsaid declaration – except me.

Lily's attempt at quashing her anger had failed. She saw that pained expression again and her cheeks burned. "Felix has never stolen anything. What was he talking about?"

"I don't know, Lily."

"But you saw him at the end – of all people to go to him." Lily gulped down her beer. "I should have gone."

Gabriel's chair seemed not to please him – he shuffled some more and his face fidgeted between pleasure and pain. "You should know he talked about you. Anyways he kept saying your name and your son's."

Something jolted inside Lily. Her beer sloshed around as she almost dropped the glass on the table. She watched the puddle form and felt the cold liquid fall to her knee. Your son – the words fell out like jigsaw pieces. They enlightened her.

Gabriel's eyes had not flickered – he studied her as he lifted the beer to his lips. "Dominic is it? I figure you guys were the last people on his mind."

There were questions she should ask, but they had been suppressed so long that now she could not discipline them into anything cogent.

"Mon fils," Jopert shouted, slapping Gabriel on the back. He grinned like a schoolboy, putting a hand to Gabriel's hair and then his shoulder. It rested there as he turned to Lily. "It's time we were going. Are you ready, because the wife's tired and she's got lunch to do when we get back."

Lily's eyes were on Jopert's hand – it was loathe to abandon Gabriel's shoulder. Even through the padded jacket his fingers would feel muscle and bone. The intimacy irked her and she rose, brusquely pushing past the table.

The ride home was just as quiet as their outward journey, but this time Lily did not notice the green hollows and copses. At the two cottages, Flora and Florette stood on their paths, brooms in hand, staring flatly at the approaching car. Jopert and his wife barely acknowledged their neighbours. At the other end of the bridge Honorine straightened herself and placed the watering can at her feet. She tugged at her cardigan, unhappy with the arrangement of buttons. And then equally discontent with her hair, her hands scurried to the chignon. Madame Jopert made a muffled noise and, when Lily turned, she saw the woman's nervous hands grasp the front of her coat.

"Now, now. Calm down – it's all over now," her husband reassured her through the rear view mirror.

Jopert dropped Lily at the couderc and, with her tulips swaying at her knees, Lily put Gabriel from her mind. She had almost forgotten the reason for the outing to La Petite Aubaine. Venetia would probably ring in the afternoon with a report of the viewing. She enjoyed the feeling of impatience and hurried despite the heavy bags. There would have been some mess still at the well, but not enough to deter anyone with romantic notions for an idyllic life.

In only a singlet vest and trousers, Baptistin lifted a hand in greeting from his bench. With her own occupied, Lily nodded back, but then saw the beads of moisture trickling down his cheeks.

"Are you alright?" she shouted out.

"Fine, fine." He waved a hand again, this time to dismiss her, and then wiped the back of it across his brow.

At the gate pillars Lily stopped mid-stride. She looked to the lichen covered roof of the well expecting to see beyond it an oblong patch of dead grass and a circle of blackened earth. She expected to see the grassy bank and the slow moving waters of the Vamaleau. But the grey canvas blocked her view and a simmering pot stood over the charcoaled earth. With pear and cherry blossom twined around his head collar, the gypsy horse snorted at Lily's arrival, tossing his head up and down. Blush pink flowers tumbled to the ground around him.

"Baptistin! You were supposed to sort it out," she bellowed, marching back with long strides. "You promised me."

The old man's eyes barely lifted from the bench this time. Standing at the open gate, Lily could see a damp stripe down his vest. His reddened chest heaved.

"You shouldn't be sitting in the sun in the middle of the day," she chided in a softer tone.

He waved again to signify that all was well, but Lily perched herself on the edge of the bench and put a hand to his brow. She turned her head towards his window – the smell of vegetables wafted out and she heard the rattle of a pan on the stove.

"You haven't had your soup yet. Are you sure you're alright?"

Baptistin nodded soberly, but from the corner of his eye, Lily saw a gleam of mischief.

"So what happened with the traveller? You told me you would sort it out."

"And I did."

"But he's still there, Baptistin. Him, his horse and his campfire."

The old man splayed out his legs and placed his hands on the bench beneath him as though he were about to make a gymnastic move. Looking across to the river, he spoke with deliberation.

"I said I would put it right and so I did. I solved your problem – the problem of selling the house to strangers. We don't want to lose our well, Lily."

Lily saw fear and anxiety in her neighbour, not malice.

"Chez Reynat needs new owners, Baptistin. It needs money spending on it and Dom and I don't have any. New people will bring new life – they'll see to all the repairs it needs."

He rocked on the bench, still gazing out to the Vamaleau.

"I remember. You were industrious when you lived here. Always wanting to improve things, Felix said. He was patient with you – it amused him, I think. Yes, we'll get people who'll come in with gusto. I've heard all about it – money and work. They'll spend the little time they have here, banging at the old place, pulling bits down. But will they get more pleasure from the old house? You put a lot of effort into it, Lily, but you didn't seem happy to me."

"I wasn't happy. But that was for different reasons," she retaliated.

"I remember a girl, laughing under the bread tree. You don't look like a woman that laughs much."

Her breath came awkwardly, her chest tightened, and she said nothing. Lily dragged her feet back to the house and bolted the door behind her. The empty room greeted her with its sad mustiness and she bent to attend to the dying embers of the fire. The ghosts of Reynat saw a child-sized woman with more life in her rebellious hair than in her pale face.

The grass needed cutting, weeds pulling, she knew, but she stayed at the French window, breathing in the cool air blowing off the water. She took a step outside and slid down to sit with her back to the gently warmed wall. The sound of the Vamaleau blotted out everything. Lily's eyelids fell, her breathing slowed, and she stopped thinking as the time of Achallat passed.

As the light faded, the Vamaleau called to Lily. It was as still as a lake. The rust coloured stones on the riverbed wavered about under the crystal water. From the flower heads strewn around the grass, Lily guessed that the viewers had brought children with them. A mist came up from the river, obscuring the hermitage and sharpening the silence. Lily turned her head jerkily. She felt someone watch her and expected to see Felix or even the gypsy, but she saw Venetia walk gracelessly down the bank, her red lips scrunched into a small circle.

"I'm really sorry," Lily began. "My neighbour misled me. I've been too…" Guilt-ridden was the word that came to mind, but she said, "easy going with him. I'll get rid of the gypsy myself."

"Gypsies are one thing. The tent was a bit of an eyesore, but that's not your problem, young woman. In fact there was no sign of the madman today. Your neighbours are your problem. Do you have any idea what the sight of a geriatric coven will do to prospective buyers?"

Lily stopped the laugh at her lips. So that explained Baptistin's pink cheeks.

"Well, I'll tell you, because I found out today. It'll send them packing. Not only are they not interested in your place, but they're not interested in anything I have to offer. They're going to look at Brittany or Spain, but they won't be back here again." Venetia waved a flat palm at Lily to check any attempt at reply. She took a deep breath and spoke the next words with patience. "People want peace and tranquillity. They want to escape the modern world, but they don't want to descend into the dark ages."

"I can see that." Lily looked back to the Vamaleau. It was unmoving, but was now opaque like one of Baptistin's thick potato soups.

"In theory we should have no problem here. There are some nice English people who've bought nearby and people like that. They like to have some neighbours not too far away."

Lily looked to the ground, unable to say anything more to excuse herself or Achallat. Between blades of grass and clover stalks, a snake made its way from the river. The colour of wet stone, it slithered towards Venetia. Lazily, it coiled itself around the heel of her shoe and held its head in the air, waving slightly as though unsure of its next move. Lily darted a look at Venetia, but the irate woman seemed blind to what was happening at her feet.

"You haven't asked me anything about your neighbours' antics so perhaps you're already acquainted with them," Venetia accused her.

Lily's eyes returned to the shoe. Emerging from the shallow margins, another snake seemed to have the same destination in mind. It reached its partner and slid along its body.

"But I'll tell you all the same. On this idyllic little lawn of yours, we found a circle of elderly people, dancing and chanting, flowers in their hair, like some fossilised relics of

Woodstock." A strange sound made Venetia pause and cock her head. Lily heard it too, but recognised it as the croaking of frogs.

"But they weren't the worst of it."

Lily had stopped listening to Venetia's tale. The crooning frogs raised their voices and flung themselves at the riverbank. She watched frogs hop, and snakes slither in a reptilian dance and, pulling herself out of paralysis, she tugged at Venetia's shoulder. "I'm sorry, Venetia, but you have to go now – I have a really busy evening planned."

Lily tripped around the creatures as she half dragged, half pushed the agent up the bank and past the campfire. Venetia seemed dumbfounded by Lily's indifferent reaction to her news.

"Have you been listening? Did you hear? I've lost clients, you do realise that?"

"Don't give up on me, Venetia. I really need to sell this place. I realise it's going to take longer than I'd hoped, but everything will be ironed out. I just need to sit down with the neighbours and explain."

"You'd better do just that. You won't do any better with the notaire, I can tell you that. News of this sort of thing travels like wildfire."

Lily shut the door of Venetia's car firmly and waved her away with a fixed smile. At the riverbank she searched, but there was no sign of wildlife in the grass. A thrush sang a piercing song from a branch of the chestnut tree; a woodpigeon waddled at its base, picking at the deadwood, searching for the ideal twig. And the river whispered soothingly. It was a perfect spring evening.

*Heard a carol, mournful, holy,
Chanted loudly, chanted lowly,
Till her blood was frozen slowly,
And her eyes were darken'd wholly,*

                Tennyson

CHAPTER EIGHTEEN

With the chores of her everyday life absent Lily was an ox missing its yoke and, like a beast of burden, she began to find herself standing motionless. It could happen in any room of the house. Sometimes she had something in her hand and, seeing it, she would remember that she was in the middle of making coffee or eating lunch. She caught sight of herself in the mirror and saw a woman with an empty life. Her face was without lines, but the obduracy in the jaw, the defensive eyes – these things aged her all the same.

She was in one of her moments of paralysis when Baptistin rapped on the French window.

"What are you doing?" he asked bluntly, taking his shoes off at the threshold. Smirking down at his stocking'd feet, he explained, "I know how you like to keep the floor clean."

She looked at him blankly and then at the knife in one hand and the book in the other. "I'm not sure."

Baptistin padded across to her. She put her full and cumbersome fists awkwardly to her hips.

"Don't think you can get in my good books just by taking your boots off. I'm not going to forget your antics last week that easily. You must be mad, all of you – drunk on that well water." She had tried to recall Venetia's last words of the tale – something about a 'high priest'. Lily looked back at Baptistin in a new light.

He pushed his shoulders back defensively. "We had good reason – and extreme measures were needed. Anyway, she won't be back for a while so it'll give you time to think."

"I don't need to think. I'm selling, so you'd all best resign yourselves to it. I'm not giving up."

His shoulders barely moved – Baptistin had another matter to raise. "Let's not go into all of that now, Lily. I'm here to ask a favour – not for myself, but for our friend. He'd like to borrow a book or two from Felix's library. I don't have many books – well, I don't have any if you want to know the truth. And Honorine's aren't to his liking." He puckered his mouth as if thinking of his neighbour's literary tastes.

Lily watched him shuffle over to the bookshelf. He pitched his head at a sharp angle to read the spines. "There's a lot of choice here."

"What friend?" Lily tapped the knife against the book.

"What friend? Our travelling friend, of course. Life can get a bit monotonous I should think in that tent of his."

Lily was outside and on the grass before Baptistin had finished speaking. She strode the length of the house and stopped herself so suddenly at the tent that she pitched forwards slightly.

"You want to borrow a book?" she yelled at the rotting canvas. "What do you think this is – a lending library as well as a campsite?"

"Now, now, calm yourself down, girl. He's an intelligent man – why shouldn't he like to read?"

Lily ignored Baptistin. Her fists rose and she saw the missile in her hand. She hurled the heavy book at the tent and watched it buckle the canvas before it slid down the side. There was a brief grunt from the interior, a sound that was stopped short as if its perpetrator swallowed the curse he was about to utter. With her legs straddling one of the guy ropes, Lily waited. She felt Baptistin's hand on hers as he snatched the knife from her fingers.

"Go ahead – help yourself to a book. In fact, help yourself to anything in the house. Read a book, have a snack, put your filthy backside on the sofa. Go ahead."

There was no reply. Lily pushed Baptistin aside and ran to the riverbank. She rowed breathlessly, feeling the blood pump in her neck, in her forehead. With the key in the lock, she lurched the door open and leaned back against it. Her head still buzzed and she needed to sit. She looked at the bed, but chose to rest on the three-legged stool.

The scent of the room – a fragrance of a sun-filled land – calmed her. When the thumping in her chest stopped, Lily swivelled round and put out a hand to the wall, letting her fingers trace the story of her painted panel. After the last scene of Felix at the window, waving melancholically, there were some faded pencil marks. She had meant to depict Mason's Sunday service near the chestnut tree, but then Gabriel had crossed the Vamaleau on Bayardo. Mason had liked one of his tiny congregation to speak – 'to be inspired' as he put it – and this had so terrified Lily that she never returned a second time. Trinity had taken to the stage confidently, even though she waffled on about nothing. "Life is a precious and fleeting gift and we should celebrate it each day," Mason had announced to his flock. Without knowing it Lily had honoured such a gift in her painting.

She had lost the skill. Her hands or her will had lost it. It seemed not to matter which. She pulled her hand away from the panel and moved to the door to sit on the flagstone, darkened with the wet of the night. There was a vague promise of sun through the mist. She saw a profile of a rider and his mount, stopping at the water's edge – a man in shadow and his bay horse with four perfectly symmetrical white socks. Lily blinked away the apparition.

*

"I'll be right back," Gabriel had said, tugging a jacket from his holdall under the bed. Bayardo was saddled up with a rolled sleeping bag attached. Gabriel stood at the door, impatient to say his farewell.

"You won't be needing those, will you?" Lily asked, alarmed. She pulled herself from their bed. With a sense of foreboding, Lily had tossed all night and then fell asleep as the doves woke. "Don't go, don't go, don't go," they seemed to purr.

Gabriel looked down at the passport and wallet in the pocket and shook his head. "No, you're right. Here, you look after them for me."

She clutched them to her chest as he smoothed down her wild morning hair, holding it back, the better to see her.

"Why don't you paint while I'm gone – it's not finished." He held her face in his hands. "I forget how young you are."

"You're coming back, aren't you?"

"It's no big deal – just a one day trek," he reassured her with a kiss on her brow.

She ached inside – the way she had ached when her father had sent her off to her aunt's house – he had the farm to see to and a son to send to school each day. No one spoke of her mother, not yet buried, but they tiptoed around the silent six-year-old. When she returned to the farm, she saw a photograph of a woman and did not recognise her mother.

Lily watched Gabriel cross the Vamaleau, Bayardo's shining hooves splashing through the causeway. He was off to find a secret waterfall that Felix had described over dinner. Ever vigilant, Felix had seen the first signs of curiosity in Gabriel's face and had jumped from the table to fetch an atlas. He had danced around Gabriel, leaning over him with the map, his eyes earnest.

"You can only get there by foot or by horse," Felix had informed him. "And even then not always. After rain the path is flooded. It is only accessible for a few weeks of the year. Yes, really, for a very short time only."

Felix studied the back of Gabriel's head, waiting for his response.

"And the moon will be full in a couple of nights – it will be a perfect time – perhaps your last chance." He waited again.

Lily had wondered at Felix's enthusiasm, but she knew that Gabriel would go. As a cockerel crowed on the couderc, she watched him ride across the causeway and disappear behind the western wall of Chez Reynat. He turned as he reached the corner, knowing she would still be at the door. He raised a hand. Lily pulled out the wooden chest from under the bed and, putting aside her dress and the Reynat veil, she took out a velvet bag. She unclasped the silver button and slid Gabriel's documents inside its satin lining. Her fingers stroked the embroidery – a yellow chested bird perched on a flowering branch.

She kept vigil from the hermitage door until dusk fell when she rowed across the river to eat with the company or rather push the food across her plate. The moon was like a nugget of amber in a black sky that night. From her bed she gazed out of the unshuttered window and followed its progress. Sleep came before the dawn.

The familiar rattling of the Renault woke her. Standing at the door, she saw the car judder over the bridge. Why she dragged out the trunk from beneath the bed, she did not know. Kneeling, she took out her bag, and fell back on her ankles. There was no need to look into its bright lining – she felt it empty and limp. Under the bed she saw only her own rucksack and a pair of espadrilles.

For weeks later the image of horse and rider stepping from the water veiled her eyes – she could see little else, even when she returned to Lack Farm. She looked out at the long fields and dry stone walls and saw the Vamaleau and Gabriel riding away from her.

*

Lily lifted herself from her cold seat. Breaking its promise, the sun had failed to overcome the haze. With boisterous honking a flight of geese announced their arrival and in a wide arc swept over the river, over the ghost-like aspen and birch, and disappeared into the greyness. Baptistin's own honking floated across. She could just make him out beside the tent. He thumped his chest with both hands as if helping out the last words that came juddering out between guffaws.

Another figure leaned against the well, his hand idly rubbing at the gypsy horse's neck beneath its mane. With drooping ears, the animal hung its head a little as it enjoyed the makeshift grooming. It took its back weight on one white socked leg while it tipped the other hind hoof to the ground. The man led the horse into the trees and Baptistin followed, cocking his head first towards the river as if aware of someone.

Lily had almost enjoyed the scene. She had caught the tone but not the words. Baptistin was unchanging – he told his stories to all – even migrating travellers. She locked the door and traipsed down the muddy path towards the Vamaleau.

Before she reached the timber mooring her feet stopped and she sucked back a noisy breath. The boat bobbed around tantalisingly a few metres from the shore, its tethering rope disappearing into the green water. Lily looked wide-eyed at the empty post. She had been so angry when she had crossed over, rowing furiously and leaping from the boat – had she tied the rope? She spent minutes trying to remember and then realised the futility of the exercise. It did not matter – her means of crossing was out of reach. She dropped to her stomach and, shuffling her body across the decking, she stretched out one arm. Failing, she pushed herself further out, hanging over the water, her muscles jittering as her fingers clawed towards the rope. Teasing her, the boat swung sideways, pulling its tether away from her reach.

Lily hauled herself up and searched the bank for something she could use and, seeing nothing, she sunk to the grass. The river mocked her fear, waiting for her to wade out, reach out for the rope and slip under. So she sat and did nothing. She felt the damp earth soak through the seat of her jeans and watched the boat until the blackbird, perched on the chimney behind her, began his end of day song. The causeway stretched out to the other bank, its green stone barely wet as the slow, lazy Vamaleau spoke softly.

Lily unlaced her boots, shoved her socks inside, and then hung them around her neck. With her jeans rolled up and her fists clenched she took one shaky step onto the wet path. A trickle of water teased her toes as she glided her foot along slowly and placed the other foot on the stone behind it. She glanced up quickly and saw the ghost of the new moon hanging above Chez Reynat's dark roof, but there were no stars out yet. She walked on, or rather slid on – she dared not raise her feet from the stone, but moved as though she skated in slow motion. Her chest was tight, her stomach knotted when she stopped. Barely lifting her head, she peered through her lashes across to Chez Reynat's bank. Her eyes were drawn to the opaque water – it swayed rhythmically beneath her. She pictured Oddo, breath held, waiting. He lay in his gravel bed with arms held out, his see-through eyes fixed on her, daring her to escape him this time. She was stuck – rooted to the path – and yet certain that she would sink like a stone. Her feet and ankles had already become cold obsidian; her fists were granite. She thought her breathing must have ceased, because she felt only ice crystallising in her chest and a mineral taste in her mouth. Chez Reynat hovered in the distance, dancing below the shining crescent. She closed her eyes to rid herself of the picture, but found herself swaying, giddy with fear. She had no thought of time. But the water was now black and the moon a brilliant diamond.

She could not look at the figure that came out of the gloom – her eyes were fixed on the dark river. It was Felix. He had come to guide her, to save her as he had done before, his feet skimming the wet path.

"Don't look down. Don't look at the water."

She tried to raise her head and managed to lift her chin from her chest.

"Keep your eyes on the tree. Can you hear the bird singing, Lily?"

It was not Felix's fussy command. The voice was unhurried, leisurely as if they had all evening to walk back to land.

"Look at the tree, Lily."

She dragged her eyes to the branches of the chestnut, its stark branches held stiffly aloft. The blackbird, having already swooped across the river so easily, hopped to a branch hanging out over the causeway. His song pierced the dusk. The figure at last reached Lily and he held out a warm hand to her granite fist. She watched his fingers as they unlocked hers. He took hold, clasping her palm to his.

Lily stole a glance and saw Gabriel's face before her eyes fled back to his hand. She pressed her icy fingers to his knuckles.

"You keep your eyes on me, Lily, and keep hold. Don't let go. We'll take it easy – one step at a time."

With her eyes fixed on Gabriel's back, Lily moved one foot in front of the other and heard the sweet song grow louder. They crept along Oddo's path and she felt blood again in her hand as it drew heat from her guide.

With grass beneath her stony feet, Lily tugged at the key at her neck and flung it into the blackness of the river.

"Take it," she spat at the Vamaleau.

It gurgled mockingly at her, its dark water rising over the path. When Lily turned Gabriel had already wandered away, his back obscure in the night.

The pale yellow woods were waning,
The broad stream in his banks complaining,

                        Tennyson

CHAPTER NINETEEN

"It's time you came home," Jack told Lily down the telephone line.

*

"It's time we went home, Liliput," Trinity had said in that first week of September.

Gabriel had left Jopert's horse in the field and Felix had driven him to the station. Mason for once was at a loss for words. Trinity brushed Lily's hair; stroked her head. She would have spoon-fed her like a baby if she could. As Lily stared at her full plate, Oki said, "we should head off – we're thinking south. Get to see the Med." He looked at Trinity hopefully.

"Sounds great, but it's back to school for us two," Trinity said with her eyes on Lily.

"There is no need to go yet." Felix had trotted in from the kitchen when he heard the conversation. "Summer is not yet over." His eyes were on Lily too.

"No, we have to go," Trinity persevered. "The holiday's over – we knew it would end." Her hand clung to Lily's waist as if she thought she needed to be propped up.

The next morning, Lily was fastening her rucksack when Felix came into the hermitage. He did not knock, and she did not notice. He walked up to the painted panel and seemed dissatisfied – he had not seen it since Lily had led Gabriel across Oddo's path.

"But you have not finished." His voice was disbelieving. "You cannot go. How can you leave it like this? Do you not remember how excited you were to paint the story? I will look after you, Lily. You are upset now, but you will forget easily enough. Oddo will help – he mends all wounds. This is your island."

He said the last words to an empty room – Lily had drifted down the riverbank towards her namesake vessel, leaving her key on the bed.

*

"You're needed," Jack insisted.

Lily listened to the list of woes from her father: the coal bunker was all but empty; there were bills unpaid; the dirt was piling up. In fact it seemed that Lack Farm was on hold. 'Your brother's forced to do the weekly shop,' Jack moaned, 'and he's better things to do.'

Lily twirled the telephone cable and it skipped along the tiles, making a satisfying noise. She flicked it against the wall as if she could swat her father away. "I know David's busy, but it's only six miles there and back, for goodness sake. The ride out'll do him good."

She pictured her brother grouchily starting up the Volvo's engine. Other than the occasional visit to the mart when he wanted to sell or buy a beast, he rarely left the farm. He relied on television to inform him of the behaviour of other human beings, wolfing down his food at the kitchen table so that he could get to the set. The discontented boy had become a solitary man, impatient with his father and blind to his sister.

Pulling her mouth into a facsimile of a smile, Lily hoped an uplifted tone would be transmitted down the line. "Can't we talk about something other than all the work I've left you. Give me some news – what's been happening?"

This was a foolish question to a man who counted himself lucky if nothing occurred and, a moment later, she heard only the ringing tone. Lily held the receiver in mid-air and bit her lip. "Okay, let's not chat," she sighed, and put it back in its cradle.

Her hands itched to do something – they missed the release of whipping the cable around. Lily looked around at the clean surfaces of Chez Reynat. Where a few weeks ago she saw effort rewarded, now she saw emptiness. The house was devoid of life. She realised the meaning of dead quiet – the absence of life. Even Felix's presence, which she had sensed at first, was lacking. Lily had heard the house creak, seen his reflection in the glass, but he had wafted away like mist. She felt as though her own steps would not resound; that if she walked, she would displace no air.

The sound of someone politely clearing his throat made Lily wheel round to face the French windows. Gabriel stood on the threshold, blocking out the meagre light of a damp day.

"Didn't want to butt in," he apologised as he took a step in, but seeing her startled look, he retraced that step and waited at the doorway, his hands dug deep in his pockets. He wore a look of wearied patience.

"I suppose I should thank you for the other day," Lily mumbled. She brought her arms across her chest. "I didn't get to thank you at the time." That was not quite true, but she excused herself – she had been in no fit state to think of common courtesies. "I didn't get to explain how I ended up out there. It must've looked daft – just standing in the middle of the river. The boat had drifted off…"

She waited for him to say, 'forget about it – none of my business.' But he studied her eyes, watched her mouth move, and listened. Her arms held her a little tighter.

"I panicked – just froze. I thought you were Felix."

A weak smile crossed his face for a moment. "Figures."

"Sorry?" Lily quizzed.

"Seems to me, you're good at getting us mixed up."

Gabriel leaned against the door and put a hand up to the lintel. This small action irritated every muscle in her body. She unclasped her arms, pulled at her hair, looked around the room and then hugged herself again, squeezing her vexed hands into her armpits.

"So tell me what you're doing here really." Her voice was brittle. "You said Felix asked for your forgiveness. Well, whatever it was for, I assume you gave it. It would be only good manners – but then manners are not one of your strong points. So, you told a dying man what he wanted to hear and then what? You're still hanging around Achallat. Haven't you got anything better to do? There's nothing for you here."

"Nothing for you either, Lily. Isn't that true? You're going to sell up and forget all about Felix and this place. Is that what your son wants too?"

"It's none of your bloody business what Dom wants. What are you doing here?"

"I made Felix a promise."

"What promise?" Lily spat out a laugh at him. "I don't remember you being so good at keeping promises."

"Maybe not," he agreed, his mouth moving stiffly.

"Why don't you go back to your kites – to your toys."

Gabriel's fingers tapped at the lintel. "Whatever happened between you and Felix…" he began.

He seemed to change his mind. It struck Lily that he laid claim to some anger too – but he held his in rein.

He had decided on his words. "I recall Felix saying Chez Reynat always chose its owners – chose those who lived in this big, old place. I don't think he'd want it put up for sale to the highest bidder. He'd want it keeping for his son and all the sons to come."

The table was between them, but Lily almost lunged at him, despite it. "You don't know what Felix would want! You obviously don't understand French law. The house is Dom's – it's his to sell. I'm just here seeing to it for him. He's got no love for the place." Saying it made her feel good. "Dominic doesn't want to have anything to do with Chez Reynat."

Gabriel nodded as though he understood perfectly and turned his back to her, choosing instead to face the river. Lily was unsure whether he spoke – his voice, so low, perhaps merged with the chattering river. She went out onto the grass and, standing beside him, she saw the muscles on his face flex and tighten.

"So what happened to your university plans? Art or history, wasn't it?" Gabriel's gaze was directed at Oddo's refuge.

Lily tried not to answer, but the words shot out. "Life never works out like we plan."

"So you came back here to Felix? Settled for life in Achallat and now you're tasting resentment, wishing you'd done something more with yourself?"

His tone knocked her own wrath sideways.

"I didn't ever resent Felix."

"No, but you're thinking at least you can make a buck out of the poor guy."

"And what about you? Where did you wander off to?" There, at last. She had asked the question. It had not escaped as a howl. It had, in the end, been uttered simply.

Lily saw him swallow hard and he took a few steps towards the river as if she had reminded him of his need to roam.

"Are you married?" She glanced at his hand, but she had searched for evidence before – as he drank his beer at the café.

"I'm married, Lily."

The words winded her. "Tell me about her," she said bravely. She itched for a fight.

He shook his head as though they had strayed into unwelcome territory. "She was just a kid." His mouth was twisted in discomfort. Lily saw apology in his mouth, but there was condemnation in his eyes.

She needed the house, needed Felix's walls around her, but before she could close the door, Gabriel spoke again.

"Before you go…" he said, turning round. "As fun as catching up has been, Lily, I came by to ask a favour. I was hoping you could spare a bed for a couple of weeks. You've got a houseful – and I feel at home here in Chez Reynat. It was always open house with Felix."

"Are you mad?"

A sudden grin spread across his face and he stared at his feet as if it embarrassed him.

"I thought that might be too much to hope for. How about you let me hole up across the water?"

For a moment she wondered what on earth he was talking about, and then she looked across to the Île des Lys.

"Why, for God's sake? I don't have the key anymore – I gave it back to its rightful owner – Oddo." She thrust out her chin, defiantly.

Gabriel nodded, taking in this information. With a wry smile he said, "I don't think he has a use for it now. Who knows, it may just turn up again. The river makes up its own mind about these things. I've got my own anyway – Felix sent me this with the letter. Pretty determined I should come."

He squeezed a hand into his pocket and pulled out the familiar iron key. This one was attached to a rough piece of twine with another smaller key. Lily did not recognise it.

She narrowed her eyes. "Is it financial? Is that why you're here? Someone's convinced you that there's something to gain?"

His expression had not altered, but Lily flinched as she uttered the last word as if she sensed a change in him. He strode the dozen steps towards her and stood so close that she could feel his breath on her face.

"What have you turned into, Lily?"

"I grew up, I suppose."

"What have you got to be bitter about? Felix? I got to thinking about you two. I remember that first morning, finding you two together. A cosy couple, even then. Before I turned up, you spent a lot of time with him. I've thought back to those things these past few weeks." His eyes had strayed back to the river; his words drifted with the water.

"You should be thankful, Lily – for the life you've got. You have a son," he declared as if she had momentarily forgotten. Lily strained to listen to each inflection in his voice.

"You've got some talent too, but I guess you're going to tell me you don't paint any more – that would figure. And you've got this place – this enchanted place – that's what Mason used to call it. There's nothing for you to be bitter about, Lily." His voice was taut like he tried to keep it leashed.

As if bored with the river, his eyes returned to her. "And you still look pretty good." He nodded, agreeing with his own judgement.

Lily felt her body become rigid like molten metal cooling. With a steel fist she would punch him; with steel fingers she would stab the eyes that so easily measured and weighed her.

Content, it seemed, that he had said all that was needed to be said, he strode off, leaving Lily to watch his easy gait and, recognising it, she knew she missed her son.

"I'll be there at the end of the month," Dom told her firmly, hearing a tone in his mother's voice that he did not comprehend.

She had telephoned him for reassurance and now she regretted it. "Take no notice of me. Everything's fine here. I'm just getting a bit restless – a bit fed up with the weather. It's all taking so long, but we were probably too optimistic. We Weavers have never sold a house before – not in living memory anyway."

The Weavers had been sown like seed at Lack Farm in the distant past. Before the present farmhouse had been built, they had lived in some simpler, humbler dwelling. Their roots dug deep into the clay earth, finding enough sustenance to survive – to keep going.

Lily bit her lip, knowing that she should ask Dominic if he had changed his mind. Did he still want to sell? But she was fearful of the answer.

"I'm coming – I've made up my mind. It'll be cool, Mum. I want to see this mad Rasputin camped in the garden."

She had told the tale too well, making her situation seem exciting – at least more exciting than the prospect of the month's vacation at Lack Farm with Granddad and Uncle David.

"I want to come and help. Anyway, I'm curious now. I don't remember anything about the place – perhaps it'll come back to me when I get there."

That was what scared her. "You'll get in my way. You'll mess up the place when I'm trying to keep it spotless for the buyers. And it's deathly dull here – it's miles from anywhere – there's never anyone in the bar down the village. And you'd have to drive everywhere." She realised that this was no different to life at Lack Farm. "Honestly, you'd hate it."

Dominic relented and Lily tried to console herself that her anxieties were for her son and his buried memories, but in truth, her fears were for herself. Dominic, Gabriel and Chez Reynat would be united – a trinity that perhaps Felix engineered.

It was the following day, a day thick with fog, when Lily first saw Gabriel cross the Vamaleau. With a holdall slung over one shoulder he stepped onto the causeway, barefoot, his jeans turned up to his shins. Before he had reached the mid-point, his figure disappeared, leeching into the mist.

The days passed: some of mist and drizzle; some of fog so dense she barely perceived the willow and its swollen buds. She saw a pointillist scene of sodden greys and sombre ochre. She felt as though she were hidden from the world, locked in a time of empty days and nights, silent, but for the owls. And each day she saw Gabriel emerge from the murk to draw water from the well and take it back to his squat on the island.

The gypsy had not broken his hibernation yet – the tent remained, but the campfire rarely burned now. Venetia made a conciliatory visit and, with the effort audible in her voice, spoke to Lily with patience and sympathy.

"I'll just take you off the books until everything's hunky-dory. It's probably for the best. Just think – the place will look so much better in a few weeks anyway, sweetie, when everything greens up and the walls don't look so... bleak. I mean, it's not that photogenic a house in winter. It needs some lightening up – a few leaves and flowers will do the world of good."

As a godmother, measuring the beauty of a plain child Venetia stood on the soft new grass and studied the cliff face of Chez Reynat's walls.

"Normally, I'd take photos, you know. It should be just a case of the right angle... but there's something about this place." She shivered and pulled the cardigan draping her shoulders a little higher. "Eerie, some might say."

"Enchanting, many have said," Lily stated defensively.

A change in the rhythm of the whispering river caught Venetia's attention and she turned to see Gabriel on his daily visit. Ploughing through the water, he seemed to enjoy kicking it aside. He carried a container over one shoulder, his fingers hooked around its handle.

Venetia's eyes lit with delight. She forgot the dour house. "I don't know about enchanting, but I see you have a man that walks on water." Her voice was breathy and she almost giggled. "What is it about Achallat? It certainly lives up to its reputation."

"I can tell you he's no holy man or saint." The words spewed out of Lily's mouth. She stepped back into the house as if, worse, he were a demon to avoid.

"But he's staying here with you? Your..." Venetia searched for a word, "guest?"

203

Without thinking Lily replied, "No, he's squatting." She sucked in a curse as she realised the effect of the term on an estate agent. "When I said squatting, I meant…"

Venetia was already striding towards her car and Lily watched it sail past the gate pillars. She knew it would be a while before she saw it again.

The fog made itself at home. It was so dense that Lily's hair was black with the wet; her face so moist that she felt part of the enveloping mist. Without wanting to, her eyes searched for the lost hermitage.

*

She had waited in Chez Reynat twenty years earlier too, but then the autumn air was crisp, the birch leaves the colour of burnt copper. She had walked to Achallat from Saint Bénigne, listening to her footsteps echo down the empty lane. With aching legs she had knocked futilely at the door of Chez Reynat and then sat on Baptistin's bench. Spotting his visitor from his open window, the old man had joined her, sitting too in silence. With a cold cup of coffee on her lap, too nauseous to drink it, she waited for Felix's return.

Felix's eyes danced as much as his feet as he ushered her into the house. She remembered that he showed no surprise – it was as if he expected her.

"Here you are, here you are," he kept repeating. "Come and sit down by the fire. Are you cold? Are you hungry?"

He put his hand to her face. It shocked her – he would have been too timid to do it just a few weeks earlier, but now with her return, he was more courageous. His hand went to her abdomen even though there was no sign of the life that was growing there.

"Fruit of the earth," he stated quietly with satisfaction.

"What can I do, Felix? I can't tell my Dad."

"So your father knows nothing of the wedding – knows nothing of Gabriel?"

Once back at the farm, Lily had doubted whether any of it had happened; she doubted whether Achallat itself were real. Now she had the evidence that it had not been a dream. She shook her head.

"Chez Reynat welcomes you with open arms – surely you know that."

"I came to find Gabriel." While she roamed the room, Felix shuffled behind her.

"Of course. He intends to come back to Achallat – I know this for sure." With the words came emphatic nodding.

"So he's still in France?" She clutched at the glimmer of hope.

"I am certain." Felix put an arm around Lily and drew her towards the sofa. He bent to the stove and rattled a poker around, sending sparks out onto the hearth. When he spoke again, his back was turned to her.

"You will stay and wait for Gabriel."

And she did. It seemed all that she could do at the time. Each day was without activity – from the plate of fresh fruit Felix brought in the morning to the bowl of hot chocolate he made at night. She stood at the window like a life-size ornament, looking out at the river as if Gabriel would ride across to her.

Her stomach began to swell as the nights grew shorter and then lengthened again, and sometime in the spring she knew that Gabriel would not return and that she would not leave Achallat. One night when her own arms were insufficient, when her skin was cold to the touch, and her bones numbed with the lack of hope, Felix succeeded in coaxing her into his bed.

Dominic was born in God's good month, as Felix called May. She telephoned her father with the news.

"A farm's no place for a baby," Jack stated. There was no chiding, no shock. He had spent months reflecting on the many fates that may have befallen his absent daughter. With no news from her, he had imagined the worst and now, almost relieved, he could name the disaster that had in fact occurred.

"Now then, I hope he's going to do right by you – this Frenchman. He knows how to do right, I suppose."

Jack did not ask the name of the father of his grandson and Lily did not tell him. That was how the lie started, she supposed now.

*

The rain was obstinate. It showed no sign of leaving Achallat. Sometimes it was barely more than a downward moving mist; sometimes it fell heavily and monotonously, bouncing off the flagstones and drowning out the sound of the river. When the rain paused Lily listened to the thundering Vamaleau – the answering chorus.

Watery days seeped into each other. Lily only knew it was Tuesday because Duffraud's van had called. She had said no more than her shopping list – the rain would have killed any conversation. She was about to turn up the volume on the old record player when a melodic tinkling joined in the cacophony of rain crashing around the house.

At the farthest French window, rain cascaded in from the lintel, splashing down like a small waterfall. The gentle noise had been the water pinging against a Chinese vase. Lily fetched towels and took a chair to the window. With water dripping down her arm, she tried to stem the flow and saw in the blackness an area less dense than the surrounding night. She stepped down from the chair and drew closer to the glass. In the midst of the steely wires of rain she saw a form, or an apparition. Lily backed away, the wet towel still in her hand. She reached the middle of the room and turned, leaping up the stairs to Felix's bedroom. Crouching, she put her face to the window.

It was no ghost, no prowling gypsy. Gabriel's jeans were jet with rain, his hair matted to his face. Like a rock that had grown out of the riverbank, he stood and looked back at her.

Lily stayed at the window and fell asleep with her head resting on her elbow at the sill. She woke with the screech of the owl and looked out at the grey before dawn. Gabriel had left. Stiff and numb, she found her bed.

In the morning Lily found a pool of water creeping from the door. The amorphous puddle was edged white as it sat on top of her many coats of beeswax. As she wrung out the cloths, Lily saw a tear fall to the bucket. 'Don't waste your tears,' she said for her father and she wiped her face roughly with her hand.

Perhaps it was the next day – Lily had lost sense of time – when the clouds were less heavy, the sky less dark. She opened one of the windows and stepped onto the sodden grass. It was clear enough for Lily to make out the hermitage and the smoke rising from its chimney. A shape moved in the pewter river. Lily studied it for a while, before she realised it was a swimmer. He moved easily, at home in water, diving into the Vamaleau from the green bank of the Île des Lys, disappearing beneath the brown surface and rising again like a water creature. Gabriel turned and reeled, throwing wave after wave onto the causeway. Eventually, he pulled out one leg onto the stone path and hoisted himself up, standing naked and shaking his hair like a dog.

That night was clearer too and Lily saw a flickering orange light on the western gable of the hermitage. Gabriel had lit a campfire somewhere near the espaliered pear, just as he had done on warm summer evenings.

A hammering woke her the next day – it vibrated through her as she lay in her narrow bed. She peered out into the drizzle and saw nothing that would account for the noise. The rhythmic boom continued and she dressed quickly, pulling on her old boots and Felix's rubber mackintosh. She followed the sound, passing the barn and crossing the lane into Claude

Jopert's pasture with its avenue of ancient oaks running along one boundary.

At the far side of the field a figure swung a large mallet in an arc and, in a graceful action, brought it down to strike a timber post. He stopped when he saw her and put aside his tool.

Lily hesitated, but Gabriel was less forbidding in daylight. She was the owner of Chez Reynat – well, more or less – and he was an interloper, cuckolding these accommodating people.

"So you've found yourself a job, then." She tried to sound both casual and dismissive.

"I'm helping out an old friend."

He claimed ownership of the hamlet's residents – they were his allies. He made it sound as though he visited Claude Jopert every Christmas – or perhaps Thanksgiving. She searched for some words to wound him, but he interrupted her quest.

"Claude's finding this kind of stuff heavy going now, but he doesn't believe in going to the hardware store and getting new. He told me that on a good farm you only buy iron and salt – that's what his father taught him. I think those days have come to an end. You'd tell Claude to sell up and move to an old folk's home. Is that right, Lily?"

He picked up the long-handled mallet again and rested it on the toe of his boot. "This place could do with young blood."

"And you've got it, I suppose."

"I wasn't thinking of myself, but they've got me now."

"What do you mean – they've got you? You think you're going to stay here? You think you can just take over the hermitage and live here permanently?"

"It crossed my mind. Achallat is a pretty special place – and my memory didn't do justice to the hermitage. It has a simple beauty I've seen nowhere else. Don't you remember that, Lily? Have you been across to look at it? I wake up each morning with that great smell – and then I have your painting too."

She did not see his expression. As soon as he spoke of the hermitage her eyes hunted for something to occupy them.

"I find it hard to think of the negatives of living here." He grinned at her through his wet hair.

"You're insane. There are too many negatives to list. You don't belong here; this isn't your place; you're trespassing. Do I need to go on?"

He seemed amused. He leaned against a sturdy piece of the fencing and folded his arms, waiting for more.

"For another thing – it's not hygienic. You can't just camp over there indefinitely."

He mulled over her words, his head to one side. "Are you inviting me to use the facilities at Chez Reynat, because if you are, I accept gladly."

"Why are you doing this? I just don't understand." Her voice caught and she wiped rain from her cheeks. There would be no tears. She had years of practice to help her control them. With the water dripping from his chin he turned back to the work in hand and picked up his mallet.

Lily barely ventured outside the thick walls of Felix's house. She bought from the visiting grocer and baker, hurrying back past the tent, now so heavy with rain that Lily doubted its occupant could do more than lie down. She bolted the door behind her, locking herself in as much as her trespassers out – she felt insubstantial as though she might merge with the landscape.

The rain had kept Baptistin at bay. One day, at the sound of her name shouted out, she jumped from her chair, but she recognised the voice the second time it hailed her. She stood in shadow to watch Gabriel, legs astride, looking from one window to the next.

He gave up waiting for her appearance and just yelled at the stone wall. "I'd like to use your boat for a while if that's okay by you. You'll get it back – you never know, you might want to pay me a visit sometime."

When he had rowed well away from the riverbank, Lily risked leaving the house to stand under the chestnut tree. On the river, he dropped the oars, letting the boat drift to rest against the causeway, and then he threw a line into the water. He sat with his back to her and she guessed that his mind was as poised as his motionless body. Did he hear the same babbling voices that she had heard that day as she too drifted on the Vamaleau? She doubted it.

*

With a swollen belly, Lily had taken the boat out with a white dress and a grey stone on her lap. She had dropped her oars and looked down into the obscure depths. Her fingers had stroked the red stitching and the pretty bird, his beak open in song for one last time and then she rolled the cloth around the stone. She had searched for the right one behind Felix's barn. Oddo spoke to her, she had thought, but then it had sounded like more than one voice – perhaps the Vamaleau was not one entity, but a host, rippling and weaving through the valley. The voices had told her she would never leave Achallat, that her husband would never return to find her, and they promised her an easy forgetfulness. With her dress she had plummeted towards the host – towards Oddo. She had recognised him instantly with his translucent skin and his clear blue eyes.

But like a good fisherman, Felix had caught her. He had dived into his river and fished her out, pulling her back to daylight and air.

"Oddo does not want you – and I will not let the river have you."

The following day Felix studied Lily hard. She felt his eyes on her as she stood at the window; as she played with his food.

"How did you manage to fall in the water from the boat?" he asked, his eyes scrutinising her face.

Lily shrugged listlessly. She was brushing her hair at her mirror, unable to escape the hard gaze.

"Why were you out there on the river? And why that dress?" Felix had tried to dispose of 'that dress' himself, telling Lily that it was only a painful memory for her. "You have no liking for the water – there was no reason for you to be there. I do not believe you were going to the island – you have not been there since…"

She shook her head and put her hands to her unborn baby.

"Lily, I am not convinced you fell."

Felix paced the floor, his hands restlessly finding each other and then making fists. With eyes like glass, he suddenly shouted, "Why will you not forget him? He is nothing – he is of no importance to us here. He deserted you, Lily. I would never have left you, no matter what. Nothing, no one could have persuaded me to leave you."

Lily put down the brush. Felix's face had reddened, the blush rising from his throat and reaching the tips of his ears.

"Why are you saying that? What do you mean?"

Felix turned for the bedroom door, muttering, "Nothing. I meant nothing."

Lily ran after him down the dark corridor and put a hand to his shoulder.

"Felix, do you know why Gabriel left me? You know, and you've never said?"

With his back to the uneven wall, Felix's eyes wandered, but found nothing on which to rest. He studied his feet for a while and then looked at Lily – oddly, she thought. The colour had left his cheeks. She waited for his words.

"There was a woman. A friend's wife, I believe."

"What woman?"

"I believe her name was Gwen. Yes, I remember – it was Gwen."

"You're just making this up," Lily accused, her eyes narrowing. "That was just some talk – Ken told me, it was just talk. How do you know all this?"

"I hear everything," Felix answered, and the blood rushed again to his face.

"I heard them talk, Lily – Mason and the other one – Oki. They talked about the woman that Gabriel left in America – somebody else's woman."

His eyes were fixed on Lily, hungry for a reaction. She turned towards her bedroom door, but her feet would not move. She swallowed again, and again, trying not to be sick. Her brow was icy cold; she blinked dry-eyed.

Her voice was even when she said, "He's gone then. I have no husband."

*

Lily remembered now as she watched Gabriel fish on the Vamaleau. That was the day that she had stopped waiting for him.

CHAPTER TWENTY

Lily listened to the symphony of raindrops, drumming at the canvas, tapping at the well roof. And then with a dissatisfied grunt, she turned away from the decrepit tent – she had studied it for long enough. The Romany was secretive, Baptistin had said, but Lily began to suspect he was part spectre.

When she spotted the large black holdall on the wellhead step, Lily realised it may be her chance to get a glimpse of the phantom. Almost on tiptoe she approached it with one eye on the tent. Her eye was drawn to the oblong bulge in the compartment on one side. The shape matched the size of a wallet. A wallet might hold an identity card – and that would have a photograph.

With her hair falling around her, Lily stooped to draw back the zipper. The unmistakeable metallic noise rang out towards the empty couderc. Lily's fingers twitched. She inched the zip along its groove until it was far enough along for her to slide her hand down the opening. Her fingers felt paper.

Behind her curtain, Lily had missed the approaching boots. Their owner scraped them along the step – to get her attention, it seemed.

"That's mine."

Jerking up, Lily came face to face with Claude Jopert. The portly man was light on his feet.

Perhaps he mistook her expression of surprise for disbelief, because Claude quickly added, "It's not mine exactly. It belongs to a friend of mine."

He scooped up the bag and jostled it from one hand to the other as if he were afraid she would wrestle it from him. "It's

Gabriel's – I mean the American's. I offered to do his washing for him. Well, not me – my wife's going to do it. I'm too set in my ways now to do that sort of thing and Marie's good at it anyway, so there's no need." His face was directed at Lily, but the farmer's eyes were on the tent. "Gabriel gave it to me this morning – here at the well. I don't know how, I just forgot it – left it here. Marie, said to me a few minutes ago – well, where's the washing then? You're getting old, Claude." Jopert slapped his forehead hard, leaving a pink imprint. "You see – I'd forgotten it. So I had to come back for it. After all, a man needs clean clothes."

Lily's head had begun to list with Jopert's first flustered words, and now she eyed him with an arched neck. Pulling her head straight, she gave it an indifferent shake.

"He's your friend, I know, Monsieur Jopert. You don't need to explain." Or make excuses, Lily almost added.

She looked at the holdall quite differently now. Her hand felt the shame of almost rummaging around in Gabriel's dirty clothes. Of course, he had no laundry facilities over at the hermitage – he would rely on the good neighbours of Achallat.

With the bag clutched to his chest Jopert trotted off towards the gate pillars. He paused and turned, but seemed not to be looking at Lily. She turned too, but saw nothing.

At the end of the couderc, Claude Jopert halted. Water had gathered at the foot of the gate and now the posts rose out of a small lagoon. At its edge, Jopert heaved the holdall over his head and launched it into the meadow as though it were an American football. Lily saw it land upside down just beyond the flood. Pulling his hat down firmly, Claude skirted the timber fence and, testing a rail, he hurdled it. He turned and gave her an amiable wave.

Lily was watching his ambling gait when something caught her eye. Pushing back wet hair and narrowing her eyes, she peered through the criss-cross of gate pillars and fence rails. It was as if curiosity aroused already, she needed to satisfy it somehow. At the edge of the field, Lily could clearly see a white envelope. Without hesitating she found the same sturdy rail and a minute later stood at the fireplace with the letter in her hand.

The ink was smudged and pellets of mud obliterated some of the words, but Lily had no difficulty in recognising Felix's handwriting. She studied the size of the envelope, the weight and bulk of the letter. Her fingers felt along the perimeter of the paper. It was simply a letter, she decided. Wiping away the dirt as best she could, she put her find on the table and stood back.

"So this is it – your letter from Felix," she said aloud. Her hand was drawn to it – she picked it up and inspected the postmark, but it was barely legible. Pulling out a chair, Lily sat down to the task, wanting to discover all she could from a stained and smudged piece of paper.

Lily listed all the people to whom Felix might have written – perhaps even Mason: he had had a sort of respect for him. Gabriel was a nobody – those had been Felix's words – a nobody. Would you think of a nobody in your final weeks? She was perplexed.

But Felix had not used that dismissive word at first, she recalled.

*

When Lily had returned to Achallat in an autumn heavy with fruit, Felix had assured her that Gabriel was due to return – he was in the south of France, travelling with his friend, Mason. Lily had not questioned how Felix had known this – she was too eager for it to be true. The leaves dropped brittle and brown and the birds fell silent.

On Christmas Eve, Felix drove Lily and Baptistin to the church of Saint Bénigne les Fontaines, and they all shared Christ's body and blood at midnight Mass. Some worshippers regarded Lily with curiosity; others shook

Felix's hand in congratulation; and one or two men slapped his back. He grinned too much for Lily's liking.

Back at Chez Reynat, Baptistin, Honorine and her husband joined them for the Réveillon – the meal in honour of the Christ-child's birth. Felix had placed candles on every surface that would accommodate one – the mantelpiece, the hearth, the treads of the staircase and of course the table, laid with the Reynat silver and Limoges porcelain. The fire blazed and Felix's cooking, which had begun early that morning, scented the house. The Réveillon would be a long drawn out affair.

Lily watched the bright faces in the candlelight as a child observes the grown-ups at a meal. She could not quite understand their joyfulness, but she was pleased for the levity of the atmosphere and relieved that she was not expected to participate. When the last course left the table and the diners sat back, glassy eyed and subdued, Felix fetched a child's recorder. With renewed spirit, the residents of Achallat sang old carols with tremulous voices, often forgetting the words.

A slab of chocolate in her hand and a brown stain at her lips, Lily gazed out and wished for snow. She wished for Gabriel too.

She was already asleep on the sofa when the guests, fatigued by their singing, departed, shouting farewells up the pitch lane. Through her own sleepy fog, Lily opened her eyes to see Felix watching her. He sat on the edge of the hearth with his elbows on his knees and his eyes black in the firelight. He had rebuilt the fire, but the candles had burnt down and the only light in the room came from the sparking logs.

"Happy Christmas. Look your sabot is here on the hearth."

Felix picked up the wooden clog and, without rising, he handed it to her, kneeling now at the foot of the sofa. Lily wriggled upright and found the box, wrapped in scarlet paper and tied with ribbon.

"Open it, open it," Felix urged.

The look in his eyes was so intense that Lily had no wish to, but with the festive paper on her knees she looked down at the gift held between her thumb and forefinger. Tiny stones decorated a gold band.

"They are rubies. This was my mother's ring and my grandmother's before that."

Felix took the ring and reached for her finger. She heard him breathe – a sound of victory it seemed to Lily. She jerked her hand away.

"What are you doing? I'm already married."

His mouth tightened and he took her other hand, sliding the band onto her middle finger.

"There is no harm in this finger, surely."

It hung slackly on Lily's small hand and, with a small but deliberate flick, the ring fell to the floor.

"What's this about Felix?" She need not have asked – she knew. She knew in church. She saw the knowing smiles; heard the whispered felicitations.

"He's not coming is he? He never was. You said you knew his address in America – I want to write to him."

Felix was not listening. He was scrabbling at the cushions, searching for the ring. When he found it he held it up to the firelight.

"It's too big for your delicate hand. I can put it on a chain for you and that way you can wear it around your neck."

"Were you lying to me?"

"Why would I lie? I know his address. You should write to him today – a Christmas letter. Tell him about your life at Achallat. You write your letter and I will post it for you. It's morning already – I'll make you some breakfast."

When he was assured that she would eat her eggs and fruit, Felix retired to bed. He was gone for the best part of the day and Lily made the most of her time alone, writing and rewriting her letter at the table with the unwashed dishes and melted beeswax around her.

She did not move from the makeshift desk. She was dissatisfied with her work: the words were insufficient; the handwriting clumsy and childish. Eventually the letter was finished, she placed it in an envelope, propped it up against a faïence candlestick and waited for Felix to wake.

*

Lily stared at this other letter, leaning against the same blue and green candlestick. She would return it to Gabriel when she next saw him, she told herself – commanded herself. But his movements were unknown to her, and she had been, after all, doing her best to avoid him. All day the letter teased her, its starkness on the dark wood catching her eye. Her mind wandered to the making of it. Felix would have closed up the house, having boxed away all his belongings for the charity shop, locked the great oak door with his ancient key and set off for the hospital with an overnight case. He must have taken a taxi or, more likely, Claude Jopert had driven him. He had remembered to take his favourite pen and some good notepaper though. That was the Felix she remembered – everything planned and thought out. She pictured him propped up against a mountain of pillows, thinking hard before he set pen to paper. Now Lily convinced herself that it was not Gabriel's letter at all – it was Felix's and he would be happy for her to read it. She could see his approving face. Have I ever hidden anything from you, Lily? Read my letter.

The matter was settled. She plucked the letter from the table and within seconds the empty envelope dropped to the floor.

"*Dear Friend,*" it began in English, setting out their relationship immediately. Lily could hardly remember Felix and Gabriel exchanging more than a few words – usually about the coffee. She was puzzled that, all these years later, Felix considered him a friend. She saw now that the whole hamlet seemed to regard Gabriel in the same light. Claude

Jopert's wife was probably at that moment hanging his T-shirts and jeans in the barn to dry. For some reason, Gabriel aroused warm-heartedness, even devotion.

"*It has been a long time since we spoke that night in Jopert's stable. Do you remember? You must, because upsetting times stay etched in our hearts. If I could take back those words, I would. Who has not tried to change the course of love.*

I am in the hospital at Aubaine. I will never return to Chez Reynat. I need to speak to you before I die. My doctor tells me that it will take only weeks, but I believe him to be an optimist. So, you see, it is a matter of urgency. There are things that cannot be told by pen and paper. I need to face you, the way I will face my Maker very soon. He will be happier with me, I think, if I have tried to make amends.

I have written to Lily yesterday. These things must be said to both of you. Perhaps you are surprised that I speak of Lily. You would think that she left Achallat too, that the summer of 1970 was forgotten here on the banks of the Vamaleau. But Lily came back to me and had a child.

I must stop – this letter is not meant for explanations. I intend that you come here to France and discover them. I want you to have questions in your mind now – questions that will be answered. The past has hidden in shadow too long."

It was signed, '*A Penitent*'.

Lily stared at the droplets of water pock-marking the window pane and searched the mist beyond. The letter was a puzzle. Had she misunderstood something?

Her eyes returned to the top of the page to read again and, perhaps, make more sense of Felix's guilt when she heard the floorboard groan. She recognised the defective piece of wood – the one that always complained near the hallway. It was as if it wished to announce the arrival of every visitor to the house.

In her haste to bring back the letter Lily had forgotten to shut the door. Seeing Gabriel stride towards her, she jumped from the chair, her cheeks hot pink in an instant. He left a trail of muddy puddles behind him, but she saw only the anger flash from his eyes.

"You've got something of mine." His words cut through the room.

Ashen faced, Lily dropped the letter to the table.

"Do you usually read other people's letters?"

"I wasn't thinking of you when I opened it – I was thinking of Felix."

Gabriel's face creased with discomfort and then gave an imperceptible nod. "Why do you always disappoint me, Lily?"

The ugly noise she heard was almost a laugh – it had erupted from her own mouth.

"That's your excuse for up and leaving? I disappointed you? Don't go into the details, please – spare my feelings. Take your letter. Felix talked a lot of nonsense – his letters are no better. Why don't you just pack your stuff and go."

"You can't get rid of me that easily, Lily."

She was dumbfounded. It had been effortless once. She had done it in her sleep: some unknown, unconscious thing. He had evaporated, almost as if he had never existed – not a trace of him left in Achallat. He had been as ephemeral as the mist on the water.

CHAPTER TWENTY-ONE

As Achallat's first lonely swallow swooped over the Vamaleau, Lily telephoned Dominic.

"Come," she said.

Two days later he swept open the oak door and dropped his bag to the floor.

His open smile seemed to assuage the ghosts of the Reynat family – the rooms seemed lighter. Lily busied herself eagerly in the kitchen and they sat opposite each other with her offering. She beamed at the two glasses, two plates, two sets of cutlery. Dominic talked of university and Lily listened, nodding to encourage him, relieved to hear of another life outside of Achallat and hopeful that they could avoid the subject of the house sale for the first evening.

Gazing up at the beams, he rose from the table and walked tentatively to the staircase as if he feared to disturb his sleeping father. Lily heard the boards creak as he roamed the first floor of the house, and then the second floor. With the used plates in her hand she listened keenly to the cautious tread. He returned, his face difficult to read as he opened drawers and pulled books from shelves. When he reached Felix's locked cupboard in the fireplace alcove, he turned to Lily.

"I can't find the key," she said with a shrug. "There's not much in there – only some old stuff about the house."

It had been the one oddity – that Felix had left his hideaway locked. Perhaps he intended that his precious papers would always remain – never to be thrown out in an overzealous houseclean. He knew Lily well, after all.

Lily studied Dominic's face, gauging his reaction to his first home.

"Weird bunch of records," Dominic declared, kneeling down to the record player and flicking through the row. He perused each sleeve, tossing some aside dismissively and studying others in depth.

"So are they yours or Papa's?"

That word 'Papa'. She felt the falsehood stab her – the very word itself had come to mean lie.

"They're not mine." She denied ownership of anything in that room. "Some of them were left here."

"Who by?"

Lily frowned, annoyed at herself – she had manoeuvred the conversation down the wrong path. "Different people. Felix liked to play host."

Dominic sat on his haunches with his back against the archaic music centre. He took in her words as if he tried to imagine Chez Reynat in a time before his birth.

"He did? Good idea too, in a place like this – you could get seriously unhinged here. I thought the farm was isolated, but this…"

"It's not isolated, Dom. There are houses all around. Chez Reynat isn't on its own."

She was surprised at herself, playing devil's advocate for the old place. They looked at each other for an instant and, recognising the familiar drawing of swords between parent and child, they laughed.

Lily saw the laugh with new eyes – that simple expression that had once bestowed pleasure to her, now caused her anguish, for she saw in it, Gabriel's face. A knot formed in her stomach as she became convinced that the two owners of the same expression would see the lie immediately.

On his first morning, Dominic explored the exterior of Chez Reynat. At first she wandered with him: checking out the enormous barn; looking down the dark tunnel of the well; gazing up at the dizzying walls. Dominic walked around the tent alone and when he headed for the river, Lily returned to the house. She had almost said, 'there's nothing interesting there, Dom,' but heard the folly in the words before they reached her tongue. Having beckoned him here, she could hardly lock him up indoors. Instead she turned her attention to the dishwashing, determined not to spy on him from the tiny kitchen window.

When Lily heard the animated voices she ignored them – she had become used to the bickering and chortling of her neighbours on the couderc. Then she dropped the cloth.

"Oh God," she moaned as if she needed his help already. She rushed to the door, but she was too late – Dominic and Gabriel were united at the well. The birch, now in full leaf, threw a flickering shadow over them. Its catkins hung low, dusting the little rust roof with their green pollen.

They stood opposite each other, mirror like; pushing their hair back with strong fingers; grinning boyishly with hands squeezed into pockets. Lily wanted to pull her son's hand down from his head, to move his legs into any other posture than the one aping his father.

Gabriel scooped a small bottle out of the bucket and gulped down the water.

"So you drink this stuff?" Dominic asked incredulously. He had peered down the well an hour earlier with Lily, disbelieving that it was still in use. "How do you know it's safe? Anything could live down there." He leaned over the void again.

Gabriel smiled and nodded. "Guess so." He held out the water. "You won't taste better."

Dominic held the bottle for a while, studied its contents, and then tipped it to his lips.

"You didn't tell me we had a lodger, Mum." Dominic spoke to Lily at the doorstep, but his eyes were pinned on the fascinating stranger.

"You want to come by and see the place? It's humble, but it's got history – a lot of history. And I'll show you a thing of wonder there." Gabriel glanced at Lily and then spoke again to the younger man. "Then maybe we could get in some fishing. Do you fish?"

"Fish? I think I caught a goldfish once at the Silsby show."

"It's time you learned."

Lily felt ice in her chest. The father would teach the son.

"Where did you get the tackle?" she demanded, lunging forward, the ice cracking through her voice. "You've been rifling through Felix's things in the barn, haven't you? It belongs to Felix – you have no right."

Under the trees, Lily heard the refrain, 'Bless our well and give a son…' She shot a look at Gabriel, almost afraid that he had heard it too; afraid that it had floated up from the floor of the well.

"I'm not a thief, Lily. Nothing's stolen. Not by me anyways." His eyes lingered a while and then flicked away.

Lily remembered the letter, and hid her thief's hands in her pockets. Dominic seemed to see a woman strange to him and he put a hand to her shoulder.

"So Mum – Papa fished. I didn't know about that. I don't remember."

Lily ignored his obvious tactics of diversion, but she looked up quickly to search Gabriel's face carefully for a reaction to Dominic's words. Would he flinch at the word 'Papa', as she did? But he had turned to face the river and she was left to study the back of his head.

Wordlessly, the pair ambled to the water's edge and Lily watched the son unknowingly copy the father's gait. Early blossom drifted like snow on the Vamaleau as Gabriel rowed Dominic to the island that was now his. Her enemy had taken her one time sanctuary, and a vengeful river separated her from her only solace – her son.

She stood under the vivid green canopy of the chestnut as the two men climbed out of her boat on the other bank. Slumping wearily to the earth, she dropped her head to her hands.

The chatter of the river rose and the trees responded, but above them both Lily recognised a purring engine as it entered the hamlet. It was nothing like the throaty drone of Claude Jopert's car or the sewing machine rattle of Honorine's. It pulled up on the other side of the well and Lily heard the door open with a feeling of greater weariness. She pushed her hair from her eyes and pulled her face into a demeanour of relaxed optimism.

Venetia spotted Lily and diverted her business-like march from the front door to skirt around the tent's guy ropes. She trod carefully through the boggy grass towards her difficult client.

"I see there's been no progress." She jerked her head in the direction of the tent.

Lily was unable to offer any excuses and was too fatigued to invent a story. She thought it would be more polite to stand, but she stayed where she was, her legs outstretched in the dirt.

"So how are you doing with your troublesome neighbours?" Venetia persisted.

"My troublesome neighbours," Lily repeated, defeat in her voice. "They don't see things quite the way we do. They think they have a mission."

"And what mission is that?" Venetia had asked the question, but already she seemed impatient with the pace of the conversation. She pulled out a cigarette from her handbag and lit up.

"To keep Chez Reynat as it is – the house, the well, the river. To keep something they think is special. To keep me here, I think."

With the cigarette between her lips, Venetia made a sniggering sound. "And why would they do that? They don't seem to think that highly of you."

"They think it's my destiny – that the river has chosen me."

Perhaps it's not me it's chosen, after all, Lily thought and her gaze wandered to the hermitage with its moat of bright spring grass. Venetia let the ash drift down as she looked at Lily askance. Suddenly she waved her hand in front of her face, her eyes and mouth creased into a frown.

"It's about time Achallat joined the real world, isn't it? I know you won't mind me saying this, and I don't mean to offend, but this house is in need of some updating – don't think I didn't notice as we did the tour. There's quite a bit of damp in there. While I'm all for rustic style, people expect a certain amount of comfort – central heating for one. As for the other houses in the hamlet… I'd love to see the inside of them. I can just imagine the plumbing. But that's why we're here."

"I should take you to Lack Farm."

"Sorry?"

When Lily did not bother to explain, Venetia smiled pertly. Her face dropped suddenly and her arm rose again – this time to shake her hair, but she had forgotten the cigarette grasped between her fingers. "You have a bit of a problem here with mosquitoes," she said hoarsely, flinging the burning stick to the ground. The odour of singed hair wafted towards Lily.

"Mosquitoes? I don't think…" Lily started to say, but then saw the thick grey mist floating around the woman. It rose and fell, but remained obstinately like a gossamer cocoon around its chosen host. Venetia's hands were now both working hard to keep the insects at bay as she began slapping at her chest, neck and arms. She clawed at her hair, shaking out the grips and slides, uttering small grunts as her palms hit their target.

Lily picked herself up from the dirt. "We should go inside."

Venetia's body began to shake, her hands flapping madly. Then she gave a strangled scream as she pulled her foot from the grass.

"What the hell is that? Snakes, snakes! My God, there are snakes everywhere!"

She hopped from foot to foot, her heels delving deeper into the mire with each step. Lily saw Venetia sway and put out an arm. And then they both heard the first croak.

With a voice intended to convey calmness, Lily said quietly, "It's only frogs. It's the time of year – they've come here to mate. They've come out of the reeds for some reason."

Lily looked back at the marshy area on the river's edge as if the reason would be apparent. The Vamaleau rumbled. Its current had paused, but the water was not still – it seemed to tremble. Venetia's cries became more frantic as she leapt from foot to foot. Aiming to leap over the creatures congregated at her feet, Venetia finally lost her balance. She wavered in mid-air at an impossible to sustain angle and then keeled over, dropping heavily to the green bog.

Paralysed, Lily watched the woman stagger upright and then, partly on her knees, haul herself up the slope like an injured animal. Venetia turned as she reached the safety of her car.

"I'll never step foot in this God forsaken hole again – and I'll make sure no client of mine does either – nor anybody else's. This place is evil. You'll never sell."

The boat stabbed at the riverbank and its two occupants jumped ashore with mimicking strides.

"Who have you fallen out with this time, Mum?" Dominic grinned as the car screeched out of the couderc.

Lily turned back to her son and forgetful husband with hollow eyes. She wanted to tell someone that she did not know what to do. She was as alone now as the day she fell into the Vamaleau. That was how she wanted to remember it. The falling through the dark waters had seemed easy and fortuitous – the solution to her problems.

The river did not call her this time, but Lily left the riverbank all the same. She pulled Felix's car keys from her pocket and tramped up the incline to the barn, calling to Dominic with an insistent voice.

"Come on, we're going to the notaire's."

"Now? It's lunchtime – it'll be closed."

Lily stopped mid-stride and turned round. She saw a recalcitrant look in his eye, but, more she saw how he now viewed her. She had changed, he thought.

"Now, Dom. That's why you're here, isn't it? Not to fish and mess about with boats, but to deal with the legal stuff. That's what we talked about on the phone."

Dominic pulled a hand through his hair. "What's up, Mum?"

"We have to find someone to sell this…" Lily stopped herself and took a deep breath. "We have to find a different agent, Dom. Are you coming?"

He walked up to her slowly and put a hand on each shoulder. "I've only just got here. It's all so different than I remembered – than I expected. I need some time – I'm not ready for the legal stuff yet."

Lily pushed his arms away and ran to the car.

At twelve thirty-five La Petite Aubaine was deserted, but Lily did not notice. She was unaware of the closed shops, the empty streets. There were no shoppers or pushchairs to avoid on the narrow pavement. She was oblivious to the stubborn rain.

Lily arrived at the doorway at the end of the rue Bonne Fontaine, checked the brass nameplate and pushed at the central knob. The door refused to move. Lily pressed the bell – and then hit it with a fist. Someone hollered from above her, from an open window above the wool shop next door.

"He's at lunch – you'll have to come back," the woman shouted. Seeing no reaction in Lily, she spoke more slowly – she was used to seeing English visitors stop at the notaire's office. "Come back at three o'clock – three o'clock. It is lunchtime. Do you understand?"

On the empty street Lily waited.

The notaire was a compact man with a face that had grown so accustomed to smiling that his mouth was fixed in a benign expression, the corners turned like tiny kiss curls. He had had a pleasurable lunch at home and now hurried through the drizzle towards his office. Recognising Lily from a distance, he gave her a nod, but as he neared her, his satisfied expression changed to one of concern. He ushered the bedraggled woman into the building and offered her a coffee, but Lily shook her head and blurted out that she no longer had a contract with Venetia Crow.

"And Dominic is here now at Achallat so we can sort out all the legal papers. I want it done as quickly as possible, monsieur."

"I am pleased your son has arrived and we can see to the rest of the paperwork, of course."

He put his hands on his handsome desk and drew his fingers along as though smoothing out the leather top. He glanced at Lily and then at the window, and then more confident that he had composed his thoughts, he cleared his throat.

"But I'm sorry that I cannot help you, Madame, with the other matter. There are so many properties at the moment. My books are quite full. I am one man and my legal work is my priority."

"But Chez Reynat isn't just another property. It's a special place."

Lily searched her mind and found Venetia's words, hoping they would inspire another property expert. "It's a rural idyll. You'll have no problem selling it. It's enchanting – it's what people are looking for – a dream."

The permanent smile fell. "I'm sorry, Madame. It's not a very populated part of France here. It's not Paris or Lyons or even Limoges. I imagine there, one can ignore one's neighbours. Here news travels. I have heard of your difficulties and I must tell you that I cannot sell your house. I cannot help you."

Sat in the Renault, Lily stared ahead at the condensation on one side of the screen and the mizzle on the other. Eventually the market square and the world disappeared from her view.

CHAPTER TWENTY-TWO

Lily walked down the long aisle to the front row, unaware of the wet sweater clinging to her back and chest. Dark stone walls, candles, deep coloured damask at the altar – these were things that comforted those that sought consolation. Around her painted Madonnas looked down with sad, knowing eyes. From the foot of Christ's cross, Mary had no help to give another mother.

Caked mud cracked underneath her as she bent down to the simple wooden chair. The soaked jeans and the sodden espadrilles scratching at her soles should have caused discomfort. She was only slightly bemused by her state. The last thing she remembered was leaving the notaire's office in La Petite Aubaine.

To one side of the nave, a tray of candles blinked on a cloth covered table. She was drawn to them, moth like, having no notion of their meaning. Did they burn to aid the souls of the dead? Or were they supplication for those still living? She counted them. Six candles: perhaps lit by six people grieving; or for six people in torment. She picked up one of the long spills and struck it to a seventh candle.

At the back of the church the door groaned and then thudded closed on its green padding.

The heavy fragrance of the building reminded Lily of the hermitage. "For you, Felix," she said into the empty nave. "I hope you've been absolved of whatever sin you imagined. I'm sure you pleased God well enough. I should have come – I'm sorry. I wished you'd drunk your water."

The flame at the new wick sparked, burning brightly as if Felix's soul had heard her and responded. It settled down and flickered weakly like the other six.

"Do you think he's listening to you?"

She had not heard the footsteps.

"I saw the Renault on the square," Gabriel said as if this explained his presence. "Claude let me borrow his car – Dom was worried about you."

She heard him say her son's name with such intimacy – not even Dominic.

"You disappeared for twenty years and now I can't get away from you – you're everywhere." She heard her voice, thin and distant.

"Isn't forgiveness the hardest thing?"

Lily was unsure what he meant. "There was nothing to forgive with Felix."

She could have said so much more – he gave me a home, he gave my son a father – even for a short while. At least Dominic has someone to call Papa.

Gabriel pulled his mouth taut.

"I lit the candle just to remember him – that's all."

Gabriel lowered himself into a chair on the front row. Leaning forward, he rested his arms on his knees as if in prayer, but his eyes were directed at Lily. He let out a long sigh.

"Was he a good father?" There was a roughness to his voice.

Many answers formed in her mind: he did his best; I didn't give him much of a chance.

"Yes." Her half-hearted reply shamed her.

Behind her, Lily felt the heat of the candles at the small of her back. Her sweater lifted from her skin, creeping away, warm and damp. But the rest of her body was gelid. Shivers juddered up her chest, one violent spasm after another. She watched Gabriel rise, take off his jacket and slip it over her shoulders. As he pulled the collar round, she felt his hands through the wet wool. At the touch, she flinched and a spasm not of cold, but of revulsion sent the jacket to the stone floor. Gabriel stooped, retrieved it, and placed it over her again.

This time she shook herself free deliberately. With a half-smile, he pushed her hair from her brow, leaving his thumbs on her cold skin for a moment.

"Always wilful, Lily."

She heard her father's rebuke, but Gabriel's tone was different. Jack always sounded so brow-beaten by what fate had handed him, so dissatisfied with his own handiwork. He had done his best with his daughter, but what is a widower to do? The look in Gabriel's eyes suggested something different as he uttered the phrase. He left the sheepskin on the floor and sat down again.

"He was a good man," she declared. Her lukewarm yes had done a disservice to Felix and she wanted to make amends.

Gabriel made a guttural noise. "Felix liked his secrets, but then so do you, Lily."

"He was a good man," she said more emphatically.

"Light your candle for him then."

"How dare you – you of all people – say anything against Felix. He was honourable."

Gabriel looked like something had hit him.

"You." She choked on the word. "You made a solemn vow seem like something of no importance. You just walked away – back to your lover. You behaved deceitfully to everyone."

Gabriel jumped up from the chair, almost kicking it away, and then fell back into it.

"You want to know about Gwen, I guess. Do you recall us talking about hell? We were on the riverbank and you were making a chain of flowers. It was too beautiful a day to talk about something like that. Even Mason came out and watched the river. Do you remember?"

"No, I don't remember."

She saw the aggrieved smile and knew he recognised the lie.

"It doesn't matter. When I got back from Vietnam I was no different to a lot of guys, I guess – messed up. I'd seen how easy it was." Lily saw him swallow. "Just like hunting. That's what some said – a good day's hunting. Life and death was easy. I just wanted to live – and I asked myself why I wasn't dead…" He stopped as if he could not quite decide on his words.

"I don't recall how it started with Gwen and it doesn't matter now – it was a long time ago. Ancient history. 'I'd like to get away from earth awhile' that's what Robert Frost wrote and that's how I felt. He didn't want fate to snatch him away though. 'Earth's the right place for love.' Perhaps I thought I was in love. Art didn't notice – and Gwen thought he didn't care. I guess she was trying to provoke him."

Gabriel stared at his shoes as he spoke and Lily wondered whether he had forgotten she was there. Medieval timbers overhead groaned, adjusting themselves infinitesimally; the church bells rang out from the tower.

"I needed to get away and Mason brought me to Europe. 'I'll guide you out of Hades,' he told me. "He rowed me across the Styx and brought me to Elysium."

Lily's back was hot now, the wool burning her skin, the smell of lanolin more powerful than the sweeter incense. Hearing the words from Gabriel's mouth was so much worse than when they came from Felix's.

"So you went back to her then."

He pushed his hands through his hair and stayed with his elbows in mid-air, his hands interlaced behind his head.

"That's not why I left Achallat."

With a soft pattering tread, the curé began to approach the couple, then changed his mind and retreated.

"Did you love him?" Gabriel asked.

"Yes."

He bent for his jacket at her feet, and then followed the clergyman.

Lily watched him walk down the aisle; watched his back disappear through the green door, and then she turned back to the candles. A statue of Saint Bénigne stood in a niche in the wall above her. He carried a pair of pails, suspended on a simple branch balanced across his shoulders. With his left hand up to steady the pole, and the other outstretched, palm upwards, he looked down on Lily with china blue eyes.

With a wet trail at her marble-cold cheeks, Lily put a forefinger and thumb to her tongue and set them to the candlewick. Her father would be proud of her, not wasting a candle. After all, there was no hope.

CHAPTER TWENTY-THREE

Lily ignored the dizzy ache in her head and the chill gripping her stomach, and walked to the riverbank as if the power of the Vamaleau was stronger than any bodily discomfort. She expected to see Dominic, lounging under one of the trees, or even on the other bank, but there was no sign of him. The empty boat swayed about, tapping at the jetty.

At the staircase she shouted his name, knowing there would be no reply. Light-headed, she reached out to the banister to steady herself. 'Empty,' she said and gazed around the room to confirm this. Catching sight of a reflection in the square panes of the window, she realised that the vacant eyed ghost was not another Reynat phantom, but herself.

Lily escaped the airless house. The fine rain had given way to a claustrophobic mist. The tent, drying out patchily, looked like a camouflage fabric with formless shapes of grey, from palest bone to ash. She stumbled at a guy rope, but she felt no irritation now. She was past that – she knew that the gypsy would never leave and that she would never be able to sell Chez Reynat. Gabriel would hound her. He was immovable, like rock, and she was just water as intangible as mist. She leaned over the well and gazed down at the emptiness.

From the black space came voices filled with joy. Lily recalled Felix's description of an ancient Achallat – a dwelling place busy with people and life. Perhaps it was another world – a place where Felix and the Reynats lived. She held her breath, concentrating, and heard Dominic's voice sounding out above the others. In his slow emphatic

French, he demanded, "You must speak more slowly, Monsieur. I speak only a little French."

Lily swayed as she pulled herself straight and pushed her body away from the wall. She tried to focus her mind. This time she heard him laughing – a loud, childish sound. It came not from the depths of the earth, but from the couderc. With a jarring pain cracking through her head, she squinted and looked down the empty lane. Baptistin's door was ajar and at his gatepost stood Séverine's scooter.

As she stood at his threshold, the assembled company turned as one to see the late arrival. Her appearance seemed unwelcome to some, but Baptistin, standing over his seated guests, beamed at her as if it were his birthday and, now that last guest had arrived, his party could begin.

Around the square table were seated most of Achallat. The twins occupied the back of the room, squashed together on one large chair; Jopert and his wife sat with their backs to Lily and the door; Honorine took up the upholstered seat next to the glowing stove; and Séverine was squeezed between the table and an overlarge dresser. Baptistin's best chair – an oak carver with sturdy arms and a high back – accommodated Dominic, who leaned forward, his folded arms on the table. Fanning herself with a folded newspaper, Honorine gestured to Jopert to open the window beside him.

With his hands full, Baptistin used his voice to entice in Lily, shouting, "Come in, come in, neighbour. We are all getting to know each other here." Clutching eight stumpy glasses, Baptistin surveyed his guests and banged down the tumblers on the table. At the centre of this sturdy, plain piece of furniture lay a tin of madeleine biscuits.

"We're just having a little get together, isn't that right, Dominic?"

Not understanding the words, but comprehending well enough the glasses and the smiles, Dominic grinned back at the old man.

"It's pastis all round except for Honorine. Is that right? And how about you, Lily?"

Confused, Lily shook her head.

At the back of the room the twins began a muffled but intense discussion about Honorine's love of tea and pink champagne. They disagreed – politely – on whether she had first tasted tea in Paris or not.

"So as I said, pastis all round except for Honorine – she'll make do with our good water."

"It's why her skin's so lovely," Florette wittered, "the champagne – and the water of course."

Flora patted Florette on the knee, partly to offer support, and partly to shut her up, but the others had hardly noticed the remark.

With all the tumblers filled the guests followed their host's example and raised their glasses, and in unison, chanted, "To Oddo and our well!"

Lily tipped the liquid to her mouth and leaned against the doorframe, her eyes fixed on Dominic. His mouth wobbled in a smile between politeness and amusement. As if he suddenly felt the scrutiny from his mother, he turned his head to her and mouthed, "I got dragged here." His eyes opened wide in mock horror.

Baptistin caught the exchange and, wiping his mouth with the back of his hand, he explained, "We were gathered around for our usual afternoon chat, Lily. Not the best of weathers to be out of doors, but neighbours like to exchange news and we have to get together now and then to make arrangements. In fact this concerns you. Are you alright? Here – take a madeleine." He thrust the tin in front of Lily and when she did not immediately take the offering, he shook it as though coaxing a puppy.

"As I was saying – we were discussing the next tea dance. Of course, it should take place on Tuesday next, but next week is Holy Week."

"We never have it in Holy Week," Honorine interjected, "because I go to Paris then. I like to see my niece and her family at this time of year. Although they are such a noisy household now – teenagers. Luckily, I still have my little apartment so I can escape the bedlam."

"And Holy Week is always so cold," Florette added helpfully.

"But before you know it the Good Lord's month will be here," Jopert said.

"That has nothing to do with it!" Baptistin thundered. "The weather doesn't stop us doing anything – and neither does your absence." He glowered at Honorine for a moment and then remembered that it was a festive occasion, and that he was the host. "Anyway Lily, we were discussing this, when up from the river came this fine young man to charm us all."

Pushing Séverine aside, Baptistin leaned over the table and put a hand to Dominic's cheek. He held it there for a moment, his eyes serious.

"Will you all look at that face!" Baptistin's cheeks lifted with delight.

"A good face," Claude agreed.

"And look at those eyes. Do you remember the man that kept pigs down river? He had sharp grey eyes too. But not like these. These are unusual – not many have eyes this colour. But they remind me of someone," Baptistin continued as though leader in the game. He glanced at Lily. "Not your eyes, Maman, eh?" and he raised his hand to ruffle the young man's hair.

Dominic looked around with a smile that promised to break into laughter.

"Tell me – what are you studying at this English university?" Baptistin asked, sharp eyed and earnest.

"Mathematics." Dominic answered with an inflection that suggested he was unsure if he had understood the question.

Baptistin turned to Jopert and then to Honorine. They all searched each other's faces for help. The leader of the group shrugged and the others followed suit. Honorine waved her fan with a quicker tempo as if irritated by the speed of the proceedings. Her chair squealed as she swivelled towards the young man.

"Tell us what your interests are – the things you do for enjoyment." Honorine enunciated very carefully for Dominic's benefit.

He threw up one eyebrow and looked to his mother for aid. With her glass drained Lily stood as if on the deck of a storm tossed ship, wide legged to avert a fall. The conversation coasted away from her.

"Nothing special," Dominic answered.

Honorine twisted her glass around on the table – Baptistin had forgotten to fill it in his eagerness to play host to the honoured guest. Looking at the empty receptacle, she asked, "Are you in any way interested in gardening?"

Dominic laughed. "Sorry? Do you want help?"

Her voice was sharper. "Cooking or history or poetry, perhaps?"

Putting both hands to his mop of hair, Dominic's shoulders began to shake. He banged the palm of his hand on the table as if to discipline himself and then looked back at Honorine more seriously.

"None of Felix's hobbies then," Jopert grumbled. As though he tired of the game, he thumped his empty tumbler on the table, but Baptistin chose to ignore it.

"You're a fine young man anyway," Baptistin said. "You look athletic to me with a body like that. I bet you do a lot of sports. And horses – do you ride?"

Lily opened her eyes. She had begun to stray into a grey shifting place, but now she looked at Baptistin. His eyes gleamed in a pink face, but she saw that his drink was untouched.

"I like sports – and horses. I grew up with horses. I have one at home." Dominic looked pleased with his own fluency.

Baptistin drew back his shoulders. He looked like a victor, triumphant at last. Reaching to the cluttered dresser, he picked up the bottle and, squeezing himself around the table, he refilled each glass generously.

"Come on, Honorine, you'll drink something stronger on this occasion – we have something to celebrate. I told you all that we would celebrate – now do you believe me?"

A small fluttering began in Lily's stomach. Breathless, she pulled her head from the door.

"Dom, we have to go now."

Baptistin put a hand up. "First, we must make a toast. After all we have a true son of Achallat here in our midst. You were born here, young man – and you were conceived here too. The conception is as important as the birth, you know."

Dominic screwed up his eyes, no longer understanding even the gist of the conversation. Baptistin began to raise his glass and then paused, his eyes off to one side as if he tugged at some thought.

"Soon it will be May – our Good Lord's month as my brother Claude likes to call it. A good month, don't you agree, Lily?"

Lily pushed her way past Jopert, but was stuck between the open window and the corner of the table.

"Dom, let's go. This is becoming a farce." She stretched out an arm to him, but the eager host pushed it down.

"You were born in May, weren't you, young man. I remember well now and I remember when your mother first arrived the summer before. We were invisible to you in those days, weren't we, Lily?" Her dark eyes pleaded with Baptistin, but the old man turned to her son.

"You belong here in Achallat, Dominic," Baptistin articulated carefully. He spoke slowly as if he wanted to be certain that the young Englishman would comprehend.

"This is your ancestral home. You have this right, not because of who your father is, but because you were born here. This is the way it has always been at Achallat. It was how it was for Felix. We did not care what his father was, or what uniform he wore. Your roots are here, do you understand? In this river, this earth, these trees. That's what matters. Legalities – what do they matter? A child inherits from his father. This does not matter to us at Achallat. We are not going to argue if things are not what they seem. At least, not as long as things remain the way they have always been – Chez Reynat belonging to a son of Achallat."

Dominic had concentrated this time and his brow furrowed as he attempted to make sense of it all.

"You know what I mean, Lily. We expect a change of heart from you. But mull it over – you don't look well. Let's say, we'll give you until the dance. What do you say?"

"I don't know what you're talking about." Lily's voice seemed far off; her head spun in the heat of the cramped room. She put both palms on the table.

"Please, Dom. Will you come with me now."

As if seeing his ashen faced mother for the first time, Dominic stood and, in his haste to reach her, he pushed past Honorine. This seemed to be the sign for the party to end because the whole assembly rose too.

"We all know the truth, Mademoiselle Weaver," Séverine said stridently. "It was apparent the day the young man arrived."

With clouded eyes Dominic halted at the door as if he half understood.

Lily raised her hand out in an imitation of the statue of Saint Bénigne. "Why won't you leave me alone? I don't want Chez Reynat. Isn't that obvious? It's like a curse on me. This whole place is cursed – not blessed like you're always saying. Look at you all!"

Séverine hobbled the few steps to Lily and settled her piercing eyes on her. "You hold a mirror to yourself. It is not

Achallat that is cursed. Look around, are you incapable of seeing the beauty here?"

Lily felt nauseous and dizzy, but she kept on walking towards the gate pillars.

"You cannot run away" Séverine shouted after her.

Dominic found Lily sitting on her bed, her agitated hands knotted together, her vacant eyes fixed on the wall. She had not heard him pace the corridor outside her room. He smiled at her the way she had done when he had been laid low with some childhood illness.

"Here you are, Mum."

Two sticks of baguette, covered in melted cheese overhung the plate in his hand.

"One of the few things I know how to do."

Dominic put it down on the coverlet and leaned back against the wall. Lily glanced at him briefly, her pale face questioning him. Birdsong pierced the quietness between them.

"So what's happening?" he eventually asked.

"I've just got a stinking headache, Dom, that's all. That bloody drink of Baptistin – I should've eaten something first."

She reached for the food as if to reassure her son that the only problem was alcohol on an empty stomach.

"I didn't understand that much, but there was something going on over there just now." He gazed out of the window as if to find some clarity. "And it's something to do with Papa and me. And Gabe?"

Lily grieved to hear him speak of Gabriel as a friend. "Will you go home if I ask you to, Dom?"

"Not the way you look, no. What's happened while you've been here? It feels like it's to do with me – I can't just walk away and forget it." His jaw stiffened as if he planned to say more, but did not quite have the courage.

He found an easier subject. "There's a lot I don't know – your painting, for one. I didn't even know you could paint. It's beautiful, Mum. How come I've never seen you do anything like that. Did you used to paint here when I was little?

"No, Dom. That was before you were born." Her voice was flattened.

"You should take it up again."

"I can't."

Dominic took her small hands in his. The nails had grown while she had been at Achallat, the skin had calmed, but the knuckles were still swollen.

"It's not these," she said, withdrawing them. "It's the eye. I don't see things the way I used to. I don't look at things the same way."

A voice floated up from the riverbank. They both looked at each other, recognising its owner.

"Gabe says he knew you and Papa a long time ago – before I was born. That he stayed here."

Lily's eyes were on her hands, because she could not bear to look at her son.

"He spoke about this great summer of love." Dominic's voice lightened and a brief smile appeared. "It sounded cool – I can imagine what it must've been like. There's something about this place."

Gabriel hollered Dominic's name again and this time the young man turned his head to the window. His feet shifted for a moment and then, having made a decision, he began to speak, but Lily put up a hand to wave him away, and he left the room.

In the following days, they settled into a wordless routine. Dominic would first make sure that she ate some breakfast and then he would cross the Vamaleau. He returned at a dusk that grew tardier as each day passed. They ate almost mutely, Dominic chiding his mother when she ate little.

"Why don't you want to talk about your painting?" he asked one day.

Lily was curled into the corner of the sofa, her eyes on the spitting wood that Dominic had just placed in the stove. The day was cold, but he had opened up all of the windows, keen to get some air into the dark house, as he told Lily.

"I recognise a lot of the scenes – like the one of home. You made it look a bit... well, lifeless. I suppose I can see your point – best not tell Granddad though. Then it's like a kind of travelogue through France. And then you got here, and – wow – the colours. There's a weird scene of a guy, standing on the river with a key and a book. What was all that about then? Is it some sort of religious thing?"

Dominic had settled with his legs flopped out before him at the foot of the chimneypiece, a bottle of beer in his hand. He tipped it to his mouth as he waited for an explanation.

"It's Oddo."

She was aware for the first time of her son's ignorance of his first home. He had never been told of the holy man; of the Reynat family; nor any of the history of Achallat. Instead of seeming puzzled, Dominic lifted his eyebrows and his eyes lit up.

"Yeah – Papa said something about Oddo at the hospital. And then Gabe told me all about the old guy – how you used to read him Oddo's book."

Dominic looked up to the space above Lily's head and offered a sudden wide smile.

"You should read it to Dom," Gabriel said from the door behind Lily.

She did not turn around. A week ago she kept him at the threshold by just a glare, but now she felt she would fail.

"I remember some of the words – beautiful words," Gabriel continued as he stepped inside the house. "Our lives are like the water, our thoughts are like the wind."

Dominic emptied the bottle and nodded sagely. "Yeah, but what does it mean?"

Gabriel came closer and stood at the end of the sofa. "I guess it means that we're not on our own – we're connected…

"That we're part of something bigger with its own force," Dominic finished for him.

The two men grinned at each other and Lily looked from her son to his father. She recognised the way Gabriel looked at Dominic – it was the loving look a parent gives a child.

Each day Lily looked out at the island, but she no longer speculated on the developing relationship between father and son. Gabriel stayed away now that he had stolen Dominic. Each evening the young man strode into the house with a keener eye and a lighter step. Lily saw him grow into someone else – he was no longer the boy from Lack Farm.

"Mum, this place is fantastic."

Lily looked up briefly from her plate and went through the motions of assenting.

"I mean, it's perfect as it is. Some people would come in here and do the place up – putting in a new kitchen and a new bathroom – remodelling as Gabe says – and they'd totally ruin it. This place is special – it shouldn't be changed. I don't want anything to change…" He stopped and shot a quick guilty eye at Lily. She poured herself more wine, her face deadpan.

"I remember so much, Mum – from my childhood, I mean."

"You do?" Lily asked, now surprised.

"Mainly memories of Papa. You know – things like being on the river with him – creeping under the willow when we played hide and seek. It's incredible isn't it? I mean, to remember it all now after all this time." Dominic's face was animated and the words rushed out, eager for air.

"I feel such a strong tie to this place. It must be in my genes or something. I mean it was my great great great whatever who built this big old house."

He gazed down at his hands, turning them to inspect their lineage as if his own fingers had cut the stone and carved it. He smiled and Lily tried to smile back, but her muscles were frozen as she waited for his next words. But Dominic said no more that night.

One evening he did not appear at dusk. Lily wandered up and down the riverbank, going past the willow until she came to the white water. She stopped and listened to the Vamaleau thunder and boil. Bats dived and swooped silently over her, hungry after their long sleep.

A sound of laughter crossed the water and, looking up, she saw two figures diving from the causeway into the river. Lily returned to the house and closed the door.

When Dominic strode in from the inky night, Lily kept her eyes to her plate of cheese.

"You didn't wait for me?" he asked, not sounding too disappointed.

"I didn't think you were coming back."

"Don't be silly."

He made a muffled splashing sound as he crossed the room and Lily noticed the puddles on the floor. She saw his bare feet – he had walked across the causeway, like a true son of Achallat.

"Mum, I've made up my mind."

His hair was still wet from the swim and his beatific face seemed to shine.

"I've decided not to sell. I've thought it through – about Papa and me and…" Dominic hugged himself briefly and then threw his hands to his hair. "But it's not about thinking, is it? It's a gut thing. I know I have to keep this place – this incredible place. And if Gabriel wants to stay, he can. I've decided."

CHAPTER TWENTY-FOUR

The door smacked against its frame, sending a shudder through Chez Reynat. Lily had sat on the edge of her bed and waited for that last sound – the signal that Dominic had left the house. She had listened to him move around – a narrative of his morning. First the opening of his own shutter and then those downstairs; then the rattling of crockery, followed by the smell of fresh coffee. He had called up the stairs several times, but at last the oak door shut and the house was quiet.

Lily crept down, ashamed of her own behaviour. She felt unable to face Dominic across the breakfast table. The window into the stove was dark, but stringy yellow flames licked across the glass pane and soared upwards with a whistling noise. Lily padded to the window and covered one foot with the other as the blast of air hurtled under the threshold. A blue sky filled the panes and thin wisps of cloud skidded across from the east.

Lily drifted into the garden, listlessly, as a child might on a friendless Sunday afternoon. Without design she ended up under the chestnut tree. It was a noise filled morning. The well's chain clinked around itself; the tree creaked; the barn door thumped out a dull, arrhythmic beat. Above her, an optimistic chaffinch started up its emphatic song and then gave in, quickly defeated. Lily's hair whipped at her face, as the wind pulled it ramrod straight. She was reminded of home, of blustery spring days at Lack Farm when only the grass seemed secure. She had not missed the farm – the animals yes, but not her life there. Lily had thought that she missed the work, at least. She had spent her days at Achallat searching for chores like one of Jack's restless collies.

She had wasted weeks. Another person might have used their time differently. Lily thought of the possibilities. She might have taken Felix's bicycle along the river past Séverine's to see how far the lane took her. She could have explored La Grande Aubaine – and found a museum, a gallery. Then there was the lake on the other side of La Petite Aubaine. She could have learned to skim stones across the water.

When Lily heard Baptistin's voice bounce around in the wind, she set off towards the trumpeting sound and found him alone at the well. He looked up suddenly and wagged a crooked finger at her.

"It's all changing now. The weather's changed – do you feel that cold wind? It's the start of Holy Week. Everything will be different now. It's the sign of new life."

He said no more, but walked away with his water container, leaving the chain to rattle. Sitting herself down on the lichen covered wall, Lily watched the wind chop at the Vamaleau, sunlight sparking off the surface. The aspen and birch leaves flashed against the sky and something else dazzled in the treetops. She pitched her head this way and that, trying to make out the object that shot beyond the branches and took a few steps towards the river to scan the sky. A small splash of red darted through the blue, hovering for a while and then plummeting, only to rise again above the hawthorn and crab. The simple diamond kite reeled above Jopert's meadow on the other side of the Vamaleau. There, the ground a little higher than at Achallat, rose above the scrubby hedgerow bordering the river.

Lily loped up to the couderc, wheeling round and walking backwards some of the time. She passed Baptistin's open windows and Honorine's white house with her neck craned to the sky. At the bridge, she paused a moment – the man-made bird had disappeared from view, but then it emerged from Florette's orchard, struggling against the wind. Lily turned right at the pear and peach trees and found herself in the rolling meadow where the farmer had once harvested his hay in the night and watched a candlelit boat cross the river.

At the field's brow, a figure leaned against the lone tree. Gabriel's face was turned to watch the kite flyer. With head raised heavenward Dominic ran backwards, hollering and shouting like a child as he attempted to control the scarlet bird.

Lily took in the huge sky around her and felt there was nothing in the world but three figures and a kite. The wind scudded against her face and buffed her icy cheeks until they glowed like fire. Exhilarated, she dropped herself to the ground and, cross-shaped, she gazed up at the mesmerising object.

With her face tingling, Lily beheld a thing of beauty. In the hand it would be just fabric, metal and string, but it had become much more. She jumped up and swivelled around on the spot, performing a wayward pirouette as she tried to keep track of the red bird. Gabriel and Dominic seemed not to have noticed her.

Mid-spin, Lily saw Achallat across the river. Some roofs rose above the trees, others crouched and hid. She set off down the gentle bank until she stood above the hedgerow. From this perspective, the tiny Île des Lys and Oddo's hermitage appeared nestled under the protection of Chez Reynat's solid walls. The trees formed a great arc that stretched from the west, downriver of the great house, to the other side of the bridge and the straggle of cottages where Séverine lived. It was a version of Achallat she had not seen before – all of its jumbled pink and grey roofs, and smoking chimneys in one scene. It was like seeing an unloved neighbour in a new light.

"It makes a fine picture," Gabriel affirmed, suddenly standing beside her. He said more, but the wind carried his words away west with the river.

The wind swept under Lily's ribs and through her chest. She was buoyed up on an unfamiliar emotion – at least one that had become a stranger, but she nodded and kept her eyes on the scene below her. She had stopped looking at the world, she suddenly realised. She had been confined by fear: afraid of the water; afraid of Achallat; afraid of everything.

Lily turned to the object of her greatest fear. "Your kite makes a good picture too." Spinning back to watch again the contest between Dominic and the wind, she said, "Someone should paint it."

Gabriel took his hands from his pocket and said something, but Lily was not listening. She ran to the gate at the end of the meadow, crossing Florette's orchard and passing over the bridge.

The wind whipped at her hair, blew at her nostrils, provoked tears. Her ear lobes stung, but Lily smiled. In a clear head, a remarkable thought arrived unannounced, as such thoughts often do. She would tell Dominic that Felix was not his father. It was so simple. She would tell Dominic and his love of Chez Reynat would weaken – it was not Reynat blood that flowed through his hands. The house would be just a house. For an instant, she felt Felix's eyes on her, but she let the wind carry him away.

She could no longer remember why the lie had taken hold. Partly out of the shame with which her father and brother had looked on her as she struggled through the door with her young son and an old suitcase. Better to tell them that she had lived with the baby's father for five years than to try to explain. Partly because Felix had wanted it so much to be true.

She would tell Dominic. Instead of the asphyxiating panic that usually took hold when this thought had crept into her head in the depths of the night, she felt calm. Baptistin and the others would have no hold over her and the tea dance would be just another tea dance. She smiled at her neighbour's empty bench and the hanging pots of pansies whipping around in the wind.

Lily walked straight to the barn. In the yawning space she knew exactly where to look and made for a shelf beyond the logs stacked neatly along one entire wall. She took a wooden box and, supporting it with both arms, she made her way around the side of the house. Lily ducked under the previous day's forgotten washing, flying horizontally on the line, straining at its tethers. She ducked under the willow's lax branches flailing about, losing its new leaves to the river. With her eye fixed on the sky, she sat on the grassy bank.

In the box she found some pencils, a stick of charcoal, tubes of paints, several brushes, and underneath everything, a sketchbook and a book of watercolour paper. Dust flew up and rushed away from her. Picking up a tube, Lily squeezed it tentatively and, satisfied with the give, she unscrewed the top. She shifted herself a little and settled into the grass, leaning forward slightly.

Lily had forgotten the process of painting. Shaking her head at herself, she took the two china beakers to the river's edge and scooped up some water in each. Sitting again, she pushed her hands through hair knotted from the wind's mischief and took a noisy breath. Suddenly noticing her shoes and, as if this might make all the difference, she kicked them off and leaned forward to massage her feet. The paper rippled at her; the kite danced. With the brush held over her lap, she closed her eyes, listening, waiting until she heard nothing inside her head.

Lily did not hear Dominic speak the first time. He had begun to walk away, his head bent as if now accustomed to his mother's distance. He had watched her from the wellhead as she sat with her back to him. With her head perfectly still, Lily's hand moved rhythmically from palette to paper to water. Fluid shapes of blues and greens floated across the paper, the foreground of river and earth merging with the sky. And in the midst of the blue, the brush placed a shot of scarlet with trailing ribbons that seemed to flutter on the paper.

"You've caught it," he said warily, as if wanting to say something more significant.

Lily put down the brush and put the book on the grass before her. She held her hair back at the nape and breathed in noisily. "I tried."

He crouched down beside and picked up the book, careful of the still wet paint. "So you found your old stuff. But why today? Why have you decided to pick up your brushes now – after all this time?"

"Because it was about time I did, I suppose. About time I got on with it." She laughed at herself and leaned back to survey her work. "It's not much – it's not great art. It's about today, that's all. The day I watched you fly a kite."

Severed branches with their new leaves freewheeled along in the thick brown water, only to be trapped by the causeway. A wagtail dropped to the wet path and inspected the potential nest material, its feathered end tapping frantically at the stone.

"I'm glad you like the place, Dom. I know that'll make Felix happy, wherever he is." She swivelled to face him and saw in his eyes that her words had been inadequate. Dominic had fallen in love with Achallat and his face shone with ardour.

"He'd want us to keep the house, Mum – I know it. I don't want to give it away, to lose it. It's like I have a piece of him now."

"Perhaps. I know it's a piece of you and him together. A piece of your childhood."

Lily settled herself into a new position so that she could look at her son comfortably. She closed her eyes and stilled her breath as she had done earlier before putting brush to paper.

"Did you miss having a father – growing up?"

"I don't think so. Not really. Now and then." The words came grudgingly. "But I had Granddad and Uncle David, anyway." Dominic's eyes wandered through the landscape. "But since I've been here I feel really close to Papa."

"Good. Felix was a good father to you while we were here and it wasn't his fault that we left – it wasn't his idea." She stopped and pulled her thoughts together again. "You won't remember, but he took you for walks along the riverbank and told you the names of the birds and the trees."

"I've never asked you why we left."

Lily drew in a noisy breath as her mouth struggled to let the words escape.

"We left because I didn't love Felix. I had never loved him."

Dominic's angelic face looked as if it had hit a brick wall – it fell inwards. She knew that what she said next would change her son's life; perhaps change the way he viewed the world.

"Felix wasn't your father – not your biological one, that is."

The words she never expected to voice had risen to the daylight and could never be taken back.

Dominic seemed to be numbed by the news. His eyes were unblinking; his lips slightly open as if he waited for words but there were none. Lily waited for a reaction, but he was motionless, his focus fixed in mid-space, and then he walked to the Vamaleau. With her eyes on his back, she flinched at the sudden sound he made – it was a laugh of sorts, a small mean utterance. When he turned, his face was ugly with derision.

"Now you tell me? So that's what it was all about. That's what was going on with the old folks the other day. They know – and you've never told me. Why now? Just when I was feeling close to Papa. You've taken him away from me again – for no good reason – just like you did when I was four. You should've kept it your nasty little secret rather than tell me now."

Lily waited. She saw his eyes rush around, searching, and then he turned back to his mother.

"So who's my real father?"

"Felix was your real father. He was a true father to you. Never forget that." She declared it with a passion that surprised her.

And then Lily answered Dominic's question.

"Your father – if that's what you want to call him – was just someone passing through. Someone who up and went. He doesn't matter." She almost said, 'a nobody'.

Her mouth closed firmly this time and she drew her knees up to her chest. Looking across at the meadow, Lily saw that the kite had come down to earth.

"So this place isn't mine then?" Dominic looked up at the high walls.

It had turned out as she had hoped. It was now so easy to say 'It isn't ours. Chez Reynat has nothing to do with us.'

Felix must have smiled, because Lily said something different.

"It is, Dom. Felix loved you. He was your father – you are his son. It's just like Baptistin said – you're a child of Achallat."

CHAPTER TWENTY-FIVE

As Trinity's voice bubbled down the line, Lily pictured her, wide-eyed with enthusiasm, a smile broad and generous.

"So how did Dom take it?"

"Not so well." Lily felt she had passed on the baton of pain to Dominic – Gabriel had handed it to her with his war wounds, and now she gave it to her son.

"So he knows that Gabriel's his father?" Trinity's tone was disbelieving.

"Of course not. Anyway, he's not a real father – not in any true sense, is he? He just gave Dom his colouring, his eyes – superficial things."

"Well... I don't think Guy would think his genes superficial, but back to the point – he'll find out, won't he? What's the point of not getting it out all in the open in one go? That's what I always do with Guy. If I've got a confession to make, I make sure I throw in everything I can think of – and then it's over with. Or were you planning to tell him a bit at a time – so that he can get used to the idea? What's the plan, Liliput?"

It had not occurred to Lily that the truth was an inevitable next step; that there was some sort of linear path that she had started out on, like a yellow brick road. She now saw that Dominic's mind would be filled with questions, and that Baptistin had perhaps already answered them in his crowded kitchen a few days earlier. Dominic may not have understood the conversation well at the time, but creative thinking might pull the threads together.

Lily left the conversation unfinished. The birth of a fluttering panic – that Dominic may turn to Gabriel for answers to his questions – impelled her to the water's edge.

She looked for the boat, and saw it, inaccessible, moored at the island. Her need to reclaim her son overcame her fear – Lily paced the riverbank only once.

Baptistin, cleaning the well chain and pulley, glanced away from his chore towards his reluctant neighbour. He dropped his hand with the oiled rag to his side as he gave Lily more attention, perhaps wondering whether she was about to dive.

Lily had stopped at the causeway. She flicked off both shoes, rolled up her jeans, and took a first step, surveying the depth of the water. It lapped over her feet, drifting around her, subdued and hushed. The river seemed to take a breath after the wind's agitation. Lily almost crawled forward, crouched over, studying her pink toes in the clear water. And then, like a marionette, she turned stiffly to look back at Chez Reynat. Lily paid no attention to Oddo – she swivelled round again and walked on to the island. She would not seize up and turn to stone; she would not sink to the riverbed. With a leap onto the grass, Lily ran up the slope without looking back.

A pair of muddy boots guarded the doorstep, together with the kite that had soared above Achallat. At the sight of the boots with their loose laces, a ripple started in Lily's stomach as she faced the closed door. She took a breath and knocked on the wood and, when this seemed too small and inadequate a gesture, she closed her hand into a tiny, hard fist and hammered at the weathered timber, causing the door to rebound in its frame. Lily waited for a moment, but sensed the emptiness inside. Cupping her hands above her brow and straining against the thickly glazed window, she saw a roughly made bed and a black bag at its foot. A long faced Oddo, book and key in hand, gazed out mournfully at her.

Lily turned the corner of the building into shin-high grass. Here were Felix's pear and peach trees, lichen-covered and heavy with blossom. Decayed and desiccated fruit from the previous season lay on the green floor. A wooden ladder rested against one of the trunks and a basket sat underneath as if Felix had quit his task one September afternoon. Sitting with his back to the gable wall, Gabriel seemed to contemplate Felix's husbandry, his fingers playing absentmindedly with a small object in his hands. He only looked at Lily briefly.

"Where's Dom?" she asked bluntly.

"Lily, you're one angry person," he said with his eyes still to the ladder. "You have a right to be with me – I made a bad decision. That's an understatement, isn't it? But it seems to me, you're angry at the whole wide world. It doesn't figure. What have you got against Achallat? And Felix? Maybe you think you made a bad decision too."

"Oh for God's sake, give me a break. You've turned into some sort of sadist. Look, I don't care about your mind games. Where's Dom?"

Lily did not know which part of her outburst had perplexed him, but he looked at her blankly.

"Is everything okay between you two?" he asked eventually. "I haven't seen him since this morning – with the kite. Perhaps you need to let him kick his heels a while. It'll work out. He's a good person."

The sun shone on Gabriel and he lowered his lids in submission. Lily pulled her eyes from his face and instead watched the small key twist about between his fingers.

"I've got some news that should please you," he announced suddenly, his eyes still closed. "I'll be leaving in a couple of days. I hope I haven't outstayed my welcome. I've one thing to thank Felix for, I guess – the invite. I'm glad I came – that was a good decision."

He nodded to himself and looked up at Lily. She had not moved from the corner of the hermitage, and he was forced to shift a little so that he could comfortably study her.

"I came to Achallat to see you, Lily. You guessed right – I didn't care much for Felix – no way would I have come just to ease his conscience."

Lily looked at the circle of charred earth between them and Gabriel must have noticed, because he moved the conversation on. "You remember our campfires? The fishing's still good. You used to gaze at the flames and talk about your life at the farm – about your father and brother."

"I did?"

"All this time I sort of imagined you back there, but then I thought you'd have done something else. Dom does the same. He stares at the fire and talks about home. Guess he takes after his mother."

Lily had left the corner of the hermitage without realising. She stood above the ring and smelled the charcoal.

"I'd like to think he has a bit of his father too," Gabriel added. "It was good to spend some time with Dom – good to get to know him. I'd like to keep in touch, but I don't want to cause any trouble with you, his Mom. I'm not going to say anything to him, Lily, you've got no need to worry."

Lily felt small and, as if trying to dispel the feeling, she pushed out her chest, but the words of ire failed to reach her tongue. "I don't know how we ended up here," she surprised herself saying. She was unsure what she meant.

"Life is a pathless wood," Gabriel remarked. He saw Lily's bewilderment. "Robert Frost again. That's how my life has seemed – except when Mason brought me here." He shook his head. "I suppose I should thank Felix for that. Do you suppose he pleased his Maker after all? One thing's been bothering me." Gabriel's hands stopped their fumbling and he held up the key between thumb and forefinger. "I've been trying to figure this out. Felix was a weird guy – no offence – but he wouldn't have sent this key unless I was meant to find something. Do you recognise it?"

Lily shook her head – she was still numb from his news.

"You want to see if it fits something at the house?" Gabriel held it out in his palm.

Lily had recovered. She waited for the rest of the ruse and then grew impatient. "What are you talking about? I'm looking for Dom – I don't have time for this nonsense. And I want you to leave him alone." The words sounded mean, selfish and she turned her back to him, ashamed of them.

Lily took ownership of her boat and rowed back to Achallat. And then she searched Achallat. Baptistin's windows were open as usual, but there was no sign of him or Dominic. She looked over the fence into Jopert's field; she trudged over the bridge to the hay meadow on the other side of the river. Lily had just passed the two cottages when she saw Dominic at the tiny bridge on the road leading to Saint Bénigne. He had not heard her. With his feet swinging above the water, Dominic sat on the low wall and tossed sticks into the stream as he had done as a small child. Lily left him to his thoughts, slightly irked that she was following Gabriel's advice.

Lily meandered back to Chez Reynat. She passed the tent and noted again its malodorous state, and for the first time wondered why the traveller would camp in permanent shade. From beyond the tangled hedge, the gypsy horse snickered and the brief, peaceful sound brought back memories of her own at Lack Farm. Lily clambered over the fence and found the horse, its head deep in lush grass. With her face to its neck, she breathed in the smell of its skin warmed by the sun, and soaked up the quietness of the creature. Looking up into its sleepy eye, she told it, "You're getting on too – like my old friend at home."

Its ears dropped sideways as she rubbed the scurfy hollow below its fringe. It dozed while Lily enjoyed the small actions of patting and stroking. Without thinking, she went through the ritual of inspection: checking its eyes; its back; its feet. She looked again at its four white socks – perfectly symmetrical. She lifted the fringe to check the pinprick star on its brow.

"You are, aren't you?" She stepped back, putting a palm to her own brow. "Bayardo. But how's that possible? Of course, you're Jopert's horse – and we're in Jopert's field."

Her brain was like a wheel, slow to start and then racing along downhill. She walked away backwards from the animal and her hands turned to her own grooming. She smoothed her hair as she tried to think, pulling it back into a ponytail and letting it drop again.

"My brain's addled, staying in this place. I'm a bloody fool," she complained to the horse.

Beyond the gate she could just make out the rust red roof of the well and the topmost corner of the ramshackle structure next to it. A tent occupied by a phantom gypsy, never seen by her or Dominic – only Baptistin. A ghost perhaps, but Venetia Crow and her clients had witnessed somebody's antics. A deranged man, Venetia had said.

Slapping the horse's shoulder in farewell, Lily ran to the end of the field. She pulled open the flap and was disappointed to find an empty tent and anaemic grass – she had expected to discover Gabriel. She crouched down onto the dying grass and looked more carefully. The turf was more sickly in the centre, but there was no other evidence of occupation. But, after all, he had found a better residence across the river.

Lily straightened herself and, with a quick look to the corners, she tugged at one guy rope, then a second. She snatched at the upright pole and yanked it out with ease. The tent toppled onto the cauldron and its charcoal bed, shrouding them both. As she strode around the tent, she yanked out one guy rope and then another. The pegs flew up and she put an arm out to shield her face. With the other upright pole hoisted out, Lily looked down at the heap with satisfaction, her arms folded to a job well done.

"What's happened to the wild man of Achallat?" Dominic stood beside Lily.

"He's gone – gone never to return."

"So you chased him off?" Dominic kicked a toe idly at the grey heap. "Like you're going to chase off Gabriel. Let's hope I haven't inherited the Weaver's paranoid unfriendliness. But who knows what I've inherited, eh."

His last words were grunted over his shoulder as he walked to a steely river. The hermitage was already lost to the dusk, but a light flickered from the island.

"Dom, Dom, stop a minute," Lily hollered.

He waited by the boat, impatient Lily, could see to share Gabriel's campfire.

"We should talk," she said, breathily as she reached him.

Dominic said nothing and bent to untie the rope.

"You spend more time at the hermitage now than you do here." She winced at her injured tone.

"Leave it, Mum," he said simply and jumped into the boat. He changed his mind and sprang back onto the jetty.

"Okay, you want to talk. I've been doing a lot of thinking. That holiday with Auntie Trin – that's when you met Papa. You always gave me the idea that it was a holiday romance."

"No, I didn't, Dom. I've never talked much about that summer. You just imagined it, that's all."

"I've been thinking. There were all these people coming and going here. All these hippies hitching round Europe, giving peace a chance, man."

He was no longer the young man that Lily had left at Aubaine station just weeks earlier. His voice whipped at her and she pulled her head back involuntarily.

"Felix liked people here," Lily said. "He liked to hear voices around him – that's what he used to say."

She had known that questions would be lining up in Dominic's head. Now they would be hurled at her. She braced herself.

"So tell me about these dropouts that Papa put up. I want to know all about that holiday."

"They were just a bunch of young men – hardly older than you," she said, looking up at him. "They were so different from the boys at home, from your uncle and Granddad. They spoke easily – and talked about everything and anything. They seemed interested in the world."

"So my dad's one of them – one of these hippies, that's what you're saying. In fact could be any one of them – isn't that right?"

Lily let her eyes fall to the ground – so much easier than seeing Dominic's contorted face. And she told him more to comfort herself. "They spoke a different language too. I remember thinking that one of them grew up on a farm, because he kept talking about his yard. I had no idea his yard had grass and trees – not cow muck and tarmac. They were different. They threw their legs all over the furniture." Lily smiled, remembering her first reactions. "And they were polite – with the people in Achallat, I mean."

Lily thought about those easy manners – they all had them, even Ken. So unlike Jack, who found words alien to his natural thought processes. When one of them met someone at the well, they automatically said, 'sir or ma'am'. It seemed to Lily incongruous with their scruffy dress and their sloppy posture, but she and Trinity were wooed by their old-fashioned courtesy.

Dominic had not been interested in her story. "So – I've worked it out that Papa could really be my real father. After all you're not sure who it is."

"He isn't, Dom." She had expected questions and instead her son had found his own answers.

"Let's see. You slept with all of them except Papa. Why did he get such a rough deal?"

"You're angry with me – furious with me…"

"No hang on," he interrupted, "tell me about them all. Rack your brain and see if you can list them for me. I need to have some idea and then I can just choose one that I like the sound of. Or choose one at random. We could cut out pieces of paper and I could pick one – a bit like a Grand National sweepstake."

Lily took the beating and then she sat down on the jetty. There was nothing else she could say, she realised. She would let him think whatever he needed to – she would protect him from the truth at whatever cost. Dominic looked exhausted by his outpouring, depleted of venom. Lily watched him row away – he would nurse his wounds with Gabriel.

CHAPTER TWENTY-SIX

As Florette had anticipated, the east wind departed with its host, Holy Week. It had been a fleeting visit. In an old cotton dress Lily sat on the edge of the table and swung her feet towards the open window. A bee poked itself inside a broom flower, its droning muffling as if a door closed behind it. A pair of orange-tip butterflies spiralled around one another and danced towards the river. Spring had settled in Achallat and Lily listened to the hamlet wake.

The sudden rise in the temperature had given the residents of Achallat reason to linger as they drew their day's supplies. Instead of the lively tone of brisk hellos and farewells with a quick reminder of meetings to be held, or news to be relayed; the speech was slower, more reflective, conveying the mulled over thoughts of the winter.

Lily had failed to catch Dominic that morning. She had hurtled down the stairs, but found the fire unlit, the coffee pot cold. Well, she could hardly expect anything different. Now as she watched him row back to Chez Reynat, Lily braced herself for more bruising.

She was finely tuned to the Vamaleau and its mood now. She had lived alone with its whispering and roaring; its goading and nagging. Lily's ears pricked before she heard anything and her eyes looked towards the bridge. And then she saw Dominic do the same, his arms pausing, the oars held above the surface of the river. The rushing water appeared like a train, crashing against boulders, surging under the flimsy craft, sliding it towards Oddo's path. It was stronger than Dominic and, despite his frantic rowing, it shoved him against the causeway. He stopped trying to row and rammed his oar against the stone, trying to regain his position. Lily leapt from the table and then slid down the bank. Almost beside her, Gabriel charged down from the well.

Dominic rowed hard. Even from where she stood, Lily could see the effort as he pulled at the oars, but he reached the reedy bank. He had conquered the river and now he strode onto the grass with the cocky confidence of youth.

"Hey there, G," he shouted, ignoring his mother and holding out his hand to Gabriel. "I've been looking for you to give you the official invite."

"What to?" Lily asked before Gabriel could say anything.

Gabriel put a hand to Dominic's shoulder. "What happened down there?"

Lily stared at the hand – it rested there, the fingers taking comfort in the touch. And she saw Claude Jopert's hand again on Gabriel's shoulder, unwilling to leave.

Dominic turned his head to the river. It had calmed itself, spilling as a thin silvery shelf over the causeway. "Weird or what?"

"It's the time of year," Lily explained, but her voice lacked conviction. "The snow's thawing in the Auvergne and there's been all that rain. Rivers are like that." It was her turn to put a hand on her son's arm. "What invitation are you talking about?"

"My party." His eyes returned to Gabriel.

"You know it's Papa's dance…" he paused and looked sideways at Lily, suddenly uncomfortable with the term.

"That's right," she reassured him, "it's your father's dance tomorrow."

"As the new owner of Chez Reynat I'm throwing the party and you're invited, G."

Gabriel smiled at his son.

"Man, it's going to be cool," Dominic predicted, throwing his hands through his dark hair.

"Cool? I wouldn't hold out much hope of that," Lily said with one eyebrow arched. "You weren't at the last one. It'll be a bit different to your usual Saturday nights at uni, I think."

"I bet Bappy and his mates know how to party. They're weird at the best of times – look how crazy they are on a glass of Pernod."

"It's a tea dance, Dom – tea. There won't be barrels of beer or cheap booze. And anyway, their eccentricity has nothing to do with alcohol – more to do with the water."

Gabriel shook his head. "They're good people here. It wasn't Felix's party, Dom. That's not the way it works in Achallat."

Lily was irked. He thought he was in tune with the place.

"The tea dance belongs to them all," he continued. "Don't think you can play the role of the big chief. It's not a case of the king is dead, long live the king."

Dominic looked bewildered.

Gabriel winked. "It may not be what you're used to at college, but I promise you the food will be great. Marie Jopert's taken over from Felix as head baker. And her cakes are good."

"Cakes? I've got that covered," Dominic said cryptically, and, as if he had received a reminder, he loped through the French window.

Lily was about to ask him if his bags were packed, but Gabriel pre-empted her.

"I'll stay for Dom's party. Let's give him a break and call it his." Gabriel smiled like an indulgent father. He held out his hand and Lily saw again the small intricate key. "Do you want to see what it fits? I'm guessing that little hideaway of his in the fireplace – where he kept those old papers. It's giving me an itch – I'd like to uncover Felix's little mystery before I go."

"You won't give up with your little games, will you? Go and sort it out yourself if you're that desperate – the door's open. I'm amazed you didn't just wander in anyway." Lily suddenly remembered Venetia's tale – a wild man in Felix's bedroom. "But you probably already have. You seem to have made yourself at home everywhere in Achallat."

Lily crossed the couderc and called out Baptistin's name, but there was no reply. At the white house, she heard a rhythmic noise of metal on earth and turned to look through the arched gateway that led to Honorine's garden. Down the path, Baptistin stooped over his rake as he pulled and pushed the tilth between rows of spiky green shoots. After several repetitions he paused and rested both hands on the top of the handle, his eyes still to the task. Lily could see the man's shoulders rise and fall as he regained his breath. He looked up when he heard the singing gate and gave Lily a skewed smile.

The words escaped out before she had reached him. "Dom knows. You can all stop your silly antics, your amateur theatrics – behaving like children. No more cavorting round with flowers in your hair, no more frightening people." She took a breath and held it, waiting for his response.

Baptistin took up his rake again and stretched it out along the soil. It grazed the small stones in its path and came to rest again at his feet.

"So you're not going to sell the Reynat house then," he said quietly, his eyes on the ground.

"I won't be threatened, Baptistin. I don't know what Dom'll want to do. He loves the place – I know that. He's a son of Achallat, just like you said."

He straightened himself and placed a hand in the hollow of his back, frowning as he did so.

"I thought you two didn't get on," Lily said, noticing his wet brow.

The skin between throat and vest was a rude, angry red. A crooked smile appeared fleetingly and then he blew heavily through fleshy lips.

"You mean the old harridan Honorine and me? She doesn't know what a rake is for." He cackled and raised the volume as he directed his voice towards the house and its gaping windows. "If I didn't do her gardening, she'd go hungry."

"That's good of you."

"It's just the way things are. We like arguing. We've done it all our lives – except when her husband was here. We're like an old married couple ourselves now – but we don't bother sharing a bed. Sharing water is as far as it gets."

With his chin on the top of the rake handle, he studied Lily. "You and Felix never rowed much. I remember you were an oddly quiet pair."

"It wasn't a marriage, and didn't pretend to be one, Baptistin."

"I suppose not. Didn't you see your parents argue though?"

Lily kicked at the dirt on the cobbled path.

"Mum died when I was six. I've never seen Dad lose his temper with anyone – not even one of his obstinate cows. He grumbles, but he doesn't shout."

Baptistin nodded knowingly.

"Some are less passionate – that's the way of it."

He returned to his task with renewed energy, sending the shiny stones flying through the air and dusting Honorine's onion crop with a layer of soil.

"He's agreed to go." Her eyes glittered like the cobbles at her feet.

"You mean Gabriel? What does your son say – you evicting his father?"

Lily bit her lip. "I haven't told him about Gabriel – I've hurt him enough. I've told him all he needs to know." More stridently, she said, "And I don't need to justify myself to you. That man's not important. It was no more than a fling to him. It was all over in weeks." Her voice sounded pitiful for a moment and she pulled herself together. "He has no rights. Felix once told me that his father wasn't important – wasn't important to the Reynat's, to Achallat. Well, it's just the same."

As she spoke, Lily felt her shameful words drop like stones. She knew nothing of Felix's father. It may have been that he grieved when he left the French hamlet. Who was she to judge a stranger?

Baptistin had stopped raking and now fidgeted. A fat stiff hand patted at his thigh while the other thumped the metal to the ground. "Let's not argue about Felix – or what Felix believed."

"Gabriel only stayed so long with your connivance – some game you were all playing."

The old man's eyes stayed glued to his feet.

Lily was fortified. "And you can take that old tent away before I burn it. Which one of you volunteered to terrify those poor people? It wasn't you obviously – you were with me on the bench. Are you going to tell me?"

With his face still pointing to his shoes, a shy smile swept across Baptistin's face.

"What's that look for? You're up to something – you're a crafty one – you." Lily narrowed her eyes.

"Me crafty? No, you mistake it for a sense of humour. Felix was the crafty one of Achallat."

"Don't be daft. Felix was straightforward."

"You think so? When he saw something he wanted, he got it – in his own way – not straightforward, no, more roundabout, more subtle. His mother was just the same – a lovely girl, but she was as wily as a fox. She liked what she saw with that soldier, and she wasn't going to let anything get in her way. I don't think he knew what hit him – he looked barely out of school."

"You've got mixed up – it was Felix's mother who was just out of school – Felix told me." On some maudlin days Felix talked of nothing else.

"She was young enough, I suppose. But she had looked around Aubaine and not seen anything that took her fancy – young men were in short supply."

The gate moaned and Gabriel sauntered through the archway, flipping the overhanging rose back with his hand. Lily watched his slow stride up the path, his eyes fixed and dark. She expected she disappointed him again in some way. The hoe fell at Lily's feet and she looked over her shoulder to see Baptistin jogging through the orderly plot towards a gate at the far end.

Before Gabriel had reached her, Lily stooped to a stone and, holding it in her flattened palm, she said, "This is all you mean to the people here."

She flung it aside with her eyes on his, but something in Gabriel had changed. He looked shell-shocked. Lily's eyes wandered to his hands. In one he held a piece of paper, in the other something she thought had floated down the Vamaleau. She focused on the crumpled white fabric – the dress she wore on the day of Oddo's feast. The dress she had taken to Oddo.

*

It had plummeted with her. Lily had rolled it around her chosen stone and pulled the rope tight. She had been satisfied with the knot. It had been more difficult to tie the rope around her wrist with just the fingers of one hand. Perhaps it would have been better tied around her feet, or her neck.

The second knot had loosened in the Vamaleau. How Felix found the dress still swaddling her perfect stone, Lily never knew, but she washed and ironed it and set it, wrapped in tissue paper, in the bottom of her chest of drawers. Lily did not look at it again until a curious four-year-old went in search of something to amuse himself.

It was a hot day. Lily had been watching the damselflies flash over the Vamaleau. She lifted her head from the sparks of electric blue and saw Dominic trailing the dress along the grass.

"Papa, Papa, tell me the name of this red bird?" He held the scarlet stitching up to his father.

Felix snatched the dress from the tiny fingers and hurled it out to the water, sending it to the river a second time. The white cotton billowed on the surface and sailed downstream, finding its own stones and boulders to wrap. Dominic did not cry. Maybe it was the questioning gaze from grey eyes, or the patient stance of the toddler – it was Felix who wept. His sobs were loud, racking, breaking to the surface with difficulty.

Lily went to the bedroom she shared with Dominic and put her son's clothes on the bed. She took only a few things of her own from the drawers: the small box with the plaited rings; her velvet bag still empty. When Felix found her stuffing the clothes and toys into a jute shopping bag he tugged at her hands.

"You were never meant for him. I found you – me, not him. The hermitage meant you for me. He was too old for you, Lily."

"Gabriel's younger than you, Felix." Lily looked at a face, raw and swollen.

"But he was rootless – just taking what he could get as he passed through. Just like my father. I wanted Dom to be free of him, to never know him. He's luckier than I was – he has me. I am his Papa."

"No, you're not," Lily said. She felt no shame in saying it then. It was later that the guilty words haunted her.

Felix walked away, past Dominic sitting with dark eyes in the corridor. He returned with a leather suitcase and some regained dignity. "Honorine has kindly offered you this. It is an old one that she no longer uses." Felix had recovered enough, but there was a limpness to him. He shuffled to her and placed the case on the bed. "You are welcome to borrow it, Lily. Honorine would like you to return it when you come back to Achallat. I told her that you had not decided how long you would remain away, but you were coming back to Chez Reynat."

*

Lily pulled her eyes from the crumpled dress and snorted. "Is that what you found with the mysterious key? You can have the bloody thing. It's just an old rag – I've already thrown the thing away once."

Her bitter laugh rang out above the birdsong. Gabriel's face was warped with discomfort, but he kept his eyes steadily on her.

"Is that what Felix thought he stole from you? All this is about a shabby wedding dress?"

Lily could see the clumsy embroidery weaving along the hem, the trailing threads. "Felix was crazy – and so are you by the look of it. I'm surrounded by madmen – it must be the water here. Or perhaps you were hoping for something more exciting."

Lily waited only a moment, and then pushed past him. He had said nothing to her. Perhaps he was perplexed to find the dress real – perhaps that summer had become a dream to him too.

With the sun sinking, Lily climbed Chez Reynat's stairs. It was the best time to take a bath – the room would be lit up with a rosy glow. And Lily loved the room. The huge old bath, chipped on its rolled edge, sat in the middle of what had once been a bedroom – Felix's grandmother had converted it.

The cause of Lily's love was not the ornate painted furniture or the silk covered chairs, now worn and frayed, but the window that old Madame Reynat had installed. The bathroom window at Lack Farm was frosted for no good reason, hiding the view outside, but protecting the decency of its users from the beast and the birds. This window stretched from almost the floor to the ceiling. It had a seat set into it and, with the windows open, Lily could lean over the iron balustrade and look down to Felix's washing line and his neat potager – if she had wished. Lily liked to push herself into the corner of the seat and gaze out at the trees disappearing into the distance. She and Trinity had shared baths when they first arrived. They had squealed like children, flooding the scrubbed grey floorboards. Then Trinity shared it with Oki. Gabriel arrived and, once more, Lily had someone to splash in the roomy bath. She would turn the tap with her toes so that his back was doused with cold water, and he would pull her foot away, smiling. Slyly, her foot would return, and Gabriel would jump, again and again, until he surged forward, whispering 'wilful girl' in her ear.

Now she threw open the windows and watched the river sliding away from Achallat. It was only passing through. It had a mission to reach the sea and, like a child who imagines the other side of the world at the end of the lane, Lily pictured Gabriel's sea – the Pacific Ocean. She saw him fly his kite, while she had bathed his child. Soon he would be gone back to his ocean.

With the sun on her face, she slipped under the hot water and imagined the Vamaleau carrying Gabriel away from her.

CHAPTER TWENTY-SEVEN

All of Achallat seemed to bounce. The neighbours shouted to each other: instructions; observations; or just made noises for the sake of it. It was that sort of day. Lily put a hand to her brow and tried to stop the world moving.

Baptistin walked with a buoyancy to his step, rolling from one foot to the other as his uneven arms swung in rhythm. He stopped by the French window and noisily took in a lungful of air.

"It's hot. It will be a hot day," he announced, smacking his chest with his palms.

Brooding with arms folded, Lily pulled herself away from the house wall and gave Baptistin a cursory look. Around her people were occupied with the preparation for Dominic's party. For that was how everyone seemed to see it – the young man as host.

"Never mind standing there, you old fool. We need more chairs," Honorine ordered Baptistin as she swept past him with a basket.

Florette – or was it Flora – trotted into the house, giggling and rolling her eyes. The bickering had already started and it made for a more entertaining afternoon. She carried a dish containing two hot roast chickens. Lily turned her head as the aroma trailed in the twin's wake.

"Her husband killed them yesterday," Baptistin said. "He raises good chickens."

"She has a husband?" Lily asked, momentarily curious.

"Of course, Flora has a husband. Florette is the spinster. Flora married in sixty-three. They lived as a threesome for ten years, but then Florette moved across the way – she didn't like living with a man. He's good with chickens and geese, but not much use at anything else. He'll be here today – it's a special occasion with the boy in charge."

"You remember what we talked about – you're not going to get him to stay – he's not wanted, remember," Lily reminded him.

"Dominic not wanted?" His jaw fell.

Lily glowered at Baptistin through half lids.

"Oh, Gabriel. You're a fool, Lily." Baptistin said no more, but walked away with a little less spring in his step.

Baptistin and Claude Jopert had tasted the wine already. Now they stopped watching the women buzz from one activity to another and instead followed the scent of sugar and vanilla seeping in with Dominic from the kitchen. The young man found a space on the table for his tray of small cakes.

"They may not look great and they're a bit on the heavy side, folks, but I can guarantee they'll make the party swing." He licked his fingers for effect.

"You make?" Jopert asked hesitantly in English. He reached out a hand, but it was slapped back instantly.

"I've counted them out," Dominic scolded with a twinkle in his eye. "One each, two tops. And not until the party starts."

Jopert frowned at the incomprehensible English, but he understood the gesture. He picked up his glass and turned his back to the temptation.

"You look like you're keeping guard, ready to turn away the riff raff," Dominic said to Lily at the doorway.

His tone was cold, but at least he was speaking now. She had kept her position as sentry with her eyes fixed on the hermitage, seeing no movement, but a wisp of smoke climbing from the chimney.

"Such a hot day," she murmured to no one.

"It will have been a cold night over there."

Lily jumped to see Séverine with a hand clinging to either side of the doorframe. Her wirewool hair had been pinned down with an assortment of slides, but, here and there, it rebelled, escaping from its shiny captors in stiff tufts.

"How's the knitting going?" Lily asked.

Séverine gave Lily a fierce smile. "It's just about finished. Then all that will be to do, will be the casting off. The tale is told. And what about your painting over there?"

"As finished as it'll ever be."

Séverine cackled. "You think you've turned your back on it? It'll knock you down on all fours yet."

The music started suddenly. A stage of sorts had been arranged on the hearth rug for Jopert and his accordion. He sat with a glass in arm's reach on the dead stove, his foot tapping out the lively rhythm. Already Flora and Florette were sweeping across the floor, spinning, two pairs of identical arms embracing each other.

At the hallway door, a tall man tucked in his head and stood stooped under the frame as if the discomfort of his posture was more bearable than a walk across the unfamiliar room. Lily recognised the priest from Felix's funeral. His jugged ears glowed a sugar pink as he wiped his feet diligently on the doormat, lengthening the process as much as he could. At last, he trekked across the floor towards the table and surveyed its bounteous fare, and with his arms at his back and his feet grounded, he dared smile out at the room.

Lily blinked away Felix on the stairs, his eyes bright and a sheepish grin on his face. Instead, she watched Dominic pull Honorine by the hand, twirling her round inexpertly, both hands in the wrong places. The dignified woman made allowances for his youth and moved around with a tense smile, her neck extended stiffly. Dominic's eyes teased the elderly woman, but Lily saw an intensity there that worried her. They were not the gentle eyes of her student son who had found an old box in the attic at Lack Farm.

Lily rubbed her brow again. She had scrubbed at it so much that it glowed pink above the rest of her pale face. The daylight dazzled. She stepped into the edge of the room, but now the glare seemed even harsher and she moved farther in. She still kept vigil.

"We're celebrating aren't we? Why are you standing here empty handed," Baptistin said to Lily, accusingly.

He stabbed a glass of sparkling wine into her hand, and, distractedly, she took it. Her eyes were on Gabriel. He waited at the French window, letting his eyes take in the party and then waved a greeting to Claude Jopert, who nodded in reply, one hand pumping the instrument back and forth while the fingers of the other tripped across the keys.

"It's not champagne mind. I hope you're not as high and mighty as Honorine. Look at her there – all coy like a sixteen-year-old with the boy."

Baptistin took a bite of cake and scowled at his sparring partner, but Honorine kept her eyes diligently on the new owner of Chez Reynat as they shuffled around in a haphazard fashion.

"Well then, here's to a good life. Drink up," Baptistin ordered, bending forward to meet the wine halfway.

With her eyes on Gabriel, Lily gulped down the honey coloured liquid.

"Here. It's an English type of patisserie is it?" Baptistin had taken out a small lump of the cake and now handed her the remainder. "He's not so skilled in the kitchen – the boy. I prefer Marie Jopert's chestnut sablés."

Lily took it absent-mindedly and ate with eyes fixed. Gabriel wore a crisp white shirt with a narrow stripe. She had only ever seen him in T-shirts and the kind of sweaters that dogs circle before settling down on. He strolled towards Lily and Baptistin, an ambiguous expression on his face.

"Marie Jopert's handiwork, I see," Lily said, her eyes still on the pressed shirt.

"I clean up okay, don't I?"

"I hope you're packed up and ready to go."

She tried to look past him, to the dancers, but her eyes shot back and fore to check on his expression. With his back to the floor Gabriel concentrated on Lily.

"Ça va, mon fils," Claude said suddenly, clutching Gabriel and leading him away towards the food. "Come and talk while I eat. All this playing works up an appetite and I want some of Flora's chicken before it all goes."

With their musician attending to his stomach's needs, the dancers left the floor – most of them trotting towards the food. As the huddle grew, Lily found herself encircled by people whose sole interest was to reach the chicken before it disappeared. She found another glass, took a long drink and caught her son's hard gaze.

When the music started up again it was not Jopert's jolly accordion, but one of the old records.

"At least it's not Glenn Miller," Lily groaned, taking another gulp of wine. Some in the hungry queue turned their heads, catching her tone. Lily felt penned in and she had to stop herself putting a hand out to push the bodies away.

Like a sea, the crowd parted, making room for an approaching figure. Gabriel came to Lily. At least he did not go through the empty ritual of smiling at her. With solemnity, he put a hand around her waist and pulled her to the deserted floor.

"Come and dance with me, Lily. The way you used to."

For a moment, she was seventeen again. She almost felt the daisies between her toes as he waltzed her around. She put her palms to his chest and allowed him to guide her to the music with two strong hands planted at the small of her back. She was too acutely aware of the smell of his hair, the feel of his shirt. They moved slowly to the plaintive song – an old Neil Young one, 'Down by the river'. The remembered lyrics struck Lily suddenly. They told of a man who had killed his lover down by the river. The singer seemed remorseful and when she glanced quickly at Gabriel's eyes, Lily looked for regret. She could see that there was no apology in his face anymore; no pained expression; no struggle taking place within him. As she and Gabriel circled the floor in slow motion she looked down at herself from above and saw, perhaps not a corpse, but someone hardly alive. She was a body without anima. Her hands rested lightly on each shoulder as she gazed blankly at the pale blue stripe of the cotton. The feet moved in rhythm, but she was going through the motions as she had done for twenty years. Felix had not rescued her at all – she lay on the riverbed with Oddo.

Lily looked into her assassin's eyes. They were not the eyes of a cold-blooded killer – they grieved.

"You raised him well, Lily. He's a son to be proud of. I'm glad I got to meet my son."

So much for being a corpse, she thought. Her chest thumped under her dress. "Sperm is overrated. There's more to fatherhood than that." She had tried to deliver the words calmly.

"I thought you'd given him to another man. When Dom arrived I tried to figure it out. I thought how you'd have been angry with me – you'd have hated me, even. But I still couldn't see how you'd have just settled for Felix. Unless it was always Felix. He stole my son – and he stole you."

They moved slowly, feet shifting together to the music, but Lily's head seemed to be moving to a different beat. She heaved her chest to find air.

"I wrote you," Gabriel said.

She watched his mouth shape the words and felt his fingers flex against her spine.

"You think I got your letter. You think I just ignored you, but I didn't."

The cotton shifted as her hands pushed at it. His heart seemed untroubled, but she felt it all the same. She took her hands down from his shoulders and, wriggling, reached back, trying to loosen his grip at her back.

"Okay, we won't talk about the letter now," Gabriel said.

Her fist went to her chest to fight the tight knot that had formed there. He bent his head and she felt his breath.

"Lily, Lily," was all that he said.

"You're a fraud. All these people here think so much of you – why? You're nobody. Nothing, that's what Felix called you. 'He's nothing – forget him,' he said. That summer was a fool's paradise – we were all play-acting some Garden of Eden. At least I had the excuse of being seventeen. Now you turn up here, pretending you were Felix's friend. All you want to do is blame your shame on Felix. I know what you're going to say – that Felix didn't send my letter. That that's what you found in Felix's cupboard."

She was winded when she had finished. She had not thought about the paper in Gabriel's hand when he walked up Honorine's path. Lily had not allowed herself to be perplexed. She had stuffed all conjecture into a recess, just as Felix had done with her letter. She had seen the cupboard gaping open and found the Reynat papers still there, neatly bound with dark blue ribbon.

The song continued its lament and the guitar wailed pitifully. Gabriel relaxed his hands and placed them at her hips, allowing her to pull herself away slightly. He made a short sound that jarred with the plaintive singer.

"When I got his letter, I was just thinking about the holidays coming up – going up to Hood and getting in some skiing. Then this letter arrives. It says you took up with Felix and you had a child. That's why I came, Lily. I didn't give a damn about a dying man's confession. I couldn't stand the guy back then – always hanging around corners, always with his eyes on you."

Lily's own eyes were black. She had stopped moving.

"I want to hear about your life," Gabriel said, changing the subject and leaning back slightly.

Lily wanted to say, 'What life? I'm practically dead, can't you see?'

"You're not going to ask me about mine?" he asked, nodding, knowing the answer. "Or about the night I left Achallat? It's time I told you."

Lily's eyes zigzagged around the room. The partygoers stood with plates in hand, studying the two dancers – or rather the two people motionless in the middle of the floor. Baptistin ate with difficulty, stooping over his food, his knotty hand gripping the plate awkwardly. Honorine pecked at one of Dominic's cakes, pinching the crumbs between her fingers.

"Felix loved his stories – well I have one about Felix."

"He kept a cheap white dress – that's all there is to be told. He liked to keep things, that's what he did. Old things – old family things."

"He kept things that weren't his."

Gabriel pulled her into motion again and her eyes moved between her partner and the room. Dominic leaned against the staircase, grim with arms folded and then Jopert put a hand to his shoulder and the young man smiled obligingly.

"I didn't get your letter, Lily. I read it for the first time yesterday. I want to tell you about that night."

"Down by the river," the singer moaned. Gabriel pulled her close again and dropped his head so that his chin touched her brow.

"Don't you get it? I don't care any more about that night," she wailed, refusing to move any more. Lily was rooted to the spot and Gabriel gave in.

Hands paused between plate and mouth; ears pricked. The bystanders looked more closely and Dominic turned from Jopert with a keener eye.

She moved her head mournfully from side to side. "It doesn't matter if Felix kept the letter. He was trying to protect me from getting hurt even more."

She remembered the look on Felix's face as he paced the room and questioned her about her fall into the Vamaleau.

His suggestion to write the letter had been for the best of reasons. He wanted to ease her pain.

"What was the point of writing to you. You'd left me." Her voice seemed strangled by the words.

"I know," Gabriel said quietly.

Jopert had gauged the situation and decided to abandon the quest for the chicken. He sauntered back to his accordion, his head forward, his hands limp at his side.

Hearing the first few bars, a few couples joined them on the floor. There were no eyes on Lily and Gabriel now, but with ears strained, the dancers twirled around them like bees round a honeypot.

Dominic was suddenly at Lily's side. "Hey there, you two. What's up?"

Lily pushed him away from the battlefield with a clenched fist. "Go and butter up your guests," she said with her eyes still on the striped shirt.

Dominic flinched at the tone in his mother's voice and turned on his heels, walking into the dusk.

"Felix looked after me. My own father told me not to bother going home. I was seventeen."

Gabriel at last let his hands drop. Everything on his face seemed to be at odds. "No excuses, Lily. I left you." He turned towards the door and abandoned her to the dancers and Jopert's music.

Lily looked around, dazed. Everyone danced with glowing faces and glassy eyes, oblivious now to the drama in their midst. The priest had climbed the table and, in a kneeling position, pulled out books, flipping open the covers, amassing a pile at his upturned feet.

Lily surveyed the table – there was little left. She picked up another of Dominic's cakes and ate it almost whole. She was in turmoil. Gabriel was leaving, but his words ate at her slowly. She looked up towards the staircase and saw Felix with white lips mouthing, 'I found you.' Lily picked up a bottle and drained the last of its contents into the nearest glass.

"A wonderful library, Madame Reynat," the priest sang out from his elevated position as he tossed another book onto the table.

His once pink face had a dewy bloom and was now the colour of alabaster. Baptistin arrived at her side and took her hand to dance, but she was already dizzy.

"Are people behaving a bit oddly?" she asked her neighbour.

Baptistin looked up at the man above them. "What can I say? I don't know what's normal for a man of the cloth." He shrugged his shoulders. "It's a hot night."

Lily listened to the maggoty words tunnelling in her mind – Gabriel's and Felix's. She plunged through the weaving dancers into the gloom and the heat struck her like a wave.

She did not have to search to find Gabriel. He sat under the chestnut tree, his elbows resting on his splayed knees. It was as if he waited for her. The only movement as she approached was at his jaw, which seemed to prepare for the coming battle.

"He was waiting for me when I got back that night – from the waterfall," Gabriel began. "The waterfall – you remember? He was so keen that I should see this force of nature. It was no great shakes."

She thought he closed his eyes, but it was hard to tell – she was standing above him and the house lights were far away.

"He was standing at the gate to Jopert's field, a torch in his hand. How long do you think he was there?" The question was not aimed at Lily – he had asked himself the question many times. "He said you were not much more than a child. That he looked on you like a daughter – and he and I were about the same age." Gabriel glanced up now at Lily with a look of distaste. He pulled at a flower at his feet and tore off a leaf.

"He said his mother was only seventeen when a soldier came to Saint Bénigne and told her she was beautiful. I said, 'Do you think I'm a Nazi?' But I didn't need to ask him. I felt like one. We were not the good guys over there – we were trespassers with loaded guns. Those people were getting killed for no good reason that I could see. They were invisible to us. I imagined Felix's father strutting into town, and then I looked at myself."

"That's stupid," Lily choked. "I don't believe he said that." But she did believe.

Her old dress stuck to her. The cotton was damp where his hands had grasped her back and a rivulet of moisture trickled at the nape of her neck.

"Felix was in love. He said the soldier had had no honour. I said, 'how can you talk about your father like that?' He said, 'he was no father to me'. He told me his mother's life was ruined and it wasn't hard for me to see you standing there with your future gone. Sounds stupid now – it didn't then. When he told me I should go, I thought, well, you'd get yourself to college. You'd helped me heal, I wasn't going to ruin your life."

"This is supposed to make things better? This is supposed to be an explanation?" Lily's voice jumped a pitch and the river seemed to quieten even more.

"You're not listening. He made me feel bad about myself again – it was easy. Nobody came out of Vietnam feeling good about themselves – except perhaps the psychos. I'd messed up back home with Art and Gwen – and then Felix said that word 'honour'."

Lily's head thumped and banged against her skull. She felt as though an elastic band was about to snap at her temple.

"I'd hoped you'd write when you were good and ready. I waited. Then I guessed you'd forgotten about us, forgotten about our summer."

She rummaged deep for a word to hurt, but her head throbbed too much, and her chest ached as if it were compressed.

"Like you forgot me, you mean? Felix wasn't my husband, but he never turned away from me. Whatever you say now – rewriting history –, it was you who walked away – Felix didn't make you. You couldn't have needed much persuading."

Gabriel got up and pulled something from the back pocket of his jeans. "I wrote you, Lily."

Lily's laugh was toneless. "Keep your bloody letters. Have you got a collection there? You'll pull a white rabbit out next. What's this one?"

It had grown dark. Gabriel's face was just a shadow, but she saw the white paper flutter as he tossed it aside. They both turned together. Dominic's eyes were wild; his face pale and damp.

"You two?" his voice cracked. "You two and Papa?"

He hit the heel of his palm against the side of his head. "I've just about taken in that you've lied to me all these years. That's a bummer enough. But now, with him here, you still weren't going to tell me."

Lily reached out a hand, but Dominic pushed it away before it had made contact, and stepped back unsteadily.

"You were supposed to be Papa's friend. And you screw around with my Mum?" Dominic shook his head, but the action unbalanced him even more. He spread his legs in an attempt to balance himself.

"Your Mom and I were married, Dom. Right here." Gabriel looked down at his feet as if checking the exact position and then looked up at the overhanging canopy. "Right under this tree."

Lily wondered whether the roaring she heard was her screaming and she held her breath to listen. But she made no sound – the thundering was just inside her head. She wanted to catch his words as they fell out into the night; wanted to suffocate them in the blackness.

Dominic looked like a cat, his eyes narrowed to slits. "Let me get this straight – my unmarried mum's really married; my dad isn't my dad. And some drifter is." The words slid out of his mouth, slightly slurred. "And it was there, staring me in the face. You and him. We're a bloody sick family, aren't we? Granddad and Uncle Dave have hardly spoken to a soul for twenty years, ashamed of you – ashamed of me – and I fly kites with my dad and don't even know."

"Dom," Lily said pathetically and reached out again, but this time, he launched himself at the grassy incline, and charged up it, staggering, until he disappeared into the night.

It was undone.

"It was no marriage – no wedding, just a rite. How do you know Dom's your son?" Her eyes glittered. "It was a summer of love, after all."

"Okay, Lily, you win – I give up."

She hardly noticed Gabriel follow in his son's tracks. There was nobody, except perhaps Oddo, to hear the noise that rose from deep inside her chest. If they had, they may have thought it the sound of a wild animal, cornered and without hope.

CHAPTER TWENTY-EIGHT

Between stiff stems something pale caught like a child's paper boat, scuttled and abandoned. The corner dipped below the water and then cartwheeled and, free at last, it floated to Lily's feet.

She bent to the rustling paper and now that she was so close to the ground Lily made out tiny blue flowers: Felix's forget-me-nots. *'Ne m'oubliez pas,'* he still reminded her. They seemed to shoot up from the soil, wriggling between her toes.

The elastic band must have finally snapped in her head, because she felt light-headed now – there was just a dark void inside. "Where are my shoes?" she said to her feet as if they would tell. She remembered the find in her hand and shook it open, squinting at it nose to paper and then with her arms outstretched. It was impossible to read in the starless night.

Lily headed for the light flooding out of almost every window of the house but, hearing Baptistin's robust singing, she decided to keep her distance from the gaiety. She peered again at the even black lines.

"Sweet Lily," it began. The writing was unknown to her. The strokes were light with some letters hardly finished: so unlike Felix's careful lettering.

"I don't know if I'm doing the right thing. It feels wrong – you're my wife, but I guess it must be right. You're seventeen and I want you to do all the things you've dreamed of. I'm hoping I'll get a letter from you – I'll be waiting for it, but if things change, if when you get back home things look different, don't worry…"

The next words were illegible, washed away in the Vamaleau. She put a finger to the paper, but still failed and moved on to the next line.

"Be happy,
Gabriel"

She pushed the paper away, tearing at it and tossing the shreds towards the river. The mournful confetti floated slowly through the still air, and then disappeared.

She had the skewed clear-headedness given by alcohol and perhaps something more. She heard Mason's words. Standing under the chestnut tree, he had said, "Shine a light on the past and then walk on." His eyes had been fixed on Gabriel, and she remembered him repeating the phrase as if he knew the mantra was of comfort to his friend.

Lily stood for a long time, a dark statue on the edge of the river. Sky, earth and water merged into an inky blankness. Her eyes searched for some light and she turned her head, expecting to see the house lit up, but she saw nothing. Lily stretched out her hands, trying to make contact with anything. She was inside a void.

And then she heard the river.

"You're always there," she said to the creeping water.

It answered her with a growl, but then Lily realised that the booming noise had come not from the Vamaleau at her feet, but from above her. Flashes lit up the sky behind the hermitage, and the image of the tiny building blinked at her with a silvery halo around it. It flickered in and out of focus, seeming to jump around its island.

A hot wind blew up from nowhere and the tree behind her moaned. And then the wind died just as suddenly.

Lily did not see the lightning strike the old tree or hear the shriek of torn timber. The crack was so loud that she thought it must be inside her head. The cold hit her chest and she heard the rushing noise of water around her, perhaps inside her.

She was in the water, under the water, falling. The water spoke in her head and Lily wondered whether her eyes were open – she could see nothing, but then her face hit air. Lily gasped at it, her mouth sucking at it, her lungs clawing at it. Another fork of lightning flashed and she caught sight of something huge sweep past her, plunging downstream. Lily sank again, slipping into the thick enfolding water.

"You again," Lily told Oddo. He stretched white fingers to her and offered a forlorn smile from his hollow mouth. "You've got your own way at last," she said. She felt the long fingers fold around her wrist, the fat ends like suckers on her skin and then another hand took hold of her arm.

Gabriel ducked involuntarily when the first lightning strike cracked through the air. The back of his neck tingled as he turned round to look at the river. He heard the crashing, but for a moment he could not make sense of the scene before his eyes. The Vamaleau churned and foamed, and, in the brief flash, he saw the huge limb of the tree struggle with the river. It tossed and spun, and then surrendered to its captor, sliding over the causeway. The reek of burning wood woke Gabriel from his daze as quickly as if it had been smelling salts. He ran down the bank. He could see nothing, but his ears were assaulted with the thundering of the river as it swept through the blackness. He looked up and down where he thought the river edge must be. There was no sign of Lily. He sprinted down towards the willow, its even blacker outline sketched against the jet sky. She was not on the riverbank. Another strike flashed. In the foam he glimpsed something – an arm, perhaps. The lightning had shown him the causeway and then it disappeared again. He ran to where it should be, pulled off his boots and ploughed into the river. His feet found the stone. Struggling against the shin-high water pushing him sideways, he propelled himself forward, trusting his feet to find the path. Halfway into the river he made out the body.

The current tossed it up and sucked it back down. He dived into the pitch and blindly found an arm.

The fingers were warm, the grip strong and Lily was out of the water, coughing violently. Her legs scuffed and bumped at the edge of the stone as her body was dragged onto the causeway and then onto something softer. Retching, she spilled Oddo's water onto the grass. Hands pushed away her hair; arms carried her and then lowered her. Lily had left a watery hell, but she seemed in a strange place – the room shook and roared violently. The eyes, inches away, and hands at her cold cheeks told her that it was her body that convulsed; her head that thundered.

The noise in Lily's head subsided, but the room still wobbled when she moved her eyes. She was still swimming in the dark. She felt hands rub her hard, but it seemed to be someone else's skin – hers was encased in a glacier, a wet sheet of ice that encircled her. Her head was raised and she felt fingers search her scalp. The grave eyes drew away and she was left alone, juddering in her freezing wrap.

When Lily heard the crack, smelt the wood singe, and felt the acrid taste on her tongue, her body told her to escape and she threw her arms out to flail about. But the hands that were not Oddo's held her still until she saw sparks at the sooted chimney and breathed in the scent of the holy man's room.

A river of jewel colours flashed at Lily as light danced around the walls and struck the painted panel. She saw Oddo, pale and anxious; saw Felix waving. He beckoned her. And then Gabriel looked down.

He sat on the edge of the bed and watched the pallor on Lily's face give way to healthier pink as the room warmed up. Her eyes, huge and black at first, began to focus on him. Her breathing steadied. He wiped at her face where the stream of water fell from his own hair. His shirt ballooned out from his chest; his jeans were like a second skin, clinging to his thighs. He unpeeled them both and climbed under the dry sheets, sliding Lily still in her wrappings towards him. With both arms he clasped her to him.

Lily soaked up the heat of his body like a lizard on a house wall. Feeling her own warm breath on his neck, she let her eyelids close.

"Stay awake," he commanded her.

She raised her lashes briefly. "Don't worry, I'm not concussed. I'm just drunk," she mumbled. "High. High as a kite." The laugh trickled up from her throat. "Hang on – I might fly off." And she gave in to the desire to sleep.

"Stay awake." He rubbed his thumb against her cheek. Her eyes remained stubbornly closed. "Talk to me."

"You talk," she sighed.

"That's not the way it works." He pushed damp strands from her brow, but hearing the sleep on her breath, he gave a short sigh. "Okay, I'll do the talking. Are you listening? I'll tell you about the ocean. It's stubborn – like you, Lily. It pounds away at the land, day in, day out. It can get bad-tempered, but it's not moody like the Vamaleau. You never turn your back on it though – it can whip your legs from under you. It doesn't lap or sigh like a sea, it roars with life."

His last words seemed to inhale and exhale like the Pacific itself and Lily lost them. She slept for a minute, perhaps seconds.

"Wilful Lily. Tell me about Oddo again, like you used to."

"The river's in my head." She breathed heavily and in a drawl said, "Anyway he's angry with me. So's the river."

"Why is Oddo angry with you, Lily?"

Lily heard the smile on Gabriel's face.

"Who knows?" she said thickly. "All this time I thought he wanted me – he pulled me in this time – or the river did. They can't make up their minds, I suppose. Didn't want me last time either. 'Come on in, the water's fine' they said." She giggled for only a second. "But they threw me back to

Felix." Gabriel's thumb stopped. The fire crackled and threw an orange light on his face.

"Forgive me, Lily," he whispered with his mouth to her ear.

Such small words, Lily thought, such easy words, but they slipped in, slid between her ribs and found her heart as though by their humble size they crept in. She opened her mouth to tell him, but he spoke again.

"It's okay." His breath warmed her still damp face. "We would've had a sweet life, Lily – here together in our little hermitage. It just didn't work out that way."

She woke to see the room ghostly with light from a half veiled moon. Gabriel lay like a stone effigy on a tomb, one hand resting on his chest, the other reaching out towards her as though reaching for his sword. She drew her fingers lightly across his face, tracing the groove of the scar. The knight slept and Lily closed her eyes again.

When she woke she felt it had been a sleep of years. Gabriel stood at the doorway, his feet still pointing into the room, but his face turned towards the blackness outside. His arms were crossed and he leaned against the doorjamb.

"Are you leaving?" She had asked the same question before. Then it had been dawn and Bayardo waited saddled for his master.

Gabriel turned. He had made a good fire: its embers still gave out enough light for Lily to make out a wry smile. There was a slight movement of the head.

"Go back to sleep, Lily. It's still the middle of the night. Achallat is dreaming."

CHAPTER TWENTY-NINE

Lily's wakening was blurred, with no definition between sleep and consciousness. Her mind, perhaps still dreaming, returned to the frosty day at Lack Farm when Felix's letter was thrust in her hand. Such a cold day, she remembered – an odd day for her past to wake and find her.

She had dreamed of the river. It slid beneath her feet, determined to be away from Achallat. With the reason of reverie, she had wondered whether it had been jealous of Célestine, who had so wished to leave. In her dream Lily listened to Gabriel's instruction. 'Don't let go of me,' he told her. 'We'll take it easy – one step at a time.'

Her shoulder throbbed. She reached tentative fingers to the site – it was swollen and tender, but there was no wound, at least. She had no need to check beneath the bed for Gabriel's things. 'Forgive me,' he had asked and she had stayed mute.

Losing him was becoming a habit. That September morning, the Renault had rattled over the Vamaleau and Jopert had guided his butterscotch cattle behind it. Mason, Ken and Oki had been dumbfounded by Gabriel's disappearance. But no one any longer said, 'When Gabe returns.' He had walked out of Eden alone. They looked at Lily as if she must be the cause, and that feeling returned to her now as she gazed up at Oddo's ornate window.

Lily wrapped a sheet around herself and stood in her shroud on the threshold. Like a spring day should be, it was bright and clear. The only reminder of the heat was on the old tree – a black and bleached wound gaping where its limb had been ripped away. Lily pulled the sheet in more tightly.

The boat stitched across the Vamaleau towards her, the black haired figure pulling the oars easily. He jumped onto the riverbank and loped up the path.

"I brought you these," Dominic said, holding out some clothes on his arm. She began to compose the words needed, but Dominic spoke first, "Gabriel told me. Told me about how you thought you were doing the right thing. He told me about Papa. But it still doesn't make it right."

"Oh." How do you tell a nineteen-year-old that a lot of life isn't right – doesn't make sense in retrospect. "I'll tell you the story of that summer when you want to hear it. I won't tell it as well as your Aunt Trin would, but you'll get the beginning, middle and end."

Dominic nodded and looked towards the smoke leaping out of Chez Reynat's chimney. It spiralled upwards and eventually became invisible. "I heard about the tree too – you nearly drowned. You were lucky."

"I had someone to look out for me."

"You think Oddo saved you?" Dominic's face showed his disbelief.

"Not Oddo. Someone flesh and blood saved me."

Lily took the jeans and sweater into the hermitage and re-emerged dressed for the weather. Dominic was sitting in her spot with his back to the pink wall. He watched the to-ing and fro-ing at the house as she used to do.

Stooping at her boot laces, she said, "Those cakes of yours were a very bad idea."

For a fleeting moment a grin swept across his face. "It would've been okay if everybody had stuck to just one. There was hardly anything in them, but I hadn't taken Friar Tuck into consideration."

"It's lucky your baking's so bad and everybody else threw them away."

"They did? That's why the birds are falling about the place then. I've had to pick half a dozen of them up already."

Lily had just got "What?" out, when she recognised the playful tone. She laughed and Dominic smiled back.

"He's gone," he told her suddenly.

She gave Dominic a weak smile. 'I give up, Lily,' Gabriel had said. And so he had.

"He gave me his address – he wants to keep in touch." Dominic played with a small piece of paper in his hand. He moved it between his fingers as if he had not yet decided whether to throw it away. "He wants me to visit him this summer. At least it'd be a change from the farm, I suppose."

Lily nodded, recognising his wish to play it down. Something else bothered her son. He stood and twisted on the spot, snatching glances at the river, the house.

"I want to give them Chez Reynat," Dominic plunged in. "It's like it already belongs to them anyway. I know you're going to say the legal stuff's going to be complicated, but we could make it out to all of them – old Bappy, Jopert and Madame." Dominic looked wistfully across the river. "I could come and see the place when I wanted."

Lily took her son's face in her hands. She saw a miracle. Somehow, Dominic had inherited the best of his two fathers. "That's a good idea, Dom." She looked across at the open French window and heard the distant chatter. "But we can't sort it out today – I've got something I have to do – that can't wait."

As Dominic rowed them across the Vamaleau, Lily's eyes avoided the disfigured tree. The smell of charcoal still hung over the water. She made Dominic stop at the halfway point and put her hand over the side of the boat. With outstretched fingers she rested her flattened hand on the surface of the water. It lapped against her palm as her body swayed to the rhythm of the Vamaleau.

Dominic asked the question with just a raised eyebrow. "Just saying goodbye," Lily answered him.

Everything was almost back to normal at Chez Reynat: the extra chairs were gone; the dishes were washed; and the table cleared. Honorine swept the floor slowly, painstakingly reaching into every nook and cranny. Baptistin leaned against the fireplace and watched, a contented look in his eye.

"Good to see the old girl work," he nodded to Lily as she stepped in through the French window. "If she can use a broom, she can use a rake, don't you think?"

Lily glanced back to Honorine to see what the reaction might be. There was none – she was lost to her task.

"And are you okay? You're not hurt?" Baptistin asked as if he suddenly remembered.

Lily felt as though she had been flayed – her back, thighs and calves were raw. But she just nodded. After weeks of indolence, there was suddenly so much to do. She put things in order in her mind: shower, pack, explain… No, there was too much and some would have to wait. "Where's Claude?" she asked Baptistin.

"He took him to the station about an hour ago." Baptistin did not need to say who was in such a hurry to leave – the residents of Achallat took Gabriel's disappearances for granted. The old man looked at the clock to confirm his words. "Claude should be back any minute. What do you want him for?"

Lily had already made for the kitchen where she found Marie Jopert. The woman glanced up from the cloth in her hand and, seeing Lily at the door, she returned her attention to the glass polishing.

"So where's Gabriel off to, Marie? Where's he catching a train to?"

Marie Jopert shrugged her shoulders. It was a tiny movement as if even that gesture were a bold statement. She pressed her fingers against the fabric and rubbed until the glass squeaked.

"Come on. It's not a secret, is it? He's taking the train to Paris and flying home? All I want to know is – will he be staying the night there?"

Marie placed the short tumbler at the end of a sparkling row. Having run out of work, she picked one of its fellows that had already received her assiduous treatment. Lily made a noise – a sort of discontented growl – that she hoped would intimidate Marie just enough to weaken her resolve. It did not work.

"Oh, for goodness sake. I'm going nowhere until you tell me. Have you thought of working for the French secret service?" Lily saw some movement on Marie's face – a flicker of a smile.

"I gave Gabriel my keys," a voice piped up from the door behind Lily. She turned to see Honorine with her broom at arm's length. Claude's wife quickly put down the glass and freed Honorine of the stick. She cleaned Honorine's house every Thursday and found the sight of her employer and a broom too incongruous to bear.

Honorine wiped her hands together quickly. "I gave him the keys to my apartment. He can send them back to me in the post. It's such a waste of money staying in hotels – the rooms are usually no better than broom cupboards." She looked at the humble implement again.

"You've got an apartment?"

Honorine looked disdainfully at Lily. "Do you take nothing in? I use it for a few weeks of the year. Really just to see my niece and her family – but I've told you this before. I should sell the place. I've been meaning to for years. It's not as nice an area as it was. Times change. Everywhere changes."

Lily found Dominic playing with Felix's fishing rod. Sat on the step beneath the wellhead he swung the line in front of him, idly watching the pendulum.

"I don't think you'll catch anything there."

"I was thinking of casting it down the well. You said you didn't know what lived down there. I could find out."

She dropped down beside him and nudged him sideways to free more of the step. "Dom, I want you to close up the house for me. You can tell Baptistin about your decision if you like, but for now I want you to lock up and then catch a train for home. I suppose you could leave it to the end of the week – the new owners will keep you in order. There won't be much to do – Baptistin already has a key. Just close all the shutters. No need to switch off the water or the electricity or anything like that. They'll be having the next dance soon enough. Leave early though to give yourself plenty of time to get across Paris. And if you ask Jopert I'm sure he'll give you a lift to the station. You might be able to get an afternoon ferry if you're lucky." Lily closed one eyelid as she concentrated her mind. "Then by the time you've changed trains again in London... Well anyway, Granddad'll pick you up whatever time you get in. He'll grumble plenty, but you should be used to that by now." The words had spilled from her tongue as fast as they formed.

Dom placed the rod on the grass and looked hard at his mother. "Where are you going to be?" Then he looked at the ground beside her and saw her bag – the one she had brought for her short stay – for Felix's funeral. "You're going home today?" His voice rose a notch.

"No, I'm not going back to the farm." Lily took a deep breath. "That took some saying. Not for a while." She plunged her hands in her pockets and looked around her. "I hope not anyway. I'm taking a holiday – an adventure. I've got a lot of catching up to do. Don't look so worried – your mum's not abandoning you. I just won't be at Granddad's, that's all. It's time I moved out – at my age – don't you think?"

CHAPTER THIRTY

Lily had cursed Jopert under her breath in the car, and now she cursed him aloud. He had driven at a stroll as though he were taking Marie to the Wednesday market and now Lily had missed her train. It snaked north out of the station as she reached the glass doors of the foyer. She would have to catch the next – whenever that was.

The one traveller arriving at La Grande Aubaine squeezed past her in the doorway with his wheeled case and his tired looking newspaper. She craned her neck to see past him. On the farthest bench a figure sat hunched forward, his elbows on his knees. Not in prayer, she guessed.

As Lily walked the platform she wondered why his soiled boots should need so much study. Lily knew mud well. She knew soil: the sticky ochre clay of Lack Farm; the gritty loam of Honorine's potager. And the rich rust earth of the Île des Lys on Gabriel's boots.

Gabriel looked up when she reached him.

She had had no time to rehearse. A train journey would have given her plenty to construct the strong argument she thought she might need.

She watched the words leave his lips, but she heard nothing as an express thundered through the station. Lily felt as though she would be sucked in its wake and she instinctively tried to dig her feet into the concrete beneath them. They both watched it follow in the trail of Lily's missed train.

She looked back at Gabriel. "What are you still doing here? Jopert dropped you off hours ago."

His boots were no longer of interest to him, but it was as if he could not find the answer for her: his eyes searched the platform. Lily found herself a perch on the end of the bench and tugged at her hair, looking sideways at him.

"Tell me about the waterfall," she said. His voice would calm her.

He took a breath and held it while he seemed to decide. "Felix's waterfall. It wasn't so great. Just like Felix to exaggerate. It took us a while to get there – not really horse friendly terrain. Bayardo lost his footing a few times. We got there late and I thought of camping out, but I wanted to get back – to Achallat. So Bayardo and I headed on back in the dark."

Lily listened to the sound of his voice, the shapes his mouth made. She was soothed. She would like him to tell her about the pathless wood. Her hands fell to her lap and she leaned into the bench as her mind tried to find the right words. What would they have been if she had run down the dewy bank and followed him that September morning? They would have been the words of a child. Only the turtle dove's song 'don't go, don't go,' came to mind now.

Gabriel must have heard the call in her eyes, because he reached out and found her hand.